PRAISE

Joy Comes in the Morning is destined to become an instant classic. This beautiful novel has the potential for being developed into other forms of media a la the works of Laura Ingalls Wilder or the Brontë sisters. Ms. Hope weaves a tale of intrigue, hardship, and love through the voices of complex and dynamic characters. She masterfully and thoughtfully blends historical fact with fiction evoking emotion and reflection from the reader. The profound subject matter of this work is tempered with enchanting twists and turns throughout, and its timeless poignancy far outshines the insipidness of many contemporary romance novels. Christian readers will be delighted to recognize the parable of the Good Samaritan underlying the piece, but Ms. Hope has made the story accessible to anyone and everyone who gives it their time and attention. A rare debut masterpiece from an author with a bright future ahead!

Lauren MJ Connelly
Published Freelance Writer and Blogger
www.puremama.com

JOY COMES IN THE MORNING

JOY COMES IN THE MORNING

Joyce Hope

Tate Publishing & *Enterprises*

Published by Tate Publishing & Enterprises, LLC
127 E. Trade Center Terrace | Mustang, Oklahoma 73064 USA
1.888.361.9473 | www.tatepublishing.com

Tate Publishing is committed to excellence in the publishing industry. The company reflects the philosophy established by the founders, based on Psalm 68:11,
"The Lord gave the word and great was the company of those who published it."

Interior design by Joey Garrett

Published in the United States of America

ISBN: 978-1-60696-529-0
1. Fiction / Christian / Historical
2. Fiction / Christian / Romance
09.03.10

DEDICATIONS

To Christ, my Savior, who shows me more and more with each passing day that I can do all things through him.

To Edward, my loving husband and perpetual source of encouragement.

Weeping may endure for a night, but joy cometh in the morning.

Psalm 30:5 (KJV)

PREFACE

Hollywood doesn't always accurately represent the details of history, I found. As a "Philly" girl, I learned the American Civil War details from a Northern point of view. It didn't faze me at all when Hollywood produced a movie that greatly vilified Dr. Henry Wirz, the only man convicted of war crimes following the Civil War. But as I researched the life of the man and his trial transcripts, my views changed completely, as did my entire perspective as to *why* we were so divided as a nation. The heroes of my novels are always employed in an occupation that represents a characteristic of Christ. While my hero in this novel remains a defender and judge whose strong voice symbolizes pure justice, the events and circumstances became rerouted due to my new perspective. In order to understand the psyche of my hero, I've written a biography of Henry Wirz and the Andersonville Trial.

Dr. Henry Wirz migrated from Switzerland to Kentucky in 1849. At the start of the Civil War, he enlisted with the Louisiana Volunteers, only to sustain a wound that incapacitated his right arm. For "war bravery," he was promoted, freed from active combat, and sent to work for Confederate prisoner-of-war camps.

In April of 1864, Wirz was made commander of southern Georgia's Andersonville Prison, built to house Union prisoners. Conditions there were horrendous. Extremely overcrowded, prisoners lived in the unsheltered open with little food, no medicines, and polluted water. Within its fourteen-month existence, it had been calculated that 13,000 of the 45,000 incarcerated died. During this time, Wirz pleaded with superiors and the Federal government to provide supplies and medicine, and to organize a prisoner exchange to relieve the gross overcrowding. He even sent four of his prisoners to Washington to plead for aid. The Union army had abolished prisoner exchange at that time, not wanting to empower the South by exchanging healthy Southern soldiers for Northern "skeletons." All medical supplies going into the South by land and sea were considered contraband, and several Southern ladies had been arrested for attempting to hide medicines beneath their clothing. Northern soldiers destroyed all sources of Southern food supplies and burned down doctors' offices as they ravaged their way through the South.

At the conclusion of the war, the bewildered Wirz was arrested for war crimes and imprisoned in a Washington DC jail. A nine-man military commission was set up to try him. The Northern press defamed him by making him out to be a murderous monster that tortured prisoners. Wirz's lawyers knew their client was doomed due to public outcry demanding his conviction and the fact that every one of their defense motions had been denied. One hundred and forty five out of one hundred and sixty witnesses testified that they never saw Wirz attempt to hurt or kill any prisoner, nor did he ever give orders for guards to kill or torture. The remaining fifteen witnesses couldn't back up their claims with evidence. The prosecution claimed that Wirz had been in conspiracy with Jefferson Davis and several others (who were still in hiding during Wirz's trial) to kill Union prisoners, so they used Wirz as their scapegoat to try to build charges against the fugitives.

After a two-month trial and no substantial evidence whatsoever, Wirz was ultimately declared guilty by the commission and sentenced to hang on the very spot where the US Supreme Court stands today. The devoted husband and father of three daughters voiced his innocence up to the very moment he climbed the stairs of the scaffold. The noose didn't break Wirz's neck. He dangled for a considerable length of time, until he strangled to death. His controversial trial was the first war crimes trial in modern history, and he was the only man tried and executed for crimes committed during the Civil War, setting direct historical precedence for the Nuremberg War Crimes Tribunal after World War II.

FEBRUARY 14, 1912

"My granddaughter should have been here a half hour ago, Viola. When she arrives, please tell her I've already gone up to the attic."

"I will, Miss Elizabeth. Will you be needing some help in climbing the stairs?"

"No, no, dear. Continue with your cooking. I can manage well enough with my cane and the banister, thank you. I suppose you can plan on serving dinner two hours from whenever Julia arrives. She surely does love your steak and kidney pie ... says it's the best to be found on either side of the Atlantic."

Elizabeth Chambers shakily rose from the kitchen table, reached for the cane that was hooked onto the back of her chair, and then stood back to admire her meticulous workmanship. Julia would never be able to guess what lay inside this colossal box, wrapped in gilded paper and frilled with satin bows and dried flowers. She emitted a short, satisfied chuckle then shuffled over to the encased stairwell that ran along the back of the kitchen to begin her climb.

When she reached the arduous finish of her three-flight trip, she surveyed her vast surroundings and realized it had been well over two years since she last visited her cache of memories. *Hmm ... where to begin! Julia needs something old. Every item up here would fulfill that requirement, and most likely even the something borrowed and something blue, but there's indisputably nothing new.*

"Whew! I best open a window first. This place needs a good airing," she mumbled to herself as she made her way over to a grouping of three windows. Two needed the strength of much younger hands to be able to pry them open. The third was just right for a petite woman of seventy-three years. She eyed the stained glass porthole window on the adjacent wall and went to unlatch it. A cool, exhilarating breeze rushed in to replace the attic's stale mustiness. She deeply inhaled its sweet essence then instantly caught her breath, startled that her peripheral vision had picked up some movement from across the room. *Stupid old woman!* Realizing she had been duped by her own reflection, she headed over to the foggy-mirrored wardrobe to take a gander at the finely lined face framed by a snow white Gibson Girl. Pleased with the image that returned her gaze, she plucked at a tendril curl and giggled like a schoolgirl as it popped back into place.

"You're not half bad looking for an old dame," she complimented herself with an added sunny smile. *He would still find me fetching,* she imagined, the sunny smile fading into a wistful stare through a pool of tears. "I miss you so, my love," she said softly, "most especially on this day."

"Is my sweet little grandmother in there?" a perky voice called from the doorway.

Elizabeth wiped her eyes with the back of her hand, forced the return of the sunny smile, dropped the cane, and held her arms out to her beloved granddaughter.

"She most certainly is!" she exclaimed as they embraced and exchanged kisses. "Where's your father?" she asked, anxious to see her son.

"Father said to tell you that he and Mother will spend all of tomorrow afternoon with you since he's with a client that could only see him today. Will brought me here in his new motorcar. Would you believe it took less than a half hour to make the ten-mile trip? It's much faster than Father's vehicle."

"Well, I still prefer a carriage. Technology sets the world at too fast a pace, and I'm not so sure that's a good thing. And you certainly could never persuade me to take a ride in the sky. Where *is* Will?"

"He'll be back in time for supper. He's running errands." Her eyes wandered over to a massive wooden trunk. "May we start there?" she asked, pointing to the object of her curiosity.

"Good a place as any. As I recall, it's filled with old clothes, photographs, and some memorable costume jewelry. Do you still want those old wingbacks?" she asked, pointing to two dusty, faded, gold brocade chairs.

"Oh yes! I adore antiques, anything American and pre Civil War. I'll have them reupholstered." She lifted up the top of the trunk and stooped down to begin her invasion. "Oh! It's Grampa," she said sadly, taking a framed picture that lay on top of the pile of memorabilia. "It's similar to the one that sits beside your music box on the table by your bedside. He was a *mighty* handsome man, even at seventy-five." She reached over to clutch her grandmother's hand and, looking up at her, said, "I remember when this photograph was taken ... several months before he died ... two years ago ... I'm so sorry, Grams! Is this going to be too upsetting for you?"

Elizabeth gulped hard and blinked back the tears. She took the picture from Julia and went to sit on a wingback. "I'll be fine. You keep looking in there, and I'll reflect on my man for a bit." She ran her fingers lightly over the glass, trying to imagine the warm feel of his well-groomed bearded face.

"Well, look at this old gown! Oh my, has fashion changed greatly over time!" Julia exclaimed, lifting a tumultuous amount of faded blue yardage from the pile of vintage clothing. "It must have been terribly awkward having to wear those crinoline 'cages' under your skirt. May they *never* come back into style! There appears to be a shell comb caught on a piece of the lace," she noted while trying to free it. "I believe it's a small mantilla comb. How lovely! I might attach my veil to this and claim it as my 'something old.' Oh, and here's Grampa's brown-corded church coat with his lovely initialed handkerchief still folded neatly in the pocket." She reached over to retrieve a piece of brown-edged paper that had fallen to the floor from another pocket. Careful not to rip the fragile sheet, she unfolded it to scan the contents. "It looks to be a poem torn from a book, but the printing is somewhat water-smeared. It reads: *Please, do not bid me farewell at daybreak. For I've come to depend on your light to shine as a beacon along my*... Grams? Whatever is the matter?" she asked, stopping at the sound of her grandmother's gasp.

A tear trickled down Elizabeth's delicate pink cheek. "He *did* keep it with him all the years we were together." She took a handkerchief from her apron pocket to pat her eyes. "Julia, I believe now is the time that I inform you of something your father and I have been meaning to tell you, but first, since today is Valentine's Day, I would like to tell you a love story..."

Joy Comes in the Morning

Please, do not bid me farewell at daybreak.
For I've come to depend on your light
to shine as a beacon along my path
as I travel the valley through night.

Cloaked in the warmth of your comfort,
secure in the strength of your care,
I can walk through the shadows of darkness
as long as I know you are there.

So near to the dawn you have brought me.
Now we watch as the gray clouds part way
for The Son to bring peace to our morning.
Might we share in the joy of the day?

Though we've come to the end of our journey,
is it time we shall say our goodbyes?
Dare would I know that you love me
by that glimmer of hope in your eyes?

For it pierces my heart like an arrow,
so I must confess what I know.
I love you, as I do no other,
and plead that you not let me go.

CHAPTER 1

August 22, 1865

Libby Prescott despised her husband. But this sentiment didn't always consume her. Before her fair-haired Adonis departed to join the Union army, her adoration for him ran so deep, she would have gladly sacrificed herself by taking his place in battle. For the last month or so, she had made it a daily ritual to pray that the good Lord would soften and change her heart, to expel the regret that Billy hadn't died in battle as had his two brothers, and that she would somehow learn to love him as she once did, even just a smidgen. But thus far God hadn't seen fit to grant her request, and tonight she realized that she hated Billy with every fiber of her aching, bruised, and abused being.

Lifting his limp hand from her shoulder, she gently set it over his gaping mouth, hoping to muffle his snores and filter out a degree of stench from his sour, whiskey-tainted breath and rotting teeth. Her nightgown clung to her body, drenched with his sweat. She knew too well that he would awaken in a few hours or less—trembling, angry, bilious, and ravenous for his habitual comfort. She planned on barricading herself in the downstairs bedroom when that happened. Now certain that he had fallen into a deep sleep, she felt confident enough to leave their bedroom to go wash her tender body and change her nightgown, if another was to be found that he hadn't already ripped.

She crept quietly down the stairs to the kitchen, disrobed, and sponged away his grime. Despite the insufficient lighting, she was sickened by the clear visibility of the many latest purple bruises that were embossed in the soft flesh of her arms and chest. She ran her fingers lightly over the areas where skin had been scraped by his rough, bewhiskered face and hoped that maybe Papa had a salve that might numb the sting.

It seemed to be an overly dark night—a quarter moon, no stars, and just a clear view from her kitchen window of the lantern-lit office in her father's house across the field.

Papa's up late. Must be nigh on to ten o'clock. What could he possibly be doing? Perhaps tending to his patients' charts? She lightly shrugged then went to the back bedroom to search through her mama's cedar chest for a white cotton nightgown and pair of crocheted slippers. After raking a brush through the tangles of her long raven curls, she secured the mass into a snood.

It was a dreadfully hot night, even for the end of August—too hot to sleep. Maybe the lull of the porch swing would relax her enough to be able to rest for a short while. But would the mosquito bites be worth the venture? She began pacing the parlor, contemplating how she might manage to find sweet solace away from the sleeping monster above her. She lay down on the divan to ponder her plight.

Lord, she prayed, *I can't bear this way of life much longer. At least the morphine and opium kept him peaceful-like, and he let me be. But he… he hurt me again tonight, Lord. Whiskey has made a beast of him, and it doesn't seem to ease the ache in his leg very much. Help me, please! What shall I do when he awakens?* She reached over to turn down the lamp wick then rested her head on the arm of the divan. Weary and worn, her heavy lids closed.

"Libby! Libby! Drat you, you witch! Where are you?" his thunderous voice bellowed.

Her eyes flew open, bulging with fear. She shuddered at the knowledge that he had consumed the last half bottle of whiskey a few hours earlier in the evening, and his throbbing leg was making him angrier than a wet hornet. The house literally quaked from the heavy thud of his left foot, his uneven stride pounding the floor above her as he stumbled into his britches then searched in the dark for that blasted leather pouch and syringe.

"Libby!" he roared. "Did you ever get my medicine from your old man? You made a promise to me, woman! You said he'd have more by today, but there's nothing in here! Where would you be putting it?"

When she heard him move closer to the upper landing of the stairs, she quietly tiptoed out the front door, down the porch steps and around to the side of the house. There would be no way on God's green earth that she could explain to him that she never restocked his whiskey supply after her father had told her parcels of morphine and opium would most certainly be delivered to his office today. And Billy didn't have enough heart left in him to make him understand that hundreds of thousands of soldiers had returned from the war with similar afflictions and his same deplorable addictions. Demand had left supplies low, and Papa's order never arrived.

Peeking into the parlor window, her eyes followed his shadow as it moved about the dimly lit room, searching through every drawer, nook, and cranny he came upon. When the shadow stopped moving at a certain point, she knew his hand was busy rummaging around the empty spaces in the bookcases. Four years departed from home, and he hadn't forgotten her special hiding place for tiny wrapped gifts and sweets for the children of visiting folk. The only items that were hidden behind the books now were... a tiny, single-barreled Derringer and three bullets! She caught her breath at the realization that she'd forgotten all about them, having lived with her father the entire time Billy was gone.

She heard the front door open. He hobbled outside, leaned over the porch railing, gagged, and relinquished whatever dinner remained in his stomach. Then he began his slow decent of the porch steps. She panicked, not being able to determine which way to go. She figured her only choice would be to run to the back of the house and take the narrow path through tall weeds to the safe harbor of her father's house. At the rate that Billy moved, she should arrive well before him. Oh, woe be to hindsight! Now she wished she had accepted Papa's suggestion to move back to his home. Only that afternoon he had warned her that the fury coming from Billy's twisted brain might be the death of her some day.

She backed away from the window, only to find a rusty bent nail that protruded from a wooden siding board had ensnared the bottom of her gown. She tugged and tugged, then giving it a decisively hard yank to rip it free, headed for the back of the house. Too late! He had already reached the back of the house from the other side, being swift in his determination. All she could do was trail him at a spaced distance. She was well aware that he assumed she was with her father. Where else *could* she be? They lived in near desolation.

"I'll kill them both!" he gruffly proclaimed, as she watched his head bob up and down as he struggled to hastily bedraggle his gimpy leg along the dirt path. When he arrived at his destination, he pounded on the door of her father's office. "Open up, old man!" he loudly demanded. "And be quick about it!"

"The door is unlocked, Billy. Come in," she heard her father call.

Hearing the door fling open and slam against the wall, she decided it would be best not to interfere in their confrontation and to simply allow her father's wise discernment deal with Billy's foul behavior. She stayed back at a good thirty paces, hiding behind a willow tree.

"Where's my medicine, old man?" he growled.

"I've decided that my daughter should move back here with me until you can gain control of yourself. Have you given any more thought to my advice at having your leg removed? I can arrange for a hospital in Philadelphia to properly remove it, and you may again live a pain-free life. I would be more than happy to pay for it," he calmly said.

"Right now, the only thing I want is my medicine! Anything! Give me *anything*!" he yelled, pummeling his fist against the wall.

"I'm going over to your house and will bring my daughter back with me," the doctor informed him in his consistently composed voice.

Libby clapped her hand over her mouth. Now Billy *knew* she wasn't in Papa's home. She strained to hear their conversation, but both men were silent for several seconds as the realization hit Billy that he now had more control over the situation than Dr. Caleb Shaw.

"If you don't get me what I need, old man, you're *dead,* just like your precious little girl! That's right! Dead! Dead and buried, and rightly deserving! She was a filthy, deceitful liar!"

Bang!

The gun! No, Lord! Not Papa! she silently screamed. Her eyes darted around the dark surroundings as she tried to perceive where she might go to find any form of human life to help her poor father and to escape this insanity. Heat lightning crackled above her, followed by a deep, resounding boom of thunder. Knowing that Billy would now come looking for her, she turned and ran through the thicket of the field as fast as nature would allow to the lane that led to her nearest neighbor's home. Tears blinded her vision; burrs, thorns, and stones ripped at her feet through her thinly knit slippers. He might be much slower than she, but he need only to saddle and mount their horse in order to gain advantage in the hunt. Finally she came to the only neighbor's home within a quarter-mile radius.

"Mr. Clark!" she screamed, using both fists to bang on his door. "Open for me, please! It's Libby Prescott, and I need your help! Please! Oh, *please* open the door! Billy has gone mad and shot Papa!" She sunk to her knees and leaned against the door, crying in anguish. Her dear papa needed help, but what was she to do? She knew the Clark's main home was in Philadelphia, but they usually spent most of the summer in this, their country house. Perhaps they had gone back to the city, there being little relief here from the intensity of this summer's heat. She slowly rose, trying to regain a steady stance on her throbbing feet, only to find herself confronted with sinister eyes that glowed golden-red in the darkness, and a low, threatening growl that would have caused her to swoon had she not been in so precarious a position.

"Esau! They wouldn't go back to the city without you!" She reached her hand out in friendship to the Clark's hunting dog. He cautiously approached and began to nuzzle her feet. "I know," she said, patting his head. "They're bleeding. Wherever could your master be, old boy?"

Forlorn and weeping, she sat down and leaned against the door again, not knowing where to turn. Then, quite suddenly, the sound of a sharp train whistle pierced the darkness. Someone who could be of help! She was aware that a couple nights per week, a freight train sporadically stopped for several hours at the abandoned Union station house up the road. She also knew that Billy could easily find her at the Clark's house, and she'd better hightail it out of there and get to the train engineer. Two pairs of cowardly eyes watched from their second-story bedroom window as their dog took it upon him to accompany the distraught young woman on her quest for assistance.

The pair reached their goal only to find the entire area shrouded in darkness. The engineer hadn't lit the old lantern that hung on a hook by the barred station door. She surmised that he was relieving himself somewhere close by or perhaps sleeping in the engine car. If only there was a way to light the lantern. She subconsciously ran her hands down her sides. Normally she kept matches in her apron, and the lack of pockets reminded her that she was attired only in a cotton nightgown. But modesty was the last rule of social etiquette on her mind at present. Her sweet father's life was in her hands. She knew she dared not cry out. Billy might be hot on her trail for all she knew, so she ardently began her search for a savior. He might possibly be sleeping in the open air, but she couldn't afford not to inspect all areas. Esau, feeling he had completed his good deed, wandered back in the direction from where they had come. It was useless to try to get into the boxcars. She hadn't the strength or the height to open the sliding panels. Elated to find a partially opened panel on the fourth car from the engine, she stood on swollen toes and peered into the opening.

"Is anyone in there? If you please, I need help! My father has been shot! Is anyone in there?" she whispered.

Blinding match-light ripped through the darkness of the boxcar interior. Throwing her forearm over her smarting eyes, she turned away. But upon hearing whispers, she instantly looked back into the car to find two grimy faces staring out at her.

"Please! How might I find the engineer?" she anxiously asked. "I must get help for my father! My husband has gone mad and shot him!"

"We'll help ya, girlie," a low female voice softly responded. "Let us help you climb up, and we'll talk about what to do. We don't be knowin' where the engineer is, and he ain't supposed to know we're in here, so hush and raise your arms on up." Two male hands reached down to pull her up and into the boxcar and plunked her down onto a cube of bound hay. The female lit another match to light a stubby candle, and Libby found herself gazing into the faces of a white woman close to her own age of twenty-five years and a brawny mulatto man in his late thirties.

"What do ya give us if we help ya?" the woman asked.

"I... I have nothing with me. Please, *please* try to understand that my father has been shot, and I need to get help quickly! We'll discuss payment later. A man is *dying*, or he may already be d..." She broke down and sobbed. "I'll be happy to give you everything I own if you'll *help* me! I *beg* of you!" she pleaded, pounding her palms on her knees.

"Supposin' we start with them rings," the man said, pointing to her left hand.

Papa always tells me that I'm gullible, she sadly thought. *And he's correct.* Knowing in her heart that they had no intention of assisting her, she chose to risk a hasty jump from the boxcar. But just as she acted, a large hand reached out, grabbed her by her hair, and flung her to the floor—and then a mighty fist rendered her unconscious.

CHAPTER 2

Early morning sun peeked through the warped gap between the sliding doors of the boxcar. Finally conscious but thoroughly disoriented, Libby surveyed her surroundings through the eye that wasn't swollen shut. Every cell of her battered body screamed out in pain. Her head pulsed so greatly, she feared it might explode from the pressure. Then, one by one, memories of last night's happenings flooded her brain. *Papa!* Panic set in, shooting enough adrenaline through her to assist in dragging her tortured torso over to the doors. Despite the fact that three fingers of her left hand were either dislocated or perhaps broken, she prepared to use what little strength she still possessed to pry open one of the doors. To her surprise, she found the feat to be effortless. But she wasn't prepared for what lay outside—strangely unfamiliar landscape. There were no heavily wooded areas or embankments along the train tracks in her hometown of Wellesley, Pennsylvania. There were no patchy beds of long onion grass or wild orange lilies either. Even the smell of the air here was different—thickly humid and fragrant.

Clinging to the door, she labored to hoist herself to a standing position. Poor, aching, shredded feet! Her once dainty pink slippers were now dirt-caked and dyed a gory shade of reddish brown by the dried blood that cemented them to her skin. Once erect, she leaned outside to capture the attention of the first passerby, but the area appeared to be desolate. About to cry out for help, the train suddenly jolted violently in preparation for departure, thrusting her from the boxcar down a grassy embankment. The trunk of a broad oak tree prevented further advancement.

"I haven't a clue as to who this girl might be, Dr. Flanagan, although her injuries and dirt have greatly disguised her features. I'm going to tell Becky to heat some water so I may bathe her," Clarissa Chambers said, heading for the bedroom door.

"Wait. Stay with me for a few moments longer, Clary. I need you to hold the ether cloth over her nose. I'm going to try to relocate her fingers, so 'tis best she stays unconscious. The pain would be too much to bear for such a scrap of a girl."

"Do you surmise that she's been ... ?" she cautiously asked.

"I'm certain. The several clusters of five bruises appear to be made by the press of strong fingers, and their locations convince me that she's been violated. Jeremy will need to fetch the sheriff to question her. I'll write a report of my findings and have it delivered to him," he said while placing his inventory back in its medical satchel.

"The poor dear can't be more than eighteen years. I do hope her assailant is found and brought to justice. Shame and condemnation on any man who would practice such brutality on so delicate a little creature!"

"I'm concerned for the women of this town. We may have a preying animal on the loose. There, now. Her fingers are back in position. I leave it to you and your wise discernment as to which of your herbal remedies would best heal her cuts, bruises, and poor mangled feet. Make certain the broken toe stays strapped to the toe beside it. The gash on the side of her head isn't deep enough to warrant stitching, but cleanse the area several times a day. I'll leave a salve to dress it after each cleaning. It will heal faster if the scab stays moist. I know I leave her in capable hands, Clary. She'll thank the Lord that she happened to wander into your care. I've done all that I'm able, so I'll take leave of you now. I'll ask Jeremy to fetch Sheriff Clayton on my way out. I'll be back on the morrow to see how well she's faring. When will Justin arrive home from Washington?"

"Any day now. His engagement celebration is to take place in ten days, but I wouldn't be surprised if he stays in Washington as long as possible. The Henry Wirz trial begins today. I know he wants to keep abreast of the proceedings."

"Ah, yes, the Andersonville trial. I have great empathy for Wirz, we both being physicians and devoted family men. Those who know him can only deem him a caring, compassionate fellow. I suspect he'll end up a pawn to get at Jeff Davis for war crimes."

"I believe that may be the way Justin feels, but he would never comment without hearing all of the evidence… I would have placed the young lady in the guest room had the walls not been freshly painted. The fumes would have only added to her discomfort," she explained as they ventured into the hallway. "Jeremy!" she called over the balcony railing.

"Mr. Jeremy gone ta fetch the sheriff, Miss Clary," Becky informed her from the downstairs foyer.

"Good! Please bring up a large basin of warm water, mild soap, and a pile of clean towels to Mr. Justin's room. I'll need your assistance in bathing the girl. Also, please boil several rusty nails in a small amount of water."

"Yas, ma'am, Miss Clary."

"She's still unconscious, Jeremy. Perhaps it wasn't wise to bring the sheriff here before we had an opportunity to question her. He's such an irritable, impatient individual. If he feels we've wasted his valuable time, he—Oh, I hear a moan! She's awake! Go tell him he may come upstairs now."

"Wait until he sees how she's been brutalized. He'll be out for blood!"

"Go!" Clary demanded, pushing her younger brother toward the stairs. She hastened back to her patient, pleased to find her fully conscious. Seating herself on the edge of the bed, she lifted Libby's hand and soothingly stroked it. "I'm pleased to see that you're finally awake," she said with a warm, friendly smile. "I want to assure you that you're in a safe home, surrounded by decent Christian folk who will care for you. My name is Clarissa Chambers, but you may call me Clary. And what is your name, miss?"

Libby stared blankly at her benefactress. "I ... I don't know. I believe I'm ... no, no, I'm ... I don't know *what* my name is ... Where am I?"

"You're in Barrister's Junction, Virginia, twenty-five miles west of Washington. Are you familiar with this area?" Libby slowly shook her head. "My brother found you lying unconscious beside our family cemetery. He carried you into our home, and for the last couple hours our family physician and I have attended to your bruises, wounds ... and other afflictions. Can you recall *nothing* of your plight?"

"No ... nothing ... nothing," she answered, staring up at the pretty, red-haired woman of about twenty-five years. Befuddled, she added, "But I suppose I'll have a cognitive thought after resting. I'm ... I'm so tired. My only wish is to sleep," she said with a weak sigh. She looked past Clary to see a gangly, tow-headed young man of about twenty years and a rugged man twice his age attempt to approach the bed.

Clary hastily stood up to mediate by placing a hand on each man's chest and, with a determined shove, attempted to force them to exit the room.

"She remembers nothing of last night's events, Sheriff; therefore, I deem it best that she rest for a while. Her memory may rekindle after she sleeps. Trauma can do odd things to the mind. Besides, you would probably prefer she not be confused when you interrogate her."

"What do you mean, she can't remember? Now you listen to

me, Clary! I only saw her face for a few seconds, but what I saw was enough to concern me for the safety of the women in this town. Any assistance she can give in apprehending her assailant might save another young woman from her same fate… or worse!"

"I tell you that she *cannot* be of any help to you at present. She can't even recall her name. Please respect my judgment. I apologize for having brought you here. Jeremy will keep you posted as to her condition and when she finally recollects. I'm as anxious as you that she remembers. Also, her presence may place this household in jeopardy."

"I'll deputize a man to keep watch over you until Justin comes home."

"I'm well able to care for my household, Sheriff!" Jeremy argued.

"Nonsense!" Clary stared hard into her brother's eyes. "Who will guard us while you're at work? The biggest help you can be is to place an article in your newspaper to draw out anyone who might know something of this girl. There must be *someone* close by who is anxious to know of her whereabouts. If her assailant tracks her to our home, Sheriff Clayton's deputy will capture him. Go on now, Jeremy. Go to work."

"You're mighty bossy," he whined indignantly. "But I suppose you're right." He started down the stairs. "I might be the boss at work, but it's undeniably a woman who is boss of this household," he mumbled.

"I'll send Dan Granger out to stay with you until Justin comes home, Clary. He has a couple weeks before he has to cut and cure his crop, so he can spare some time. Now be certain to send word when your patient appears ready to discuss her attack."

"*Must* you send Dan Granger?" she asked with red cheeks and flaring eyes.

"He's the only man available for the time being. Try to look past your past."

"Well… well, you can just tell him… tell him you forbid him to speak to me while he's working this case," she said adamantly.

"Now you know I can't command anything of the sort." He grabbed his hat from the coat rack and walked out on to the porch. "Write him a note stating your demands, and have Jeremy give it to him," he suggested with a chuckle and a tip of his hat.

Libby closed her eye, the excruciating pain in her head overshadowing any curiosity as to her caretakers or comfortable place of confinement. The faint, musky scent of leather and bay rum relayed the fact that she was resting in a man's bedchamber. All five senses felt razor sharp, rubbed raw by a plight from which she had no recollection, and her body craved sweet sleep. She would search her mind for her identity later… later. She began to drift.

"I shall call you 'Sparrow' for now," Clary told Libby, setting a tray of bathing supplies on the night table. "Sparrow, because God's eye is always on the sparrow, and he sent you to us for protection. You need not help to remove your nightgown. Becky and I shall do all of the work." She took a cup from the tray and ladled out a spoonful of murky water. "Open your mouth for a blood strengthener."

Libby swallowed the bitter potion and shivered. "Rusty nails!" She gagged.

Clary looked surprised. "How did you know?"

Libby stared blankly at her.

"Do not fret. The taste won't remain long. I've made a tea of white willow bark sweetened with a good bit of honey to help you sleep and ease inflammation. Becky will hold your head steady while I feed it to you. Then we'll bathe you. I've made several poultices of eucalyptus and yarrow to help numb and heal your wounds. When you've slept for a while, we'll sit you up to soak your feet in a basin of warm witch hazel water."

“Have you myrrh and lavender? Both work well with witch hazel to disinfect.” She furrowed her brow. *Why would I recall that?*

Clary looked at Becky and smiled. “Our little sparrow can’t remember her name, but her knowledge of healing aids may be our first clue to her identity.”

CHAPTER 3

Clary pulled the drapes open then turned to observe her patient. "You're looking well today, Sparrow," she remarked, nodding to Becky to set the breakfast tray on the bed. "Do you realize you just slept for twenty hours? You weren't even aware that Dr. Flanagan examined you yesterday afternoon. Before you eat, I'll take you to the wash closet. You, my dear, are in for a delight, for we recently were blessed with in-house plumbing!" She peeled the light blanket off Libby and placed an arm around her waist to help her stand. "I'll help you down the stairs."

Libby caught her breath the instant she put her weight on her feet. She looked down to see two puffy blobs of tattered flesh. Their unsightliness brought tears to her eyes.

Clary kissed her cheek. "Poor little dear. This will be the only time you'll be on your feet today. I have a surprise! Dr. Flanagan left a wheeled chair with us so that I might take you outside to enjoy the fresh air. We'll put the roses back in those pale little cheeks. You must be pleased that you can now see from both eyes. What color *are* your eyes? I do declare I've never seen such dark eyes. Almost black, yet they have a blue cast to them. You need not respond to my constant prattle. I speak too frequently, and I know you may not be feeling well enough to converse."

"I would very much like to converse with you. I'll be forever grateful for your care and hospitality. When I finally realize my identity, I pray I'm able to repay your kindness."

"Nonsense! As a Christian I'm called to charity, and charity requires or accepts no repayment. It's a gift of hope. Perhaps it would be best that I help you into a tub of warm water and feed you breakfast while you soak."

"Your garden is quite impressive, Clary! The varieties of herbs and flowers are delightfully fragrant. And the size! *Surely* you don't care for it all by yourself. Oh! Do I see purple echinacea cone blooms? They have a wonderfully antiseptic quality when blended into soap, so I suppose you must also grow meadowsweet? The combination of echinacea and meadowsweet makes such a lovely, comforting cup of tea on a chilly winter's day."

Clary stooped down in front of the wheeled chair. "The mind is queer, isn't it? It can recollect bits and pieces of trivial subject matter but can't seem to recall something as important as one's own name and identity. I suppose God made it that way as a protective measure, to blot out times we can't face until we're able. You must have experienced excruciating trauma, my little friend. Your speech tells me that you've received an education, but I suspect you weren't raised in this vicinity. Your accent, I would wager, is derived from the northern regions of this country." She smiled. "But I can forgive you for that. We can't help where we're raised, can we?" She stood back up and repositioned herself behind the chair. "I began to build this garden over four years ago. It was only a small portion of the size it is today. I've always been fascinated by the natural healing remedies provided by the good Lord. When my cousin, Surgeon General Sam Moore, called upon his fellow Confederates to grow and gather wild herbs to make medicines to aid our soldiers, I decided to grow all I could, especially hypericum."

"St. John's Wort," mumbled Libby.

"Correct. Tomorrow you shall meet Dr. Flanagan. He traveled with the Irish brigade during the war and made good use of my medicinal concoctions. Have you any recollection of the war?"

She shrugged and, with little conviction, said, "I vaguely

remember … A young man is coming to us." She pointed toward the house.

"That would be my youngest brother, Jeremy. His passion for journalism led him to purchase his own printing press, which produces a newspaper named *The Barrister's Beacon*. His 'on the scene' coverage of the battle at Fort Stevens, back in '64, was quite exceptional. Mr. Lincoln was in attendance, and Jeremy's photographer was able to take a candid shot of him. I must show it to you. While I'm proud of Jeremy and his newfound success, I feel it best not to allow my feelings to be known to him. It's difficult enough being the only female child sandwiched between a household of brothers. The competition is fierce! I have three other brothers. Joshua is twenty-four years of age, exactly one year younger than me. He and his wife, Lydia, own a small horse farm in the next county. They've given me a precious baby niece, Laurel. We nearly lost Josh. He survived two gunshot wounds received while fighting in the battle at Gettysburg."

"Oh!"

"Did I say something that incited a memory?"

"No, no. When you said 'two gunshot wounds,' a flash went through my head, but I still can recall nothing."

"I also had a brother, Jeffrey, who would be twenty-eight years of age. He was killed several years ago while fighting in the first battle at Shiloh. He had no children but left a wife named Betsy. She remarried a month ago."

"Betsy … *Betsy*?" Libby squealed excitedly. "I believe that's *my* name!"

"Come quickly!" Clary called to her brother. "Our young lady seems to have recalled her name! It's Betsy! Perhaps she'll remember her last name shortly."

Jeremy quickened the stride of his final twenty yards to greet them. He grinned at Libby. "Well, good morning to you, Miss Betsy. I'm pleased to finally make your acquaintance."

Libby held out her hand to him. "I now can thank another of my benefactors. Thank you kindly, Mr. Jeremy, for caring enough to take me into your home," she said, with a shy softness. Her pale cheeks flushed to pink at the recollection that he was the one who had carried her scantily clad body into his home.

Sensitive to her embarrassment, he said, "I couldn't take my eyes off your poor, bruised face. But I must say, for the short time you've been with us, your wounds seem to be healing right nicely. My sister is quite the herbal expert. Had she been born a man, she would be a great physician or scientist today."

"I would be just as great a physician or scientist as a *woman*... most likely *better* than any man," Clary said defiantly. "But unfortunately for me, society requires that most of my waking hours be spent taking charge of the menial tasks involved in caring for a household of helpless men... for now. But someday, someday I'm going to travel the world and discover something that will truly be deemed beneficial to mankind."

"Her independent, superior attitude has cost my sister many a romance, including one with the gentleman who sits on the porch bench, watching as you take your little stroll," he said with a smirk.

"Hush! Betsy will believe we spend most of our time on the battlefield." She waived him on in agitation. "Go... go tell Becky to give Dan his meal... and you had best go back to work."

He winked at Libby. "Great satisfaction in 'getting her goat,'" he said with a chuckle.

"I wish he had gone to England to live with Mother and Father," Clary grumbled when he was out of earshot. "The continental experience might help to mature him."

"Your parents live in England?"

"My father works as President Johnson's trade ambassador to France and England. He's required to live in either France or England for nine months out of the year. My parents are fortunate to own a lovely manor house in the English countryside. My grandmother died prior to the war. She willed *this* house to the five of us grandchildren, and my father's house, for the three months of the year that he and Mother are in the States, is the one you see across the field," she explained, pointing the way.

"Across the field," Libby echoed in unexplainable wonder.

"Yes. Becky, her husband, Abel, and little Vie live in an apartment at the back of the house. Abel has done an admirable job at maintaining our properties."

"I suppose Becky and Abel are your slaves?"

Clary laughed. "It hasn't been legal for anyone to own a slave for quite some time, but in answer to your question: hardly, dear. We here are all servants and none of us slaves. Becky and Abel are paid and given room and board. We're one big family that works together. Why, last Christmas, my brother gave Abel two acres of land on the other side of the woods to build a home of his own. Take care that you not adhere to the notion that all Southerners are slavers. The vast majority of soldiers who fought in the war never owned a slave. Most fought for the preservation of the South and to prevent Northern aggression due to the great imbalance of state representation in Congress and the Senate. Now, miss, we'll soak your feet and massage them with aloe ointment."

This bed is so... incredibly comfortable. Thank you for bringing me to Clary, Lord. Help me to remember, please... please... sleepy... so sleepy, drifted through Libby's mind as she began to doze off. *The sound of the gentle rainfall is lovely... and smells so fresh... as does this bed.* "Is that you, Clary? I thought you retired for the evening," she dreamily murmured at the sound of footsteps.

"Forgive me for disturbing your rest, young lady. I only want to remove a few personal items from my room," a deep, masculine voice informed her.

"Please light a lamp so that you may see what you're doing, sir."

"The name is Justin, miss, but I'll properly introduce myself to you in the morning. I've found what I need, so please go back to sleep. My sister would behead me if she knew I awakened you."

Libby giddily giggled. "Then it will be our little secret. I surely wouldn't want to be responsible for anyone having to lose his head over me. Goodnight. Oh, but where will you sleep?"

"In the guest room. Pay me no mind. Goodnight, Miss Betsy."

Such a remarkably rich voice! I would like to hear him sing. She lightly laughed, then turned on to her side to hug her pillow. The bedtime potion that had been administered to her was working so well, she floated away into the night.

"Please, no breakfast! I feel as though I should vomit. Please take the food away! I can't tolerate the smell!" Libby gagged. "Oh! Forgive me! I'm ever so grateful for your hospitality, but I know you would be quite unhappy if I ruined your lovely bed linens."

Clary handed the tray to Becky to return to the kitchen. "We'll try again later. Today I would like to get you up and dressed, since the swelling in your feet has gone down considerably. Becky and I took up the hems of two of my frocks, so you'll have clothing to wear. My brother, Justin, arrived home late last night, and Mr. Granger apprised him of your situation. I'll introduce you to him after we make you presentable. Come with me to my bedroom. You may sit at my dressing table while I brush your hair."

Libby cautiously stood up and was surprised that she felt little pain in her feet. She followed Clary and sat down in front of the mirror. "My injuries are much better today, Clary, but my stomach is irritable. I'm sorry I couldn't eat your food. My behavior was very ungracious and rude!"

Clary carefully worked the brush through the mass of heavy, tangled curls. "Oh fie! You need not apologize. Last night's elixir must have disagreed with your stomach."

"I don't believe so. I slept well."

"Your hair is so … so *abundant.* Do forgive me. Did I hurt you?" she asked, struggling to detangle the knots. "I must work carefully around your head abrasion."

"Clary, you've told me nothing about Justin."

"True. We never did come to speak of him. Well, he's my oldest sibling and is thirty years of age. Most working weeks he resides in Washington. I'm proud to say that he's a West Point *and* Harvard Law School graduate, who didn't participate in active combat during the war, but instead served in military tribunals as a ranking captain. For the last three months, he's been employed by the law firm of Dupont, Dupont, and Dupont as a barrister who hopes to add a 'Chambers' on to the list of Duponts. This will most likely happen shortly, for Justin is now officially engaged to Susanna Dupont, daughter of Dupont, the first. The lady is a tall, willowy creature, with alabaster skin, a swanlike neck, golden hair, and the strong will of a spoiled child."

"You don't care for her?"

"I like her well enough, I suppose. She's pleasant. It's just that … I believe she has dreams for my brother that he'll never be able to envision. And he's someone who would surrender his happiness to please her. Now don't misunderstand me. He's not easily manipulated or simple-minded. Indeed, he has brilliant intellect. He merely has a tender heart for the needs of others and justice for all. Perhaps he *will* find happiness in fulfilling her dreams," she said with a wave of the brush.

"What is it that she wants for him? No snood. A ribbon, please."

"She wishes for him to eventually enter the political arena, as her father has been attempting," Clary explained while tying Libby's hair back with a wide red ribbon. "Charles Dupont is a barrel-chested, rotund scalawag with lofty goals, who hopes to one day become this country's president. The man is too full of himself to be truly concerned for the well-being of his fellow countrymen. My brother merely wishes to help reconstruct this country by ensuring that everyone is treated fairly and that no individual may take advantage of another. He's not politically motivated, merely a true defender of the weak and helpless. I believe that Susanna may find him lacking in ambition."

"I'm sorry for him," Libby said sympathetically. "But if she loves him, she'll accept his goals. His happiness will be hers."

"Now what would a young girl like you know about love? You can't be more than seventeen years of age," Clary noted, staring at their cheek-to-cheek reflection in the mirror.

"I believe I may be sixteen. Yes, I seem to recollect that I'm sixteen, and I don't need to know about love to be able to pity his situation."

Clary laughed. "And so wise for a young girl of sixteen. Now we'll remove your nightgown, and you may wear my lovely red and white crepe de chine frock. Your bosom is fuller than mine, so you should fill out the bodice quite nicely."

"Clary, why didn't you marry Mr. Granger? He looks at you with admiring eyes."

"The man I'll someday marry, hopefully before I'm officially labeled 'spinster,' will be highly intelligent and lacking Dan Granger's 'stubborn as a mule' disposition. I believe the final argument we had, before we parted ways, had to do with choosing the most beneficial fertilizer for his tobacco crop."

"Wonderful! I see Dr. Flanagan's silver mare outside," Clary told Libby as they descended the stairs. "He and Justin may be eating breakfast. Come, now. You need not be bashful. Both men are gentlemen and will do their best to put you at ease."

When they entered the kitchen, the men stood up to receive them.

"My, Clary, our patient is looking well this morning. And she even smiles!" the good doctor exclaimed as he and Justin pulled chairs from the table for the ladies.

"I would like to introduce you to my little pet, Betsy. Betsy, meet your highly competent physician, Dr. James Flanagan, and my handsome brother, Justin." She took Libby's right hand and held it out for Justin to take. Libby shyly looked down, away from the caring brown eyes that boldly studied her face.

"Good morning, Miss Betsy. I trust you slept well?" he asked with a knowing smile.

She looked up at him and returned his smile. "Most definitely, thank you. Your bed is quite comfortable."

"Do you see, Doctor, that she has bruising only around her eye and upper cheek? The rest of the bruises and scrapes have almost completely faded," Clary proudly pointed out when they were all seated.

"I do. We make a remarkable team. I would hire you as my assistant if Mrs. Flanagan were not already my office helper." He turned to cast scrutinizing eyes upon his patient. It was now fairly clear as to her appearance before the assault, and somehow she looked familiar to him, as though he had met her at some place in time.

"I'm surprised you didn't stay longer in Washington, Justin," Clary remarked. "I know the great interest you've shown in the Andersonville trial."

"Military trials are closed to the public, and now that I'm back in civilian life—"

The kitchen door suddenly flew open, banged against the stove, and then slammed shut.

"Misser Jussin! You home!" a little voice gleefully shrieked.

Libby and Clary laughed as a tiny child rushed in to throw herself into Justin's open arms.

"I miss you," she told him with a peck to his cheek.

The door flew open again, but this time an angry Becky came in to claim her overzealous three-year-old.

"I tole you ta wait till the doctor leave before goin' in ta see Mr. Justin!"

Justin held the child's round cherub face to his cheek. "Have you met our little Vie, Miss Betsy?" Libby shook her head. "She's a bundle of energy. Abel probably had her locked down until you were well enough to handle her exuberance. She's not interrupting anything important, Becky. I'll give her some strawberry preserves on bread. May I fix something for you?" he asked Libby as he stood up and sat Vie on his chair.

"Betsy was unable to eat her breakfast this morning. Perhaps she would like some bread and preserves," suggested Clary.

"I suppose a crust of bread and some weak tea might settle my stomach," said Libby. "Nothing else, please." She glanced at the doctor. His relentless stare caused her to fidget.

"You pwiddy," Vie told Libby. "Mama say dey gonna catch da bad man dat hurt you an' 'whoop his hide.' I know what 'whoop' be. What be 'hide'?"

"It's the place where Mama Becky places your whoopings," Clary laughingly explained.

Libby decided she had best quell the staring doctor's curiosity. "I really am doing quite well, sir. Almost back to my normal self," she said with a light, nervous giggle as tears pooled in her eyes. "Whoever that may be."

Vie looked at Libby through large, soulful eyes. "Don' cwy, Miz Bitsy. Jesus an' Misser Jussin take care o' you."

"Thank you, sweet little girl. You've given me cheer," Libby said with a broad smile.

"Now, little Miss Viola, if you'll take your bread outside so that I may speak with Miss Betsy for a few moments, I'll give you a pony ride before your nap this afternoon. Do we have an agreement?" Justin asked.

"Gweemint," she said, reaching her little hand up to shake his.

He handed the child her bread, took the tray from the counter, and motioned for Libby to follow him to his office library. He instructed her to take a seat in one of the gold brocade wing chairs, placed the tray of bread and tea on the small round table next to her, and then took a seat in the twin wing chair on the other side of the table.

"Dr. Flanagan has a matter to discuss with Clary, so I thought I would take this opportunity to ask you several questions and put you at ease as to what you can expect from us while you're in our home. I'll also need to set down a couple rules for your own protection. But first of all, are you a person of faith, Miss Betsy?"

"I know my Savior. Of that, I've not forgotten," she said, reaching for her cup of tea.

"Splendid! We attend church every Sunday. I'll exempt you from tomorrow, but you should be feeling well enough to attend next week."

"Perhaps I shan't be here next week. Someone may claim me, or I may realize my identity."

"If that be the case, I'll be content. However, we would never release you to any individual we consider an unfit caretaker. You're most welcome in our home until you feel comfortable enough to move on. Now, I must insist that you never answer the door or step outside without a chaperone. The article that my brother placed in his newspaper gives no inkling as to where you may be. All inquiries are to be made directly to him at his workplace, but this doesn't mean you're safe. Someone may have followed you here." He reached across the table to rest his hand on hers as she went to pick up the crust of bread. "I don't want you to be afraid. Everything possible is being done to assure your safety and discover your identity."

"I've sent to Jefferson Medical School in Philadelphia asking for any current publications they may have on the study of *memory loss*," the doctor told Clary as she escorted him to the front door. "I don't pretend to be very knowledgeable about the disorder, but I've witnessed several cases over the course of the war. The science of the mind is not exacting, merely speculative."

"Do you surmise that her memory will return after her head completely heals?"

"I can't rightly say. There appears to be no swelling of her brain or noticeable brain damage, but if I were to surmise, I would say most of her memory loss is due to shock at having experienced horrific trauma. Time will tell. Also, I must say that her look is familiar to me. I'll have to mull it over. Perhaps Mrs. Flanagan will recognize the girl. She can accompany me on my next visit to your home. A good day to you, Clary."

CHAPTER 4

A dozen weary men with shovels and muddy boots sat on Dr. Shaw's front porch awaiting further instructions and the latest prognosis on Dr. Shaw's condition to be given by his associate, Dr. Tim Morrow. Reverend Shelton had arrived early that morning to keep watch over and pray for his dear friend, Caleb. It had been a very frustrating and grueling three days of working through several downpours and trudging through thick mud, digging up any suspicious area of loose soil that might possibly be the grave of Libby Prescott. After a time, Sally Morrow appeared before the group with a pitcher of lemonade to refill their glasses. Her expression was gravely solemn.

"I'm sorrowed to say that the good doctor is barely alive, gentlemen. The bullet lies close to his heart, and he has simply lost too much blood. Tim believes he's trying to hold on until he knows his daughter has been found to receive a proper burial, and for his son, Ben, to be located and brought to his bedside. If you're not already aware, the Academy of Natural Science in Philadelphia employs Ben when he's not teaching science at Boston University. His superiors telegraphed us that he's on an assignment of a botanical nature. It may take several days to find him, because he and his associate are camping in the Poconos."

"We covered every inch of land within the radius of a mile, Mrs. Too bad the Clarks must have headed back to Philadelphia. We sure could have used ole Esau's help. The sheriff's hounds keep losing her scent. Guess the ground's too waterlogged. Found this pink snood ahangin' on a low tree branch on the other side of the field," reported Andy Stone, the next closest neighbor to the Prescotts. He handed it to Sally then thoughtfully scratched his head. "It stumps me that we didn't come across even a drop of blood in or around the Prescott house. Besides, how could Billy manage to carry her very far to bury her what with his ailin' leg and all... unless he strangled her and loaded her onto his horse."

"We'll leave Billy up to the law," Mrs. Morrow said, with an impatient wave of her hand. "My main concern is that we find the dear girl's body so that her father may die without questions."

Reverend Shelton and Dr. Morrow came outside to face the men. They didn't need to utter a word. Caleb Shaw was gone. Sally buried her face in her hands and sobbed. Tears could be seen in the eyes of even the burliest of the men. Several had daughters of their own. What a tragedy to die without the peace of knowing.

"Gentlemen," Reverend Shelton reminded them, "at least Caleb had peace in knowing where he was headed."

"What do we do now?" several asked.

"Nothing," said the doctor. "I'm afraid Billy's the only one who can finalize this hunt."

"Go home, gentlemen. I'll see some of you tomorrow at Sunday service. Thank you for your efforts," the reverend said, and then he headed back inside to arrange the funeral.

Maggie Clark opened the window of their sixth-floor suite overlooking Chestnut Street. The sticky summer rain had finally stopped, and she was dying for a breath of fresh air, along with some relief from the city heat. She batted at an unwelcome fly and reached for the Monday newspaper to deal the pest its final blow. After flicking the tiny corpse out the window, she sat down and began leafing through the pages, trying to determine if there were any upcoming social events posted for which she knew she would be receiving an invitation. But it was a small block in the obituaries that commanded her attention. With newspaper in hand, she bounded out into the hall and down all six flights of stairs to search for her husband. She found him berating a cowering desk clerk for two days of tardiness. As she rushed at them, Harry Clark reeled around with a raised, threatening hand.

"Don't interrupt me, Maggie! I'm not finished with this soon-to-be-discharged 'good for nothing.' Go back upstairs!"

She knew better than to argue. She had felt the sting of his hand on her cheek far too often over the course of their fifteen-year marriage. After climbing back up the six flights, she dropped into the nearest chair to the window, unbuttoned her bodice, and used the newspaper to fan away the perspiration droplets from her chest. Ten minutes later, her husband returned, walking an angry gait with a scowl plastered on his bloated face.

"Now tell me what in blazes has you all fired up!"

She held the obituary page up to him. He snatched it from her hand and began to read:

> Died: Dr. Caleb Stanton Shaw, 55, of Wellesley, PA, from a gunshot wound to the area of his heart, allegedly inflicted by his son-in-law three days prior to his death. The doctor was able to give his associate some details of a discussion that induced a scuffle between he and his son-in-law, after the younger man informed him that he had murdered and buried his wife, the doctor's only daughter. Her remains have yet to be found and exhumed. A son, Benjamin Adam, survives the doctor.

"Do you not see?" Maggie asked in a high-pitched voice, agitated by the dull expression on her husband's face.

"What's there to see? She was screaming her head off that Billy shot her father. We just went through a war, Maggie. Thousands of men that were shot died," he said with a shrug, tossing the newspaper on the floor.

Maggie put her face in her hands and wept for the good doctor and his daughter ... and the fact that *she* had to be married to the most dimwitted, uncompassionate, cowardly man in the city of Philadelphia. She began to wonder how they had ever come so far—to own a bustling hotel and fine dining room.

"She was trying to tell us that her father had been shot, but *after* Billy told Caleb that he had killed and buried her!" She rolled her eyes and threw her hands up in the air at the fact that his dull expression remained unchanged. "She's alive ... somewhere!" she screamed at him. "I wish the newspaper had given more details. I suppose that because he's not a Philadelphia resident anymore—"

The dull expression instantly transformed into a threatening glare.

"Now you see here, woman! You let what happened forty miles from here *be*. I forbid you to get involved in this! It could ruin our reputation and business."

"It wouldn't if we had helped the poor girl when she came to us," she sadly stated.

"I was just protecting us from Billy. Guess he caught up to her and killed her after she stopped at our house."

"If that be the case, then I would feel even worse than I do right now, if that were possible, because we could have prevented another murder."

He pointed his finger close to her face. "You heard me! You're to keep your mouth shut!"

It was a dark and gloomy Tuesday—a perfect afternoon for a funeral of one so well loved. A major percentage of the Wellesley population attended, all garbed in their black crape finery, with black umbrellas in hand. The rain stopped long enough for Reverend Shelton to say what had to be said and to pray that Libby Prescott's body would be found, or that Billy would eventually lead the sheriff to her remains. He reminded the crowd that father and daughter were together again, happy in the best possible place.

When the crowd finally disbanded, a lone figure stood by the graveside of his father. Ben Shaw didn't care to speak to anyone. He only wished to be alone with his father for a time, to meditate and attempt to shake off the guilt that he hadn't been present to prevent all of this heartbreak. Sally Morrow looked back to see him standing there and went to stand by his side.

"We were afraid you wouldn't be here in time," she softly said, placing a gentle hand on his shoulder.

He glanced at her with a half smile. "I know folks have always thought of me as being somewhat odd. I was standing at the back of the crowd." He sighed. "I simply don't care to speak with anyone today. I'm still trying to understand the events leading up to this tragedy."

"Stay with Tim and me, Ben. Don't go back to your father's house just yet. It's too soon. We'll talk after you've had a good night's rest. You'll want all of the details."

"You're very kind. I believe I would like to stay at your home. You've always been like part of my family… family to all of us."

The sky opened up again, and rain poured down over the casket and the two mourners who stood beside it. Ben positioned his hat over his black, tasseled curls and took Sally's outreached hand that drew him beneath her umbrella. He was special to her. She had always harbored high hopes that he and her Emma Jean would someday marry but had come to accept the fact that Ben was married to his research. She doubted that any woman could draw him away from so dear a career.

"I'll make you a good supper, and then you may retire for the night. All of your questions will be answered in the morning."

"Good afternoon," Libby called to Jeremy from the bench where she was soaking her feet in a basin of warm water, lavender, and salts. "It's a lovely, bright Tuesday afternoon, is it not?" she asked as he moseyed up the porch steps and stood before the two women. "Did you have a pleasant day at work?"

"Sit with Betsy for a moment, Jeremy," ordered Clary, accepting the newspaper he handed her. "I need to discuss the week's menus with Becky. Justin insists that she always have a chaperone, and she should soak for another fifteen minutes."

"Certainly." He took Clary's place and turned to look at Libby with questioning eyes.

"Yes?" she asked.

"I'm surprised you're not curious as to whether there have been any responses to my article concerning you. You've not asked even once."

"I supposed you would inform me without having to ask. Well, has anyone come forward?" she cautiously asked.

"Two, actually. An old woman who refuses to believe her granddaughter is dead and has been searching for her for twenty years." He touched his finger to the side of his head and rolled his eyes. "Then late this morning, a gentleman came to us with the news that his wife had left him last week, but he didn't give us the correct information on two bits of information we purposely left out of the article. His wife is a half-foot taller than you and missing two teeth of obvious notice when she smiles. Smile for me, Miss Betsy. Ah, yes. A perfect set," he remarked. "And because your teeth are so pearly white and perfect, this is for you." He handed her a small brown sack.

She peeked inside and giggled. "Not so pearly white and perfect if I eat all of these by myself. Share them with me, please, and thank you. It was very kind of you to think of me," she said, holding the sack of assorted sweets up to him. He popped a peppermint drop in his mouth, and she watched as his eyes traveled up the hundred-yard path that led to the road. He had noticed the clomping sound of the horse's hooves before her.

"I do believe we're to have company, Susanna and one of her snooty younger sisters, Charlotte."

"I wasn't aware that Miss Susanna lived in Barrister's Junction. I was under the impression that her home was in Washington."

"Her family lives close enough that I had the displeasure of attending school with Charlotte for a couple of years until she was sent to some uppity finishing school for young ladies. The Duponts are an 'old money' family, and their estate lies five miles east of here. They also lease a large suite in one of the grandest hotels in Washington, the Willard. Justin may have told Susanna of you after church this past Sunday. Their engagement reception is to be in the town hall this upcoming Saturday evening, so she may be calling to discuss the event and most certainly to catch a glimpse of our 'mystery lady.'" He gave her hair a tug. "Whatever the case, I prefer not to be present when they land." He rose and called for Clary to replace him. "I happily leave them to you," he informed her when she stepped back out on to the porch. He gave a brisk wave to the approaching women then disappeared into the house, much to the disappointment of Charlotte.

"Oh dear!" Clary whispered to Libby. "I doubt that Justin was expecting her visit, since he's extraordinarily busy today. I suppose *we'll* have to receive them. I'm sure their curiosity concerning you has lured them here."

"May I have a towel to dry my feet and slippers to cover them, please?" she asked with frantic eyes, not wishing for the ladies to view her still unsightly feet.

"Certainly. I realize you'd prefer they not gawk at you, but prepare yourself to be visually examined from head to toe. Do not allow yourself to be intimidated by Charlotte. She's the epitome of snobbery." She called to Becky to bring a towel and knit slippers just as the ladies stepped down from their buggy and started up the walkway to the porch. It was Justin who retrieved their request, handed them to Clary, and bounded down the steps to greet the women. He kissed Susanna's cheek, offered an arm to each lady, and escorted them up to the porch to perform introductions.

"Do forgive us for stopping by without notice," Susanna begged of Clary. "My sister and I were out for a ride on this lovely day and agreed that we just *had* to meet your young charge."

Simultaneously she and Charlotte looked down at the embarrassed Libby, who was trying desperately to pull the slippers over her soggy feet while looking up at the women with a sheepish smile. Susanna returned the smile, but Charlotte's expression remained lifeless. Libby finally managed to stand and found that it was indeed intimidating to stand before these two tall, fair-haired women with lavender-blue eyes. Both stood at least half a head taller than she, were impeccably groomed and coiffed, and were attired in the finest summer silk frocks.

Susanna rested a hand on Justin's arm, batted her eyelashes at him, and resituated a stray lock of his deep mahogany brown hair. "Oh my!" she gushingly exclaimed. "I do declare she's the sweetest little ole thing." She looked at Libby and, with the most sympathetic tone she could muster, said, "You poor, dear child! Your mama and papa must be beside themselves with worry."

Justin interrupted. "Suppose we go into the house, ladies. I'll ask Becky to prepare an afternoon tea, but I'm sorry to say that I'll only be able to spend a few minutes with you. I have a brief that must be completed before tomorrow." He held the door for the two Duponts, who splendidly swept past him through the doorway, followed by an amused Clary, and Libby, who felt as plain and awkward as a scullery maid in the midst of high society. Justin took hold of Libby's arm. "Please don't feel as if you need to socialize with Susanna and her sister," he whispered. "If you're not feeling well, go lie down, and I'll make your apologies. Clary told me you've been feeling ill upon waking for the last several mornings, and any time spent with Charlotte might be too tedious for you."

She looked up into his kind eyes with relief radiating from hers. "Thank you," she whispered back. "I'll accept your offer."

"Misser Jussin!" Vie called, running up to the porch. "We go pony ridin'?"

"I have visitors, Vie. Perhaps before supper, if I finish my work. If I'm unable, then Jeremy will take you."

"Hawoe, Miz Bitsy. You feew bedder taday?"

"Very well, thank you, dear," she said, taking the child's hand and walking her into the entryway foyer. "Would you like to come upstairs with me? You and I can take a little nap together so you're rested for your pony ride with Mr. Justin."

Both Miss Duponts reeled around in indignant shock. After a full minute, Charlotte opened her mouth to spew a bit of venom.

"*Surely* you're not taking that ... that *pickaninny* upstairs to lie with you on your bed, Miss Betsy!" she haughtily exclaimed.

"Why, yes, Miss Dupont. I *surely* am," she responded with equal haughtiness, marching the child past the two gaping-mouthed women. As they started up the stairs, Libby smiled upon hearing Clary snort in an effort to prevent a burst of laughter.

"What be a 'pickanee,' Miz Bitsy?"

"A word we shouldn't say."

"Why?"

"Because."

"'Cause why?"

"Just because, Vie."

"But—"

"Enough."

Vie fell asleep almost immediately, but Libby lay unable to sleep, thinking about Justin and the ladies downstairs enjoying their afternoon tea. It was ungracious to have responded to Charlotte in such a cold manner, and she knew she had to apologize to her benefactors. Justin must think her most ungrateful to treat his guests with such blatant rudeness. *Remember your place. Always know that you are here by the goodness of their charitable hearts.*

An hour later, she heard chatter on the porch below her open window. She heard Clary bid the ladies a good day, re-enter the house, and shut the front door.

"If it were not for her lily-white complexion, I might believe Miss Betsy to be a wild gypsy girl," she heard Charlotte say to Susanna.

Susanna giggled. "You may be correct. Have you *ever* seen such eyes of black and hair so disheveled? Or perhaps she's mulatto. She pays no mind to napping with a pickaninny."

Libby went to the window to see if Justin was accompanying the ladies to their carriage, but he was nowhere in view. Her teary eyes smarted at their hurtful words.

Abel was showing Justin a window on the side of the house that looked as if someone had attempted to pry it open with a sharp object. They heard the ladies' unkind assessment of Libby, and it bothered Justin. He immediately went to the front walk-way as they drove away then looked up at his open bedroom win-dow in time to see Libby back away from it. He decided to speak to Susanna concerning the matter.

CHAPTER 5

"Good morning, Ben. I hope you slept well," said Sally Morrow to her guest who had just wandered into the kitchen. "Tim had to go to his office earlier than usual but said he would be home to take lunch with us. I'll give you all the details of the week's events and answer your questions after you eat. We'll take our coffee into the parlor to have our discussion. I remember how much you loved buckwheat cakes and syrup as a boy. Your mama said you would eat them for every meal if she allowed."

"Please don't go to any trouble. I'm afraid my stomach is twisted into a knot… but they *do* look mighty good," he added, looking over her shoulder to the skillet.

After a silent breakfast, Sally picked up a tray from the counter and asked him to follow her into the parlor.

"You probably wonder why I haven't been anxiously asking you for details. I suppose I'm a coward. I've been afraid to know the facts because it all seems to be one horrific nightmare," he said, taking the tray from her and placing it on the tea table. When she sat down, he poured a cup of coffee for each of them then nervously paced the floor in anticipation of her information. After blotting up several splashes of coffee from the hardwood floor, he decided he best sit down. "When Billy came home to Libby six months ago, I was there to meet him," he began.

"His leg was badly mangled, and he was addicted to opium to ease the pain. My father later wrote that he had begun giving Billy morphine, since he seemed to need something more potent to ease the persistent suffering. He had also been trying to encourage him to have the leg amputated. When I came home for a visit late last spring, Billy appeared quite mellow. I knew he would never be his lighthearted self again, but at least he seemed to be cordial and kind to my sister. A month later my father wrote that because the demand for the opiates was so great, his shipments were becoming sporadic, so Billy had turned to hard liquor for pain relief.

"Unfortunately, it greatly altered Billy's disposition, and he had become abusive toward Libby, so vilely so, that Father requested she move back to his home. She adamantly rejected the idea, insisting she had taken an oath to be his wife for better or worse, and hoped he would return to the man she married if she could persuade him to have his leg removed. Since both of Billy's brothers died while having amputations, he refused. As Billy's behavior became progressively more violent, my father wrote that he felt a need to purchase a gun, perchance."

He slowly shook his head. "For the last several years, my associate and I have been experimenting with all species of botanical life hoping to create medicines equally effective as the opiates, but without their addictive powers and side effects. While our research produced several quality remedies, none were as potent and effective as that which had already been discovered." He gulped down the entire cup of coffee then stood up to pace again. He turned to look at his hostess. "Forgive me. I should be listening to *your* summary."

"As you know, Wednesday is the day your father works at Tim's office. Last Wednesday, when Caleb failed to show, I went alone to search for him because Tim had an overload of patients to see. We wondered if he had a broken wheel or perhaps might be ill. I found no stranded buggies along the five-mile stretch, and when I arrived at his home, I walked around to the office and was surprised to see the door wide open. There was a good deal of blood on the floor in the doorway and several smeared drops on the stoop. I saw that your father lay slumped over his desk. He had placed his handkerchief over the wound that lay close to his heart, and then he must have immediately lost consciousness. The way he was positioned, the edge of the desk pressed against the wound and helped to prevent blood loss. I knew he was alive by the pulse in his neck. While I hated the thought of leaving him, I knew I had to fetch Tim.

"As soon as Tim and I moved him to a prone position, the wound began to bleed profusely. The bullet was lodged too close to his heart to risk attempting to remove it. Tim knew his time was short. I began searching the office for clues as to what happened, and it struck me that there was blood by the door, but none on the floor from the doorway to the desk. A single-barreled *empty* pistol lay on the desk. I walked outside and around to the back of the house, and low and behold, I found Billy lying in the mud with a gunshot wound to his head and a small, single-barreled Colt Derringer in his hand. He also had a pulse. Tim told me to go to the Clark home for help in moving Billy to shelter, but the Clark's house was vacant and boarded up. I had just met Mrs. Clark at the mercantile the morning before, and she was purchasing food items for their stay. I suppose they were called back to Philadelphia, perhaps a problem with their business. Fortunately, I was able to locate Andy Stone. He assisted Tim in carrying Billy to a bedroom then went to fetch the police.

"For the short time that your father maintained consciousness, he was able to tell us that Billy had come to him like a madman, demanding medicine and threatening to kill him if he didn't get what he wanted, just as he had killed and buried Libby. He said she had deceived him and deserved to die. Billy pulled a gun from his pocket, but Caleb had been prepared to deal with his insanity and took a gun from his open desk drawer and shot him. Billy was able to spontaneously shoot back, then reeled through the doorway, fell to the ground, and must have crawled to the back of the house before losing consciousness. Caleb knew he had hit Billy but didn't realize where. He begged us to find Libby's body for a proper burial and then lost consciousness for three days before he died.

"I think the saddest part of this whole unnatural event was watching the tears pour from your father's eyes at the guilt and shame he felt at not protecting Libby beforehand. He asked that we lay her to rest beside her mother and him."

Ben took a handkerchief from his trouser pocket and pressed it to his eyes for a few seconds, then stared at the impeccably embroidered initials and finely crocheted edging that Libby had designed on the simple white square of cotton cloth. He faintly smiled, remembering that Libby had kept herself occupied by embroidering garnishments on every plain piece of fabric in sight—her way of keeping busy until Billy returned to her. He rubbed his thumb over the fleur-de-lis design that she was so fond of embroidering. *This sort of situation simply doesn't happen in the lives of well-bred, Christian people. Why would God allow this? There was not a sweeter, more genteel woman than Libby or a man as kind and righteous as Father*. "And what of Billy?" he asked.

Sally shrugged. "His parents claimed him. The sheriff has stationed a deputy at their home. The bullet is lodged too deeply in his brain to remove. There have been cases of men who live through a gunshot wound to the head and are eventually able to speak, but please, don't allow your hopes to soar."

He deeply sighed. "I feel so helpless. What more can be done to discover my sister's body?"

"Nothing, I'm afraid. Nothing."

"Supper's on the table, y'all," Becky called up the stairs. She walked out on to the front porch to relieve Justin from having to take another turn around the property leading her child atop a beloved pony. "Come, chil.' You bes' get washed up fo' supper. You be takin' 'nough of Mr. Justin's time. He got things to do."

"Jus' one mo' turn, Mama?"

"You heared me, chil.' You git a whoopin' if yer not in by the time I counts ta ten. One … two … "

Justin lifted her off the pony. "You obey your mama now, Vie. Besides, how can I take you for a pony ride tomorrow if I can't replenish my strength with your mama's fine cooking tonight?"

She smiled up at him. "Fank you fo' da ride, Misser Jussin. Go pwenish."

Clary and Libby were just beginning to descend the stairs when Justin entered the foyer. He waited at the bottom of the steps to escort the ladies into the dining room.

"I must say you're looking pert. How are you feeling?" he asked of Libby.

"I feel quite well, Mr. Chambers, but for a touch of malaise in the early morning. It's difficult to eat breakfast."

"Well, you more than make up for it at suppertime," he somberly stated, recalling her piled-high plate from last night's repast.

She spun around to face him with a hand clamped over her mouth. "Oh, please do forgive me! I wasn't aware that I was making a hog of myself!" she explained, clearly mortified.

He and Clary burst into laughter. "He speaks in jest, Betsy." She gave her brother a rough shove. "Tell her you're jesting!"

"It's true. I am. You ladies are far too concerned with impressing men by eating small, ladylike portions. We men are perfectly aware you eat your fill in private. It does my heart good to see a petite young lady with the uninhibited appetite of a man at least twice her size." He gave her a tongue-in-cheek smile.

She blushed and shyly smiled back at him. She liked his disposition—caring, kind, friendly, yet firm and authoritative. And he certainly was handsome! She admired the masculine bone structure of his face, his dark brown hair and mustache with just a tinge of russet highlights, and the becoming cleft in his square jaw. She pictured him standing at Susanna's side. They made a stunning couple, Susanna being slender, tall, and fair, and Justin being robust in physique, tanned, a few inches taller. *Silly girl,* she thought wistfully. *He's nearly twice your age. Besides, he's promised, and what female could possibly compete with Susanna Dupont?*

"I have something for you, Miss Betsy," he said, reaching into his vest pocket. He handed her a small envelope made of costly linen paper.

She pulled out a folded note, read the contents, and then stared at him with a mask of confusion and flushed cheeks. It was an invitation to his and Susanna's engagement reception, simply addressed to "Miss Betsy" and personally signed by Susanna. She was sure that Justin had instigated this distribution. He had visited with Susanna this morning, while delivering a report to her father. "May we discuss this later, perhaps after supper?" she asked.

"I see no need for discussion. The reception is in three days. You should be feeling well enough to attend. I won't permit you to stay alone in this house. Jeremy will be your escort as well as Clary's."

"I'll ask Becky if she'll allow me to stay with her for the time—"

"No. Becky, Abel, and Vie need to spend their evenings alone, as a family, and I believe they have a church social to attend that evening. You'll come with us."

"But I have no formal clothing—"

"That is easily remedied. Clary will take you to my mother's home to look through her wardrobe." He scanned her figure. "Your size is similar."

"But ... but ... I'll only be attending because ... because ..." she tried to explain, becoming too frustrated to put her feelings into words.

He pulled out a dining room chair for her to sit down then cut her off. "No more discussion for now," he said firmly, taking his seat at the head of the table.

Tears pooled in her eyes. She knew that he had seen her at his bedroom window the day before, and he knew she had heard the comments made by the Miss Duponts. She was certain that he had coerced Susanna into sending the invitation. Hoping for support, she turned to look pleadingly at Clary, but Clary merely kept her eyes lowered.

"Good evening to you, family, and Miss Betsy," Jeremy said, bounding into the room. "I was worried I would be late for supper." He took his seat and dropped his napkin onto his lap. "Why so solemn?"

"I was just telling Miss Betsy that you'll be her escort to the reception," Justin informed him.

He looked at Libby and grinned. "Is that a sobering notion to you, Miss Betsy? I would be delighted to be your escort, if you'll permit me. I was hoping you would come. Now the other ladies in attendance might not think me so desperate, having to attend as my *sister's* escort." When he saw that Libby didn't return his smile, he began to make faces at her until she surrendered.

She laughed. "If it will help to ensure your popularity, then I'm content to know that my presence will have some merit." She glanced over at Justin then down to her plate.

"The two of you laugh at my expense!" Clary exclaimed indignantly.

Libby rested a hand on Clary's shoulder. "Not at *your* expense at all. I was also considering that I would be doing you a service by giving him someone else to vex and squabble with besides you for the entire evening." They all laughed.

"Shall we thank the Lord for our food?" Justin asked, reaching to take her hand in fellowship.

After supper, the men went into the parlor to discuss the day's events while the ladies went to clean up the kitchen.

"I wash the supper dishes every evening," Clary explained. "After a long work day, Becky takes half of the food to her home, then stays there to enjoy time with her family."

"I'm glad to be able to help you. If… if you please, I… I would like to have the responsibility of attending to other chores to help earn my keep. I … I'm feeling well enough to be a help to you … and … and it would help to ease some of the anxiety in not knowing … " She weakly sank down onto a kitchen chair, buried her face in her hands, and sobbed.

Clary dried her hands and sat down beside Libby to comfort her. "Are you really so distressed that Justin insists you attend his reception?"

"Oh no! That's not the matter." With a pained face, she said, "It's simply the stress of not knowing, not having the ability to recall my identity combined with the great fear of finally learning. What if I'm not happy with *who* I am? The way I came to you persuades me to believe that I may have a sordid or blemished past, having associated with disreputable individuals."

"Betsy, I do believe that you may have associated with disreputable individuals but not by your consent. You're clearly a well-bred young lady who became a victim."

"Jeremy believes that I don't show enough interest as to who may inquire after me through his article. I suppose my lack of questioning has to do with the fact that I'm afraid, so terribly afraid! I may not know my identity, but I'm absolutely certain that sheer terror lies in waiting."

"There, there," Clary softly said in a comforting tone, hugging Libby's head to her shoulder. "When the beast arrives, we'll face him together … all of us. Now, shall we dwell on a subject that is uplifting?" She handed Libby a cloth to dry the dishes. "I've been sorting through my mind which of my mother's evening gowns would be most befitting to your lovely sort of 'exotic' appearance, and a certain one stands out. I think you'll be well pleased with it."

"Do you suppose your parents regret that they're not able to attend the reception?"

Clary rolled her eyes and smiled. "Perhaps for Justin's sake. However, while they're somewhat fond of Susanna, they hold no affection for her haughty mother and think even less of her pompous father. Mark my words, this reception has been arranged for the furtherance of *his* political career. Everyone who is 'somcone' will have been invited, and Mr. Charles Dupont will waltz his way about the ballroom serenading every ear that he's able to capture."

"Do I hear two gossiping ladies?" Jeremy peeked around the kitchen doorjamb.

"You hear two ladies discussing truth," Clary answered.

He discharged a wicked laugh. "I'm thankful that I'm not the one who is marrying into that family of vampires."

"You know you would thoroughly enjoy having either Charlotte *or* Caroline sink their teeth into your scrawny neck."

"Caroline perhaps, but I believe Charlotte's main problem is that she needs to be kissed, and who in his right mind would be willing to do that?"

"You?" Clary asked, wide-eyed.

"No, ma'am! I plan to stay as far away from them as possible for the entirety of Saturday evening. I'll be wherever there is food." He looked thoughtfully into space. "I must say, though, that despite Miss Caroline's reputation as being 'dumb as a door-knocker,' she turned out to be quite the beauty in her eighteenth year. I've never been partial to fair-haired, frail ladies with no depth to their pale blue eyes. Caroline looks nothing like her sisters. There's a certain warmth and pleasantness about her brown eyes and chestnut hair ... and full red lips ..." He was quickly brought back to his senses when the women began to giggle at his daydream. He cleared his throat. "I just came from discussing a pertinent matter with Justin. He may wish to speak with you, Miss Betsy, so you best hurry with the dishes."

CHAPTER 6

Startled by determined pounding on the kitchen door, Clary dropped her dishtowel and dashed to open it. "Whatever is wrong, Becky?"

"Vie's got a terrible ailin' belly. Do you have somethin' I can give 'er, Miss Clary?"

"Of course. Come in while I get it for you." She looked at Libby. "Suppose you get the poetry book you were reading from the library. We'll read on the front porch while there's still daylight."

Libby wandered up the hall from the kitchen to the library. Seeing that the door was fully shut, she lingered for a few seconds, wondering if she should disturb Justin perchance he was absorbed in work. Deciding against an intrusion and about to turn away, the door suddenly flew open, and Justin slammed against her. He gripped her shoulders and stepped back.

"Excuse me!" he profusely apologized, and then bent down to retrieve his shirt button. "I didn't mean to fly at you. I hope I didn't hurt you."

She giggled. "I'm fine." She retied the ribbon bow on her bodice, its loop having plucked the loose button from his shirt. She held out her hand to him. "Give me the button. Tomorrow I'll sew it back on."

He pressed his hand against her back to direct her into the library. "I was coming to look for you." He closed the door behind them. "Sit down, please," he instructed, pointing to one of the gold wing chairs. He took a seat on the other.

"Clary and I were going to read on the porch before it becomes too dark. I was about to look for a book." Her eyes wandered over to his beautiful, glossy piano.

"I notice you look longingly at the piano every time you're in this room. Do you play?" He gestured for her to go sit at the keyboard.

"I believe so, because I can picture the keys and their sounds in my mind. But I prefer to test my ability when no one is present and my fingers are not quite so sore. Why do you wish to speak with me?"

"Jeremy told me of a tattered young woman who inquired after you this afternoon. She looked to be in her mid-twenties and smelled as if she hadn't bathed in weeks. Her speech was so poor he was surprised that she could read. And since there are no pictures of you in his newspaper, she had to be able to read.

"Jeremy was impressed by the fact that she described you so well. His article only stated that you lost your memory and gave a brief description of your appearance, hoping anyone who inquired would be able to provide the unpublished details. She was able to tell him that you disappeared the night before you wandered on to our property and described you as having waist-length black curly hair, dark eyes, short in stature, and wearing only a white nightgown. She kept anxiously asking if you had regained your memory and seemed determined to find out where you were lodging. Jeremy told her you still had no memory then began questioning her concerning her relationship to you. She merely stated that you were a visiting cousin who had mysteriously wandered off into the night. When he asked her what *your* name was and where *she* lived, a rock broke through a window. When he turned away from her, she took off running up the road to meet up with a woman who was also shabbily clothed. Needless to say, Jeremy alerted the sheriff." He watched her closely, waiting to see if a facial expression would reveal any recollection, but she merely stared back with large frightened eyes looking out from an ashen face.

"This is what I feared," she whispered, beginning to tremble. "I can recall no one who looks as you described, and I have no desire to know more of her." She quickly rose then clutched a hand to her head and began to slowly slump to the floor. Justin caught her around the waist and swept her up into his arms, deciding to carry her upstairs to lie on his bed rather than trying to deposit her alongside the stack of papers and books piled on the love seat.

"What has happened to Betsy?" an alarmed Clary asked upon approaching them in the hallway.

"She fainted. Find Jeremy and tell him to fetch Dr. Flanagan," he ordered from the top of the stairs. Gently laying her on his bed, he sat down alongside her and stared down at her lifeless face, which was frightfully pale beneath the faint yellow bruising that stained the delicate skin around her left eye and cheekbone. For the very first time, he began to wonder what the story was behind this mystery person. Up until now, he hadn't really given her much thought since she was in the capable hands of his sister. His mind had been occupied every moment of every day with his career and upcoming marriage. He doubted that she was sixteen. Her mannerisms and the maturity he read in her eyes told him so. He studied her face until her lashes began to flutter. "Miss Betsy," he said softly, with his face close to hers.

Her eyes suddenly sprang open, and she instantly shrank back with a start. Realizing that friend rather than foe sat regarding her helplessness, she smiled and looked bashfully away with crimson flushed cheeks.

"Miss Betsy." He laid a hand on her cheek to turn her face back to look at him.

She closed her eyes again. The heat of his hand burned her skin, and she felt as though the insides of her head were swirling round and round.

"I've sent for Dr. Flanagan. You lost consciousness. Are you all right?" At her continued silence, he removed his hand from her cheek, sat up straight, and sighed, trying to determine how he might coax a response from her. "Why won't you *answer* me?" he asked in a compellingly compassionate tone.

She turned away from him again and tightly pursed her lips to keep from giggling in embarrassment. *A grown woman would look him in the eye and tell him she's fine. He must think me a dolt. Force yourself to look at him!* She opened her eyes and turned her sights back to his face. Staring into his concerned eyes, she blatantly said, "Forgive my childish behavior. I suppose I'm not used to men carrying me upstairs to their bed then sitting so close to my side."

This time *his* face flushed to scarlet, and he bolted to a standing position. "Then it is I who must ask for forgiveness. I suppose I was too intent upon your state of—" He stopped when she began to laugh uproariously.

"I was trying to tell you that I'm embarrassed, but it came out as sounding offensive. Please pay me no mind, Mr. Chambers," she said, trying to gain control of her laughter.

His mouth broke into a broad grin. "Please discontinue with the 'Mr. Chambers,'" he implored. "Because you're sleeping in my bed, I feel you're justified in calling me Justin ... and I hope *that* didn't come out as sounding offensive." They both heartily laughed.

"I see that my patient has recovered nicely," Clary commented from the doorway, with one hand on a hip and a glass of water in the other.

Libby propped herself up on her elbows. "I'm feeling well. I don't know what came over me. My hope is that the doctor won't be available to visit." She lay back down again, thinking what a burden she must be to this undeserving family. *Please, Lord, allow me to be able to repay them for their kindnesses when my trial is through.*

Justin headed for the door. "If you'll excuse me, ladies, I'm off to borrow a few books from a neighboring barrister."

"Justin!" Libby called to him. "It's time that I return your bed to you and move to the guest room," she said, scooting back against the headboard.

He turned to look at her. "No, Miss Betsy. You're comfortably settled, and I'll be heading back to Washington in a few days." He turned to leave again.

"Justin!" she called again. "It's simply 'Betsy'... and thank you."

He smiled and nodded his head to her. "Good evening... Betsy."

Libby listened to his footstep as he descended the stairs then looked at Clary. It was difficult to read the expression on Clary's face—amused or confused.

"Here's some water," Clary said, approaching the bed to sit on its edge.

Libby took a few sips then set the glass and the button that was clenched in her other hand on the night table. She told Clary everything Justin had told her.

"But, if you please, right now I would rather not speculate as to who the young woman might be. I feel so foolish," Libby admitted. "The room began to swirl, possibly I stood up too quickly, then behaved as a silly child. Oh! And Vie?"

Clary laughed. "She told her mother she wanted to test the taste of dirt and had sampled some from several places on the property. I suppose we'll have to teach her to cook shortly to divert her experiments into more palatable cuisine. She'll be fine. What she ate will pass in time."

Libby laughed. "I enjoy her. She's so bright! It would be lovely if she became as fine a cook as her mother."

"She's a delight... I hear hooves." When she went to the window, a look of disappointment crossed her face. "Jeremy brought Mrs. Flanagan. She's a perceptive woman, but she's not a physician. I suppose the doctor was called elsewhere." She thumped on the glass to let them know they should come up to Justin's room then went to light a couple lamps. They listened to the footsteps making their way up the stairs. Jeremy knocked on the doorjamb.

"The doctor is delivering Martha O'Leary's baby, but Mrs. Flanagan insisted on visiting with you. Justin stopped her in the hallway. She'll be up in a minute. Feeling better, Betsy?" he asked.

"Yes, thank you. I believe I merely stood up too quickly. I suppose my head is not completely healed. Perhaps that is why I'm still unable to recall," she reflected.

"Call when you need for me to deliver her back to her house. I'll be behind the house helping Abel haul a crate from the barn to the front lawn."

A plump, silver-haired woman, dressed entirely in black save for a ruffle of white lace on her bonnet, suddenly filled the doorway, waiting for an invitation.

"Do come in and meet my Betsy," Clary offered, pointing to the sturdy leather chair by the window. "Betsy, this is Fiona Flanagan, the wife of your physician."

Fiona ignored the chair, deciding to settle herself on the edge of the bed to better interrogate Libby. "So, my dear, what would be ailing you this evening?" she asked in a heavy Irish brogue. "Don't be shying from me now. I may not be a doctor, but I've been living with one long enough to have acquired quite a medical education. My Jamie is helping to bring a babe into the world this evening. I've been meaning to pay you a visit, so I reckoned now is good a time as any."

"Truly, ma'am, I'm feeling quite well. I merely swooned from having stood up too quickly," Libby explained, feeling ill at ease by the older woman's intrusive stare.

"Does your stomach feel poorly and is your appetite light?"

"Not this evening, but the last few mornings I've felt ill upon waking." She giggled. "I certainly ate enough this evening to make a grown man sick to his stomach. You stare at me knowingly, ma'am. Why is that?" she asked, looking to Clary to divert the bold woman's appraising eyes.

"You look vaguely familiar to me, young miss...but from somewhere in the past...long before you would have been in this world."

"You believe in reincarnation and living other lives?" Libby asked wide-eyed and innocently.

Fiona bellowed a booming laugh and slapped her knee. "You misunderstand what I say. No, miss. I'm a Christian woman. I believe in no such malarkey. To put it simply, I must have come across someone in my past who looked very much like you. I must say you look the picture of perfect health. I'm sure you have Clary to thank for that."

"She's an excellent nurse, ma'am."

"That she is. I'm going to take leave of you now. I'll most likely be seeing you in church this Sunday but will be saying prayers for you before then." She took Libby's hand, gave it a light squeeze, and then looked at Clary. "Would you be kind enough to talk with me for a moment...downstairs?"

Clary followed the woman down the stairs and into the library for privacy.

"I'll be blunt. I believe the young woman may be carrying a child."

"Fiona!"

Fiona held up her hand. "Hear me, please. She experiences nausea each morning, yet eats like a sailor in the evening. Her pallor is rosy, her eyes glow, yet she becomes dizzy and swoons."

"But—"

Fiona held her hand up again. "Be certain she eats plenty of greens and fruit, meat without fat, three glasses of milk each day...and if she asks for no rags during the next few weeks, you'll know for sure."

"But if she was violated only eight days ago, surely it would be too soon to display any symptoms—"

"Who's to say that she hasn't been with a man before she was violated?"

"But she's not much more than a child!"

"Is she? She cannot remember her name. How can she remember her age if she has no recollection of who she is? She may not even be 'Betsy.'"

"I find what you say to be astounding, but I can't bring this information to her until I'm absolutely positive."

"That would be wise. We shouldn't complicate her life any more than it is at present. Such news might only cause her to regress rather than bring her to the knowledge of her identity. When you're sure, Jamie will give her an examination to confirm the fact. For now, the plan is to keep her safe and fed well."

"Dare I mention this to my brothers?"

"You should … to Justin most especially. He's taken responsibility for her while she's under your roof. I must leave now. I'll have Jeremy deposit me at the O'Leary's. The babe should have been born by now."

"I'll go look for him. Thank you for visiting," Clary said, opening the door to find Jeremy waiting in the hall. She suspiciously eyed his red cheeks. When he shrugged and rolled his eyes at her, she knew he had been eavesdropping into their conversation. "I'll speak with you later," she told him in a threatening tone. She turned around to bid farewell to her visitor then headed back upstairs.

Libby was standing by the window, watching as Jeremy helped Fiona into the buggy. "She's a very … *large* person," she expressed to Clary then began to laugh. "I mean, not so much large in size, but—"

Clary laughed also. "I understood you. She's quite a dominant character."

"Who did she lose in the war?"

"Her brother, this past March. I'm afraid my brother's reception may seem more as a funeral rather than a gala occasion. So many families have lost their men. The majority of guests will be attired in black, and few will dance. But you, my dear girl," she added, placing her arm around Libby's shoulders, "you shall be adorned in a lovely gown of robin's egg blue, frosted with yards and yards of white lace, imported from Brittany."

Libby turned to her with misty eyes and kissed her cheek. "I love you as a sister and the very dearest of friends. You're so kind to me. You truly exemplify God's love."

CHAPTER 7

"I'll fetch the sewing basket from the kitchen cupboard and bring it outside to you. Go on now," Clary said to Libby, giving her a light push. "I must help Becky hang the wash then gather the ripe fruits and vegetables from the garden. Abel is repairing a porch rail and has already been instructed to keep watch over you at all times. If he should have to leave, you're to immediately come back inside."

"I feel as a small child," Libby complained. "Rather than trouble him, might I sew in the library? I believe Justin may be visiting with Miss Susanna, so the room is vacant."

"No. Justin went into town to buy supplies. Why not take advantage of the fresh air and bright sunlight?"

"Why doesn't Justin visit with Miss Susanna very often? If he were my beau, I would like to see him as frequently as possible."

"Frankly, I've been wondering the same. I suppose a heavy social schedule consumes much of her time. Now, I also have a small pile of clothing that needs minor repairs. It should keep you busy for some time. By the time you finish, you should be ready to eat something. Becky will make you a nice ripe tomato and onion sandwich. I fear there are enough tomatoes in the garden to last us until Christmas," she said with a great sigh. "After dinner, we'll look through my mother's wardrobe. Go on now."

Libby went outside and sat down on the bench. Abel nodded, and she smiled and nodded back at him. "Where is Vie this morning?"

"She be playin' with her friend Tildy, miss. She live on down the road."

A three-year-old child may wander down the road alone, but I must have a watchdog at all times! Be thankful. Always remember to be thankful for the thought they put into caring for you. She noticed that Abel had already repaired the porch rail and was assembling a pile of wooden pieces.

"What are you constructing, Abel?"

"I been a meanin' ta put dis togedder fer a long time. Mr. Justin ask me ta do it las' night. It be a porch swing wifout da chains, an' da seat glide back 'n forf. It be a puzzle fer sure," he acknowledged, staring at the pile and scratching his head.

"I believe I see Justin coming up the road. Perhaps you'll be able to figure it out between the two of you."

Clary came outside and set a large sewing basket and a smaller basket filled with work projects next to the bench. "Go to it, young lady. Oh, I see Justin coming. He'll help you with that, Abel. He's the one who ordered it and read the directions on how to assemble it, so he should be a great help to you. I'll bring some lemonade out in a bit."

"Yas, em, Miss Clary," he said, watching Justin tie his horse to the hitching post.

Libby took the button from her apron pocket and searched through the pile of clothes for Justin's shirt. Figuring he left it upstairs, she stood up to go look for it.

"Betsy!" Justin called. "Wait, please." He ran up the porch steps. "I see my sister has given you some repair work. If you have my button, I'll give you the shirt. This is the only one I had to wear since today is wash day," he explained, disrobing to the waist. He stood in front of her with a bare torso and his arm extended with the offer of his shirt. Red-faced, she accepted it and hastily sat back down to busy herself.

He turned to regard Abel. "I figured you might have trouble with that. I'll help you put it together since I have a few hours to spare. That sun certainly feels good, doesn't it?" He stretched his arms up. "It'll be invigorating to do some manual labor for a change."

Libby kept her head lowered, pretending to be fully occupied with securing his button but admiring his broad chest and shoulders above a firm, fit waistline by looking over at him through her eyelashes. *What a finely built man! Concentrate on your work, Betsy!*

She finished sewing on the button and, after removing the handkerchief from the pocket, held the shirt up to shake it out and fold it. Feeling strangely compelled to search through the sewing basket for a crochet hook, she decided to make a fine white edging to sew around the perimeter of the plain white handkerchief. Surprised that it took her very little time, she decided to embroider his initials onto a corner.

"What's your middle name, Justin?" she asked.

He stopped what he was doing and wiped the sweat from his brow with the back of his hand. "Samuel. Why?"

"You shall see," she simply said.

After embroidering a bold, black JSC on one corner, she took blue thread and embroidered an intricate fleur-de-lis design beneath the initials, as well as one on the opposite corner. Pleased with her work, she was amazed at how very little time it took her to complete her task.

After a while, Clary came outside with a tray of four glasses of lemonade. She set it down beside Libby then descended the steps to assess the men's progress.

"Now I have an idea of how this monstrosity will look," she commented. She looked at her brother and heavily sighed. "You *do* know that you're beet-red, do you not? You may not feel it now, but tomorrow morning I have a feeling I'll be required to give you an aloe and rosemary oil rub," she informed him in a condescending tone.

He laughed wickedly and gestured that he planned to grab and hug her.

"Don't dare to touch me! You're drenched with perspiration.

I'll go get your handkerchief. And put a shirt on. There are ladies present."

"I see *one* lady," he teased. "Does it offend you that I'm not wearing a shirt, Betsy?"

Without looking up from her work, she began to giggle. "I refuse to answer on the grounds that it may incriminate me if I say what I am thinking, Counselor."

Clary went to sit beside Libby and picked up the handkerchief. "This is lovely! Did you do this? I don't recall Justin owning one so ornate."

"Yes," Libby answered shyly. "The three petals of the iris symbolize the Trinity."

"Come see what our young lady has made for you, Justin. Her workmanship is perfection." She handed him the handkerchief.

"This *is* beautiful! Thank you kindly, Betsy," he said warmly, smiling appreciatively at her. "And I certainly would never use it to wipe away perspiration. This would look well with the initials displayed above the pocket of my Sunday frock coat." He picked up a glass of lemonade, handed it to Abel, and then took the final one from the tray for himself.

"I'm taking Betsy over to Father's house after dinner. I need a few moments of your time to speak with you in private. Are you going to visit with Susanna today?"

"No. The Dupont women are invited to a high tea at four o'clock, so I'll visit with her tomorrow. Later this afternoon I'll be spending time with Richard Dupont, working on the fundamentals of an upcoming case. Suppose we plan a picnic for Sunday afternoon. Susanna will accompany us home from church. Well, ladies, I leave the remainder of the swing construction to Abel. I'm going inside to bathe before dinner."

"Becky just finished serving dinner in the dining room." Clary closed the door to the library and moved a few steps closer to Justin's desk. "Shall I bring you a tray?"

"No, I'll come to the dining room. What is it that you wanted to speak about in private? Will it take long?"

"No, only one simple statement. Fiona Flanagan surmises that Betsy may be carrying a child." She waited, expecting to see a reaction of surprise, shock—any sort of reaction.

He merely nodded. "Jeremy told me of this late last evening," he said with a shrug, then sat back in his chair. "Why should it be a surprise? We know almost as little of her now as the moment she arrived. Why couldn't she be carrying a child?"

Her eyes flared with indignation. "Because... because she's not much more than a child and is most likely not married! Do you see a husband? If she was your wife, wouldn't you be frantically searching for her?" she asked in agitated excitability.

He stood up and came around the desk to place a comforting arm around her shoulders. "Calm yourself, little sister. All we can do is to continue to be her friends and caretakers. Only the Lord can fit the pieces of her life back together again, in *his* perfect timing. Be anxious for nothing."

"Well... well, I'm angry that Jeremy told you! I told him to leave it to me to tell you. After Betsy retired last night, I confronted Jeremy with the fact that I knew he had been eavesdropping into my conversation with Fiona. He had the *audacity* to tell me that he would investigate the brothels in the Washington area to see if they were missing a young lady. I nearly slapped his face! How preposterous! Is he so *stupid* that he doesn't know that women of *that* caliber lack sweet little Betsy's apparent good breeding and spiritual commitment, and those... those *women* have ways of not *coming* with child and have ways of ridding themselves of it should they happen to—"

"Clary. *Again, I say*... calm yourself. Most likely his intent was to torment you." He kissed her cheek. "Or it may simply be

Jeremy's journalistic nature that spurs his curiosity. Did you forget what a terror he was as a child?"

She had to laugh. "Yes. How well I remember. There had to be a story behind every happening, no matter how trivial. We'll not talk of this to Betsy, at present."

"Agreed. Let's go eat. All of that hard labor has made me ravenous."

"Your parents' home is lovely, Clary. I'm particularly charmed by the Far Eastern decor," Libby commented, her eyes taking in every piece of art and ornament.

"That, my dear, is the joy of being married to a man whose career deals in the laws of importing and exporting. The contacts my father has made with ambassadors of other countries has provided my mother with all of this. Most are gifts. Wait until you see her wardrobe! I'll show you a few of the very latest garments and fabrics from Paris that have yet to be brought to the fashion industry of this country. Come," she beckoned, starting up the spiral stairway in the foyer.

"Why are her gowns here and not with her in England?"

"Her mourning period for my brother, and her brother, who was killed in battle last winter, will be over shortly. She's been wearing black frocks for most of the past three years. My parents will be home in time for Christmas, and Mother will take her colorful gowns with her back to England in April."

"Why do *you* not wear mourning clothing?"

"I did for a short period. When you know me better, you'll realize that I don't adhere well to tradition, and surprisingly, I've never been ostracized for my practices... although I do believe some people find me to be somewhat odd. This way. Their bedroom is on the right. The gown you shall wear is still set on the figure. Mother was about to have the waist let out by a couple of inches, so it should fit you perfectly left just the way it is."

"What about shoes? It's strenuous to walk any distance, much less dance."

"No one expects you to dance. Jeremy and I have never had much interest in dancing, so the three of us will simply sit, eat, and gossip about the strangeness of some of the guests. I have a solution to your shoe problem. I recall a pair of white shoes made of a soft, brocade fabric. The heels are not too high, and we'll cut a cross in the fabric so that your broken toe has no pressure on it."

"Oh, I couldn't allow you to ruin your mother's shoes! She may not even think well of my borrowing her gown," Libby protested.

"You don't know my sweet, generous mother. If she were here with us, she would suggest doing the same with the shoes and give you the gown rather than lend it to you," Clary proudly informed her. She opened the door to her parents' room. "The sewing room and wardrobe are behind the door on the other side of the room."

"This has to be the largest bedchamber I've ever seen . . . I believe . . . Well, it would have to be!" Libby declared in awe.

"It *is* grand, is it not? I suppose since Justin is the 'rightful heir,' this will be his and Susanna's bedroom some day," she said wistfully. "Though I suspect that this house would not be grand enough to suit Susanna. Here it is," she said, pointing to the garment form. "Does it please you?"

"Please me? It's the most beautiful gown in existence!" Libby exclaimed delightedly, lifting the skirt and running her hand over the silk and lace. "This is *too* fine! I couldn't wear this."

"You most certainly shall, my dear. I'm going to go search for the shoes now. I believe they may be in a storage room they plan to convert to a wash closet during their next stay. Stay and look through the wardrobe. You'll find amazing things," she said on her way out the door. Halfway down the stairs she halted, startled to see the front door slowly open, and smiled in relief when she saw Vie's tiny round face peak in. The child's eyes lit up when she saw Clary.

"Hawoe, Miz Cwary. I wookin' fo' Miz Bitsy. She be wif you? I gots a pwesent fo' her," she said, holding up a grubby bit of fabric, gathered and tied with a string.

"She's upstairs. May I see your gift?" Clary asked.

Vie came fully inside and went to hand it to her. "It be wots o' money fo' dis pwesent. Miz Bitsy gonna wuv it," she said proudly. "It make her feew bedder."

Clary lightly squeezed the fabric then rubbed her thumb and forefinger over the object, which felt like a ring.

"Vie, suppose we show this to your mama first? Then we'll rewrap it and give it to Miss Betsy if your mama approves. If your mama says no, then we'll wrap up something else to give to her. Where did you get this?"

"But, Miz Cwary, da wady say to give dis to da pwiddy wady wif da wong bwack hair. Dat be Miz Bitsy," she explained, ready to burst into tears.

Clary gave her a hug. "I'll make sure you have a lovely gift to give to her, but right now I would like for us to show it to your mama. You may also tell us something about the lady who gave this to you," she said, pulling the string from the fabric to find a thin gold band embedded with several diamond chips. She held it up to the sunlight to see if there was any engraving on the inside but found none. Nonetheless, she knew it was not a piece of paste jewelry. She dropped the ring into her apron pocket, took Vie's arm to draw her further into the foyer, and then stuck her head out the door to peruse the grounds, hoping the woman that Vie spoke to might be loitering. When she saw no one, she closed the door and turned to the child.

"What did the lady look like?"

"She not be pwiddy, wike you an' Miz Bitsy. She gots a dirdy face an' po' cwose."

"I want you to go back to my house and wait in the kitchen with your mama. I'll be over in a few minutes. I don't want you to say anything about this ring to Miss Betsy until I tell you that you may. If you obey me, I promise I'll bring a lovely shell mantilla comb with me. You may wrap it in pretty paper, and Miss Betsy will wear it to Mr. Justin's reception on Saturday."

The soulful dark eyes lit up at the offer of fine paper to wrap up the comb. "Dat be good, Miz Cwary. I go ta Mama now," she said, heading out the door.

Clary slowly walked from the foyer down the hallway to the storage room. She took the ring from her apron pocket and tried to slip it on the third finger of her left hand, but even with force, she couldn't move it down past the first joint. It had to belong to a small woman—someone petite, like Betsy. She stood in front of the storage room door for a moment and deeply sighed, wondering if she should show the ring to Betsy but deciding to talk it over with Justin first. Her main concern was for Betsy's safety, and she knew Justin would feel the same. She also surmised that it might not be wise to allow Vie to go to her friend's home without a chaperone. The woman the child described sounded much the same as the disheveled, lowbred woman who had visited Jeremy—and a large rock had interrupted *that* confrontation. She opened the door to the closet but stopped short of her search when she heard music coming from the grand piano in the occasional room—beautiful, flawlessly played music—a Chopin Polonaise! She dropped the ring back in her apron pocket, quickly rummaged through several boxes to find the shoes, and then tiptoed into the occasional room not wishing to disturb the musician before the finale.

When the piece came to an end, Betsy stared down at the keys and shook her head in amazement, realizing the knowledge that she was blessed with musical ability must have slipped away with her identity. She gave a startled jump as Clary clapped her hands in delight.

"I've never heard it played with such communication or precision. Beautiful, Betsy!"

Libby giggled. "This piano is so lovely I couldn't resist testing the sound of the keys. I surprise myself a bit more with each passing day," she said incredulously. "I wonder what I'll learn of myself tomorrow. I should keep a journal of my discoveries. On August 31, I learned I could sew, embroider, crochet, and play the piano. What will September 1 bring? September 1," she said thoughtfully. "That date seems familiar to me."

"Thank you for bringing me to the station, Sally," Ben said, climbing down from her buggy. "When I return in a couple weeks, I'll bring Libby's belongings from her house to Father's. Please tell Dr. Tim to help himself to any of Father's possessions that relate to medicine. I've no use for any of it."

"You wouldn't like to keep certain items for sentimental reasons? His microscope?"

"No, I already own two. I separated Father's library and crated his science and theology books to be shipped to Boston. The house is mine now, but I'll probably not be able to visit very often," he said sadly. "I may have to sell it. I've requested a leave of absence from my teaching position for the semester following Christmas holiday. I'll better sort through Libby's personal items at that time. This week I'll be spending most of my time at the Academy, and then I have some business to take care of at the Smithsonian in Washington on behalf of the Academy. I'll return to Boston after that."

"I'll send you a telegraph should there be any new developments concerning Libby. Will you be selling her house?"

"No. This morning I told Billy's parents to make good use of it. Perhaps Billy's sister, Lavinia, will want it since she's engaged to be married. Billy and his brothers put a year of hard labor into building it. Isn't it ironic that Billy should die today, September 1? He... he died on what would have been my sister's twenty-sixth birthday," he said somberly.

CHAPTER 8

"I feel so badly for Vie, Justin! Becky spanked her for talking to a stranger and accepting the ring. She's confined to her room from yesterday until this evening, and she's not permitted to play at Tildy's house for two weeks. Her little heart was in the right place, but I didn't feel it was my place to interfere with the way Becky disciplines. Perhaps you can make Becky understand that I promised Vie could give to Betsy Mother's tiny shell mantilla comb wrapped up in special paper. I don't want to renege on my promise. I feel *so* badly…"

"I'll talk with her. Are we in agreement that it's best to find and interrogate this strange woman before we show the ring to Betsy?"

"Yes. It's Betsy's biggest fear that her past may have held associations with disreputable people."

"I've sent word to the sheriff that the woman who approached Vie may also be the one who spoke to Jeremy and asked him to assign a deputy to stay with you when I leave for Washington on Monday. I'll be home the following weekend to see our niece." He smiled and winked at her. "I requested that the deputy be anyone but Granger."

"Thank you kindly. You and Betsy have something in common, you know."

"And what would that be?"

"You're both blessed with great musical aptitude. You should hear her play the piano, and her singing voice is magnificent! She wasn't at all bashful in practicing most of yesterday, while you and Jeremy were gone from the house. Next weekend, when Josh and Lydia visit, we should plan a small musical soirée."

"Clary," he said solemnly, "surely you must realize that Betsy won't be here forever. She could leave us at any time and may even have a husband for all we know. I'll say again to you that I don't believe she's a mere sixteen, and I know you really don't believe so either. Set your mind on not becoming too attached to her."

"She can always be my friend, no matter whom she is or where she comes from."

He nodded. "It *is* good to see you have a close female friend."

She blushed. "I know people think I'm 'different.' But Betsy seems to understand me and respects my interests. Did you spend all of yesterday with Susanna?"

"An hour at dinnertime. Most of the day I spent discussing a case with Charles then spent the evening conversing with him and Mrs. Dupont. It seems the sisters need from last evening until this evening to prepare themselves for the reception." He chuckled. "Why does it take so long for women to prepare for social functions? It'll take less than an hour for me to bathe and dress."

Clary shrugged. "Not all women. I should go wake Betsy from her nap. I know you have to leave before we three, so will you please first talk to Becky while I draw a hot bath for you?" She reached into her apron pocket and took out the shell comb, a folded sheet of flower-embossed paper, and yellow ribbon. "Please give this to her. Request that she wrap it and have Vie give it to Betsy before they go to their church social."

"I'll do that for you if you promise not to put anything in my bath water except for a bar of soap."

"Come out, Clary! You and Betsy have spent the last two hours in there. Whatever could you be doing for all that time? It only takes ten minutes to bathe. There won't be time for me to use the tub!" yelled Jeremy, banging his fist on the wash closet door.

"Go bathe the way you did before we had the plumbing installed," suggested Clary.

"Why don't *you* go bathe in the pond?" he angrily answered.

"We have conditioning oils in our hair, and it's too soon to rinse them out," Clary explained.

"I think we should have another wash closet added on to the house, one for the ladies and one for the men," they heard him mutter.

The women giggled. "That will be the day, when homes have *two* wash closets," Clary said to Libby. "Can you imagine that? Such luxury!"

"I'll give you ten more minutes before I break the door down," he seriously warned, causing them to break out into hysterical laughter as he walked away.

"I love the smell of the oil," commented Libby. "What did you make it with?"

"It's merely a blend of oils and juices from a lemon, aloe leaves, sunflower seeds, and chamomile. Your hair is guaranteed to be shiny, tame, and smell heavenly."

"You're so inventive! You should market your beauty products for women. I notice you have several full jars and bottles on your dressing table."

"All are my own concoctions. I've even made a fine cream with a zinc oxide base, combined with several skin-conditioning herbs, powdered corn silk, and clay dust to add color. I use it to help disguise my freckles and will use it to camouflage your little bit of bruising. Perhaps I *will* have my own business some day," she said with conviction. "Becky and her family are going to their church supper in an hour. We best rinse off so Becky has time to help style our hair. If it's pinned while wet, it will look smooth and glossy and be dry by the time we reach our destination. Hold still while I pour this pitcher of water over your hair, then I'll lean over the tub so you can pour the other pitcher over mine."

"Will your brother Joshua and his wife be at the reception?"

"No. The baby is only six weeks old, so they won't want to leave her with a caretaker. But you shall meet them next weekend. They're coming here for a four-day visit. I haven't seen my niece since the day she was born. I'm sure her look has changed considerably."

Please, Lord. Allow me to still be here at that time. I so love them all.

"There couldn't be a lovelier shell comb in the entire world!" praised Libby, bending down to kiss the beaming little face. "I'll cherish it forever. Thank you, Vie."

"Mama fix yo' hair so pwiddy, Miz Bitsy. Ya put da comb stickin up on top o' yo' head . . . wike a pwincess do."

"You're correct. It does rather look like a small crown," Libby said, placing the mantilla in front of the piled-high rolled curls and plaits on the top of her head. "And thank *you*, Becky. You did a wonderful job. I feel several inches taller."

"You welcome, Miss Betsy. I help you in the gown when you git in the petticoats an' crinoline. No cinchin' yo' waist, though," Becky said, looking over at Clary for approval.

"She's right, Betsy. Your waist is tiny enough," Clary said, thinking about a possible pregnancy.

"Good! Then I'll be able to breathe well and eat much. I'm *ravenous*!" Libby exclaimed, raising her arms up for Becky to carefully pull the gown over her head and secure the hooks, buttons, and bows while Clary massaged a small amount of her beauty cream into her faintly bruised skin.

"Just a touch of rouge on your cheeks and lips, and you'll be finished. I don't find the pale look that's presently fashionable to be at all becoming. You, Betsy, look like the queen of Spain!

Come stand by the full-length mirror," she said, taking Libby's arm.

"The green in your gown brings out the bit of green in your brown eyes, Clary. You look beautiful!" Libby exclaimed, before regarding her own reflection in the mirror.

"Thank you. Betsy?"

Libby stared at her own reflection in speechless awe. "I have a memory," she finally said in a small, quivering voice. "Of my mother ... the way she looked when I was Vie's age. Our appearance is almost identical. I recall that she was finely dressed, preparing to leave for a special social gathering. Now if only I could recall her name ... my name. I ... I'm no longer certain that I'm Betsy. I believe that she is Betsy, but then ... who am I?" She went to sit down on the leather chair. "My head aches," she said, rubbing her temples.

"You rest. I'll give you a dose of feverfew and make you a cup of willow bark tea. They should help. Perhaps you should also eat a small bit before we leave," Clary said on her way out to gather the medicinal aids. "Becky, if you don't leave soon, you'll arrive at the church too late for your gospel sing."

Becky and Vie followed Clary downstairs. "Vie, you go on ta' yo' papa. I be out in a minute." When Vie was out of earshot, she said, "I believes it jus' the baby. It can make a body dizzy-like."

"You really believe the same as Fiona Flanagan ... that Betsy is carrying a child?"

"I think it before Miss Fiona come here. I feeled the same when I be carrying Vie. An' you 'member when Miss Lydia come a visitin' in early spring? She keeped asayin' she be light-headed, an' she glad she feeled good in the mornin' 'gain. An' *whooeee*, she eat a lot o' supper!"

Clary plunked herself down on the foyer bench. "Yes, now that you mention it, I remember that certain odors repulsed her to nausea. Time will tell. There's still the possibility that Betsy sustained more damage to her head than—"

Becky shook her head. "That don't make yo' belly sick jus' in the mornin' or eat like a man in the evenin.'"

Jeremy stuck his head in through the front door, ready to yell that he had brought the carriage to the front of the house and was ready to leave.

"I see you're ready," he said to Clary. "Where's Betsy?"

"Right here," Libby called down from the top of the steps.

Jeremy stepped inside to stand at the base of the stairs and stared with a gaping mouth at the vision that descended. "My *stars*!" he exclaimed. "Betsy! You'll cause every woman in the ballroom to bristle with envy!"

Clary and Becky exchanged glances, each hoping Libby hadn't heard any of their conversation.

"I was about to make your tea, Betsy," Clary said, standing up to go to the kitchen.

"I'm fine now," Libby said.

"You surely are!" commented Jeremy with eyes as round as saucers.

"You can shut your mouth now, Jeremy. Betsy, maybe you should eat some bread along the way. Your head no longer aches?"

"No. It vanished as quickly as it came."

"I git yo' bread befo' I leave," offered Becky.

"May I have a thick helping of butter on the top, please? Oh, and maybe some slices of your delicious pickled peppers on top of that?" she asked, oblivious to the overt look of disdain on their faces at her unpalatable request.

CHAPTER 9

"Will you look at that!" commented Jeremy when they arrived at the town hall. "Dupont has hired valets to park the transportation." He jumped down from the driver's seat to help the ladies out of the carriage then waved the reins at one of the young men dressed in colonial garb. "Did we misunderstand? Is this a costume ball?"

Clary rolled her eyes at him. "The valets are dressed in that fashion so you're able to distinguish them from the guests. *Please* try to appear as if you have some breeding. And do remove the chewing gum from your mouth. You look like a cow."

"A bull, you mean," he said, forcefully spit-shooting his gum onto a bush.

Libby giggled. "I have a feeling I'm going to have to seat myself between the two of you for the entire evening."

"I won't argue with that arrangement," he said, offering an arm to each lady. "The one pleasant statement I'll make to you this evening, sister, is that you look very pretty. However did you accomplish that monumentally impossible feat?"

"I've decided that I shall ignore you for the entire affair," she said, turning down his arm and walking ahead of them.

He turned to Libby. "I know your foot is still tender and you're not used to wearing shoes. We'll walk slowly. Oh, I forgot something! Stand here for a moment." He ran back to the carriage, reached beneath the driver's seat, and quickly put his hand behind his back. When he returned he presented her with a small bouquet, arranged with fragrant herbs and tiny, deep pink and white roses. "Your tussie-mussie, my lady," he said, with a bow.

She smiled and curtsied. "Why, thank you, sir. It's lovely. You really *can* be quite charming. Look to your right. Is that Charlotte Dupont coming this way? She's waving to you."

His face turned crimson, and with desperate eyes, he surveyed all directions but realized there was no way to escape a confrontation. He and Libby stood in place, waiting for her to reach them.

"Why, Jeremy Chambers, I do *declare* you're a mighty handsome sight this evening," she cooed, with a flutter of her lashes.

"Good evening to you, Charlotte. You've already met Betsy."

"Why, yes, I have." Charlotte haughtily appraised Libby from head to toe. "I must say you're recovering nicely, Miss Betsy ... and are attired quite regally."

"Thank you, Miss Dupont. I must say that I find relief in not looking like a wild-haired gypsy for a change," Libby returned with a light laugh. She stared directly into the young woman's defensively horrified eyes, forcing her to blush and look down at the tips of her costly shoes. "Miss Charlotte," Libby added, taking the initiative to be charitable, "I would like to apologize to you for my rude behavior when you came to visit the Chambers.' My tone of voice was truly ungracious. Do forgive me," Libby said warmly, extending her hand in friendship.

Charlotte regarded her with surprise, and her eyes clearly displayed that she had dropped her defenses. Her face lit up, and her smile was charming as she took Libby's hand. "I have nothing to forgive, Miss Betsy. It is I who must apologize. I pray I didn't wound you with my unkind remarks and snobbery."

"Please call me Betsy, Charlotte. Yes, I was hurt for an instant but would like to put our initial meeting behind us and begin afresh." She held out her hand for Charlotte to take then turned to look at Jeremy and gave him an impish grin. He shook his head in disbelief. "It didn't take a kiss," she mouthed at him. "You look lovely in your lavender gown," she complimented her new friend. "I know that Jeremy will want to sign his name to several choices on your dance card."

"Hurry," Clary called to them. "It looks as if it may rain," she said with raised eyebrows when she saw Libby and Charlotte hand in hand.

They entered the door to the immense foyer of the grand ballroom and stood in line waiting to be announced and presented to Mr. and Mrs. Dupont and Justin and Susanna.

"I certainly don't care to be presented to my own parents," said Charlotte. "Come aside with me, Jeremy… if Betsy approves, of course. I would like you to sign my dance card for at least a waltz or two and several reels."

"I'm Betsy's attendant this evening. She's unable to dance, so—"

"Go with Charlotte, Jeremy. I can't expect you to sit beside me all evening. Enjoy yourself," Libby said, waving him on. She and Clary watched in amusement as Charlotte took possessive hold of his arm to escort him away from the crowd. When he turned and shot them a vilely disgruntled look, the women giggled at his displeasure.

"However did you win her majesty's favor?" Clary sarcastically asked.

"With honesty and an offer of friendship. I hope this line moves quickly. The food smells wonderful."

"See how the men stare at you, Betsy? The younger men can't take their eyes from you. You'll probably receive many invitations to dance."

"I believe they're regarding you, Clary."

"No, I guarantee they're flirtatiously eying *you*. I've known most of these men for years and attended school with several. My appearance is nothing new to them."

"I honestly have no interest in speaking or dancing with any men. I only wish to eat. My stomach is grumbling, and a bit too loudly. Must we be announced? Is there a way to enter the ballroom unnoticed?" she asked, with pleading eyes.

Clary took her arm. "I've attended several socials held in this ballroom and know there's a door behind the drapes to the left of the door where Justin and Susanna are standing. It enters on to the stage where the musicians are seated. They haven't begun to play, so we'll slip nonchalantly past them and go down the steps to the tables of food."

They had almost reached their destination when Clary heard her name called. They turned to find themselves confronted by Justin. Then quite strangely, with none uttering a single, solitary word, and almost as if rehearsed, Clary solemnly took several steps backward to witness what she saw beginning to play out before her—a look in her brother's eyes she had never seen before, as he drank in the essence of the beautiful, raven-haired young woman who stood before him. She noticed that he almost seemed to have stopped breathing and that his countenance had caught Libby so off-guard, her breathing had became labored as she stared into the eyes of the man who appeared entranced, yet fully aware of his surroundings.

"Please forgive my boldness, Betsy," he finally managed to softly plead along with a slight bow. "And forgive me, Susanna," he whispered. He closed his eyes and took a deep breath, then opened them to focus on Clary. She stared blankly back at him, all the while her heart was pounding with joy at the realization that her brother—*hopefully*—was really *not* in love with Susanna Dupont. She reasoned that God might have sent this endearing little creature into their lives for the sake of Justin.

"Justin, my dear, I wondered where you disappeared to," Susanna said as she approached him and rested her hand on his shoulder. "Good evening, Clary, Miss Betsy. You both look enchanting this evening. Come, Justin. We're holding up the reception line." She gently tugged at his arm and smiled coquettishly before leading him away.

Clary looked wide-eyed at Libby. "Well!" was the only word she could exhale.

"What … what just happened?" Libby panted, still slightly out of breath with her hand over her heart.

"I'm not quite sure. Come, we'll get you a plate of food."

"I don't believe I'm so hungry anymore. May we sit down for a few moments?"

"Of course," she said, pulling the drape aside to expose the hidden door.

"I see you ladies have the same idea," a male voice commented from behind them. "Forget all of the formal folderol, and get to the food! May I join you?"

Clary laughed. "Good evening, Richard. Of course you may. I'd like to introduce you to my sweet friend, Betsy. I'm sure my brother has told you of her. Betsy, I'd like you to meet Richard Dupont, third on the list of Duponts, nephew of Charles, son of Robert, and cousin of Susanna. Richard is to become a father shortly. I imagine a night on the town would have been too much of a strain on Amy?"

"I thought it best she stay home. She's due to deliver any time now." He reached for Libby's hand. "I'm honored to meet you, Miss Betsy. Justin has told me all he knows of you. I pray that your life will soon straighten out."

"I also, thank you. It's a pleasure to meet you," she said shyly, taking his hand.

"Suppose you ladies sit down, and I'll bring you each a plate of food. Have you any special preferences?"

Libby giggled. "Anything that's even remotely edible."

"That's very sweet of you," Clary said. "Betsy should stay off of her feet as much as possible."

Once all of the attendees crowded the ballroom, Libby noticed that more than half of them were attired entirely in black. So many somber faces—so little laughter for so festive an occasion. Susanna, in her exquisite gown of Chinese rose silk, stood up to take the arm of her father. He escorted her to the center floor of the ballroom, and the small orchestra began the evening's festivities with a waltz. Several minutes later, other couples joined them.

"Why doesn't Susanna dance the first dance with Justin?" Libby asked Clary.

Clary shrugged. "Justin never did care much for dancing, despite his great love of music. He'll dance a few dances with her, but he would rather sit and watch or appreciate the sound of a good orchestra or chamber ensemble."

"She looks so beautiful tonight," Libby said wistfully, watching as Susanna took on another partner.

"She doesn't hold a candle to you," Jeremy said, his head intruding between the two conversing women. "You *do* know I should be angry with the two of you after placing me in the awkward position of having to sign for six dances with Charlotte... but turns out, she kisses *very* well. Seems that's what *I* needed," he announced with a broad grin.

"Jeremy! Go away if you plan on talking this way for the entire evening," chided Clary. "Go back to Charlotte. Richard Dupont will be our companion. He's going to bring us buffet plates... although he certainly is taking his time."

"I'm afraid he isn't. One of his servants just came to take him home. His wife is in labor. I'll get your food, Betsy. Do you notice the way Susanna tries to capture the eyes of every man in the room? I hope Justin know what he's getting himself into."

It's true, Libby thought. *She smiles and looks coyly at every male who happens to look her way. Justin is the most handsome man in the room, and he possesses so many other admirable qualities. Does he notice her behavior? Why does she require so much attention when she has Justin for a beau?*

"He's intelligent enough to know what he's doing." Clary smiled. "You shall see. I believe all will be well," she said definitively. "Oh no, here comes Charles Dupont! Jeremy, would you like to wager? I'll bet you two bits that as soon as I introduce him to Betsy, he'll say a few compassionate words to her then immediately tell his plan that if elected to Congress, he'll single-handedly rid the entire thirty-six states of all forms of erotica and boast of how he actively endorsed the Collamer's Bill. He knows, Betsy, that despite the fact that we women aren't permitted to vote, we'll be impressed by the fact that he wants to 'purify' our men's minds; therefore we'll try to influence them to vote for him."

"You have him pegged, sister, so no, I'll not wager with you because I know he'll do as you say. Smile, Betsy. I see three gentlemen heading this way who seem anxiously determined to make your acquaintance."

"Who could *possibly* be at our door at seven o'clock on a Saturday evening?" Sally Morrow asked her husband. "I know there are no babies to be delivered for at least another month, and there's no sickness going around."

Dr. Morrow looked up from his newspaper. "Well, my dear, the only way you'll find out is to go open the door."

Sally went to the kitchen, wondering why the caller had chosen *that* door rather than the front door. Her eyes widened in surprise at who was standing on the stoop.

"Mrs. Clark? Do come in. Is your husband with you?" Maggie Clark shook her head. "I thought you had gone back to Philadelphia." She closed the door and gestured for her guest to sit at the kitchen table. "I'll make tea."

"I left my husband, and he doesn't know where I am. I've rented a buggy and must be back at the train station within the next hour to go to my mother's home in Reading. I... I just had to talk to you for a few moments before I move on, concerning a subject that has been weighing heavily on my heart and mind."

Dr. Morrow came out to the kitchen to see who was visiting and was as surprised as his wife at their caller.

"Good evening, Doctor," she greeted him, flush-faced and nervous. "I was telling your wife that I left my husband. I've been putting away small sums of money over time in preparation for this day. I can no longer bear to be with him. He's a cowardly man who sorely lacks honor and integrity, and I know he would beat me to death if he knew I had come to you. I … I don't know how to begin."

"Take your time," Sally said, sitting down at the table.

"Please don't bother with tea, thank you. I have no time." Tears slid down her cheeks. "Our behavior was reprehensible. First, I must ask you if the police have caught Billy Prescott. I read Dr. Shaw's obituary."

"Billy was never on the run," Dr. Morrow said. "Dr. Shaw shot him in the head almost the very second before Billy shot *him*. Billy died very early yesterday morning. We were hoping he would revive long enough to tell us what he had done with Libby's body."

Mrs. Clark appeared stunned. "The newspaper mentioned nothing of Billy having been shot."

"Perhaps not the Philadelphia newspapers, but the *Wellesley Times* mentioned the fact," Sally said.

"Then … then Billy *couldn't* have killed Libby! She's alive, *somewhere*!"

"Whatever are you talking about? How do you know anything of this affair? You had gone back to the city," Sally said with indignant skepticism.

"No, no, we were right here! It was late Tuesday night, August 22, when Libby came pounding on our door, pleading for help. She was screaming that Billy had shot her papa and begged that we help her. Harry told me to be still, that Billy was crazy and would kill us if we got involved. After a while she wandered off into the night with Esau. Esau came back alone some time later. Harry ordered me to quickly pack up to leave the house immediately. He had the doors and windows boarded up by sunrise. He was *so* afraid that Billy would approach us or that someone would ask us to allow Esau to help find Libby, he poisoned the poor animal the moment we returned to Philadelphia. He wanted nothing to do with the whole situation.

"After reading the obituary, we assumed Billy had caught up with Libby and killed her. I couldn't bear the thought that we could have saved her life had we sheltered her ... but had I known that Billy was on his deathbed ..." She began to tremble with sobs. "It changes everything. I know she's alive! But why is it that she didn't know Billy had been shot, unless she didn't care about that fact and was only concerned for her father's welfare. Billy was a *vile* man! Only she can shed light on that. I'm rambling. Forgive me. From the little we could see from our bedroom window, it appeared that she might have been wearing only a nightgown or a shift. But how could she simply disappear into thin air?"

Dr. and Mrs. Morrow just stared at one another, desperately trying to comprehend and sort out what was being relayed to them. Dr. Morrow abruptly stood up.

"I'm going into Wellesley to talk to the sheriff and send a wire to Ben. We'll have to organize a new search, but this time it will have to be door to door. I pray to God that she hasn't met with foul play. I dare not be optimistic about that, however, for she's been gone for eleven days now. Please, Mrs. Clark, will you accompany me to make a statement? I'll make certain that you get to the train station. Also, please know that no one will blame you personally, but your husband is another matter. You show great fortitude in coming to us now."

"Yes, I'll gladly come with you." She breathed a great sigh of relief at finally being unburdened and forgiven then said a silent prayer for Libby's safe return.

CHAPTER 10

"Here's a bonnet, Betsy. It's not my intention to goad you, but Jeremy and Justin are waiting in the carriage. Church begins in a half hour, and the ride takes at least twenty minutes," Clary said, setting a floral-trimmed straw bonnet on Libby's head and tying the ribbon into a bow beneath her chin.

Libby gulped down the last few swallows of gingerroot tea. "Forgive me, but his morning my stomach is giving me more problems than usual."

"That's simply because you're being rushed. I've wrapped a crust of bread in a napkin for you to eat along the way. Come," she said, taking her hand.

Justin jumped down to help the ladies into the carriage, and although he smiled at Libby, he seemed to go out of his way to avoid eye contact when she returned his smile.

"I was surprised when you said that Becky and Abel don't attend your church," Libby said, once seated.

"Let's say that Becky and Abel prefer a much more 'spirited' church service than ours offers," Jeremy said with a chuckle. "Their church is one hundred percent black. We have a few black families that attend our church, though."

"You appear solemn this morning, Justin. Fatigued from last night's festivities?" Clary asked with a light snicker.

"Simply pensive. There's much on my mind."

Clary looked down and smiled smugly to herself. She reached over to take Libby's hand. "Are you feeling any better, dear?"

"Yes," she replied, nibbling on her bread. "It's so odd that I should feel this way each morning. I certainly hope it ends soon."

"Justin, have you given any more thought as to why the side window of the library is damaged?" Clary asked. "Do you really believe someone may have tried to break in?"

"Only our little brother. Several weeks ago, Jeremy tried to pry it open with his pocketknife. No one was home, and he had forgotten his house key," he said, giving Jeremy an elbow to the ribs.

They arrived a full ten minutes before the service was to begin, and after helping the women from the carriage, Justin persuaded them to go in ahead of him. He had promised Susanna he would wait for her so they could sit together. But when she failed to show on time, he waited a few more minutes until he heard the sound of the organ then went in to seat himself beside Libby. He was genuinely surprised to see Jeremy sitting beside Charlotte on the pew in front of them. He also took note that Dr. and Mrs. Flanagan sat on the pew in front of Jeremy and Charlotte. When the service was over, he planned on inviting them to the picnic. He had several questions to ask the doctor concerning Betsy's progress—or lack thereof.

Seeing that there was no hymnal for Justin, Libby moved hers over to share with him as the congregation stood up to sing "Come Thou Fount of Every Blessing." Almost to the finish of the first stanza, Clary stopped singing to watch several people, including the doctor and his wife, turn to search for the couple who harmonized the soprano and baritone parts so beautifully together. Fiona Flanagan excitedly whispered something into her husband's ear, and he nodded enthusiastically. After finishing the fourth stanza, Justin turned to look at Libby, and she shyly smiled at him.

That was very enjoyable. Perfect harmony! "I do believe we make beautiful music together," Libby whispered to him, then immediately blushed crimson at having realized the faux pas of her selected choice of words. "What I meant to say—"

"You needn't correct yourself," he whispered, with an amused smile. "I understood what you meant."

Justin was pleased that Reverend Crabtree chose to speak on the subject of God's promise of deliverance through trials. It was the sort of message that Betsy needed to hear. He suspected that she felt ultimately secure in the comfort and loving friendship of his home and family. Perhaps that's why she didn't seem too concerned that she hadn't regained her memory and seemed to go out of her way to avoid even *attempting* to remember. But he also knew that her biggest trial lay ahead of her, when she finally had to face the circumstances that had brought her to them. And they would need to help her fully realize Psalm 91 and the key verse from Psalm 30 that the reverend had quoted: "Weeping may endure for a night, but joy cometh in the morning."

He looked about him at the three hundred or so church members. Over half were attired entirely in black. He could clearly picture the faces of Jeffrey and Uncle Seth before him, reminding him of the trials his family had weathered not too far in the past and the devastating one that he had endured some seven years ago. Yes, this message was dedicated to many.

He silently prayed for wisdom in helping the young lady who sat beside him. Then he thanked the Lord that her battered body was healing and if she *was* carrying a child that she would love and accept it. His mind jolted back to his surroundings when Libby slipped the hymnal in front of him and the congregation began to sing "A Mighty Fortress Is Our God." He had to marvel at the quality blending of his voice with hers.

After the service, Reverend Crabtree stood by the door to greet his congregation. Clary introduced Libby to him.

"I'm happy to meet you, Miss Betsy," he said upon taking her outreached hand. "Justin told me of your situation last Sunday, so I've been praying for you throughout the week. You're one of the main reasons I chose to preach today's sermon subject."

"Thank you, Reverend Shelton. It was truly a message of hope," Libby said warmly.

"He's Reverend Crabtree, Betsy," Clary corrected.

"I ... oh dear! Forgive me. I ... I seem to have had a flash of memory. Reverend Shelton ... he's a friend, I believe. He may pastor the church I attend."

"We'll have to look into the names of every pastor in the vicinity," Justin whispered to Jeremy. "Good morning, Charlotte," Justin greeted the young woman standing beside Jeremy. "And where might Susanna be this morning?"

"She should be waiting outside. I couldn't seem to pry her from her bed. She begged that I allow her to sleep a while longer, claiming she was exhausted and her feet ached from hours of dancing last night, so I had one of our servants leave me by the church. Father, Mother, and Caroline went back to Washington early this morning. Jeremy invited me to your picnic. It's all right, is it not?" she anxiously asked as the five of them descended the church steps.

"Certainly it's all right," he assured her, wondering what had gotten into Jeremy. "I do believe I see my lady talking with someone by the old willow tree," he noted, picking up his pace to join her.

Libby stopped walking to watch as he went to stand by her side. For some odd reason, she felt a tug at her heart when he said the words "my lady." It seemed to overshadow the fact that a hidden part of her life had just surfaced. Justin kissed Susanna's cheek, put his arm around her shoulders, and shook hands with the man to whom she was speaking. Quite suddenly the arm that embraced Susanna dropped back to his side, and the two men walked away from her. Even from a distance, Libby could tell by the expression on Susanna's face that she was commencing to seethe.

"That's Sheriff Clayton, Betsy," said Clary. "Perhaps he feels that now is the time for him to speak with you."

"What could I possibly tell him?" she asked, a look of alarm growing on her face. "I still remember nothing of importance."

"We'll find out in a bit. Here come Dr. and Mrs. Flanagan. Jeremy, suppose you and Charlotte wait for us in the carriage. Justin will most likely come home in Susanna's buggy, so there won't be enough room for Betsy and me," she said.

"Top of the mornin' to you, ladies! The Mrs. and I have been speaking of the fine sound we heard coming from you and Justin, Miss Betsy," the doctor said.

"Your voice quality tells me that you have had some training," Fiona said, sharply studying Libby's face. "Do you suppose your *mother* may have taught you to sing so well?"

"She also plays the piano beautifully," Clary interjected.

Libby stared blankly at the couple who studied her face as if expecting to hear some sort of divine revelation. "I can't recall if she taught me, but she may have. I *do* clearly remember that my mother and I look similar, but when she was very young. I can't envision her present-day appearance."

"Betsy had a recollection of her mother's appearance last evening, while we were dressing for Justin's reception," explained Clary.

Fiona and the doctor looked at one another and nodded.

"Excuse me," Justin said, coming between Clary and Libby. "Good morning, Fiona and James. I had planned to invite you to our home for a picnic this afternoon, but a matter has come up that requires the attention of my family and possibly Betsy. So I would like to extend the invitation for next Saturday, when my brother and his family will be visiting."

"That would be lovely," said Fiona. "We may have some interesting information for you by then. What time?"

"Plan to come at noon." He turned his attention to Libby, but she was busy surveying her surroundings to locate Susanna's whereabouts, until her eyes became magnetized to a tin star pinned to a brawny chest. She jumped and openly shuddered. Justin encircled his arm around her shoulders, completely disregarding the overtly glaring eyes of his approaching intended one. "Calm yourself," he softly said to Libby. "You, also," he said to Susanna when she came to stand by his other side.

Sensing the building of tension, the Flanagans bid them a fast, fond farewell and scurried to their carriage.

"Well, what would you have me do?" asked Susanna. "Now that there will be no picnic, would you prefer that I return home?" she asked in a cynical tone.

"I'm sorry that our planned day has been interfered with, my dear, but I was hoping you would realize and understand that there's a pressing matter to attend to." He lifted her hand and kissed it.

"Will someone *please* tell us what has happened?" Clary impatiently asked. "You, Sheriff, you tell us."

"Miss Dupont knows, but I'm not certain if it's advisable for Miss Betsy to hear just yet." He looked at Susanna, hoping she would take Libby aside for a few moments so that he could make a few decisions with Clary and Justin. But she merely stood in place, impatiently tapping her toe on the ground and glaring at Libby through vinegary eyes.

Justin took Susanna aside and for a moment spoke quietly to her, then kissed her forehead. She turned back to Libby and begrudgingly held a hand out to her.

Clary gave Libby a light push to go to her. *Spoiled, spoiled child! When will Justin's eyes be opened to Susanna?*

Susanna and Libby stood in unadulterated silence, spaced a foot apart, their backs leaning against a broad tree trunk, and staring at the trio who were conversing some fifty feet away.

"I'll allow you to explain, Sheriff," said Justin.

"Well, Clary, it seems that an hour ago, your mystery woman may be the one who was brought in a wagon by her grandmother to the infirmary for the indigent. It seems that she was almost beaten to death by her common-law husband, a large mulatto man in his late thirties named Josiah Staples. The young woman's name is Lottie Harmon. She hasn't been conscious long enough to be cognitive, just keeps drifting in and out. Her grandmother claims he beat her in a drunken rage because she had returned something that he had stolen to its rightful owner. Needless to say, I'll need Jeremy to identify her as the one who came to him inquiring after Miss Betsy, and—"

"No! Not Betsy," said Clary with determined firmness. "I'm assuming that this Josiah person may have been the one who harmed … and … and possibly violated Betsy, then dislocated her fingers trying to remove her ring. It would be too much of a shock for her to handle. She needs to remember much more of her past before she's ready to identify her attacker."

"Then how do you propose we prosecute this man when we catch him?"

Clary's eyes widened. "You mean he's on the run? You haven't caught him yet?" He nodded. "Then she's not safe. Someone must guard her day and night."

"Don't you suppose she'll wonder why she's being watch-dogged?" he asked, becoming impatient with her uncooperativeness.

"Clary," said Justin, "Betsy knows that a woman inquired after her through Jeremy. Suppose we leave it up to her as to whether she's up to identifying her. I can't see that this will do any harm. We'll be with her. All she has to do is to determine whether she might have interacted with this woman."

"Well," she said reluctantly, "I suppose you're right." She looked back to the two mutes leaning against the tree. "Susanna?"

"She and Charlotte can take their buggy and wait for us at home. We'll tell Jeremy what's expected of him and take our carriage."

He walked over to the two women and directed his explanation to Susanna. She walked off in a huff to meet with her sister. Clary watched him relay what was to take place to Libby and saw her nod in agreement.

"We owe you an explanation," Justin told Libby before they entered the infirmary. "We believe the woman you're about to identify approached Vie and gave her a ring that might possibly belong to you, a thin gold band set with three diamond chips. She directed Vie to give it to you, but Clary intercepted it. Do you recall owning such a ring?"

"Um ... yes ... yes, I do! It's my mother's wedding ring. My father bought her a new one as an anniversary gift. I remember! She gave it to me as a keepsake, but I don't remember it having been stolen," she said, looking confused.

"Suppose we let Jeremy see if he can identify her first," Justin suggested as they walked up the hallway to Lottie's room.

Jeremy and the sheriff went in and came out less than a minute later.

"It's the woman who came to *The Beacon*, but the only way I know is because she has a distinctly obvious raised mole on her left earlobe." He looked squarely at Justin. "Prepare yourselves. She's been beaten to a pulp."

Clary and Libby cringed. "Will she heal?" Libby anxiously inquired of the doctor.

He shook his head. "Only by a miracle. A nurse took her grandmother to the kitchen for sustenance. You may want to question her," he said to Jeremy.

"I'll do that, thank you. Justin, you should go in with Betsy. Clary can come with me."

Justin reached for Libby's hand and opened the door. As they approached the bed, he put his arm protectively around her shoulders. He hoped she wouldn't faint from the sour, repugnant odor that permeated the room.

When Libby looked down at the woman's twisted, swollen, bruised, and slashed face, she gasped and looked up into Justin's eyes with an expression of sheer horror.

"I couldn't possibly identify this person! There's no way of knowing what she looks like! Oh, Justin!" she exclaimed, bursting into tears.

Seeing that the woman was attempting to open her eyelids, the doctor hastily moved to her side to check her pulse.

Lottie looked up at Libby through two narrow, blood-caked slits, and with labored breathing managed to whisper what sounded like "forgive me," then closed her eyes.

"Justin! What can we do to help her?" Libby cried, burying her face in his chest.

"There's nothing anyone can do for her," said the doctor. "She's gone."

Libby flung her arms around Justin's neck and nestled her head to his shoulder. "She's lost!" she cried.

He held her close and comforting, wondering what words would calm her. "We don't know that she's lost, and it's not ours to assume. Only the Lord knows her heart," he finally said. "Remember, though once misguided, she tried to do what was right in the end. Perhaps she had made her heart right with God. Come, now. We'll go back out into the hallway. I'm concerned that the stench in this room may cause you to fall ill."

Jeremy, Clary, Sheriff Clayton, and a poorly dressed, grimy woman in her late sixties were waiting outside the door. When the doctor told the woman that her granddaughter had died, she didn't appear forlorn.

"She was a good girl till she got mixed up with that no-good Josiah Staples. That man is pure evil! He took her away from me for three whole months. They only got back here couple o' weeks ago. Don't know where they been all that time. She only says that Josiah stealed something from some poor lady, and she feeled sorry for her and wanted to give it back. That's all I know and can tell you." She looked at the doctor. "If someone can load her back into the wagon, I'll take her home and bury her."

The expression on Libby's face projected such a mixture of outrage and distraught that Justin reached into his pocket and pulled out a sum of money. "Take this and use it for a proper burial, ma'am. She deserves that much after all she's been through."

The woman didn't hesitate to take the money and, without so

much as a "thank you," began to walk away from them. "Watch your backs," she warned them over her shoulder. "Josiah Staples was never a good man, and now he's a murderer."

CHAPTER 11

Libby couldn't bring herself to speak a solitary word for the entire trip back to the house. The strain of fatigue and sadness in her eyes prompted Clary to suggest she take a nap.

"No," she said as they walked up the path to the house and a waiting Charlotte. "I prefer to stay awake. Lottie's poor, broken face is branded into my brain. I know I couldn't rest."

"Where is Susanna?" Justin inquired of Charlotte.

"We passed a friend out on the road. Susanna decided to visit with her, and I decided to wait here." She looked across the lawn to see Vie coming toward them. "That child was about to visit until she saw me sitting here. There was nothing I could say to persuade her to wait with me for your arrival. I … I would like to win her favor," she stammered. "I know I must guard what comes out of my mouth. I don't mean to be uppity … it's … it's simply that I've discovered I'm quite socially inept. I find it difficult to interact with ease." They quietly listened as she attempted to explain herself. Flustered, she turned to Libby. "But enough about my shortcomings. How are you, dear girl?" she asked, offering her hand to escort Libby into the house and up to the bedroom.

Justin grabbed Jeremy's shoulder. "Whatever did you do to her?" he asked incredulously.

Jeremy grinned. "Just taught her how to not take herself so seriously."

"Hmm … so that's all it took, and you taught her in just one evening. Perhaps I should test your tactic on Susanna. You must educate me later this evening."

"Misser Jussin! Misser Jermy! We havin' a picnic?" asked Vie, racing up the porch steps to catch up with them.

"It's good the sheriff didn't ask that Vie identify the woman," whispered Jeremy.

"I seriously doubt that he would have asked a small child to look at that woman's face. She would have nightmares for months," Justin whispered back. He turned to take the child's hand. "No, Vie. We'll have our picnic next Saturday, when Mr. Josh, Miss Lydia, and baby Laurel come to visit. But you're welcome to have dinner with us. Suppose you go upstairs and tell the ladies that the men are going to make dinner for a change."

"Mama say dat be women works, not mens."

"I can't promise that it will taste as good as your mama's cooking, but we'll try to make it as palatable as possible."

"What be 'palable'?"

Justin gave her a light push at the bottom of the stairs. "Go up and ask Miss Clary."

"And tell Miss Charlotte that I said she's to be sweet to you," called Jeremy.

Libby sat down on the bed next to Charlotte and gave her the details of the late morning's ordeal while waiting for Clary to bring her wedding band.

"I suppose you'll have to identify the man when they capture him," said Charlotte.

Libby shrugged. "I doubt that I could. I don't remember any such man. I can't even recall ever seeing Lottie. But I *do* remember my mother's ring," she said, accepting her keepsake from Clary and immediately sliding it down the third finger of her left hand. A perfect fit.

She's accustomed to wearing her mother's ring on her marriage fin-

ger, Clary thought with satisfaction. *I suppose I may now safely assume that she has no husband.*

"Oh! Miz Cwary give you da ring?" Vie asked with excitement upon entering the room. "It be aw wight now?"

"Yes, Vie. It seems that it already belonged to her," Clary explained.

"Excuse me," said Libby. She stood up and headed for the door. "I must use the wash closet."

Vie suspiciously eyed Charlotte and stepped back a pace. "Misser Jermy say ta tell you ta be thweet ta me," she announced, with her nose in the air.

Charlotte clapped a hand on her chest in a defensive gesture then burst into laughter. She reached up and pulled a tiny gold butterfly pin from her hair and ran it through several cornrows on top of the child's head.

"You may have my butterfly as a peace offering. That means that I would like to be your friend," she offered with a smile.

Vie stood very still, staring into space for a moment, deep in thought. She gave a little nod, then reached into her pocket and held her closed hand out to Charlotte. "Then here be my piece of a off ring." She dropped a gold band onto Charlotte's open hand. Both Charlotte and Clary gasped.

"Where did you get that?" Clary quickly demanded to know. When she saw the frightened look in the child's eyes, she took the ring from Charlotte's still open hand, instructed her not to say anything about it to Libby, and then escorted the child down the steps and over to Mama Becky.

Twenty minutes later, Clary came back without Vie to find everyone seated and eating dinner at the dining room table. She found it strange that Susanna had not yet arrived.

"Where is Susanna?" she testily asked.

"She most likely is having too lovely a time with her friend Louise," answered Charlotte.

Clary took her seat and looked over at Justin. He didn't seem at all concerned that Susanna preferred to spend her time with someone other than him. She could feel her blood begin to boil. *What sort of asinine relationship is this?*

Justin looked up from his plate. "We already said grace. Where is Vie?"

"She had to return home. I'll explain why later."

"You do know, Charlotte, if you would have removed your petticoats like Betsy and Clary did before coming to the table, you would be able to sit closer and not drop so much food onto your lap," commented Jeremy.

Charlotte turned scarlet, and Justin reached over to swat the back of Jeremy's head.

"Well, ladies, I haven't heard any compliments on the gourmet fare we've served you," said Justin.

"That's because we're eating Becky's picnic ham, chicken, and sweet potato pie that she left in the kitchen. We'll thank her, but you did a fine job at setting the table. All of the silverware is in its proper place. Is something wrong, Charlotte?" asked Clary. "You look puzzled."

"I suppose I'm not used to anyone speaking during meals at my house."

"What a lovely idea! Suppose we remain quiet and simply eat," Clary crossly suggested.

Justin stared hard at Clary's face. He knew something was "ruffling her feathers." When she glared at him, he directed his focus over to Libby. He noticed that she barely touched her food. Normally her appetite was ferocious by this time of day. She also appeared uncommonly pale, and her present demeanor of mourning touched his heart. He continued to regard her, taking notice that her long, thick black lashes seemed to cast a shadow over her cheeks as she concentrated so intently on rearranging bits of food around her plate with her fork. He found it pleasing the way her waist-length black curls were simply and loosely tied back with a wide red ribbon and the charming way tiny spiral curls framed her lovely face … and certainly the way the outer corners of her large black eyes tilted slightly upward was most becoming. Her small hands and feet were almost childlike in size, but her figure told him that she was no child. The fullness of her bosom and shapeliness of her body were definitely not that of a child.

She looked up suddenly and shyly smiled at him. He flashed a quick broad grin then focused back on eating the remaining food on his plate. Clary keenly observed their interaction with a faint smile of satisfaction.

"Hello, all," Susanna said, waltzing into the room. "Forgive my tardiness." She gave Justin a light peck on the check then sat down on the only unoccupied chair. "I passed Louise Childress along the road and decided to visit with her for a bit. I had been meaning to ask her if she would be one of my bridesmaids and decided that this was as good a time as any. She'll make number eight, besides my two sisters. Please pass the chicken, Charlotte. I'm famished. Is there no one to serve cool water or tea? Oh, that's right, today is Sunday, so your servants have the day off. I forgot, not having gone to church, and—" She suddenly stopped talking, aware that all eyes were upon her.

"Are you certain that no one talks during meals at your house, Charlotte?" Justin asked.

Susanna looked seriously ahead, as if she were trying to digest Justin's question and everyone's stare, then waved her hand at him and giggled. "Silly goose! I'm simply excited. Coordinating a wedding takes much thought and planning. As each idea falls into place, I become *excited.*"

Who's the silly goose? wondered Clary. "Betsy, I'm concerned for your health. Please go upstairs and rest. You may have your appetite back after you sleep for a bit. This morning was very trying." She put her hand over Libby's. "Go, dear."

"Yes, please go rest," encouraged Susanna. "You look as if

you're drained of blood. You need not remain here on Charlotte's and my account."

"Susanna," said Charlotte. "Eat . . . so that Clary and I may clear the table."

"Please tell Betsy I'll call on her the middle of next week," Libby heard Charlotte say to Clary on the front porch. She hastily rose from the bed to look out the window. Justin and Jeremy were escorting the ladies to their buggy. Justin gave Susanna a kiss on the cheek before departure, and then he turned around to see Jeremy holding Charlotte in a death-grip, passionately kissing her lips. He then helped the flushed and happy Charlotte into the buggy, and the men waved as they drove off.

"You had better slow down," Justin advised Jeremy. "You'll have the young woman believing you're in love with her."

Does Susanna ever wonder if you're really in love with her, Justin? Clary thought, once inside the house. "I would like to speak with you in the library for a moment, Justin. Alone!" she called over her shoulder.

"I have two concerns," she said, once he closed the library door behind them and went to sit at his desk. "First, although you'll most likely tell me that it's none of my concern, I would like to comment that I feel you and Susanna have a truly strange relationship. You never spend time together. Even Betsy noticed. She told me that, if you were her beau, she would want to spend as much time with you as possible."

He gave her an amused grin. "She did, did she? Clary, Susanna and I have our whole life to spend together. At present we're simply involved with wedding and career responsibilities. Our time together will come after we're married."

"Perhaps you'll find out that you spent so much time with your 'responsibilities' that you never found out if you're actually compatible, and when it's too late."

His grin faded. "You're correct. I *will* tell you that it's none of your concern," he said somberly.

She slapped her hand on his desk then began to pace the room so that he wouldn't notice her tears of frustration.

"Is there something else?" he asked.

She took the ring from her pocket and placed it on the desk in front of him. "Vie was about to give it to Charlotte as a gift. Betsy wasn't in the room, so I immediately whisked Vie over to Becky to question her about where she had gotten it. Look at the engraving."

He took a magnifying glass from his desk drawer and went to the window to hold the ring up to the light. "The letters are almost too small to read… possibly because the ring is so tiny. It looks like: W & E 6/2/60." He sat back down. "Do you believe this belongs to Betsy?"

"Vie claims that she found it. Lottie Harmon had *not* given it to her… and if the engraved date is a wedding day, then it couldn't possibly belong to Betsy. I realize that you feel Betsy is older than sixteen, but even if she's eighteen, she would have only been thirteen on her wedding day. That would be preposterous!"

"The name 'Betsy' is often used as a shortened name for 'Elizabeth.' Do you suppose the 'E' stands for 'Elizabeth'?"

"Fiona Flanagan suggested that her name may not even be Betsy, since she can't remember who she is. And *Jeffrey's* wife wasn't Elizabeth, just Betsy Lynn. And what about Betsy Holden?"

"I seriously doubt that our Betsy's given name is *Bethesda*," he said, rolling his eyes.

"I would like to hold on to this ring for a while, until I feel the time is right. Becky told Vie she's not to mention anything about the ring to Betsy."

"I can't see the harm in showing it to her. Do you have some sort of hidden agenda? I almost have the feeling that you don't want Betsy to remember her past life."

"That is ridiculous! I won't even give you the courtesy of

responding to your suggestion." She went to open the door when she heard a knock. "What is it?" she asked gruffly of Jeremy.

"You certainly are snappish! What is your problem?" he asked, somewhat taken aback. "I only came to inform you that the sheriff's deputy just told me Josiah Staples is in custody. Seems he was riding the rails and was arrested when he tried to exit a boxcar in York, Pennsylvania. Sheriff Clayton figured that the quickest means of escape would be by freight train, so he got hold of the train's scheduled stops then wired the police in each town along the route to keep a lookout. He jumped out of the train, right into a pair of handcuffs. It'll make a great story for tomorrow's edition. I'm going to ride over to the sheriff's office to get more details," he said excitedly. "The deputy said ole Josiah had quite a roll of money in his pocket," he called over his shoulder. "Hello, Betsy. Justin and Clary are in the library," they heard him say before exiting the house.

Clary turned to Justin. "I've said all I have to say, so I'm going to prepare something to eat for Betsy. I'm glad we won't need a stranger in the house to look after us while you're gone."

CHAPTER 12

"Come in," Justin called, responding to a knock on the library door.

"I'm sorry to disturb you," said Libby, opening the door just enough to stick her head through. "I would like to read more from Clary's poetry book." When he nodded, she went to retrieve it from the bookshelf. "Clary's resting upstairs. She claims that her head is aching. Since I'm no longer required to have a chaperone, I'll take the book out on the porch to watch the sunset." She regarded him for a moment. "You're leaving for Washington tomorrow?" she asked shyly.

He looked up from his paperwork. "Yes, very early in the morning, but I'll be home late Thursday evening."

"Well…um…have a safe trip," she said, about to exit the room.

"It's only a bit over an hour's train ride…Betsy?" He sensed that she needed to talk with him.

"Yes, Justin?" she asked, turning around to go stand in front of his desk. "What are you reading from your Bible?"

"I'm going over and writing down some of the points the reverend made in his sermon this morning, rereading Psalms 91 and 30." He leaned back in his chair and smiled warmly at her. "Is there something you need to discuss with me?" he asked in a tender sort of way.

"There is *so* much I would like to discuss with you, but I'm afraid you would never be able to spare so much time. Any spare time you have should—"

"Be spent with Susanna," he said, thinking he was completing her sentence. "My sister tells me that you feel Susanna and I don't spend enough time together."

She deeply blushed. "I … I … it's none of my affair how much time you spend with Susanna. I was about to suggest that you'll need any spare time you might have this evening to pack your clothing and prepare for your trip back to the city." She looked down, unable to accept the amused twinkle in his eyes.

"Well, it just so happens, young lady, I have the hour until sunset to spend time listening to you release all of the questions, anxieties, and frustrations that have built up inside of you over the past couple of weeks." He stood up. "Suppose I join you on the porch glider."

She set the book back on the shelf, and followed him out to the porch. After they sat down, she took a small paper sack from her apron pocket and held it up to him.

"Would you like one?" she asked. He took the sack from her and looked inside. "Candy. Jeremy bought them for me. I can't … I *shouldn't* eat them all."

He spent a moment trying to decide which flavor he was in the mood for then popped a peppermint drop into his mouth.

"You can't mix peppermint drops with other flavors," she said. "They make all the other flavors taste like peppermint."

He nodded. They were quiet for a few moments. "It's pleasant to feel a cool breeze for a change," he finally commented.

"Yes," she said. "I imagine we'll see a lovely orange, early harvest sunset this evening."

"I believe you may be correct. Now suppose you tell me what is on your mind."

"Well, first I would like you to know how very much I appreciate all of you. Not many families would take a perfect stranger into their home and treat him … or her as one of their own. This morning, when you handed a sum of money to Lottie's grandmother, it struck me greatly that I've imposed on your hospitality to the degree of *absurdity*. You've clothed me, fed me, attended to my medical care, and spent compassionate time guarding my sanity and person. And then paying for a proper burial for my alleged attacker? It... it would be *ludicrous* for me to assume that I, a complete stranger, am not a burden and an imposition into your peaceful lives..."

He reached over and took her hand. The earnestness in her voice and the overwrought frustration she seemed to feel in her helplessness brought a mist to his eyes. When she began to weep, he handed her his handkerchief.

"It's not nearly as intricately made as the one you embroidered for me, but it will suffice," he said. "Betsy, I would like to tell you a story about a little red-haired girl."

"You may, if there's a point to be made," she said with a light sniff and a giggle.

"A lawyer always strives to make a point. Once there was a little red-haired girl with large, greenish-brown, *inquisitive* eyes. After completing her very first day at school, she told her mother that no one wanted to be her friend. The girls didn't like her freckles and carrot-red hair, and the boys thought she was too smart because she could correctly answer every question the teacher asked. When not at school, she spent most of her time reading everything she could get her hands on. The girl had two older brothers and two younger brothers. All of their achievements were recognized and praised by family and teachers, but no one seemed to notice or care that the little girl was far more brilliant than any of her brothers. She became so reclusive that her mother became her only true friend. Her mother was the only one who praised her little inventions and listened patiently to her ideas.

"When the little girl became sixteen years of age, she still had no female friends, but because the so-called 'ugly duckling' had transformed into a lovely swan, young men began to take notice of her. They would call upon her father to ask permission to court her, but none remained very long. They found her interests and superior intellect to be tedious. Only one man remained long enough for *her* to take the initiative to rebuff, the man who guarded you the first few days you were with us. Finally a young woman, she had to face the fact that her mother was required to leave her for a good portion of every year. She became so lonely, she eventually didn't even care to communicate with her brothers, just spent her days helping Becky with household chores and shutting herself off from the rest of the world by growing herbs and experimenting with their properties to be implemented into medicines and beauty potions.

"You, of course, know that I'm speaking of Clary. Betsy, when last I arrived home from Washington, I saw such a change in my sister, one that I had never witnessed before. There was sparkle and renewed life in her eyes. You, Betsy, have given my sister a much-needed purpose. You think you need her? I will tell you that she needs you more so. So the point that I'm trying to make is that you are not an imposition; you are a godsend."

Libby looked down at the large, well-manicured hand that firmly grasped hers. "If what you are telling me is so, then my great debt to you is somewhat lessened," she said softly. She looked up into the warm brown eyes that were fixed upon her face. "However, the fact remains that I'm still greatly indebted to you and thank the Lord many times each day that he led me to your safe haven."

He gave her fingers a light squeeze before releasing her hand then folded his arms across his chest. "Suppose we move on to another matter. What else would you like to discuss?"

"Well, I've been haphazardly reading through several of your law books, particularly the *Rudiments of Defense and Defending*. So much of what I've read puzzles me. I would like to know and understand the heart of a defense attorney," she said solemnly. "Will you enlighten me?"

He burst into laughter but quickly sobered when he realized the intent seriousness of her inquiry. "The way in which you regard me, miss, persuades me to believe that you find attorneys that defend to be a sinister lot."

"I simply cannot comprehend how a righteous man can defend that which he knows to be unlawful and sinful in the eyes of God."

"Are you telling me you don't feel that every individual deserves a fair trial?" he asked.

"But what is a fair trial? An individual who requires the services of a defense attorney is most likely guilty of his crime and possibly has even relayed so to said attorney. Is it fair to those whom the defendant has victimized that a skillful individual attempt to discredit the victim and work toward securing the lightest punishment or possibly even freedom for the defendant?"

He sat quietly pondering for a moment. *What a strange young woman. No one has ever before confronted me with these notions.* "I believe that you've steered your thinking toward what the dangerous criminal deserves, and no doubt Lottie Harmon's tragic death has influenced you. Do you believe that the woman who steals bread to feed her hungry children deserves the same punishment as, shall we say, Josiah Staples?"

"No, certainly not. I... I possibly am not expressing myself well. Have you ever defended an individual but, because you knew he was guilty of a heinous crime, couldn't bring yourself to do an effective job at securing the lightest possible punishment, that your conscience wouldn't allow it?"

"Betsy, are you a sinner?" When she nodded, he asked, "Do you believe that Christ is your defender before God?" She nodded again. "And are you confident that Christ is the most competent defender you could possibly have?"

"Certainly! However, he'll only represent me if I've repented and am sorry for my wrongdoing. How many of your defendants *truly* repent and ask for forgiveness? God's law and man's law are not one and the same, as far as I can see."

He said nothing for a moment. Her point was impacting him somewhat, but she needed to understand man's system of law.

"Betsy, didn't you read that it's not the responsibility of a defense attorney to prove guilt or innocence? It's the prosecutor's job to prove guilt beyond the shadow of a doubt. It almost works like a system of checks and balances. My job is simply to assure that the prosecution hasn't overstepped itself by presenting falsehoods or misrepresentations. The fate of the defendant remains in the hands of judge and jury."

He sighed and shook his head. "I suppose the problem with man's law is that we're all sinners: defender, prosecutor, the accused, and the jury. So our system can never be truly just or perfect as in God's law. I will tell you, though, that I've not had the opportunity of actually solely defending an individual. Until now I've prepared the research briefs for certain cases, and during the war I was able to acquire experience in judgments and sentencing, but according to set military law. I'm required to prepare and present one pro bono case assigned to my firm by Virginia's state prosecutors. If my efforts in handling and representing the case are satisfactory, I may begin to accept and defend cases of my own and thus be given full partnership in the Dupont firm. Pro bono means—"

"Free of charge," she finished for him. She took a deep breath and rested her hand on his forearm. "Perhaps it would be best to broach this subject at some other time. It's becoming too dark to see. I apologize if I've caused you to feel that I think less of you because of your occupation. My intent was merely to learn. I have only the highest regard for you."

He stood up and took her hand to help her stand. "I will tell you that you are not sixteen years of age. Suppose we go inside. If you're willing, I should very much like to hear you play the Chopin Polonaise you played for my sister. Perhaps she'll feel well enough to join us."

"I'll play for you if you do the same for me."

"I must warn you that my ability to play the piano merits very little consideration. My voice is my forte."

"Then you shall sing," she said, following him into the house.

"May we try 'I Sing the Mighty Power of God'? I believe we would harmonize well together."

He took her arm. "Step carefully until I light a lamp. I'm curious as to where Jeremy disappeared."

"I'm willing to wager that he's visiting with Charlotte."

"It's amazing, the change in that young woman. She's now friendly toward you, and Jeremy certainly finds her appealing."

"She simply needed someone to help her break free from her own personal prison. She realizes she can be her true self with Jeremy and he won't run from her. She doesn't have to put on the façade that her social circle requires of her."

He lit one of the foyer lamps then turned to look at her. "As I said before, you are not a girl of just sixteen years."

"What age do you surmise that I am?"

He stepped back a stride to scrutinize her appearance through narrowed eye. "Hmm … I would say … *nineteen*." He stroked his chin. "Yes, at least nineteen, still young enough to be considered a little sister. You'll be my adopted little sister. I know Clary would approve," he said with a chuckle, and then placed a hand on her cascade of curls to guide her into the library. "After I light some lamps, I'll get us something to eat while you're limbering up your fingers."

Clary stood listening to their conversation on the upper landing of the foyer. *No, Justin, I would not approve. I want her to be so much more to you than a sister.* She tiptoed back to her room and gently shut the door.

"Shall I awaken Clary?"

"No. Let her sleep. Her workload will be heavy this week, preparing for my brother's family. Now don't begin playing until I return," he said, heading for the kitchen.

Libby adjusted the piano stool and sat down to practice her scales until Justin returned with two glasses of milk and a few slices of cake. He set the tray on the table between the wing chairs then sat down and began eating a slice of cake. He nodded for her to begin, but her eyes were glued to his thick slice of butter cake. He stood up, broke a piece from it, and placed it in her eager mouth. "You'll get more after the Polonaise," he promised, sitting back down again. "Now begin."

When she finished, he applauded with vigor. "That was *excellent*! All of Chopin's music is infused with such depth of passion. You communicate the work the way it was meant to be played. *Bravo*!"

"Now it's your turn to play and my turn to eat," she said, rising from the stool to go sit on the other wingback.

"I have an idea," he said, going out into the hallway. He came back with the backless bench that sat against the wall near the front door. "There's enough room on this bench for both of us to play. We'll try some duets. You'll have to sit on a few books to be at the right height, however." He selected a few books from the bookcase, placed one on top of the other on the bench, and gestured for her to sit down. He then perused the selection of books on the bottom shelf of the bookcase, pulled out a hymnal, and handed it to her. "Choose what you like," he offered.

She scanned the index and found "I Sing the Mighty Power of God."

"You may hold the page open while I play. Let's sing all stanzas…and please feel free to improvise. After that we'll sing 'All Creatures of Our God and King,' and then perhaps we can try that new hymn we sang in church, 'Praise to the Lord, the Almighty.' If it's too new to be in this hymnal, I'll have to play it by ear. I hope you know all of the words."

When they finished their personal concert, she clapped with glee, bouncing up and down on the bench until the pile of books slid and began to topple. She would have fallen to the floor had he not grabbed her in time. They heartily laughed and, after finally gaining some composure, turned to look at one another. She could read the admiration in his eyes and recognized it in his voice when he said, "You, Betsy, are a refreshing delight!"

"May anyone join this party?" Jeremy asked from the doorway.

"This party is disbanding. I've already taken up too much of Justin's time. He needs to prepare for his trip and get a good night's rest, but there's a piece of cake left," Libby informed him. She went to the bookcase to retrieve the book of poetry then headed for the door. "Good night, gentlemen. If I'm claimed before you arrive home this Thursday, Justin … well … " She turned to give him a shy, demure smile before exiting. "It has been wonderful knowing you."

CHAPTER 13

The chimes of the mantle clock played their final tones of the day, proclaiming midnight. Justin lifted his weary head up from his folded arms and looked about the room. A glance at the clock told him he had fallen asleep over his paperwork at least two hours earlier. He groaned at the realization that the night would only allow him a mere five hours of sleep before his departure to the city. Dread nudged him as he thought of all the work he still hadn't completed and the fact that Susanna would have every evening of the upcoming week saturated with social events she expected him to attend. He almost wished she would decide to stay home with Charlotte this week, so he could rest and catch up.

Betsy's presence had claimed much of his precious time and thought over the past days. He could picture her gleefully clapping, her curls bobbing as she bounced up and down on their makeshift piano bench. A faint smile touched his lips as he decided that he didn't regret the time lost. This evening had been most enjoyable. He clasped his hands together behind his head and sat back in his chair. A kitten—that's what she reminded him of, with her soft demeanor and the slant of her large eyes. She didn't possess the classic beauty that had first attracted him to Susanna—although Susanna would do well to have some color added to her pallid cheeks—but Betsy's appearance was mighty appealing, yes, *mighty* appealing. *But beauty is fleeting.* He chuckled. *We men are so incredibly base. Why must we always first focus on a woman's beauty?* An image of Betsy so regally attired in a gown of robin's egg blue flashed before his eyes.

Taking his watch from his pocket, he compared its time with the time on the mantle clock. Twenty-three minutes off—time to take it to the watchmaker for an oiling and adjustment. But he knew he owned another, a fine, ornate, Girard-Perregaux silver pocket watch that had belonged to his grandfather, only it lay in his top dresser drawer. Dare he risk sneaking into his room? Realizing the necessity of carrying an accurate, reliable timepiece, he decided in favor of the intrusion. He unbuttoned his shirt and extinguished the lamps. Using the moonlight to guide him, he placed the bench back at its rightful place in the foyer then ascended the stairs. Hearing what sounded like muffled cries, he halted and listened. Whatever it was, it ceased.

Very cautiously, he turned the knob of his bedroom door. The lamp on the bed table was still lit, and Betsy's head and upper back lay propped on several pillows. The book of poetry was still clutched in her hand that hung over the side of the bed. He quickly found the watch and stashed it in his pocket, then went to take the book from her hand and snuff the lamplight. When he came close to the bed, he observed that her face was stained with tears, and his heart went out to her at the frustration she must be privately enduring. As he removed the book and placed her hand beneath the blanket, she began to cry out.

"I despise you!" She sobbed. "You're a *murderer*! Keep away from me! I *never* want to see your horrid face again!" she exclaimed, her voice becoming progressively louder.

"Whatever is wrong with Betsy?" Clary asked, rushing in to stand beside Justin.

"Betsy! Betsy!" he said, lightly shaking her by her shoulders. "You're safe. You've just had a frightening dream. Hush, now. You're safe," he said soothingly, stroking her cheek.

She opened her eyes and stared at them, curious as to why they were standing over her.

"You must have had a nightmare about Josiah Staples," Clary

said, sitting on the edge of the bed. "Would you like me to sleep beside you for tonight?"

"No," she answered, somewhat disoriented. Her eyes having focused on Justin's concerned face and bared chest, she subconsciously pulled the blanket up over her lace-adorned breasts. "The face I saw in my dream seemed vaguely familiar to me... but I don't know how... or where... and he was fair-haired, not mulatto. I'm sorry I awakened you. I'll be fine by myself. Please return to your beds."

Clary kissed Libby's cheek. "Tomorrow we'll go into town to shop. We'll have a lovely time. Goodnight, dear."

Justin extinguished the lamp then bent down to kiss her forehead. "Sweet dreams, little sister," he whispered in her ear.

After shutting the door behind them, he whispered to Clary, "It appears that the mystery deepens."

Libby shivered and nestled beneath the blanket. The sweet aura of his face so close to hers, his gentle kiss, and the scent of his cologne caused her heart to race. Thoughts of him overshadowed the troubling nightmare, enabling her to fall into a deep, restful sleep.

"I'm overjoyed!" Libby exclaimed, sitting down at the breakfast table. "My stomach is ready for a thick stack of Becky's griddlecakes, two boiled eggs, and a large cup of coffee. I feel marvelous this morning, a completely settled stomach!"

"Well, if you don't feel sick now, you certainly shall after eating all of that," commented Clary, placing a small pitcher of syrup beside Libby's plate. She and Becky sat down across from her to sip their coffee.

"Where is Vie?" she asked Becky.

"She be helpin' her papa this mornin.'" She glanced at Clary. They had just agreed that it might be a good idea to keep Vie away from Betsy for a while. At least they shouldn't be left alone together. Becky was fairly sure that Vie had lied concerning how she acquired the engraved wedding band, most likely due to the fear of the "switch" striking her bottom.

"Oh … Well, I hope she comes to visit later. These are wonderful, Becky! You put pecans in them. What a tasty touch. Clary, have you some old pieces of cloth I might have?" she asked.

Clary turned to smile smugly at Becky. "Why, yes, I do. There's a large pillow cover in the hall stairwell closet that's stuffed with clean cloths. Help yourself."

"I hope I'll find some that are suitable."

Clary furrowed her brow. "How *suitable* must they be … considering?"

"I prefer that the pieces be white and without holes or rips."

Clary shrugged. "I told you she's not pregnant," she mouthed to Becky while Libby concentrated on loading up her fork.

"Have you some pink or white yarn I may use to crochet a bonnet, shawl, and booties for your baby niece?" Libby asked.

"That's a lovely thought," said Clary. "We'll purchase some in town, along with tiny rosettes to adorn them."

Libby looked up suddenly. "I promise to pay back the money for any items we might purchase. Am I being presumptuous in thinking that you have money to purchase the items I want? If it's a hardship, please inform me."

"Not at all. I have a healthy allowance. Both of my brothers have excellent incomes, and my mother sends money to help manage this house and hers."

"Oh, I forget, Miss Clary. Somethin' come from Miss Chloe, delivered early this mornin' while you was gatherin' eggs," Becky said, leaving the table to retrieve the letter.

Clary eagerly unfolded it. "I had Jeremy send a wire explaining your situation to Mother the day after you arrived, Betsy, but she must have posted this letter first, for there's no mention of you. Possibly the Trans-Atlantic wires are down again, and she never even received it. She states that Father has purchased tickets to sail on December 11, and they'll return to England on April 5, the day after Justin's *wedding*." She rolled her eyes at Libby then finished the letter in silence. "We'll have a good sum of money to buy what we need," she said, holding up a hundred dollar note. "First stop, the bank."

Justin's head nodded, and he could barely keep his heavy eyelids open as the train continued to journey toward its next stop. He wasn't in the mood to play delivery boy for the Dupont brothers this afternoon. And what he wouldn't give for a few hours of sound sleep.

He suddenly jolted upright, smiled, and nodded to the young man who took a seat across from him. But the man seemed too caught up in his own thoughts to acknowledge the greeting. Justin noticed that his eyes seemed to have a faraway look to them, and a certain degree of melancholy. Interesting eyes—large, thick-lashed, coal-black eyes, their outer corners tilting slightly upward ... similar to ... He lightly chuckled and looked out at the passing scenery. He must be delirious with fatigue if every individual he encountered appeared to have Betsy's eyes.

He looked back to the young man again as the train slowed down for its next stop and watched him stand up and rake his fingers through his black curly hair then take a handkerchief from his vest pocket to wipe the beads of perspiration from his brow. Justin's eyes instantly riveted to the initials and blue fleur-de-lis design embroidered on its corner. The young man hastily made his way to the open door and disappeared into the crowd on the platform, leaving Justin with an eerie sense of uneasiness.

"The sun is before us," Libby noted to Clary. "I expected that we would be traveling eastward." She rested a hand on top of her straw bonnet to keep the breeze from relocating it to the back of her head.

"No, a few miles west. You'll like the town of Barrister's Junction. It's charming. The storefronts are still as they were fifty years ago. I'll take you to Jeremy's office after dinner. Most of the towns going eastward along the routes to Washington have become small cities, with houses rising up in all directions. Sadly, I imagine Barrister's will be the same within time."

"Hold up there, ladies!" a male voice yelled. They turned around to see a carriage coming along side of their buggy.

"Good afternoon, Richard. I believe congratulations are in order. I hear Amy delivered a healthy baby boy," Clary said, coming to a full stop.

"A *strapping* boy, weighing in at nine pounds. We named him Jonathan."

"Betsy and I must visit with Amy and *Jonathan* as soon as she feels well enough to receive visitors. I suspect that his arrival is keeping you in Barrister's Junction."

"Not at all. Didn't Justin tell you that I'm in the process of separating myself from my father and uncle's firm?"

"No!" Clary answered, anxious to hear the details. "Tell us more, please."

"I'm surprised Justin didn't tell you that I offered him a partnership. Nathan Wentworth is planning to go into partnership with me, and I was hoping we would finally settle as Dupont, Wentworth, and Chambers. We'll be primarily handling civil cases, and I've already secured several large government contracts. I recently purchased the building on the corner of Main and Barlow, the three-story with the Georgian architecture."

"I know the building. It's a handsome structure. Did my brother give you a *coherent* explanation as to why he rejected your proposal?" Clary asked, feeling anger on the rise.

"Perhaps Susanna's influence." He laughed. "I suppose he finds greater intrigue in criminal law and defending the corrupt."

Clary knew differently but remained mum on the issue. She

smiled sweetly. "Well, good day, Richard. Betsy and I would like to have dinner at the White Swan Café, so we best be on our way before it closes for the remainder of the afternoon."

He tipped his hat. "Good day to you, ladies." He sped on past them.

Libby reached over to pull the brim of Clary's bonnet further down over her forehead. "Your fair skin burns so easily in the sun," she commented.

"If my face is red, it has nothing to do with the sun. How could Justin keep this information from me?" she fairly shouted. "I plan to tear into him once he's home again!" She slapped the reins down hard over the horse's back.

Libby laughed. "Do you suppose he refrained from confiding in you due to your temper?"

"You don't understand. A guaranteed partnership with a firm that handles only civil cases and reconstruction matters is exactly what is best suited for Justin. I would like to wring Susanna's neck!"

"Now, now," Libby said soothingly. "We don't know for certain that Susanna is completely responsible. After all, Justin has a fine mind of his own. Suppose we put this subject aside for now. Tell me of what sort of dishes the White Swan Café specializes. I'm famished."

"A boy just delivered a telegram from Philadelphia, Tim," Sally Morrow said upon entering her husband's office. "It seems that Ben is nowhere to be found, but the science academy administrator suggested that he may have gone to the Smithsonian earlier than planned since he's a member of the Megatherium Club. They're having a conference, and Ben is expected to lecture on his summer's findings in the Poconos. Have any of the men returned with any sort of hopeful news?" she asked anxiously.

"If they had, I would have come to you immediately, my dear," he said, looking up from his stack of patients' charts.

"Well, I know you've been extra busy with Caleb's patients and all. I thought perhaps—"

"If someone had come back with even a tidbit of positive information, I would have immediately rushed home to tell you. Half a dozen wrestlers could not have held me back. There's someone at the door now. Please go see who it is."

She opened the door to see Andy Stone standing on the stoop.

"Good evening to you, Mrs. I just wanted you to know that me and the other men knocked on every door within a mile of the Prescott house, and we don't know any more than we did when we started. There wasn't a soul could offer a clue as to where Libby could be. We took a couple of the sheriff's hounds again, but they only led us to the Clark place. They took a real interest in some blood splotches that were on the porch in front of their door. Figured they must have come from an animal that Esau caught. And again, they just kept leading us to the train tracks. Lots of big puddles of water still over there. They must have lost her scent. Probably too much time has gone by to even bother using the hounds."

"It may just be that the blood near the door belonged to Libby. Perhaps Billy hurt her before he shot Caleb. Oh dear! I best tell Tim what you've told me. You *are* planning on resuming your search tomorrow morning, aren't you?"

"Sheriff says he can't see no use." He shrugged. "We been everywhere. He's wired all the neighboring town police to keep an eye out for her. Ain't much else can be done."

"Thank you, Andy. I need to speak with Tim now. Have a good evening," she said, shutting the door to rush back to her husband.

"It was Andy, but with no news whatsoever. Their search came up dry. However, I have a new concern. Andy says the sheriff's hounds showed a great deal of interest in some blood splotches that were in front on the Clarks' door, and they lost Libby's scent by the train tracks again. Do you suppose Billy hurt her before he shot Caleb?"

Tim sat back in his chair and took a deep, sustained breath. "If she was screaming for help, like Maggie Clark said, she probably would have mentioned that *she* was wounded also. And why didn't the hounds find other splotches between the Clarks' and the train? The blood by the door probably came from an animal that Esau hunted down. *Bloodhounds* have a fascination with *blood*, you know, thus their name. Puzzles me a bit that she wasn't screaming that Billy was shot also. The mystery deepens, my dear. One would almost surmise that a phantom train whisked her off into the night."

Sally looked thoughtful for a moment. "I'm speculating, of course, but the Clarks' porch is covered, so the torrential rains that took place after Libby disappeared wouldn't wash away the blood by the door, but once she left the porch ..."

He nodded. "I understand what you are saying."

"What about a literal train?" she suggested, her eyes lighting up. "Do trains still stop at the old Wellesley station?"

"Don't rightly know, but I doubt it ... not since the war. But it may be worth checking into, only I doubt she would board a train if she were desperately trying to find help for her father, especially a freight train." *Hmm ... unless she met with foul play.* "I do know for sure that passenger trains haven't stopped there since back in '61."

"I'm going to go send a wire to the Smithsonian now. I pray to God that Ben can be found. I'll be back to prepare your supper in an hour."

CHAPTER 14

"Breakfast, Betsy!" Clary called from the bottom of the steps.

"No breakfast, please. I feel ill. The smell of food would only cause me to vomit," Libby called back.

"She's sick *again*?" Jeremy asked while descending the stairs.

"I'm afraid so. But she'll feel better in an hour or two and make up for what she didn't eat for breakfast at dinnertime... I would guess," she said wryly, with an added great sigh. "Why are you leaving for work at this hour?"

"I have an appointment with the sheriff. He's going to allow me time to ask Josiah Staples a few questions. I want to get to him before he's assigned an attorney. He was only extradited by the York, Pennsylvania, police yesterday afternoon."

"I hate the thought that Betsy will eventually have to witness at that man's trial."

"Be of good cheer, sister! Maybe she'll *never* regain her memory." He snickered. "Wouldn't you *love* that? Then you *just* may get to keep her," he said, pinching her cheek on his way out.

She slammed the door shut behind him and went to the stairwell closet door. The pillow cover of rags still stood in its place, untouched. She decided to take it upstairs to Libby.

"Betsy, may I come in?" she asked, with a light knock on the door.

"Please do," she said. "I've just started to crochet the booties. Have you a chore for me?"

Clary placed the bundle on the bed and saw that Libby was

dressed and sitting by the window with a large ball of pale pink yarn on her lap.

"There's nothing to do at present. Abel is going to take the rugs outside and polish the floors this morning. Becky and I will beat the rugs. I'll find something for you to do. I'm surprised you haven't looked through the rags yet."

Libby looked up from her crocheting. "I decided to wait and crochet the booties, bonnet, and shawl first, since there is so little time before your niece arrives. You appear glum. Have you a matter to discuss?"

"I'm not quite sure how you can 'wait.' Exactly what do you need the rags for?"

"To keep my hands busy while I wait for the pieces of my life to fall back into place. If I find some white cloths with no holes or rips, I'll make handkerchiefs from them similar to the one I crocheted and embroidered for Justin," she said matter-of-factly.

Clary stared at Libby for several seconds then covered her face with her hands and laughed herself to tears. A couple minutes later she looked up to see that Libby sat speechless, her mouth wide open, and eyes glassy with tears. When her lower lip began to quiver, she hastily looked down at her lap.

Clary rushed over to cuddle her. "Oh, my sweet dear!" she exclaimed. "You think I'm laughing at *you*, but I'm not! I'm laughing at myself, believe it or not. Yes, I most certainly am," she explained, breaking into laughter again. "All along, I thought you wanted them for ... your menstrual cycle."

"Oh!" Libby said, finally smiling. "I thought that maybe you found it nonsensical that I like to reuse old fabric and found the notion to be too practical and ridiculous."

Clary kissed Libby's cheek then backed up to sit on the edge of the bed, deciding that this might be the time to discuss Betsy's possible "condition."

"Betsy ... perchance ... have you given thought as to why you've felt ill for most of the mornings you've been with us?"

"I suppose I'm still convalescing."

"You didn't ask for the rags for—"

"I've been here only two weeks," she interrupted.

"Why do you suppose you feel so completely hearty from mid-morning until bedtime?"

"What are you suggesting?" she asked, fidgeting in her chair, her eyes intently focused on her crocheting.

"Betsy, when you first came to us, Dr. Flanagan examined you and determined that you may have been violated."

Libby's head jerked upright, her eyes enormous with horror. "*By Josiah Staples?* But ... but ..."

"No, no. What I mean to say is that we don't know if Josiah Staples violated you. But even if he did and you conceived by him, you wouldn't be far enough along to show the symptoms of your possible 'condition.' You would have had to have been with another man well before Josiah Staples," she said, with a soft kindness to her voice.

All color drained from Libby's cheeks. "Are you suggesting that I'm ... I have a *child* growing inside of me?"

"Yes," Clary simply said.

"That is entirely unthinkable! I've been with no man! I *know* this to be true! It's true because I would never disobey God's commandment by fornicating."

She appeared so distressed that Clary wished she hadn't brought the matter up until absolutely necessary. "Suppose we wait a while longer before visiting Dr. Flanagan for an examination. But you *do* realize if you haven't begun your menses within the next two weeks ..."

"Who else knows of what you're telling me?" she asked with trepidation.

"The Flanagans, my brothers, and Becky."

She blushed with embarrassment at the unwarranted shame she felt and covered her face with her hands for a moment. "Clary?" she finally asked. "Why is it that no one appears to be searching for me? I know I have a mother and father. I've pictured them in my mind. Why haven't they found me? Have I shamed them so that they don't care to find me? Who *am I*?" she asked in exasperation.

Clary slowly shook her head. "I apologize to you. This was *not* the time in your recovery to confront you with our suppositions. Dearest," she said, kneeling in front of Libby and taking her hand. "You will discover everything you need to know in God's good time. You're *his* child, and he loves you dearly. That wondrous fact alone should be enough to sustain you for now. Now dry your pretty eyes. Suppose you take your crocheting out to the front porch. The lovely fresh air will comfort you. This afternoon, I shall take you behind the house to my shed. It's the place where I dry herbs and press the oils from seeds, petals, and leaves. We'll make lotions for Lydia's skin and hair as a gift to take home with her and put to good use the colorful jars and bottles I purchased yesterday. We may even experiment with making scented candles with the oils we extract and distill. I have several bricks of paraffin wax and a good amount of stearic acid. We'll have a fine time."

Libby looked up from her pea shelling to see Jeremy tie his horse to the post. "You're home early," she called. "Supper won't be for another hour."

He came up on to the porch and sat beside her. "It's almost six o'clock," he said, reaching for a few raw peas. "You're just accustomed to my being late all the time."

She lightly slapped his hand. "No samples. We didn't have time to pick a large quantity of vegetables today. Clary spent most of the afternoon teaching me to make lotions and perfume, and we experimented with making candles that smell wonderful. Charlotte joined us for a few hours," she added, looking up to study his face.

"I'll be visiting with that lady this evening. Only my sister can get peas to grow so late in summer," he commented. He leaned over to sniff her neck. "I thought you smelled especially delicious today. Rather fruity."

"She's wearing my recipe for lemon verbena cologne," Clary interjected as she stepped out on to the porch to take the shelled peas back to the kitchen.

"Why does it smell so much more fragrant on her than it does on you?" he asked.

She swatted him on the back of the head. "Betsy, please take the peas to the kitchen. I would like to speak to Jeremy for a moment alone."

"You need not send me away. I know you're going to tell him of our discussion this morning and the fact that I know he knows," she said.

Clary looked sharply at Jeremy. "I told Betsy that she might possibly be carrying a child and Dr. Flanagan's prognosis from when he first examined her. She also knows that you and Justin are aware, but you are not to breathe a *word* of this to a soul, most especially Charlotte!"

He rolled his eyes. "Do you think I haven't the sense I was born with?"

"I think you have much less than what you were born with," she said, taking the bowl from Libby and heading back inside.

"It's not easy being the youngest sibling in a family. They always treat you as a child."

"I know." She laughed. "My brother doesn't feel that I can do anything of merit on my own. He's forever a fountain of advice."

They locked eyes for several seconds, and then Libby began to bounce up and down on the bench. "I have a *brother*!" she announced in astonished awe.

"Well, now. We've established that you have a father, a mother, and most likely an *older* brother. Can you remember their names?"

"Sadly, no, not yet. I'm going inside to tell Clary the news," she said excitedly, jumping up from her seat. She stopped short of the door and turned back to him. "I suppose I should ask if you questioned Josiah Staples," she said, her tone changing to one of somberness.

"I did, or tried. He was very uncooperative with me. I learned virtually nothing."

She was undecided whether to be relieved or disappointed. "I hope Josiah Staples is prosecuted to the fullest extent of the law. I will never be able to forget Lottie Harmon's disfigured face and broken body and the fact that her grandmother showed so little remorse. She had no one who truly loved her by her bedside when she died," she said with tears in her eyes. "It will haunt me until the day I die."

"Betsy!" shouted Clary, shaking her by the shoulders. "Wake up! You're having another nightmare."

Libby sprang upright to a seated position, and her eyes began to explore all corners of the moonlit room. "He has murder in his eyes!" she fearfully exclaimed, her eyes darting in all directions. "He finally found me and plans to kill me! You came in time to scare him off. He has a gun." She pointed to the window. "He climbed out through there."

Clary turned to see Jeremy standing behind her. "I believe she's still asleep. It's as if she knows we're here, yet she doesn't. I'm talking to you, and her eyes keep moving about the room as if she's searching for something."

"Betsy!" Jeremy exclaimed, taking her by the shoulders and staring into her eyes. "It's just a nightmare. No one was in this room. The windows are still latched."

Libby stared ahead through glazed eyes. "He'll try again. You see," she whimpered, "I never bought his whiskey. He can't live without his whiskey. He becomes a ferocious animal without it," she explained with tears trickling down her cheeks.

Jeremy looked back at Clary. "What shall I do? Slap her face, maybe?"

"That may work... but *lightly*... No! Move aside. I'll try it." She pushed Libby's head and shoulders back down on the pillow and lightly slapped her cheek. "Betsy!"

Libby gasped and finally focused directly on Clary's face. "What are you *doing*?"

"You had another nightmare, and we couldn't wake you without a jolt. You are *completely* safe. Josiah Staples is in prison. Perhaps tomorrow it would be best if you could see for yourself. It may put your mind to rest."

"The man that frightens me is not Josiah Staples," she insisted. "He's fair-haired, and his evil eyes burn with rage, like a madman, as how I imagine Satan to be!"

"It doesn't appear that any such man is searching for you," said Jeremy. "Besides, if this man is as determined to get at you as you say, he would have found you by now. And no one else has come to *The Beacon* to inquire after you."

"Would you like me to stay with you for the rest of the night?" asked Clary. "The bed is large enough for two."

"Yes, please," she anxiously responded. "I'm so terribly sorry to be such a nuisance."

Hearing the sound of voices below her window, Libby climbed out of bed to see Dr. Flanagan hitching his mare to the post. After having complained of fatigue, no appetite, and an aching lower back, Clary had insisted she sleep for another couple of hours. But rambling thoughts wouldn't allow her to take advantage of such luxury. She was too elated at the thought of Justin returning home the next night and realized that she greatly missed him. There seemed to be a certain indescribable comfort in his presence. She wandered over to his dresser and lightly ran her fingers over its finely etched surface then reached for one of the toiletry bottles that were grouped together on a doily. She uncorked it and sniffed. *Hair tonic*, she surmised, recalling the scent of his hair when he bent down to kiss her forehead. *You must desist from these thoughts! He belongs to another.*

Feeling the thud of the front door shutting beneath her floor, she tiptoed over to open the bedroom door just a crack and could tell by the fading tone of their voices that Clary and the doctor were moving toward the kitchen. Hopefully they would let her be, thinking she was still sleeping. She was curious as to why the doctor was paying a visit but not curious enough to eavesdrop into their conversation.

The notion that she might be carrying a child struck terror down to the very core of her being. And if perchance she actually was... She shook her head in defiance. Impossible! But... but what *if*? Bearing the shame and humiliation would be inconceivable. Justin would think her a whore. *Everyone* would think her a whore.

Father, I cannot believe that my spirit is immoral. My faith in you and my desire to please you would never allow me to be promiscuous. Please give me a sense of peace that you'll be with me throughout this nightmare and the hope that there will be great joy when I finally awaken. I cannot comprehend why you've allowed me to suffer this trial, but I trust that I'll have learned much of value when it is over.

Dr. Flanagan looked across the kitchen table to Clary's questioning eyes. "I told you I was going to send to Jefferson Medical School for pertinent new information on the subject of memory loss. Well, yesterday I received a very large parcel of publications that have been written and printed since the end of the war until now. The degrees and types of amnesia that soldiers suffered have lent a clearer understanding into the workings of the mind. Many had amnesia caused by head wounds, but a large percentage of amnesiacs were so due to the trauma of war itself. We now have countless case histories to study.

"From what you've told me of Betsy's behavior, her spurts of memory about her family, and her nightmares, I can safely conclude that her loss of memory is not injury caused, but *trauma* related. She's remembering pieces of her past that occurred during a secure time in her life and not allowing herself to come past that point. You may have given her memory more of a jolt had you shown her the engraved wedding band before informing her that she may be pregnant. If it *is* her ring and she's married, then her good moral sense would allow her to accept a pregnancy more readily and possibly bring her memory up to present day."

"But she can't be married. She would have been too young."

He shrugged. "Who knows her true age? Also, I personally find it difficult to believe a man would beat a woman unconscious to steal two thin gold wedding bands. They're not worth that much. So don't be surprised if yet another ring or piece of her jewelry comes into the picture."

Clary eyes grew larger. "Last evening Jeremy told me the owner of Vale Jewelers came to Sheriff Clayton with a diamond ring that he had purchased from Josiah Staples. When he read Jeremy's article about Josiah beating Lottie to death, he thought he'd best come forward with the ring, as not to implicate himself in any sort of crime, and ... but ... did it ever occur to you that Josiah might have beaten Betsy unconscious if he planned to violate her, to keep her from screaming?"

The doctor looked thoughtful. "This whole matter is very confusing and mysterious, and I would assume that if she were married, her husband would be frantically searching for her. Now I want to tell you something that will even further complicate the affair, but think of it more as a hunch."

"Yes? Tell me, please," she begged.

"You may think I'm daft when you hear what I have to say, but Fiona believes what I'm about to tell you to be truth. I'm still waiting to get word—"

"Tell me!" she impatiently implored, leaning forward in her seat.

"I believe I may have known Betsy's mother," he simply said.

"No!" she exclaimed, sitting upright again.

"Yes ... a native of Martinique, with a singing voice of an angel. Thirty-five years ago, when I was a student at Jefferson Medical College in Philadelphia, I became fast friends with an amiable medical student, one year my junior. When I graduated, Fiona and I returned to Ireland for several years, so I lost track of him.

"During the time we attended school together, he fell madly in love with the daughter of a science professor. The professor was an interesting fellow. His family owned a vast sugar plantation in Martinique, and his uncle was governor of the island at that time. It had always been his dream to study and teach in the States, so he forsook his family's heritage to move to America, bringing along his wife and young daughter. The daughter grew into a lovely young woman, with dark, exotic-looking eyes and long, curly, raven hair. She was a petite woman, but her soprano voice... her voice could fill a ballroom and shatter glass. She enjoyed singing at soirees and was often asked to sing in city-sponsored recitals. Fiona and I attended many of her concerts, but my friend never missed a one of her singing engagements. Her name was Babette Arnaud.

"I can't tell you if they ever married, but I will tell you that your Betsy is an exact replica of the woman. When Fiona and I heard her sing on Sunday, we both immediately thought of Babette. I've taken the liberty of wiring the college to send any information they might have concerning my friend or Babette Arnaud's whereabouts. As I said, it's a hunch. I've had no response from the school as of yet."

"I... I'm speechless. You... you've left me speechless!" she sputtered. "I don't know whether to laugh at the preposterousness or..." She covered her face with her hands for several seconds then looked him squarely in the eyes. "Do you realize what the chances are that Betsy could be the daughter of Babette Arnaud?"

"I only said it was a hunch. But if you could place the Babette of thirty-five years ago alongside your Betsy and ask them to sing a duet, you would swear you were viewing identical twins. Say nothing to Betsy until we have confirming information. It's not wise to pressure or prod an amnesiac. The shock might cause more damage and could quite possibly cause regression. I hope to have some news by your picnic on Saturday."

CHAPTER 15

"You seem to enjoy sitting at my brother's desk," Clary noted. She sat down on a wing chair. "Are you *still* reading that book of poetry?"

Libby looked up with misty eyes and a bittersweet smile. "Yes. I could read it over and over again. So lovely and heart-warming. I choose to sit here because the light from the window behind me is perfect for reading. I also read some of the passages Justin marked in his Bible. I like to read the notes that he writes on the margins. They give me some insight as to how he thinks."

"Do you feel closer to him when you sit in his chair?" she asked with a cheeky smile.

Libby blushed. "Whatever do you mean? I… I believe that I don't know him well enough to need his closeness. Clary? How did Justin come to know Susanna?"

"Do you recall Richard Dupont telling us that he's taking a Nathan Wentworth as his partner?"

"Yes."

"Well, Nathan is five years Justin's senior and two years widowed. He has a younger brother, Edward, who is Justin's age. Both Justin and Edward graduated from Harvard Law School in the spring of '61, when Edward had been engaged to marry Susanna for about one year. So initially Justin met her at their graduation, when Charles Dupont brought his family to Boston for the commencement.

"I believe that Charles planned on taking Edward as a junior partner, but Edward broke his engagement to Susanna by the end of the summer of '61 and went off to war. Why he did so remains a mystery. The Wentworths are quite a wealthy family, so Edward could have easily found himself out of battle's way, if you understand the gist of my meaning. Well, he never returned home. It was rumored that he married a widow and settled down in New England.

"Charles approached Justin with the offer of partnership toward the end of '63 and said he would keep the position open until he was able to fill it, whenever the war ended. Justin visited Charles' estate many times and was quite taken in by Susanna's obvious charms, which I fear are not enough, no ... no, I won't speak against her," she said with a disgusted sort of sigh. "They became engaged immediately after the war was officially over and Justin returned home to stay. She and her family attend our church infrequently when they're staying at their estate, but since Charles purchased a suite in Washington, they seem to prefer the city life."

"Susanna could not possibly be thirty years old."

"No, she's younger than I, twenty-four. Perhaps she wasn't mature enough to marry Edward at the time, but I dare not speculate. Justin was also engaged once, when he was twenty-three, to the daughter of Reverend Crabtree. Her name was Mary Anne. She died of pneumonia after a bout with influenza, three months into their engagement. You don't believe my information?" she asked, seeing Libby's eyes widen and face blanch.

"Yes," she murmured softly. "Yes. I find it easy to believe that Justin was once engaged." She put her face in her hands and began to weep. "My mother is dead. She died of pneumonia," she cried mournfully. "My sweet mama is dead! In my mind's eye I see her lying so still on her bed ... and men carrying her covered body away. My papa won't speak to me ... No, he *can't* speak to me. He's too grief stricken!"

Clary came to take her in her arms. "Are you certain that what you're remembering is actually so?"

"I know it is so!"

"Miss Clary, it be 'leven a clock. Time ta git Miss Lydia an' Mr. Josh," announced Becky from the doorway. "You want Abel ta fetch 'em instead?" she asked, observing Libby's emotional state.

"No. I would like to meet their train, and I think the outing will do Betsy some good." Come, dear," she said soothingly, taking Libby's hand. "You should not sit here and dwell upon it. Accompany me to the train station." She took a handkerchief from her apron pocket and patted Libby's eyes. "Use the wash closet first. I'll be waiting in the carriage for you."

"There they are!" Clary squealed excitedly. "I'm anxious to see how greatly my niece has changed!" She jumped down from the carriage, hurriedly hitched the horses to a post, ran up to the platform, gave her brother and sister-in-law each a peck on the cheek, and then tore the baby away from Lydia. She stared down at the tiny face for a few seconds then looked at Lydia. "She's *so* beautiful!" Libby could hear her say, apparently awestruck by the soft little bundle in her arms. "Now she has an abundance of hair, and it appears to have a bit of red in it. Hopefully it will be *dark* red like your hair, Lydia."

Libby observed the trio from the carriage and noted the similarities between Josh and Justin. Both men were a couple inches shorter than Jeremy but heartier in build than Jeremy's slender lankiness. Josh wore his mustache cut similarly to Justin's, but he hadn't Justin's cleft in his square chin, and his hair was a slightly lighter shade of brown with russet highlights. *They're quite a handsome family. I wish I could recall, in greater detail, the appearance of my family.*

"Pick up your valises, Josh, and come meet my Betsy. Two weeks ago, when I last wrote to you, Lydia, she was still not faring too well. But look at her now!" she said proudly as they followed her to the carriage.

Libby returned the couple's friendly smiles. "So pleased to meet you," she said shyly.

"You are absolutely correct, Clary. She's a perfect picture of good health. We weren't expecting such a pretty young lady! We're pleased to meet you too, Betsy," said Lydia, with warmth radiating from her periwinkle blue eyes.

Clary held the baby up to Libby. "Please take her for a moment, Betsy, while we stash the valises and situate ourselves."

Libby eagerly took the baby and drew the blanket aside to look at her face. She was startled at the miniature size of the sleeping infant, and wondered if the bonnet, shawl, and booties might not be too large for her.

"She's a very tiny six-week-old," Lydia offered, observing Libby's handling of her child. "She was a mere five pounds at birth. I suppose she'll be petite, as I am. But despite her small size, I still gained enough weight so that folks must have imagined I was carrying a mammoth-sized child inside of me."

"I thought you looked lovely, my darling," said Josh, gently kissing his wife's lips. "And now you're nearly back to your original weight and have developed the figure of a fully blossomed woman."

Libby giggled at his frankness and the blush he evoked to his wife's sweet, heart-shaped face.

"What he says is true," she said to Libby. "Before Laurel, I had the figure of a twelve-year-old girl … or boy."

"Will you take the reins, Josh?" asked Clary.

"For now. Did Jeremy take his horse or buggy to work today?" he asked.

"The buggy. Why?"

"Would it offend you ladies if I were to stay behind and spend the afternoon with Jeremy at *The Beacon*? You could leave me in front of his door."

"That's fine by me," said Clary. "You would most likely be bored by our conversation and afternoon plans."

He looked at his wife. "Are you sure you don't mind, Liddy?"

"Excuse me?" Libby asked, quickly looking up from the baby's face to Josh.

He smiled. "Liddy… I was speaking to my wife," he said kindly.

The color drained from Libby's face, now certain that her name was not Betsy. She decided to think on it for a while and not bring the realization to light until Josh and Lydia returned to their home on Monday morning.

"You're very pensive," Clary commented to Libby as they neared home.

"I don't wish to interrupt your conversation with Lydia. Besides, I enjoy watching the baby as she sleeps. She makes all sorts of amusing faces. I'm anxious to see her eyes open so that I might entice her to smile."

"She really hasn't smiled a true smile yet, one that you know she is actually responding to your attention," Lydia said.

"Well, ladies, shall we go for a stroll after dinner? Justin brought our baby buggy and cradle down from the attic before he left on Monday. Becky should have dinner on the table as soon as we arrive home," said Clary. "You must be famished, Betsy. You haven't eaten since last evening. You are *so* pale. Are you unwell?"

"I suppose I'm hungry. I'm anxious for you to show Lydia the gifts you made for her." She turned to Lydia and said, "Wait until you see what Clary has done with a plain candle. We filled canning jars with candle wax scented with fragrant oils. I believe there will be a whole market for them within time. It's so lovely to sit in a hot tub of water, with the relaxing scent of lavender or vanilla in the air. We're going to try lemon or maybe cinnamon and clove next."

"What a unique idea, Clary. What *will* you come up with next?"

This has to be the sweetest time of day. Libby draped a washcloth of warm water over her chest and listened to the faint sound of the mantle clock chime ten times. Josh and his family were snuggly situated in the guest room at the senior Chambers' home, and Clary and Jeremy were most likely fast asleep. *It's so peaceful to be left alone with my thoughts and to enjoy a warm bath with the heavy fragrance of lavender in the air.* She exhaled a contented sigh.

It had been such a pleasant day. Lydia was truly a personable young woman and baby Laurel a delight to cuddle and coo over. She was thankful that Josh and Lydia had refrained from any attempt to cajole memories from her with prying questions, although she suspected that Jeremy had apprised Josh of all he knew of her while they were alone together.

Justin was expected to return from Washington near midnight, so she figured she best dry herself and retire to her bedroom for the night. She had no desire to confront him en route wearing nothing but a nightgown.

Stepping out of the tub, she unplugged the drain and reached for a luxurious white Turkish towel. But before drying herself, she went to stand before the full-length wall mirror to survey her naked body. *Hmm*... Was it her imagination, or did her breasts appear fuller than they were a mere two weeks earlier? She could picture Lydia feeding her baby and thought how satisfying it must feel to be a mother and how fulfilling to have the capability of personally nourishing her child.

Her eyes traveled down her torso, and she rested a hand on her lower abdomen. Although flat, she couldn't help but wonder if there might possibly be a miniature human being growing inside of her. Lydia had said she didn't "show" until she was four and a half months into her pregnancy, and about that same time she had felt a light fluttering in her pelvic area. Libby shook her head determinedly. *No! It simply could not be.*

She finished drying off, poured a pitcher of clear water around the tub to wash down the soap silt, and then turned her attention to the chore of brushing out her hair. Feeling the house tremor a bit, she wondered if someone was still wandering about. She pulled the pins from her hair to allow the thick curls to fall to her waist, quickly raked a brush through the mass, and then slipped into her nightgown. She noticed that Clary's pink boudoir gown was hanging by a hook on the back of the wash room door. It was tempting to borrow it to wear over her gown, just in case Jeremy was still up and about. Quite certain that Clary wouldn't mind, she wrapped the frilly garment around her nightgown, secured the pearl buttons, tied the sash around her waist, then hung her frock on the door hook and placed her petticoat in the "to-be-washed" sack beneath the linen shelves.

After extinguishing two of the three candles, she decided to use the third to help navigate to her room. As she neared the library door, she could see light and knew that Justin was home and most likely waiting for a turn to use the wash closet. She snuffed the candle in hopes of quietly tiptoeing past the door without him noticing her.

"Did you decide to take up smoking, Betsy?" he inquiringly called. "I see that you weren't claimed while I was gone."

These candles smell heavenly while they're burning but surely put out a phenomenal amount of smoke when they're snuffed. She peeked around the doorjamb. "Oh ... good evening, Justin," she said with a giggle. "I wasn't expecting you home for another hour."

"I left Washington earlier than expected. Susanna wasn't feeling well and decided to retire for the evening."

"Nothing serious, I hope."

"I'm certain that it's not. Come in and speak with me. Why are you hiding? Do you feel that you're not properly attired to make your presence known to me?"

"Well," she said shyly, "I'm wearing only my nightgown and Clary's boudoir gown."

"Then you're covered from neck to toe, as much coverage as when you're wearing a frock. Come in here and enlighten me to the week's happenings." He sat back in his desk chair and motioned for her to enter. When she timidly stood in the doorway for a few seconds, he boldly stared at her with a smile playing on his lips. *My stars, she's lovely!*

She slowly approached his desk, trying to avert his gaze. What she had read in his eyes gave her goosebumps. Making her way to his chair, she handed him the candle then dropped to her knees and reached beneath the desk. "I left a crewel basket beneath your desk," she explained, looking up at him. "I hope you don't mind that I used your desk to crochet. The lighting is exceptional at this spot."

He leaned over to lift a lock of her hair. "Smells somewhat like my sister's recipe for lemon verbena cologne ... but different," he said, sniffing the lock then laying it back down over her shoulder.

"She infused several of the bottles of lemon verbena with lavender stalks and lavender oil this time. It's an experiment. Do you like it?" she asked as she stood back up.

"Very much so." He sniffed the candle then set it on the desk.

"Oh, and we experimented with making jar candles infused with different oils. Can you smell the lavender in the air?"

"I did when I stood by the wash closet door. I only smell smoke now." He grinned when she blushed. "I knew it was you bathing because you were softly singing." He stood up, took the basket from her and placed it on the desk, then took her by her wrist and escorted her to the love seat. "Come sit beside me, little sister, and tell me what you recalled of your life while I was gone," he said, sitting down with his back against its high arm so that he could look at her.

"First, I must say that your brother and sister-in-law are delightful. And wait until you see baby Laurel! She's so tiny and fragile, you just may be afraid to hold her," she commented with sparkling eyes as she sat down beside him with her back against the other arm of the love seat.

He laughed. "I'm certain she won't break, and pleased that they entertained you so well."

Quite suddenly she became serious and looked squarely into his eyes. "I asked Clary to purchase several items at the mercantile. I fully intend to repay your family for all that I bought. I'll sell my ring, if I must."

She didn't say "rings," so I must conclude that Clary still hasn't shown her the other wedding band. He made a mental note to speak to Clary concerning the matter. He was beginning to get the impression that Clary was subconsciously retarding Betsy's rehabilitation. She seemed to be quite astute concerning her bodily recovery but was not putting forth any effort into jolting her memory. "You owe us nothing, and I won't hear you speak of it again," he said with a kind firmness. "Now tell me what you've remembered."

"I know that Clary has made you aware that I might possibly be carrying a child," she said, nervously looking down at her lap then back up to his face and into his receptive eyes. "I... I honestly cannot believe I could have been promiscuous," she said earnestly. "But how do I prove otherwise if it turns out to be that..."

He reached over and lightly ran his knuckles up and down her cheek then took her hand. "Perhaps Clary shouldn't have mentioned the possibility until it became indisputably apparent to *you.* But no matter if you are or you're not, God knows the purity of your heart. I want you to know that you'll always have the support of my family and only the highest regard. Now tell me all you've remembered."

"I recalled that I have a brother," she said excitedly. "I was merely conversing with Jeremy, and the memory popped into my head and fell out of my mouth."

He chuckled at her expressiveness. "Can you recall his appearance and name?"

She shook her head. "No. He's much taller than I... and I

know he's older. I only remember that my father calls him 'Son.' I believe he may be away at school."

"Where?" he asked anxiously, thinking of the young man he had seen on the train. "Can you recall where he attends school?"

"Up," she said, pointing to the ceiling. "I believe... up. Somehow I recall my father saying we'll go *up* to visit with him. Perhaps for graduation." She shrugged.

"Can you describe him? Is he fair or dark?"

"I believe we're all dark-haired. But there *is* someone fair-haired. I've had nightmares of him. He has the eyes of Satan, and he intends to harm me," she explained with fear in her voice.

"If someone other than Josiah Staples were after you, don't you think he would have caught up with you by now? Would you feel more at ease with a guard?"

She shrugged again, not wishing to be more of a burden. Tears welled, and she looked away from his tender eyes. "I believe my mother has died," she said in a soft, trembling voice. "Clary says my memory may not be so, but I clearly see her lying so still on her bed and then her swaddled body being taken through the front door by several men attired in black. She... she died of pneumonia," she said timidly, knowing he had lost a love similarly. "Clary told me of Mary Anne. That's how I recalled the facts of my mother."

He gently took her in his arms and held her, for her sake and his own. "Weep, Betsy. Allow all of the frustration to flow from you," he whispered into her ear as he tightened his hold on her.

She relaxed in his arms for a moment, relishing the strength in his offered security but keenly aware that she was beginning to feel more for him than she ought. The sobering fact that he was taken demanded that she back away from his grasp. She gently pulled loose from his hold and sat back. "I... I... Please tell me how your week went," she stammered, trying not to look at him but feeling his eyes fixed upon her face.

He said nothing for a full moment then took a deep breath and sat back. "The week was fairly monotonous," he said blandly.

"Susanna and I attended a soiree on Tuesday evening, where the hostess introduced a young pianist who entertained us for an hour. I thought how you might have enjoyed it. He seemed to fixate on Beethoven's works, but he *did* play one Chopin Polonaise, though not as well as you play." He suddenly stood up. "I almost forgot; I have something for you and Clary." He went to the desk, opened his leather valise, and took out two round tins, each painted with a lovely European pastoral scene. "Yesterday afternoon, Susanna came to my office and insisted I escort her to a chocolate exhibition sponsored by the Tobler Chocolatiers of Switzerland and the Cadbury Company of England. I knew that if Clary learned of it and I hadn't bought her a sampler of chocolate shells and creams, she would behead me." He held one out to her.

She stood up to take it from him and opened the lid to appraise the contents. "Oh … they're lovely!" she exclaimed. "I believe that nothing on earth smells more heavenly than chocolate," she said, deeply breathing in their fragrance.

"Then my sister will simply have to put the scent into candle form for you," he said with a chuckle, and then sat down behind his desk again.

Having secured the lid on the tin, she regarded him with a thoughtful smile. "You must be exhausted," she said softly, "so I'll leave you now." She pressed the tin to her breast and shyly approached him to kiss his cheek. "Thank you for remembering me, and thank you for the time you took to speak with me," she said with sincerity. She walked toward the door then turned to see him touch his fingers to her kiss. "May you have a good night's rest."

"Sleep well, Betsy." He sat back in his chair and thought, *a "thank you" and a kiss*. Not so much as a "thank you" from Susanna for the enormous, heart-shaped tin of chocolates he had bought for her—merely a glare of annoyance when he informed her that one of the two smaller tins he purchased was for Betsy.

CHAPTER 16

Rising well before the rest of the household, Justin ventured downstairs and seated himself behind his desk in order to complete a report due to Charles Dupont by the next Monday. After two hours of driving concentration, he snuffed the lamp to greet the sunlight and sat back in his chair, satisfied that he was able to complete his monotonous chore and now free to spend uninterrupted time with his family. He could hear Becky shuffling about the kitchen beginning to prepare breakfast for the group and hoped there might be enough time to read a Bible passage and pray without interruption, as he was accustomed to doing each morning before the start of the workday.

His eyes scanned the desk for his Bible and found it on the opposite corner to where he usually placed it. *Betsy… Betsy must have displaced it.* The crewel basket was still sitting on his desk where he had set it when he took it from her last night. He decided to search through its contents to find out what had occupied her during the week, and removed the pink bonnet, shawl, and booties set she had crocheted for Laurel. He couldn't help but laugh, wondering if she had misjudged the size of his niece. Surely the pieces were too tiny to fit anything human, but they certainly were detailed and well made. Lydia would appreciate the time and effort Betsy spent in designing them.

He set them back inside the basket and opened his Bible to Psalm 57. Finding that the passage had already been marked with a foot-long strand of pink yarn, he was pleased that Betsy was drawing comfort in devoting time to reading God's Word.

His mind wandered again, and he wondered what Clary's plans were for the day, hoping they didn't include Josh and him. It had been too many months since he'd been able to spend private time with his brother. *Hunting*. Josh had always enjoyed hunting. Perhaps they might shoot a couple wild turkeys or pheasant to prepare for tomorrow's picnic and Sunday supper. He hoped that Jeremy wouldn't decide to tag along because he needed to speak with Josh on a level where Jeremy's immaturity and caustic humor might interfere into the seriousness of the subject. Josh had always been a levelheaded individual, who knew exactly what he wanted from life and relationships then strove toward that end. And certainly the war and near-death experience helped to mold his indomitable character. How many young men of twenty-four years were five years happily married, a father, and owned a successfully operated horse farm?

He suddenly looked up, thinking he had heard a light knock on the closed library door. Deciding it was merely his imagination, he continued to stare at the door in an attempt to conjure up the image of Betsy standing in the doorway when she had made her presence known to him last night. He smiled at how she appeared to be somewhat abashed at how she was attired and wondered who concocted the rules of society, to deem that which is correct and proper. After all, she was covered from neck to toe. But he also recalled how warm, soft, and cuddly she felt in his arms, smelling so intoxicatingly sweet, and a twinge of guilt attacked his conscience at the fact that she might possibly have a husband and that he was engaged. He had no right to take liberties with her vulnerability. Or was he mistaken in deeming his action self-centered? She certainly seemed to *need* for him to hold her at the time.

He tried to picture Susanna attired in a lacey, frilly, pink boudoir gown, with her golden hair hanging long and loose, and realized she had never shown herself to him with her hair down during the entire two years they had been courting. Come to think of it, he didn't *know* if Susanna was soft, warm, and cuddly, because every time he attempted to hold her, she would complain that he might muss her and remind him that her desire in life was to look forever beautiful to him. *Look, but don't touch.* Hopefully she wouldn't make it a practice to be so completely inaccessible after they married.

His thoughts traveled back to Betsy again and immediately jumped to the man he had seen on the train. She had said she thought her brother might attend a distant school, so he most likely could only be in his early twenties, at most, but the man on the train had to be close to thirty and lacked the affectations of a mere student. He slowly shook his head, wondering if the "Betsy mystery" would ever be solved. Clary certainly would be pleased if the mystery went on forever. *Rather selfish of her,* he thought, despite the fact that he was none too anxious for her to leave them either. He decided not to explore the reason *why* and instead focus on a time of intimacy with God until called to breakfast, but…

"Come in," he invited, now certain he had heard a knock on the door.

The door opened just wide enough for Libby's head to pass through. "I'm sorry to disturb you, but I came downstairs in order to help Becky make breakfast, there being several more mouths to feed than usual."

He sat back and grinned at her. "And she declined your offer."

She looked surprised. "Why…yes. I suppose you know her well. The kitchen appears to be her domain only," she said with a giggle. "May I come in to take my crochet work upstairs?"

"I already invited you in. Your arm isn't long enough to reach my desk from where you're standing, so I suppose you'll *have* to come in, unless you expect me to get up and bring it to you," he said, playing with her.

"I'll get it," she said shyly, opening the door further and approaching his desk.

"A new frock?" he asked, taking in every detail of the deep rose garment that so beautifully accentuated her loveliness. Or was it her loveliness that accentuated the frock?

"No," she said softly, disengaging herself from his audacious eyes. When she went to take the basket from his desk, he rested his hand over hers. "It… the frock belongs to your mother," she stammered, looking down at their hands. "Clary received a letter from your mother yesterday stating that I may borrow whatever I like. I only chose this *one* because the color is lovely, and it fits well. I don't plan on asking for another. The two that Clary lent me and this one…"

"Betsy." She looked at his face, to warm brown eyes that exuded tenderness. "You may borrow your heart's desire of anything we own," he said softly, not removing his hand from hers. "Will you stay a few moments to have devotions with me?"

She appeared confused for a moment. Does he always shower such warmth and tenderness on all who come to know him? She recalled Clary telling of his kind heart for the needs of others. *Perhaps his manner is also his way of displaying his concern for those he pities, and I don't wish to be pitied by him. Father, help me to remember so I can move on, and he may go on with his life and plans without interference on my part.* Realizing that her prayer was half-hearted, she decided not to explore the reason *why* and smiled sweetly at him. "I would be pleased to have devotions with you, Counselor."

"Suppose we sit on the chairs." When they were seated, he asked, "Am I to surmise, young lady, that since you attempted to help with breakfast, you awoke feeling well?"

"I *did*," she said, sounding surprised. "Marvelous! Perhaps I'm through with that phase of my recovery." When he furrowed his brow, she added, "Or through with a phase of my *impossible* 'condition,'" she said, with a roll of her eyes.

"Are you fond of children, Betsy?"

"I believe that I am. I find it effortless to love children when I hold your precious niece in my arms or listen to the sincere and innocent way Vie attempts to express herself," she said with a light laugh. "And you?"

He nodded. "Yes, very much so. Vie's presence makes me realize that I would like several of my own that are every bit as precocious as she. I'm anxious to see my niece. I took the liberty of inspecting the items you made for her to wear."

She giggled. "I hope they passed inspection. Unfortunately, they won't fit her for a while. At present they would swallow her." She giggled some more at the expression on his face. "There's that furrowed brow again," she said, observing him with questioning eyes.

"They're too *big*? Impossible! No one could be so small!" he laughingly commented.

"I asked a woman in the mercantile if she would allow me to measure her baby son's head and feet because there was no pattern to be had, but when I saw Laurel, I realized he was twice her size. What passage will you read?" she asked, looking over at his open Bible.

"I'd like to read Psalm 57, but since I found a pink marker holding that specific page, I assume—"

"No, no," she interrupted. "I finished with Psalm 56 just yesterday. You must like the Psalms as well as I do. They give me tremendous comfort."

"I enjoy the Psalms because they teach that even the strongest and most powerful of men have the ability to realize their need for God's love and forgiveness. They're not ashamed or afraid to publicly praise God or freely express their vulnerabilities, weaknesses, and passions to him, and they're *still* considered to be the 'manliest' men in history, a great example to those of us who consider themselves invincible pillars of strength," he added with a wink and broad smile. "Take verse one: David, a man who has the ability to slay giants, tells God that he needs protection from Saul and wants to safely hide in the protectiveness offered beneath

God's wings. And the second verse shows he wasn't too 'manly' to cry or admit that he powerfully feared those who planned to kill him. Well, I'll read aloud the entire passage before we're interrupted." When he finished reading, he looked over to see a faint, thoughtful smile on her lips.

"Taking refuge *in the shadow of His wings* paints such a lovely picture," she said softly. "I can just imagine a soaring, watchful eagle swooping down to spread his vast wings protectively over one of his fledglings—"

"Breakfas' ready, Mr. Justin. Mr. Josh an' Miss Lydia headin' cross the field," said Becky, thumping on the library door.

"Thank you, Becky. Please seat them in the dining room if we're not out to join them momentarily," Justin called back. He sat back in his chair and looked at Libby with regret. "I suppose our time has come to a close, but I would like to finish with prayer." They closed their eyes, and he thanked the Lord for healing her then asked him to protect her, to restore her memory, and to make his will known to her. She prayed to thank the Lord for protecting her by leading her to the Chambers' loving home and asked him to reward them for their kindnesses.

"Thank you for sharing your time with God," she said when he went to open the door for her. "I hope we'll have devotions together again … and maybe practice duets together if I'm still here."

"We will, even if you *are* claimed. I won't believe you were brought into our fellowship to suddenly leave and never to be heard from again," he said with sincerity. "We'll simply have to adopt you as our sister. I'll draw up the papers when I return to Washington," he said with a chuckle.

She laughed. "I believe you should give your parents a choice as to whether they would appreciate suddenly having a daughter they've never met."

"What have you to say, Clary?" he asked, watching her descend the stairs. "Shall we adopt Betsy as our sister?"

"I would adore having Betsy as my sister." *My sister-in-law!*

Josh and Lydia entered into the foyer, and Justin kissed Lydia, shook Josh's hand, and then took the tiny bundle from Lydia's arms. He studied Laurel's face for a few seconds then turned to Libby. "You *are* correct, madam. I've never seen a human being so small… or so incredibly beautiful," he said, gently kissing the sleeping baby's petal-soft cheek.

"The most beautiful until you have one of your own," Lydia remarked.

In his mind's eye he tried to picture Susanna with a round, protruding midsection. While he could clearly see her, the picture also painted a very misery-laden expression on her face. He seriously doubted that she would be pleased with any change to her perfect figure. But perhaps seeing Laurel and holding her might influence a change of heart. He returned the baby to her mother's arms.

"Shall we have breakfast?" he asked, gesturing to the dining room door. "I found *two* cradles in the attic, Lydia, so you'll have a place to lay Laurel while you're eating."

"Thank you. You can't imagine how much I appreciate that."

"You're quite welcome. Will you please say the blessing for the food, Josh?" Justin asked when they were seated.

After Josh finished, Lydia said, "Josh and I were discussing the day's plan, Justin, and he said he hadn't gone hunting with you since before the war."

"Ah! Great minds think alike." Justin looked at Josh. "I was going to ask you if you would like to go hunting today, and if you're agreeable, I prefer that Jeremy not go with us, for I would like to have private time with you."

"You need not be concerned about Jeremy. He told me that today he planned on showing Charlotte Dupont his newspaper operation and taking her to the White Swan for dinner. I do believe our little brother is smitten, and I have to admit I'm surprised. I thought he disliked Susanna's sisters."

"He seems to have the innate ability to draw out the true Charlotte, and we all find her to be very likeable," explained Clary.

It's a pity that what we see in Susanna is the only true Susanna. "Where *is* Jeremy?" she wondered aloud.

"Mr. Jeremy lef' fo' work 'bout an hour ago," Becky informed them while filling their coffee cups.

"Thank you, Becky," said Libby, setting her cup back on the saucer. "I hope we'll see Vie today. I've hardly seen her all week and miss her," she commented, feeling that they almost seemed to be trying to keep the child away from her since, well, last Sunday. She noticed that Justin was staring hard at Clary's face, but Clary kept her eyes averted.

"She be over later ta see the baby," Becky told Libby.

"Please pass the boiled eggs, Liddy," said Josh.

Lydia and Libby both reached for the eggs, but Libby quickly withdrew her hand when she realized he wasn't speaking to her.

"Is something wrong, Betsy?" asked Clary. "Your face is masked with worry."

"It's nothing I wish to discuss at present. I'll speak with you on the matter when Josh and Lydia have returned home," she said quietly, concentrating on her food.

"I'm pleased that you have an appetite this morning," Clary said.

Libby nodded but kept her eyes focused on her plate. Too many small memories had flashed through her head since Josh and Lydia's arrival—almost to the point of being overwhelming and frightening. Her father's appearance seemed to age with every picture of him. She was fearful that he might have died also, as did her mother. Perhaps that was the reason no one was searching for her. But what about her brother? Maybe he didn't know she was missing. Maybe no one knew how or where to reach him. Or perhaps she had so shamed her family that they no longer wished to associate with her. But the picture that frightened her the most was the face of a man with ghastly yellow hair, eyes bulging with madness, and an enormous, blood-red mouth that continually screamed her name… "Libby!" She caught her breath, gasped, and then jolted upright to see that all eyes were upon her.

"*Excuse me!*" she exclaimed, her eyes frantically traveling from one pair of questioning eyes to the next. She stood up to exit the room. "I ... I need to rest. It's only a headache," she assured them on her way out to go to her bedroom.

Clary and Justin both stood up to go after her.

"Sit down, Clary. Let me tend to her this time," Justin insisted, and she very obligingly submitted to his command.

He raced up the stairs two at a time and, standing by his bedroom door, could hear her sobbing and talking simultaneously. Putting his ear to the door, he discerned that she was praying in such anguish, it broke his heart. She always seemed to display such a cheerful front when she socialized with his family, and he realized that she was finally becoming overwhelmed and broken by her circumstance. He knocked on the door.

"Betsy? May I come in?"

"I beg you to go down and spend time with your brother," she insisted.

"Not until I've seen for myself that you're calm and in better spirits. I would like to come in," he insisted.

"Then do. It is, after all, your room," she said in a muffled voice.

He opened the door to find her lying on the bed with her face buried in her pillow. He approached the bed gingerly, not quite knowing what to say to console her. He found it ironic that Justin Chambers, Esquire, was attending a situation that rendered him at a loss for words. He took a seat on the edge of the bed and was about put his hand out to rub her back, until his better judgment told him that he needed to control his handling of her. He rested his hand on his knee instead.

"Betsy," he began.

"*Not* Betsy!" she blurted. "My name is not Betsy. I believe that to be my mother's name." She rolled over to face him. "My name is Libby. A monster who continually screams my name has told me so."

He studied her face to read if she was jesting with him and

realized she was deadly serious. His heart pounded at the realization that her brain might possibly be damaged. She lay so stone still, staring up into his eyes with eyes so black that their pupils were indistinguishable—like two enormous, glistening black buttons. He forced himself to withdraw his eyes from hers and focused them on the oil painting above his bed.

"You think I'm insane?" she softly asked.

"No," he quickly answered, looking back at her face. "I don't think you're insane. But I can't help but wonder if you sustained more damage to your head than realized."

"It's the conglomeration of haunting nightmares and disjointed memories," she said, sitting up.

He stood up and wedged the pillows between her back and the headboard, then sat back down on the edge of the bed to talk to her. "What does this 'monster' look like? Are you speaking literally, or is it a man who *looks* like a monster? Are you certain you're not having nightmares about Josiah Staples?"

She vehemently shook her head. "I have no memory of Josiah Staples' appearance, only a description given by Jeremy. I... I don't mean a literal monster, but a horrifying man with exaggerated facial features. Hate and madness burn in his eyes. I know he's searching for me, but each time he comes close, I wake up. Last night, I could hear him calling my name over and over again. Each time he called 'Libby,' his voice became louder and more hideously strained. He's... terrifying!" she exclaimed, bursting into tears.

He took her in his arms and soothingly rocked her.

"I... I'm *so* confused," she whispered into his ear, "and must honestly admit that I cannot recall anything about a war. I recall talk of the *possibility* of a war. But how could I possibly forget something so horrific that lasted for such an expanse of time? And I don't know if the pieces of my life that I recall are actually so. My father doesn't appear the same in any of my recollections. He ages too quickly... " She pulled back and looked at him with panic in her eyes. "I fear I may be losing my mind!"

He took her face in his hands and gently planted a kiss on each cheek. "Poor little dear," he said softly. "You aren't losing your mind. Before you began to remember, there was no confusion in your head. You simply could recall nothing. As time progresses, Bet—Libby, you'll begin to put all of the pieces of the puzzle together, and it will all make perfect sense. But you need to be calm, patient, and unafraid. Do you recall Romans 8:28?"

"Yes ... I do. 'All things work together for good to them that love God.'" She smiled. "'Thy word have I hid in my heart.' A far safer place than my head," she added, laughing through her tears.

He took her back in his arms again and securely held her, unaware that Clary had just backed away from the door and was cautiously tiptoeing down the stairs, deciding it to be in everyone's best interest to allow Justin to take charge of Betsy's emotional recovery.

"Can you remember your entire name? Do you suppose 'Libby' could be used for the name Elizabeth? 'Betsy' is also used for Elizabeth."

She clutched his shoulders and pulled back far enough to look at his face. "I believe that my name *is* Elizabeth ... Elizabeth Shaw ... of *Philadelphia.*" Her face lit up at the unexpected revelation.

He looked puzzled. "Philadelphia! Are you certain? How could you possibly be found lying battered and unconscious near our cemetery, wearing only your nightgown? Philadelphia is one hundred and fifty miles from here. Surely if you were visiting friends or relatives, someone would have claimed you by now."

"Well, it's a relief to know I'm not a visiting cousin of Lottie Harmon, or her grandmother would have said so," she said with a sigh. She withdrew her hands from his shoulders to rest them on her lap.

"I'm now more skeptical than before I entered this room. Before Josh and I go hunting, I'll send a wire to the Philadelphia police, inquiring about a possible missing Elizabeth Shaw, and ask that they respond to my office in Washington as well as here," he said, standing up to return to the dining room.

She bounded from the bed to stand by his side. "Please, Justin! May we please not discuss this again until Josh and Lydia return home? Send your wire, but I would prefer to tell Clary of my supposed identity this Monday morning. Please?" she asked, setting her hand on his forearm.

He covered her hand with his and turned to face her. "I'll respect what you ask, but it's going to be very difficult to return to Washington on Monday morning knowing what I know now."

"You said you would ask that a response be sent to your office, so you *will* know, whether here or there."

CHAPTER 17

"Someone is knocking on the front door, Justin!" yelled Clary from the kitchen. "Please see who is there. Becky and I are in the middle of preparing food for the picnic, and our hands are caked with sticky flour."

Justin opened the door and was surprised to find a messenger boy waiting for him. He took a coin from his pocket, handed it to the boy, and then went back to the library to read the note written by Dr. Flanagan stating that a close friend of his and Fiona had died. They were going to spend the weekend visiting with his loved ones to help arrange his funeral. But the doctor's last sentence puzzled him—something about informing Clary that they still had not received any information on the "hunch." He went out to the kitchen to show the note to his sister. She read it while he held it up to her face and merely shrugged.

"What does this mean?" he demanded to know.

"It's too preposterous and ludicrous to be worthy of a sensible discussion," she said. "The turkey you shot will be enough meat for two meals, but next time you go hunting, *you* can clean whatever you shoot."

"I shot it; you clean it. It's the way of life, little sister. The man hunts it down; the woman cleans and cooks it," he said, giving a swat to her behind.

"Whoever made up that *rule* should be shot, but I suppose if you men had to dig out the innards of every critter you shot, we would starve to death, because you would never be able to stomach the gruesome task."

"Becky, if you will excuse my sister, I would like to have a private word with her in the library before the rest of the party comes together." He handed Clary a cloth to wipe her hands.

"Really, Justin, what could there be to discuss? I'm too busy," she whined in protest.

"This will only take a minute," he insisted, clenching his arm tightly around her shoulders. "Besides, I have a surprise for you."

"You're finally going to give me my tin of chocolate?" she asked smugly, trying to place as much physical resistance as possible into his control of her.

When he finally got her into the library, he shut the door behind them and went to get her candy from his desk drawer.

"It's exactly the same as Betsy's," she commented.

"I forgot to give it to you yesterday. Why haven't you given her the engraved wedding band?"

"Thank you for the chocolate," she said, taking off the lid and stuffing her mouth. "By 'her' I assume you mean Betsy. Mmmm, these are wonderful! Why didn't you tell me that Richard Dupont offered you a partnership?" she asked simply, taking inventory of her chocolates and not focusing on him.

He leaned back against his desk and folded his arms across his chest.

When he failed to respond, she looked up and asked, "*Well?*"

"Clary, the fact that 'Betsy' is under *our* roof places her under *our* care and *our* protection. My career is mine solely, so I owe an explanation to no one."

"You do to Susanna. Is she the reason why you haven't accepted a position that would give you so much more fulfillment than your present position?"

"Why are you keeping Vie away from her? Are you afraid that she'll mention the ring?" he asked, ignoring her question.

"Did Jeremy tell you there's a third ring that may possibly

belong to Betsy, one with a large diamond? Josiah Staples sold it to Mr. Vale, and after Mr. Vale read *The Beacon* and found out that Josiah was suspected as having beaten Lottie to death over returning stolen jewelry to its owner, he turned the ring over to the sheriff."

"No, he didn't. Our little brother's time appears to be too consumed with entertaining Charlotte. But whether the diamond ring belongs to 'Betsy' or not, I *insist* that you show her the engraved band the moment Josh and Lydia leave here."

"I will if you tell me why you didn't accept Richard's offer," she answered with a noncommittal casualness.

"If you don't give it to her, I *will*!" he exclaimed impatiently, his voice tinged with rising anger. "I'm coming to believe that you're sabotaging her recovery. Why is that?"

Not willing to give him an answer, she turned and went to the door. But before she exited, she turned back to look at him and said, "Stop and think hard and honestly about how you'll feel when she finally leaves this house, and you'll begin to understand."

"Love is not selfish, Clary," he called after her.

"It can be ... and she just parked her buggy at the post," she called back from the hallway window. "Oh my stars! You will not believe your eyes when you see Susanna and Charlotte!" she exclaimed with an explosion of uproarious laughter.

Jeremy bounded down the stairs to rush outside to greet Charlotte, and Libby just reached the bottom of the steps to meet with Justin and Clary as they ventured outdoors to welcome the sisters.

"Well, don't you look as if you just stepped away from the farm," they could hear Jeremy say to Charlotte.

Charlotte burst out laughing. "May I remind you that you said we might go fishing?"

"It seems that Jeremy finally found someone who appreciates his sense of humor," Justin commented to Libby.

"Whatever do you mean, Counselor?" she asked with an amused smile. "I find his humor to be enchanting."

He looked at her with screwed up eyes. "I can't believe you're serious," he said, holding the door open for her and Clary to pass in front of him.

Clary held her tin of chocolates up to Libby. "Charlotte looks like the shepherdess on the lid of this tin. I can't believe Susanna would be seen riding in the same buggy."

They remained on the porch and focused on Jeremy assisting Charlotte from the buggy, trying desperately to refrain from laughing at the young woman dressed in an apron-topped schoolgirl pinafore and hair styled into braids that encircled her head. But Clary found it was even more difficult not to laugh at Susanna.

"My dear, I told you we were having a picnic, not a garden party," Justin commented to Susanna, his eyes taking in the lemon-yellow gown, with matching bonnet, reticule, and parasol, all intricately detailed with white embroidered flowers. "How will you sit on the ground as you're attired?"

"You'll simply have to bring a chair outside for me to sit on," she said, planting a kiss on the cheek. "Do I look beautiful enough for you? That was my goal when I dressed this morning," she said, regarding him with anxious eyes.

Clary turned to Libby and rolled her eyes. "Have you ever encountered such a dolt?"

Libby turned to stare hard at Clary. "I can't help but pity her. She's very insecure concerning her beauty. She'll never feel beautiful enough to satisfy herself or think she's beautiful enough to please anyone else. I believe she'll find great displeasure and anguish in growing old because she has been taught to place far too much importance on physical beauty. And Charlotte might be the same if it were not for Jeremy."

"You've demonstrated charity, and I must admit that Justin *is* correct. You're definitely not sixteen. Forgive me for speaking so unkindly of her. I know my words are displeasing to God," she said, opening the door to reenter the house.

"I see that Vie is making her way across the field. Am I permitted to speak to her today?" Libby asked with a faint smile.

"I have no idea what you mean," Clary answered, looking down at the porch floorboards as Libby passed in front of her.

"Misser Jussin!" Vie called. "I gots ta talk ta you."

"You're in need of a lawyer, young lady?" he asked as she approached him and Susanna.

"How you know?" she asked, wide-eyed. "But wif no udder peoples lissinin,'" she said, looking up at Susanna.

"My dear," he said, turning to Susanna, "suppose you go inside with the other ladies. I'll be with you in a moment, or you might want to visit with Lydia, Josh, and Laurel. They're around back. I'm sure you don't want to go fishing with Jeremy and Charlotte."

"Hardly," she answered in an irritated tone. "And later I would like to speak with you concerning the unfavorable changes your brother has made in the disposition of my sister. But for now I'll visit with Lydia. I haven't viewed her baby yet." She properly stationed the parasol over her head and sashayed away from them.

Justin took Vie's hand. "Come. We'll sit on the porch steps. Now what seems to be the problem, little lady?"

"I sceered dat Jesus don' wuv me no mo' 'cause I do somethin' bad," she explained while situating herself on his lap.

"Jesus loves you just the same, whether you're a good girl or a bad girl. But when you're a bad girl, he wants you to tell him what you did that was wrong and tell him you're sorry. Are you sorry?"

She nodded. "I sawwy I say a fib ta Mama, but I sceered she whoop me if I towed her da troof. I towed Mama dat I finded da ring I give ta Miz Charwit, but da wady dat give me Miz Bitsy's ring give me dat one too."

"Why didn't you wrap up both rings to give to Miss Betsy at one time?"

"'Cause I wan' a give her two pwesents so she keep bein' happy.

Mama an' Miz Cwary make me sceered, 'cause dey don' wike dat I wanna give da *firs'* ring."

"I believe that Miss Clary and your mama already know you got the second ring from the same lady, but they're waiting for you to tell your mama the truth. I'll make a deal with you. I'll be your defender and go with you to your mama if you promise to tell her exactly what you told me, and you promise not to talk about the second ring at all to anyone while Miss Lydia and Mr. Josh are here."

"You make Mama not whoop me?" she asked, sliding off his lap and taking his hand.

"I can't promise that she won't spank you. I can try to help her understand why you did what you did, but she's the judge and jury. If she feels your lie warrants a spanking, you'll have to accept her decision. But even if she does spank you, you'll still feel better because you won't be scared anymore, and the matter will be at an end. Do you understand?"

She nodded and started up the steps only to see her mother standing in the doorway holding her arms out for her to come to her.

"I'm not goin' ta whoop you. You bein' scared of gettin' a whoopin' for a week be 'nough punishment," she explained, hugging her, "but you never fib ta yo' mama 'gain, hear?"

"I pwomise, Mama."

Libby stood watching by the parlor window, touched by the loving way Justin handled the child. She wished the window had been open so she could have heard their conversation.

"Little girl!" Susanna called to Vie from her throne-like chair that Justin had brought from the parlor and placed beneath the shading branches of a broad oak tree. "Go to my carriage and bring me my sketch portfolio. It's beneath the driver's seat." She unlatched the tortoiseshell clasp of her reticule to search for a penny.

Justin put his hand over hers. "No. Ask her to *please* get it for you. Vie isn't a servant or slave, but she'll be happy to bring it to you for a smile of appreciation and a thank you."

"Whatever you say," she said, with a wave of her hand. "I'd like to sketch your family. Have you an easel that I might use so my gown won't become soiled?"

When their attention was captured by a feminine shriek, they saw that Jeremy was chasing Charlotte across the field holding a line of hooked trout above her head. Susanna rose from her chair and stomped her foot.

"You *must* talk to your brother concerning his behavior, Justin. I'll have you know that my mother is not at all pleased that Charlotte is developing habits that defy the high standards of our upbringing."

"Now, Susanna," he said soothingly. "Look around you. Everyone is laughing at their shenanigans. They're simply enjoying themselves, and I must admit I've never seen Charlotte so happy and relaxed."

Her glaring eyes traveled from one amused spectator to the next, so she decided to air her complaints to Justin when they were alone. She forced a sweet smile. "Will you be a dear and bring me an easel?" She sat back down and accepted the sketch portfolio that Vie brought to her.

"*Thank you*, Vie," Justin said, looking at Susanna.

"Oh yes, thank you, little girl. Mr. Justin and Mr. Josh are going to make ice cream later this afternoon. You may have some." She looked up at Justin. "*What?*"

He looked into her eyes and faintly shook his head. "I'll look for an easel. I remember seeing one in the attic while I was searching for a cradle for Laurel. Perhaps you would like to hold Laurel?" he asked, studying her face.

"I will... but later... after she has digested Lydia's milk." She smiled and batted her eyelashes. "You wouldn't want baby's vomit to ruin this beautiful frock, would you?"

As she watched him walk toward the house, she decided she'd best try to be more compliant to his requests. He appeared to be a bit miffed and abrupt with her this afternoon, and knowing how often he had voiced his desire of wanting several children of his own, she decided it would be in her own best interest to show some attention to Laurel.

Justin lifted Vie off the pony after completing a three-round prance of the entire property. "So what do you think of baby Laurel, young lady?" he asked.

"She be too widdle to pway wif, but she don' cwy wots, wike Tildy's baby bwudder. We pway games now?"

"No. I must go help Miss Clary and Mr. Josh. Perhaps Li—Betsy will play a game with you." He watched her run gleefully over to Libby then turned to see Susanna in the distance, thoroughly absorbed in sketching Lydia. Except for the movement of the hand that sketched her subject, he noted that she appeared to be a work of art—a beautiful, chiseled marble statue, every fine line perfect in form and dimension, yet somewhat unattainable, devoid of inner depth, almost *inanimate*. Just as well. He could never again allow himself to love as deeply as he had loved Mary Anne.

He could see bits of rose-colored frock weaving around the bushes and trees and lightly laughed as he watched Vie jump up and down, delightedly clapping her hands. "Lovely" was really quite different than "beauty," he determined. While beauty in itself was meant to be admired for its sole fascination, loveliness not only encompassed beauty but was also *life* itself—with its sparkling eyes, glowing pink cheeks, and an infectious laugh as light, fresh, and unpretentious as a cool babbling brook. To be lovely was to possess a kind heart, depth of character, and the ability to give joy by pretending to play "hide and seek" with a tot ... *Elizabeth.*

"Justin!" Josh yelled from the kitchen door. "I called you several times. Wake up! Clary put all the mixings in the ice cream churn. We'll take turns churning."

"You first," Justin called back. "I want to look at Susanna's sketches." He went to stand behind her chair. "Wonderful work," he praised her. "The picture looks exactly like Lydia. Who else have you sketched while I was gone?"

"Wherever were you for so long?" she asked, taking three sheets of paper from her portfolio. "Oh dear! The one of you is a bit smudged," she said, handing it to him to appraise.

"I took Vie over to see how far her father and his friends had progressed at laying the foundation for his house." He looked at the paper. "I believe you've made me far more handsome than I actually am ... and sketched all from memory!"

She handed him a sketch of Josh. "I never realized how much he looks like you until I studied his face. Clary refused to sit still for me, so the last one is Betsy." She handed it to him. "You don't think it looks like her?" she asked, noticing the somewhat critical glare in his eyes.

"It's very good, but ... I believe her eyes are larger and tilt up slightly more at the outer corners, rather like a kitten, and her face is not so round at the chin. And see here?" He put the sketch down on the arm of the chair and pointed to the mouth. "Her lips are much fuller and cheekbones more pronounced." When he sensed her seething, he added, "But it really is very good, especially considering you don't see her every day, as we do." He quickly kissed her cheek. "Suppose you take a rest from your work and come with me to look at the baby?"

She reluctantly took his arm, hoping he wouldn't insist that she hold the child. "Let me just *look* at her for a moment. I know! Suppose Lydia holds her and I'll sketch them together."

"How can you look at that precious little face and not want to cuddle her?" he asked, taking the baby from her cradle and placing her in Susanna's arms. When Laurel instantly squalled, Susanna nearly threw her back into Justin's arms.

Lydia took her baby from him and kindly said to Susanna, "It's time for her feeding again. I'm certain she's hungry. Perhaps you'll want to hold her later, when she's not fussing."

"Yes … yes, of course I would like to hold her later. She's an adorable child." She took hold of Justin's arm. "We should go help Josh make the ice cream. Look at the sky. I hope it doesn't rain on our picnic," she said, relieved to lead him away from the disconcerting confrontation.

"If it rains we'll move the picnic into the house. I'm thankful that we've been blessed with perfect weather so far today. After supper we'll have an old-fashioned hymn-sing around the piano."

"Oh! Didn't I tell you that I planned to return home early this evening? Remember, tomorrow I'm to hostess the art museum's newest private exhibit. I'd like to retire early, because I must leave for the city at daybreak."

"No, you did *not* tell me. I knew you were asked to hostess the exhibit, but you never mentioned that it was to take place on Sunday. This will be the second Sunday that you've missed church, and I thought you would come home with us afterward." He stopped walking, turned to her, and took her by the shoulders. "I hope that I'm wrong to be concerned that spiritual matters mean little to you."

"Well … well, you *certainly* would be wrong!" she sputtered, becoming a bit unguarded by his direct sternness. But she quickly regained her composure and touched her hand to his cheek. "It's only this one time," she said to coyly pacify him. "I promise we'll go to church together next Sunday. And you need not see me home this evening. I'll leave well before dark. You stay here and enjoy your family since you see so little of them."

CHAPTER 18

"We'll take the dessert dishes to the kitchen, and then we best leave to put Laurel to bed," Lydia said to Clary. "We're fortunate that she sleeps through the night. I've no desire to disrupt her schedule, but I *am* very sorry that our visit has come to an end." She turned to Libby. "I believe, Betsy, that I'm compelled to hire you as our nanny. You won Laurel's first true smile, and I could see the joy on her face as she listened to your glorious voice. You and Justin sing in perfect harmony. I can't remember when I've been so entertained... lovely gifts given to Laurel and me... and such delicious strawberry ice cream!" She laughed. "My words ramble because our time together has been *so* precious," she tenderly said, taking Libby's hand. "Truthfully, when you are claimed, please do stay in touch with us. You're such a dear! I pray that all goes well with you."

Justin playfully put his arm around Libby's shoulders. "Didn't Clary mention that we plan to adopt her?"

Lydia laughed, but he couldn't seem to read the expression on Josh's face.

Jeremy suddenly appeared at the library door. "I deposited my lady safely back at her home, was able to dodge Mrs. Dupont, and am glad I arrived back here in time to bid you a fond farewell. It's a pity that you have to leave at daybreak."

"I have a farm to run," said Josh, "but we'll be back in a month. Justin and I decided to surprise the parents by installing their wash closet since the fixtures have already arrived from England.

I trust you'll add your hands to the chore? Abel has agreed to help in exchange for building supplies for his house."

"Certainly I'll help. Do you think we can complete the job in a weekend?"

"With some hired help, the four of us working, and the fact that I have experience in this area, yes." He put his hand out to shake hands with Jeremy. "It's time to bed my family down for the night." He turned to Justin, whose arm still encircled Libby's shoulders. "We'll meet you outside at sunrise. Goodnight, Betsy. It was truly a pleasure meeting you." He extended his hand.

She accepted it with tears in her eyes. The warmth of their kindness and loving natures had touched her deeply. She hoped that this would not be a final farewell. Justin looked down at her face, gave her shoulder a comforting little squeeze, and then put his arm down to his side and followed his guests to the front door.

Clary kissed the baby and Lydia then turned to Libby. "I'm in dire need of a warm, soothing bath. I'll worry about the dishes tomorrow. Suppose we sleep a bit later than usual. I'll see you in the morning." She looked at Justin as he closed the front door. "And I'll see *you* in two weeks, and promise to attend to your command upon waking tomorrow morning," she added, discerning the stern look he gave her. "Goodnight." She kissed Libby then headed up the stairs.

Libby instantly looked up into Justin's eyes. "Two weeks?" she asked faintly, clearly surprised that he wouldn't be home the next weekend. "I'm sorry. It really is none of my business how long you'll be away. But," she added shyly, looking down at the floor, "I hope I'll be able to see you one last time before I leave here."

He put his hand beneath her chin and lifted her face to look at him. "Come into the library. I have something to show you." He directed her into the library, removed a piece of paper from the top drawer of his desk, and handed it to her. It was a telegram sent by the Philadelphia center-city precinct police stating that they had not been alerted by anyone to be on the lookout for a missing Elizabeth Shaw, nor had any of the other precincts.

Libby backed up against the love seat, dropped down onto it, and rested her face in her hands. She slowly shook her head. "It makes no sense. It simply makes no sense." She took her hands from her face when she felt him sit beside her. "They responded almost instantaneously."

"It was delivered while I was taking Vie for her pony ride." He was somewhat surprised that she didn't appear to be at all disconcerted by the telegram.

She was well aware that reading the telegram should have wreaked havoc on her senses, raising all sorts of questions. Was she really who she thought she was? Why was no one looking for her? Was she losing her mind? But the only thought on which she could dwell was the fact that he was going away for two weeks, and she wanted to beg him to come home next weekend.

"I have a required, full-day seminar to attend next Saturday and promised Susanna that I would escort her to a reception for governors and their wives on Sunday afternoon, to be held at the White House. Mrs. Johnson has been ill, so the president asked Mrs. Dupont if she would hostess the event for him," he explained, seemingly reading her mind.

"Oh my!" she exclaimed with sparkling eyes. "How exciting!"

He faintly smiled. "It will most likely be very dull. Mrs. Johnson is often ill. My mother was asked to hostess an event in her place the end of last February. Our entire family attended the boring reception, but Mrs. Lincoln decided to take Mrs. Johnson's place at the last moment, much to the relief of my mother. I don't understand why these functions are planned to take place on the Lord's Day."

She nodded slightly in agreement. "Did you know Mr. Lincoln?"

"Quite well. He's the one who appointed my father as Trade Ambassador."

"I don't understand how … "

"How a good Confederate family would consort with a

Republican president?" he finished her sentence. "Mary Lincoln is a Southerner whose family, the Todds, owned slaves. Her half brothers fought for the Confederacy, and Andrew Johnson is a Democrat who hails from Tennessee."

"But Josh and Jeffrey fought for the Confederacy, and Clary made medicines for Confederate soldiers."

"But all three of them still admired the president's stand on slavery, and no family was sorrier than we were when he was murdered. I imagine he might be alive today had he just held on to his opinion until calmer times and not ended up a martyr to the voting rights of the black man. Elizabeth," he said, desiring to change the subject, "you have enough concerns without worrying about the logistics of the war."

She nodded. "Do you attend church when you're in Washington?" she asked, loving the way he called her Elizabeth.

"Yes, one of Susanna's choosing. The minister's preaching is far too wishy-washy to suit my preference. He's terrified he'll offend someone of importance by attempting to enforce God's laws for living. It's difficult to feel intimacy with God in so icy-cold an environment. I believe I'll have to put my foot down and insist that we attend another." When Libby began to giggle at the suggestion, he threw his head back and laughed. "I'll wager that your little mind is placing the odds against me and that my intended will win. You're insightful to her stubborn nature. Do you find me to be wishy-washy and weak?"

She laughed. "Not at all, Counselor, merely attentive to the one you love. I find that to be admirable."

He instantly became sober, somewhat bothered by what she had just said.

She stood up. "I won't even deem you weak if you assist me in the very womanly chore of washing and drying the dishes." She smiled and held her hand out for him to take. "Please? I would like to do it for Clary. Over the last few days, she gave herself completely to the pleasure of your family and had little time to rest. But if you're too tired, I'll understand, and you may retire, but I still intend to tidy the kitchen."

He took her hand and stood up. "Of course I'll help you. It's only nine o'clock. By the way, you didn't seem to notice that when we sang 'Oh Worship the King' in church this morning, I pointed out to you the words, 'Our shield and *defender.*' *Defender*, Elizabeth."

"Ohhh ... and here I thought that *you* thought I had lost my place and merely wanted to point it out," she said with a knowing giggle.

Justin stood outside of his bedroom and slowly turned the doorknob, hating that he might disturb her sleep. But Abel and Josh's family were outside in the carriage, waiting to be taken to the train station. He knew there were items in his armoire needed for his extended stay in Washington that he had neglected to acquire the night before. He had been enjoying her company far too much to think about packing for the morrow's trip.

Stepping quietly across the room, he pulled the drapes open to allow just enough light to locate the needed items. After placing several toiletries and two carefully folded shirts in the valise he had left in the hallway, he turned to shut the door but realized he had forgotten to close the drapes, knowing that in approximately thirty minutes the sun would be shining directly on her face.

Looking over to see her resting so peacefully, he approached his bed to gaze down at her, regretfully, perhaps for the last time. Dark curls seemed to spill everywhere—over her pillow and the one beside it and over the edge of the bed. He couldn't help but watch her sleep, mesmerized by the gentle rise and fall of her lace-adorned bosom with every shallow breath she took. Suddenly aware that he had stopped breathing for the last several seconds, he inhaled then stared thoughtfully at her for one moment more—just enough time to allow temptation to overtake his sensibility. He bent down to place a gentle, lingering kiss on her lips then went to pull the drapes shut and close the door behind him. He stood grounded for a moment, wondering if he should feel guilt at kissing her—because he felt no guilt at all.

Ben Shaw managed to push his way through the crowd and step into the train just as the porter snapped the doors shut behind him. He immediately ran a hand up and down his back, relieved that none of his garb had become wedged between the closed doors as had happened to him more than once. He set his valise on the floor then scanned the rows of seats hoping to find a vacancy, but a sleepy-eyed passenger occupied every single one. It really didn't matter, he figured, because he would be changing trains after two more stops.

He reached into his vest pocket and took out the telegram of hope to read it again for the hundredth time. *If Libby is alive, Lord, my faith in you will be restored.* He neatly folded the telegram, placed it back in his pocket, and took out a handkerchief to blot the perspiration from his brow.

His peripheral vision told him that a young man sitting three rows down the aisle seemed to be boldly surveying him. The man looked somewhat familiar, but he couldn't put a name to the face. He smiled and nodded to the man, hoping he would eventually lose interest and turn his attention to someone else—but no. He continued to stare in such a blatant manner that Ben wondered if he should approach him to ask if there was a matter to be settled between them. He decided that if he angrily glared at the man, he might look away—but no.

The man took a handkerchief from his vest pocket, folded and neatly stuffed it into his coat pocket with embroidered initials and a fleur-de-lis pattern standing upright from the pocket fold, then immediately focused back on Ben. Ben could feel hot blood engorge his cheeks as his eyes focused on the object of adornment. Surely there were other women in this vast world who had a passion for embroidering fleur-de-lis emblems on handkerchiefs. Most certainly there had to be.

The train stopped, the door opened, several people left the train, and a flood of passengers entered. When the train started up again, he could see that the man was still sitting in the same seat, still staring. He decided not to allow anything to interfere with his present jubilant state of mind and directed his eyes to the window across the aisle. But unable to help himself, his eyes had focused back on the handkerchief. The man suddenly stood up, grabbed his valise from beneath his seat, and wove around the many other standing passengers to stand beside him.

"Handsome workmanship, isn't it?" Justin asked Ben, placing his thumb beneath the embroidery. "I noticed that when you took your handkerchief out a few moments ago, it looked very similar to mine. Where did you purchase it?"

"It wasn't purchased, sir. The workmanship is my sister's. She believes the three petals of the iris represent the Trinity. I own several dozen that are similar."

"I see. Mine was also not purchased but embroidered by a lovely young lady who just happened to make her way to my home three weeks ago. Strangely, she looks somewhat like you, but only stands about this tall," he said, placing his hand on the base of his collarbone.

"And where is it that you live?" Ben cautiously asked, feeling the beat of his heart pounding in his ears.

"Twenty-five miles west of Washington, in the town of Barrister's Junction."

"Oh," Ben blandly mumbled in a dejected tone.

The train stopped again, the door opened, and Ben turned away from Justin to exit.

"The young woman who embroidered mine is named Elizabeth Shaw," Justin called to him.

Ben didn't exit the door. He turned back to Justin with a blood-drained face and knees that were about to go out from under him. "I don't see how that could be," he weakly said, clearly dumbstruck by the announcement.

"I believe I may have someone who belongs to you," Justin said with a smile of assurance. "Stay on the train until the next stop. There's a small café there that serves a hearty breakfast, where we can discuss whether our seamstress is one, the same."

Libby sat down on the porch glider to wait for Clary to finish eating a belated breakfast. The overwhelming stench of pork sausage frying in the kitchen caused her stomach to churn, and there seemed to be no place to escape. Even the fresh air appeared tainted by the foul odor. She decided to move farther away from the house and left the porch to walk the path that led up to the road.

When the nausea finally subsided, her mind drifted back to her conversation with Justin. Should she even bother to tell Clary that her name is Elizabeth Shaw of Philadelphia? Apparently, she might not be. *Oh, Lord,* she prayed, *when will this nightmare end? I need you so! Help me remember the facts of my life as they actually are. Please keep me from going mad!*

She was grateful there was no nightmare last night. Actually, what little of a dream she remembered had been rather sweet. She ran her fingers lightly over her mouth, recalling the warm feel of Justin's lips on hers. *But he belongs to another, and you belong to… anyone?* He had only been gone for several hours, and she realized she missed him—far more than she had a right. Susanna would hate her if she were able to read her mind. But shouldn't she be feeling guilt at her thoughts? She realized she felt no guilt at all. But she *was* a bit disappointed in herself at not being able to feel empathy for Susanna, as she should. If their roles were reversed, she would want Susanna as distanced from him as possible.

"There you are," called Clary, turning to shut the front door behind her. "I brought you some gingerroot tea and a scrap of bread. Are you feeling any better?"

Libby walked back to the porch. "Yes. The fresh air helped." Her eyes followed Clary's eyes until they focused up to the road, where a buggy pulled by a silver mare turned down the path heading toward them.

"Dr. Flanagan," Clary said softly as she seated herself on the glider. It was obviously clear by her facial expression that she wasn't pleased by his unexpected visit.

"What do you think he wants?" asked Libby.

Clary patted the seat next to her. "Come sit beside me. My intuition tells me that we would do well to be seated when he gives his information." She handed her the tea and crust of bread.

"Good morning to you, ladies," the doctor said somberly. He climbed down from his buggy, walked up to the porch to stand behind the glider, and then reached over Clary's shoulder to hand her a folded sheet of paper.

She unfolded the letter with a small newspaper clipping attached to it. After scanning the contents, she said, "Suppose we go into the house and discuss this." She turned to Libby. "You stay here and finish your tea and bread. We'll be but a few minutes," she assured her, standing to escort the doctor into the house.

No sooner had they closed the front door behind them than a messenger rode his horse down the path to deliver a telegram to Justin. Libby accepted it and sat back down on the glider to sip her tea. She regarded the folded note, curious as to its contents. If it contained important information, someone would have to forward it to him, she reasoned. After all, he wouldn't be home for two weeks. She didn't wish to disturb the doctor and Clary, having been given the distinct impression that she wouldn't be welcome to intrude into their little tete-a-tete.

Then it dawned on her that the wire may possibly contain some information that pertained to her... and after all, she *did* have the right to know. She unfolded the note and saw that it had been sent by the Philadelphia center-city police headquarters. It read:

> *Sir—We just received information that a Dr. Morrow requests that we be on the lookout for a female in her mid-twenties bearing a similar description to the one you gave in your inquiry about an Elizabeth Shaw of Philadelphia. Morrow is searching for an Elizabeth (Libby) Prescott of Wellesley, PA. It had been thought that her husband had murdered her and her father—her remains as yet to be found. New information suggests that she may be alive. Please wire immediately if you have information.*

Libby bolted out of her seat to stand on wobbly legs and watched as the teacup and saucer fell to the porch floor, shattered into a hundred pieces, then faded from view.

Clary pressed a cool wet cloth to Libby's forehead. "She's coming to," she called to the doctor when she heard his footsteps on the stairs.

He opened his medical bag to find a disinfectant for the half dozen scrapes and cuts on one of her forearms. As he dressed the wounds, she opened her eyes and stared dully up at their faces. When he finished, he caressed her cheek in a sympathetic gesture then sat down on the edge of the bed to talk to her.

"I'm sorry you had to read that telegram before we had a chance to speak with you," he said with a soft kindness.

She faintly smiled. "I suppose it serves me right for reading a telegram that wasn't addressed to me." Tears pooled in her eyes. "And I suppose this is the day and time that I'm meant to face reality," she said with a great sad sigh. "My papa has died, and I could do *nothing* to come to his aid. Please ... please will you both leave me be for a while, so that I may sort out the facts of my life and try to place them in order?"

Clary reached into her apron pocket and took out Libby's ring. "This may help," she said, holding it out to her. "Now I'm sorry I didn't give this to you sooner."

Libby regarded it for a moment and, once clearly recognizing it, refused to accept it. She turned away from them and closed her eyes. "Sell it to help pay for my keep," she said. "I hate him and want no reminders of him, and I hope he's in police custody and receives the death penalty for the misery he has caused," she added bitterly.

"He's dead, Libby. Father shot him first," a male voice interjected from the doorway.

"*Ben?*" she shrieked, abruptly turning to look toward the direction the voice had come from. She jumped up from the bed and threw herself into her brother's waiting arms. Each sobbing, they held tightly to one another.

"My sweet baby sister," Ben softly said, hugging her head to his neck.

"Come, let's leave them be," Justin suggested to his sister and the doctor. "We'll talk downstairs and compare what we've learned concerning this tragic situation."

CHAPTER 19

"*Astonishing!*" Clary exclaimed after listening to Justin relay to her and Dr. Flanagan what he had learned from Ben during their trip home from Washington.

Justin took his handkerchief from his pocket. "It was this piece of cloth that brought us together. Ironically, it was Elizabeth's workmanship in symbolizing the Trinity that drew Ben and me together. I never mentioned to you, but I saw Ben once before on the train. His look is so similar to his sister, and when he took his handkerchief out to wipe his brow, I couldn't get his face out of my mind. It had to be divine intervention that brought us together the second time. God certainly works things out in interesting and spectacular ways. Who would have thought? Now only Elizabeth can tell us how she came to be in our backyard." He looked at the doctor. "Do you suppose she's completely regained her memory?"

"I believe she will within the next day or so, for now she's been given enough personal information to joggle her memory. This is truly amazing! My friend, who teaches at Jefferson Medical College, sent me all he could find about Caleb Shaw, that he had indeed married Babette Cecile Arnaud in 1832. She bore him two children, Benjamin Adam and Elizabeth Jeanette. The family moved from Philadelphia to Wellesley in 1855, but Babette died of pneumonia shortly after the move. My friend also sent me Caleb's obituary. The only thing I didn't learn was that Libby's husband had been shot and died."

"I can't realize the fact that she's older than I. My poor little dear," Clary said sadly. "I believe she feels responsible that her father didn't receive the help he needed. She's going to need a strong shoulder to lean on to help her get through the sorrow, depression, and guilt," she said, fixing her eyes on her brother's broad shoulders. "And if she happens to be with child... well, that's another problem. How will she support and raise a child on her own?"

"She has her faith... and Ben and us," said Justin. "She has enough support to admirably come through this trying time." He looked over at the doorway to see Ben standing alongside a perplexed Jeremy.

"I met up with this fellow in the foyer as he came down the stairs," Jeremy explained, looking at the trio for answers. "He rather looks like Betsy."

Ben smiled. "If you're referring to *Libby*, I'm her brother, Ben. Our mother was named 'Betsy' by our father, but spelled B-E-T-C-I-E to shorten her name of Babette Cecile."

"So finally someone has come to claim her," he responded. "Where is she?"

Clary stood up and offered her seat and the vacant one beside her to the men, while Justin completed the introductions and explained to Jeremy what had been learned that morning.

"Astounding! But... but how did she end up next to the cemetery behind our house?" Jeremy asked.

"By train," answered Ben.

"You *cannot* be serious!" exclaimed Clary. "What young woman would travel one hundred and fifty miles from home wearing only a nightgown?" She giggled while setting the table with refreshments of tea, biscuits, and honey.

"Freight train, ma'am," answered Ben, "and not by her own volition. I prefer that she tell you all in her own words exactly what befell her the night of August 22." He stood up to offer Clary his seat.

"Sit back down, Ben. I'll get a chair from the dining room for her," said Justin.

"She must be hungry," said Clary to Ben. "She hasn't been feeling well most mornings and hasn't eaten anything since last evening. I should take her some food."

"No. Allow her sleep for a while ... if she's able."

"Shall I take her some chamomile tea?"

Ben smiled at her. "You're very kind. Libby is extremely grateful to you ... to all of you. But no ... she's suffering from brain exhaustion. I believe she may sleep for quite some time. I mixed a sleeping powder into a glass of water for her. I always carry it with me to help me rest peacefully when I travel."

"I hope it didn't contain white willow bark, because she's been nauseous for the entire morning. I made her gingerroot tea earlier, although I suspect she never got to drink it."

"No white willow bark. My powder is mainly composed of passionflower and valerian root. Libby told me that you're a self-taught herbalist. Her praise of your knowledge has enticed me to ask you for a tour of your garden and the shed where you perform your ... *experiments*," he said with a touch of mysteriousness to his voice.

She giggled and blushed. "I'd be happy to take you on a tour. I have nothing to be ashamed of or to hide," she proudly proclaimed.

"Clary was a godsend to me during the war," offered Dr. Flanagan. "I could always depend on her to smuggle specific herbs and medical remedies to wherever I was camped, and she even concocted several medicines of her own that proved quite effective in helping to care for my patients."

"How intriguing! And you were never arrested for smuggling?"

Clary laughed. "Three times stopped, but never searched or arrested. It helped to have a brother who worked in tribunals. I always carried papers with written proof of his rank and position."

"And if they happened to find contraband on her person, I

suppose I would have found myself standing *before* a military tribunal," Justin wryly commented.

"Well, now I'm *most* anxious to see your work," he said to her with twinkling eyes. "I hope you're able to patent your findings. It's very important that you do, to protect yourself from being labeled a 'quack.' It's becoming more and more difficult to convince the American Medical Association of the need for advanced herbal research. Part of the problem with herbal medicines is that it's difficult to determine and control quality and regulate proper dosages. I've also heard rumors that several of the board believe herbal remedies to be an outdated form of Indian witchery and therefore lacking sophistication to gain acceptance into today's modern world of medicine."

Clary laughed. "An interesting rumor, but I've not taken the time to patent any of my remedies, although I agree with you. Perhaps you can instruct me on how to go about filing for a patent. I would like to hear of your summer's findings in the Poconos. Justin told me that you're a member of the Smithsonian's Megatherium Club."

"That's correct. The purpose of my most recent visit was to lecture on the properties of the species I had found and to properly name them to take their place in the museum's herbarium. We now have approximately 50,000 samples on record."

"Fascinating!" she commented, her eyes glued to his face, intently absorbing every word he spoke. "I'll take you outside as soon as you finish eating. I hope you'll stay overnight with us."

"Suppose he takes my room, and I'll sleep over at the parents' house," suggested Jeremy. "Surely you weren't planning on just taking our girl and running."

"I have to be back at Boston University by Monday, the next. There's a substitute teaching in my place at present. I honestly don't wish to move Libby so quickly, but I feel—"

"Then don't move her at all," Clary interrupted. "Did she tell you that she is most likely carrying a child?" she cautiously asked him.

His eyes widened. "No! Oh, my dear Lord," he said, looking up prayerfully and slowly shaking his head. "She'll need you more than ever now." He looked at Justin. "I have to confess that over the last three weeks, my faith has diminished to the point of near paganism. But today my faith has been completely restored and multiplied. The Lord took us this far, and I know he'll see us through any future event."

"What sort of lodging do you have in Boston?" Justin asked.

"I have only one room in a boarding house. Finding any sort of lodging in Boston is as scarce as hen's teeth while school is in session. Libby will have to live alone at my father's house until Christmastime. I've already been granted a leave of absence for the semester following Christmas. I had planned on using that time to sort out my father's and Libby's personal effects."

"My sister doesn't want Elizabeth to leave here," Justin told him. "She fits so nicely into our family."

"She missed her birthday! May I suggest we have a birthday party for her tomorrow evening?" Clary asked. She looked at Justin. "Oh ... I suppose you'll have to return to Washington this evening or tomorrow morning." *I know you don't want her to leave here either.*

"Have your party. I'll stay home until Wednesday morning. Charles already knows what has taken place here and was surprisingly understanding. After I stopped at the firm to explain why I needed to return home, Ben wired Dr. Morrow to inform him as to Elizabeth's whereabouts." He looked at Ben and chuckled. "You had best send a follow up letter explaining the details. I'm sure your wire has stunned them."

"Libby and I will write a letter together. I'd like to stay until Saturday, if I may," Ben said. "If my sister feels secure enough to leave here, then I'll take her to my father's house before I go on to Boston. But if she doesn't ... "

"She'll stay with us. Please, Ben, allow her to stay here as long as possible, even if it means that she stays until after Christmas when you're able to care for her. If she's with child, she should have those around her who will love and encourage her. Please?" Clary asked, staring longingly into his eyes.

"All of you are amazing," he said, smiling appreciatively at Clary. "She's been here for only three weeks, and you've made her one of your own."

"That's because she's so loveable, and we enjoy how she entertains us with her great musical ability," Justin said with a light laugh.

Yes, she's very loveable, isn't she, Justin? Clary silently affirmed. She turned back to Ben with pleading eyes.

"If her desire is to stay here, then I have no right to interfere with her wishes. She deserves peace and the love of good people. However, the only way I'll agree completely to the arrangement is if you promise to take my note to pay for her keep."

"Well, considering her appetite from noon until bedtime, are you certain you can afford it?" asked Jeremy, followed up by a swat to the back of his head by both Clary and Justin.

"I must interrupt to make a serious point," said Dr. Flanagan. "There's the matter that she'll need to be examined to confirm a pregnancy and determine the date the child should arrive." He looked at Ben. "You're her brother; 'tis best that you try to convince her that an examination is inevitable and in her best interest."

"I'll do that in private, this evening. Her resentment toward Billy may cause her to wish she wasn't carrying his child."

"You may be wrong about that. She seems to love children, and she can't blame the child for the sins of the father. She may resent it for a while, but I'll wager that when she feels it moving inside of her, her love will overtake any resentment," said Justin.

"Justin and Be—*Libby* have had several heart-to-heart conversations during her stay here, not the sort of talks a girl has with her *brother*," Clary explained wryly, rolling her eyes at Justin and Jeremy.

"Well, Miss Clarissa, I've eaten all I'm able and now ask that you escort me about the grounds." Ben placed his folded napkin on the table, stood up, and offered his arm to Clary.

They ran into Becky on their way out the door, and Clary explained what had taken place, introduced her to Ben, and told her they would be preparing a birthday party the next day for twenty-six-year-old Libby. As Clary and Ben walked off toward the gardens, Justin and Jeremy heard Becky say to herself, "White folks! They got mo' problems!"

CHAPTER 20

Justin leaned back in his desk chair and stared out the window at a sun that was about to disappear over the horizon, thinking how the house seemed disturbingly quiet. Elizabeth was still sleeping, and Clary, Ben, Jeremy, and Charlotte-come-lately were all over at the parents' house appraising a crate of imports that had arrived that noon, sent from England by his mother. That sort of thing bored Justin, but he knew if Susanna were visiting, she would insist that he go with her to scout for any possible treasure that she might claim for their future household.

Susanna. He knew for sure she would pay a visit tomorrow, angry that he hadn't personally told her of Ben's reunion with Elizabeth. No, she wouldn't be happy learning of it through her father. He picked up the stack of papers he had sorted through and underscored, placed them back into his leather case, then took his Bible from the corner of his desk and turned to Psalm 58.

Although he had read this particular Psalm several times before, it meant more to him now, with its theme of justice—or lack thereof. Even as far back as Old Testament days, men had to plead to God for justice and deliverance from corrupt politicians and twisted laws. Charles Dupont flashed through his mind. His intuition told him that something wasn't quite right in his dealings, but he couldn't put a finger on any particular incident that suggested overt corruption was in the making. He had been lightly rebuffed when he asked Charles what the contents of the packages were that he was told to deliver to select law firms and politicians' offices. Perhaps Clary was correct. He wondered if this might be the time to accept Richard's offer of partnership, but a voice inside of him firmly commanded him to wait. Could Richard possibly be aware of dishonest dealings at hand? Perhaps that's why he chose to disassociate himself from the Dupont firm, not daring to voice any suspicions due to his father's position.

"Good evening. Where is everyone?" a soft, sleepy little voice came from the doorway.

He quickly looked up to see Libby waiting to be invited into the library. His eyes brightened and heart beat faster at the sight of her. "They're on a treasure hunt at my parents' home. A crate arrived from England this afternoon," he explained. He stood up with the intention of going to take her arm to draw her into the room, but when her lower lip began to quiver, he instead found himself drawing her into his arms to hold her.

"You poor sweet thing," she heard him softly say. "What you must have gone through, and I know I'm still not aware of *every* sordid detail of your ordeal." He strengthened his hold on her, and she clung tightly to him, her tears dampening his cheek.

"Oh, Justin!" She softly sobbed. "My wonderful Papa was so undeserving of his fate! I was so foolish in believing they would help me. *So* foolish!"

"Shhh ... hush, now. There was absolutely *nothing* you could do to help him. Let's go to the kitchen to get you some supper. When you've finished eating, I'll listen to all that's on your heart." He took her by her shoulders and stepped back to study her face for a moment, then took a handkerchief from his pocket to pat away her tears before escorting her to the kitchen.

He set a plate of leftovers before her then sat down beside her to share half of her custard so that she wouldn't feel uncomfortable at eating alone. All the time, he fought a powerful urge to take her back in his arms to comfort her. *Yes. This little creature most certainly is extremely loveable. Lord, I've made a commitment to Susanna. I can't go back on my promise to her, and this is not a good time to place any more confusion into Elizabeth's life. Give me wisdom in dealing with my emotions, please.*

"Where would you like to go to talk?" he asked after she finished eating what seemed to be much less than usual.

"We hardly ever sit in the parlor. May we sit on the divan in that room? I suppose they'll return shortly..."

"The crate is colossal in size, and your brother seemed interested in looking over the great number of artifacts from different countries, so they'll most likely have enough to fascinate them for quite some time."

"My brother has always talked about traveling to foreign countries. It's his dream to climb the hills of Scotland and Ireland and the mountains of Switzerland, in hopes of discovering a world-saving species of medicinal plant life." She giggled as they seated themselves on the divan.

"Hmm. Where have I heard that dream before?"

"Clary!" they both exclaimed in unison, and then burst out laughing.

"Are you certain you feel comfortable in telling me so many personal details?" he asked in a manner that had become solemn.

"Oh yes. I'm very comfortable in speaking with you about *anything*. The horror really began several months prior to August 22. My husband, Wilton, most folks called him 'Billy,' was shot twice in the same leg near the finish of the war. He managed to convince his attending doctor not to amputate the leg. His two older brothers died while having limbs amputated, so Billy was fearful of the same end. It appeared that one of the bullets could be removed, but the second shattered and the pieces lodged in his bone. Needless to say, he became dependent on the morphine administered to him, and when he arrived home, his nature remained fairly calm due to the fact that my father kept him sedated with morphine or opium, whichever was to be had.

"Over the next couple of months, Billy couldn't seem to get enough of the opiates to relieve the pain, which he described as throbbing and relentless. I realize you know that hundreds of thousands of soldiers returned from war addicted to the opiates, and I know you're well able to reason that, with so much demand, shortage was inevitable. I didn't know what to do with him. He couldn't sleep, he lost his appetite, and his hair was turning gray and shedding in clumps. One would have guessed that he was twice his age of twenty-five, but still, nothing or no one could convince him to have his leg amputated, even at one of the best, well-equipped medical facilities in Philadelphia." She stopped for a second to collect her thoughts.

"All during that time, he tried to be as civil to me as possible. I felt such *pity* for him, until I made a foolish choice. Billy's father suggested that perhaps a portion of whiskey might help to ease the pain. Although alcohol consumption defies my personal convictions, I wondered if he might find some relief in it but was too naïve to realize the damage it could do in altering a person's disposition. My father warned me that it might have an adverse effect on his nature.

"Over the weeks, as I watched him consume more and greater quantities of whiskey, I also witnessed an alarming transformation in his character, a gradual metamorphosis into a cruel, sadistic, heartless monster. If I failed to be at his beckoning call at every moment of the day, he would slap my face and scream that I didn't love him and say he wished he had never married me. I … I could do *nothing* to please him. Several times I had to go to my father for medical attention for infected cuts and bruises. Billy would take hold of me and pinch my arms with his unkempt, filthy nails until I would scream and cry from the pain and beg him to stop. And"—she blushed and looked down at her lap—"at night, in bed, he would attempt to strangle me until near unconsciousness while forcing himself … " She looked away from him as tears began to pour down her cheeks. "He seemed to gain pleasure from inflicting pain upon me."

Justin swallowed hard and reached over to take her hand. "Please don't feel that you need to go on if … "

She looked back to him. "Yes, yes, I do. If I tried to leave the bed before he fell asleep, he would yank me back by my hair then slap me, and ... " she softly said, placing her hand on her breasts, "sometimes he would even punch me ... on particularly sensitive areas of my body." She took hold of a stray wisp of hair and nervously twisted it around her finger. "I couldn't tell my father everything. He was concerned enough for my safety. Had I told him all, he would have worried so, and I knew it would do no good to go to the police. A woman is her husband's property. He may do with her what he may, short of murder. Then there was the matter of my faith. I married him for better or worse."

"But he *was* a good husband to you before his injury?"

"Yes, but we were only married for less than a year before he went away to war. He and his brothers built me a lovely little house on my father's property during the time of our engagement. His manner toward me was always loving and respectful. Everyone who knew him considered him pleasant and lighthearted. He worked as a carpenter after we married, and every Friday he would never fail to bring me a large bouquet of flowers. I only saw him a total of three short times during his four years from home. With every visit, however, I saw changes in him. He had once been a man of faith, but the harshness of battle turned him into a coarse, uncouth, swearing man."

"The indescribable atrocities of war changed many men for the worse, Elizabeth."

"I realize that, but believe that had he not been shot and in such pain, he might have eventually returned to his former self. I'll never forgive myself for leading him into an addiction with such powerful consequences."

"But your heart was in the right place. You simply couldn't bear to see him suffer," he said kindly. "Now tell me the sequence of events that took place on August 22."

"That day, at noon time, I went to my father's house to bring him lunch, as was my usual practice. Papa told me he was almost certain that a supply of morphine was to be delivered to his office that afternoon, that he had received a telegram stating so. It would be the first delivery in nearly two months. I told him that I was very relieved because Billy wasn't doing well. The whiskey didn't seem to ease the ache in his leg, and he couldn't relax enough to be able to sleep.

"Papa gave me a vial of sleeping powder and told me to lace Billy's food with it. He said he was terribly concerned for my welfare and wished that I would move into his home so that he could watch over me. He said that he knew Billy's behavior was far more abusive than I had confided to him and that he feared for my life. He didn't believe that Billy would ever regain his sanity even if he did have his leg amputated.

"I took the vial back to my house and laced Billy's lunch. After he fell asleep, I went back to my father's house to wait for the morphine. A backordered carton of syringes from Sears catalog arrived, but not the morphine.

"By the afternoon's end, it was too late to ride to the nearest establishment that sold whiskey. I knew there was only a partial bottle left at home, so I decided I would also lace his supper with the sleeping powder. If I could keep him asleep through the entire night, the morphine might arrive early the next morning, or I could ride out to purchase the liquor.

"But Billy never fell asleep after supper. He just sat and finished off the remaining whiskey. I sat across from him, perplexed as to how he could not be exhausted from the mixture of liquor and sleeping powder. He seemed to have completely forgotten that I had promised him morphine. Then ... then he roughly took my arm and told me we were going to bed early and demanded that I prepare myself. He ... he was so vile toward me. He ... he hurt me with the weight of him upon me ... and his rough hands and whiskers ..."

After she had finished conveying all of the sordid facts of the night's dark and fearsome journey, she said, "The next thing I knew, I was lying on your bed being attended to by Clary and Dr. Flanagan. What I really find to be strange, now that I'm able to recall, is that my fall from the train seemed to have been broken somehow, as if I had dropped onto a feather pillow before rolling down the embankment."

He gave her hand a squeeze then looked down at his lap, but not before she saw that he was blinking hard to hold back the tears. Over the last few years, he had heard enough heinous testimony to fill volumes, but he never felt a fury rise inside of him that he did this very moment at the thought that anyone, no matter how demented, could possibly inflict such pain and harm on this delicate little woman, so sweet and precious. It seemed intrusively personal to him, and he realized he actually hurt for her and could say nothing for one long moment.

"There are freight train tracks that run along the northern edge of the woods behind this house, but the trains never stop there. The nearest station is a good two miles away. What does that tell you?" he softly asked.

"I suppose it must have been God's doing," she said with a faint smile. "I must have wandered through the woods to your backyard. It's odd that I've never noticed the sound of a train passing by the entire time I've been here."

"Clary told me you wouldn't accept your wedding band, and I'm wondering why you haven't asked about your diamond ring, considering its probable worth."

She blankly stared at him. "I own no diamond ring, only my wedding band and my mother's. They're not worth the value of a life, Lottie's life."

"Then Staples must have stolen the diamond ring from someone else. The value of your rings must have seemed great to someone who never had much." He laid her hand back on her lap, touched his fingertips to her cheek, and looked into her eyes. "Elizabeth," he tenderly said her name. He was unable to finish his sentiment when he saw the glow of lamplight pass in front of the window.

"So you're finally awake," commented Ben as the four came charging in through the front door and filed into the parlor.

"I slept for a short while but spent most of the time trying to fit the pieces of the puzzle together." She saw that their arms were loaded up with boxes. "It appears that your treasure hunt went well," she noted.

"Very well," Clary said, placing a box on the tea table in front of Justin. "Open it," she instructed him. "Mother sent it to you and Susanna. I find it astounding that not one piece broke during shipping."

Justin lifted the lid and took out the largest of the enclosed items, each one wrapped in cotton batting and velvet. He unwrapped and held it up to the lamplight.

"They're imported from Prague. Have you ever seen anything so lovely?" asked Clary, taking a wrapped goblet from the box. She unwrapped and displayed it next to the pitcher that Justin held. "Green crystal, etched with a silver renaissance scene. Look at the cut of the pitcher. Have you ever beheld anything so ornate?"

"A bit overdone in my opinion," answered Justin. "What say *you*, Ben? Do you like it?"

"The women like it. I suppose that's all that matters," he said with a chuckle.

"Susanna will adore the set," offered Charlotte, "although blue is her favorite color. Perhaps you should give this to her the very moment she arrives here tomorrow, before she reprimands you for not coming to her first with your news. It should catch her off guard," she added with a sly smile.

Justin laughed and said to Jeremy, "Now I understand why you like this young lady so well. She's smart as a whip."

"Why he *loves* me, you mean," she answered for Jeremy.

Justin loudly and intentionally cleared his throat and stood up. "Suppose we go to the kitchen for cocoa?" He looked down at Libby. "Ben wants to talk with you alone. We'll bring cocoa to you in a few moments."

"How are you faring, sweets?" Ben asked, sitting down beside his sister.

"Surprisingly well. I suppose it helped to be able to talk with Justin about the details of my life prior to settling myself beside their family graveyard."

"He's a good man. A good family. God couldn't have deposited you at a better place," he said with a broad grin. "Tomorrow Clarissa wants to take us into Barrister's Junction to show me Jeremy's place of work and to take you shopping for some necessities. I would also like to post a letter to the Morrows. It would be kind if you would write a few lines to reassure them that you're doing well." He stopped for a moment.

She looked at him with questioning eyes. "Yes? You look as if you have more to say."

"You now need to make your statement to the sheriff and identify your attacker. Also, I would like for you to visit Dr. Flanagan's office. Wouldn't you like to be certain?" he asked, with eyes fixed upon her midsection.

"I'm already certain that I want no part of *him* growing inside of me," she said bitterly.

"There's nothing you can do if there is, other than to accept it. Do you realize that if there *is* a child growing inside of you, what a miracle it is?"

"I suppose you're referring to the fact that since Billy was overly drugged or drunk most of the time …"

"No. The fact that after all of the physical punishment you experienced, being thrown from a train, and suffering emotional and mental trauma, a child still continues to grow in you. I call that a miracle. If you are, then it's meant to be."

"I'll go for an examination if you insist, but after regaining my memory I already feel certain that I am. I recalled pondering the possibility before August 22. Wouldn't you prefer that I'm examined by Dr. Tim after I return home?"

He looked surprised by her question. "You don't wish to stay here until I'm able to stay at home with you?"

"I wouldn't have the gall to ask to stay here after already taking so much of their valuable time, although I'm not so sure I could bear leaving them."

He regarded her with a confused stare. "Forgive me, but I assumed you would be jumping for joy at their proposal that you stay with them until after Christmas."

"But they haven't brought the matter to me."

"Aha! There's the problem. Clarissa and Justin have already begged me to allow you to stay here. They seem anxious to care for you."

Her eyes lit up. "I wasn't aware!" she exclaimed, bouncing up and down on the divan. "Now I'm jumping for joy!"

CHAPTER 21

"Are you going to town with us, Justin?" asked Clary, setting a box on his desk. "Becky's going to bake Libby's birthday cake while we're gone. We'll be home sometime late in the afternoon. I'd like to take Ben and Libby to the White Swan for dinner. It seems that Libby has taken quite a fancy to their liver and onion pie. *Ugh*!" she said, with a shiver. "Here are three beautiful, cloth-bound journals, assembled in London. Would you like one?"

He laughed. "That little woman certainly relishes her food ... any food. I have to stay here to finish up a report and wait for Susanna. Charlotte telling her that she's invited to Elizabeth's birthday party may smooth her ruffled feathers. But do you feel it's in good taste to have a party, considering Elizabeth's father died only recently?" He lifted the journals out. "Very nice workmanship. I have no use for a journal, though," he said, placing them back in the box.

"It will be nothing lavish, just a remembrance to cheer her. Did you hear her cry out in her sleep last night? Ben said she had another nightmare about Billy. I would have thought the nightmares would stop once she regained her memory."

He nodded. "I heard her, but when I opened my bedroom door, I could see that Ben was going to her. Have you offered a journal to Elizabeth?"

"No, but I was planning to." She picked up the box and turned to leave.

He sat back in his chair and tapped his pen on the desk. "Wait.

Leave the journal with the roses on the cover. I would like to give it to Elizabeth along with some instructions that might help to obliterate her nightmares."

"Mr. Justin, a young man wearin' a uniform jus' come with a letter for Cap'ain Justin Chambers," Becky announced from the doorway. "He be waitin' for an answer."

"Thank you, Becky." He stood up and took the note from her to read its contents.

"Who is it from?" Clary asked, overtly interested due to the fact that it was addressed to *Captain* Justin Chambers.

"This is remarkable! I've been asked to serve as an alternate for the commission hearing the Henry Wirz testimony. It appears that one of the alternates has become too ill to be present, and my name was suggested as a possible replacement." He looked down and read aloud, "By an undisclosed source that stands firm in the belief of your ability to deploy wisdom and fairness in your judgments."

"But the trial has been going on for over three weeks now," she said, smiling at how pleased he appeared.

"That is so. I'll simply have to study the transcript."

"I believe you've already made your decision. But what will Charles say?"

"There isn't much he *can* say. It's my civic duty, and it wouldn't look well for him politically if he didn't temporarily relinquish me graciously to serve my country. Besides, I'm not working on anything at present that could be considered detrimental to the firm. I've been mostly playing errand boy for Charles the last few weeks. I'll write a note of explanation for you to wire to him while you're in Barrister's this morning. The tribunal would like a response immediately if I'm to report tomorrow."

He went to his desk to write a response and took it out to the messenger. "I'm returning an affirmative response," he said, already knowing the protocol. The boy handed him a sealed copy of the trial transcript in return for the note.

Clary looked up. *Thank you, God! This is exactly what he needs.*

Forgive my anger that he hadn't accepted Richard's offer. I should have known you were leading him toward greater things, and it's always best to "wait upon the Lord."

Justin tucked the last sheet of the trial transcript back into its envelope and glanced over at the clock. Time had flown, and it was now one o'clock in the afternoon. He was amazed that Susanna hadn't shown up at his door yet. Taking the bowl of beef stew from the tray of dinner Becky brought to him, he shoveled a heaping spoonful into his mouth and sat back to ponder the pages he had just read. He couldn't help but pity Wirz. The poor man could barely sit through the proceedings due to an injury sustained during the surrender process between Generals Sherman and Johnston. A chaise finally had to be brought into the courtroom for him to lie down. He wagered that Wirz now wished that he had never moved from Switzerland to this country, no matter how lucrative his Kentucky and Louisiana medical practices had become.

Colonel Chipman. He had met that pompous blowhard once, at a military gala. Pity he was in charge of the prosecution. There probably wasn't a defender in Washington who could be considered a worthy adversary to his manipulative ways. Yes, the defense was definitely going to have a difficult time of it. Three out of the five defense attorneys had already resigned, and rumor had it that the remaining two, Baker and Schade, had threatened to withdraw their services after every one of their motions had been denied. The only good that had come from this trial, thus far, was that the final indictment against Robert E. Lee had been dropped. He almost wished he had been asked to work for the defense. As an alternate, it would be unlikely that he would be permitted to voice his opinion unless the member of the commission to whom he was assigned became ill and couldn't serve.

Well, no sense dwelling on it at present. There would be time for that after all of the evidence was in.

He finished up his stew, set the bowl back on the tray, and inhaled deeply. Becky must have put Elizabeth's birthday cake in the oven a short while ago. The air in the house was thick with its tantalizing aroma. Elizabeth. She looked so sweet standing in the doorway to shyly bid him a good morning and to congratulate him on his appointment. Attired in a borrowed black crape frock and a black bonnet adorned with a single red rose, she still looked fetching. All that black only seemed to accentuate the loveliness of her large dark eyes, "peaches and cream" complexion, and pink lips. He was pleased that Ben had agreed that she should stay with them until after Christmas but knew her extended stay would only make it more difficult to release their little friend when it came time for her to return home.

Becky came in to take his tray to the kitchen. "Miss Susanna jus' hitch her horse, Mr. Justin. You want me to get the door?"

"Thank you, Becky, but I'll go to her." He went to stand by the front door and braced himself for an onslaught of admonishments but was taken aback when Susanna merrily waved to him while reaching beneath the driver's seat of her buggy.

"I'll be there in a moment, Justin," she called to him. "I couldn't come without a gift for the birthday girl, so I went into town to shop this morning, and I do believe I found the perfect item." She held up a large valise made of the finest leather and embossed fabric. "Now she'll have something to carry home the clothes and things you all have given to her. I've been told a bit of her story by my father and Charlotte," she said on her way up the porch steps, "but Charlotte wouldn't tell me Miss Libby's age. She begged that I ask you ... but no ... allow me to guess." She giggled upon entering the foyer through the door he held open for her. "Um ... I would guess that she's eighteen, since she was married." She dropped the valise on the floor, took Justin's face in her hands, and kissed him full on the mouth.

"Twenty-six," he loudly blurted, clearly unnerved by this rare show of affection.

She backed several steps away from him, and he watched as the smile of glee faded from her lips. "You jest with me," she said somberly, staring into his eyes. "She's not a mere girl?"

"I couldn't have answered more truthfully," he responded, tearing his eyes from hers to look down at the valise. "I'm certain she'll appreciate your fine gift when it's time for her to return home. Come with me to the parlor. I'll apprise you of the details of her situation and tell you of a surprising visit I had this morning."

He sat her down and relayed as much of Elizabeth's personal history as he felt he should but was careful to leave out the most intimate facts and that she might possibly be pregnant with Billy's child. His better judgment told him that certain details were not his to tell.

"Oh dear!" Susanna said when he finished with the first half of his news. "How horrible to have gone through all that she's weathered," she said with surprising sympathy. "I cannot *possibly* imagine," she said, slowly shaking her head. "You ... you say she's staying here for a while longer?"

"That's correct, until after Christmas, when her brother is able to live with her for several months. It would be too difficult for her to go home to live by herself and have to face all of her past trauma with no support. Clary is anxious that her friend stay here until she's able to move on by herself."

"Clary's friend," she said very softly. She looked at him and sadly sighed, wondering if he realized that she was not stupid or blind. "I suppose what must be, must be," she said weakly. "She ... she has no other family to care for her?"

"Her brother told me their grandparents are deceased, and the only familiar living relative is their father's older sister. She resides with her husband in England, and they have no children of their own. They know none of their relatives living in Martinique, because their grandfather was disinherited by his family when he gave up his birthright."

"Oh … I see. You have other information?" she hurriedly asked, thinking she might burst into tears should they continue with their present topic of conversation.

He told her of his appointment. "I wired your father already. Our client load is small, so he shouldn't be too put out. Besides, the way the trial seems to be going, it may finish shortly."

"I believe my father has completely thrown his energies into acquiring a nomination to run for Congress. He told Mother he wasn't going to accept new clients for the next few months, so he'll not be disturbed if you take a leave of absence." She looked longingly at him for a moment. "I … I really am pleased for you, you know."

He took her hand and kissed it. "I know you are. Thank you, my dear. Oh, I have something for you." He stood up and held his hand out to her. "It's hidden beneath my desk." He took her into the library and handed her the box. "My mother sent it from England," he explained, with a twinkle in his eye.

She unwrapped the pitcher and a goblet then counted aloud the five remaining goblets. "Oh, they're lovely!" she exclaimed, holding the green pitcher up to the light of the window. "But I wonder if they come in blue."

An hour before suppertime, the trio returned from town to find Justin and Susanna sitting on the porch glider, held hostage by the incessant chatter of Vie. When the child spotted the carriage turning toward the path, she ran down the steps to greet them.

"Happy birfday, Miz Lizzybits," she shouted, jumping up and down. "Mama say yo' name weally be Lizzybits, so now I be Vi-o-la."

"Why, thank you, *Viola*, but my birthday was actually a couple of weeks ago," answered Libby as Ben helped her and Clary down from the carriage.

"Dey be pwesents in dem sacks?" she asked, pointing to the many parcels beneath the carriage seats.

"No presents," answered Libby. "Mostly clothing and kitchen and sewing supplies."

"You gonna make cwose fo' yo' baby?" she innocently asked. "Where *is* yo' baby?"

Everyone pretended not to hear the questions, but Susanna immediately turned to lock eyes with Justin. He said nothing, merely patted her hand, and stood up to help carry the parcels into the house. He came down the steps to stand behind Libby, and when she turned to hand him a box of mason jars, she looked up into his eyes and nodded slightly.

"When?" he whispered.

"End of March," she whispered back. "I identified Josiah Staples as the man who beat and robbed me," she added in her normal range of voice. "He couldn't see me, thank goodness, but I could see him. Now that I've identified him, the sheriff says he'll be moved to a holding jail until his murder trial. If I press charges, there might possibly be two trials, one for assault and robbery, and the other for Lottie's murder. The sheriff said it was unlikely that the state would pay expenses for two trials, though. The public defender that also works for the firm of Perry and Glass has been assigned to Staples."

"That would be Arthur Campbell. Strange..." Justin said with skepticism. He recalled being taken aback by Campbell's gray, sickly pallor when he'd delivered a package from Charles to Campbell's firm only last week. "The man has been diagnosed with lung cancer, and it's well known that he was absent more days in the last few months than days worked."

"I have more to tell you but will do so later this evening," she whispered. Looking up to the porch, she saw a pair of glaring eyes. "Good afternoon, Miss Susanna," she cheerfully called, with a broad smile. "You certainly look lovely this afternoon."

"Good afternoon, Miss Libby... and thank you," she responded, somewhat satisfied to see the "birthday girl" attired in mourning clothes. She was convinced that no one could be deemed attractive shrouded entirely in black, yet it did seem to enhance her dark eyes and rosy cheeks. She opened her reticule to make sure she hadn't forgotten her lip and cheek rouge. Then her eyes lit up, and she eagerly went to take the parcel Libby was carrying up the steps. "Allow me to take that," she gaily insisted. "You shouldn't lift in your condition. Congratulations to you! You must be very excited!"

Libby blushed and handed her the less-than-one-pound bag of knitting yarn. "I … um … thank you. You haven't been introduced to my brother." She turned around to capture her brother's attention, but he and Clary were still standing beside the carriage deeply immersed in a private conversation.

Seeing her discomfort, Justin interrupted their conversation. "Ben," he called. "You haven't met my lady yet." Ben went to him, and Clary took hold of Vie's arm to walk her to the back of the house and into the kitchen for a reprimand from her mother.

"I'm so pleased to meet you, Miss Susanna. May I say that my sister is correct? She told me how beautiful a lady you are," he said, determining that she would be flattered by his assessment.

She fluttered her eyelashes and gave him the brightest smile she could conjure. "Well, aren't *you* the little ole charmer," she gushed. She rested her hand on his arm and in a deeply compassionate tone added, "I'm so *terribly* sorry to hear of your misfortune. I know I would be beside myself if I lost my dear papa, but I suppose there's great satisfaction in knowing that your papa's murderer is dead."

"*Susanna!*" Justin abruptly exclaimed, taking her arm to draw her away from Ben. He whispered something into her ear that persuaded her to nod and smile. They both went into the house and left Libby and Ben standing alone on the porch.

Ben looked at Libby with his eyebrows moving up and down in rapid succession. She burst out laughing. "Well, she *is* beautiful," she simply said.

"And that's about all," he responded. He slowly shook his

head, not quite understanding exactly what it was in Susanna that would entice a levelheaded man like Justin to marry her. He was equally puzzled that no man had claimed Clarissa as his own. Now there was the ideal woman. Besides pretty, she had a charming personality, could brilliantly hold up her end of a conversation, and was as intelligent as any man he had ever met. There also was nothing false about the woman. She spoke her mind with a gentility that could never offend. She ... hmm. He opened the door for his sister.

"Suppose you go upstairs and rest until supper," he suggested. "I'll sort out the parcels that are yours and bring them up to you later." When she started up the stairs, he added, "Libby, I'm glad you chose to buy colorful frocks today. No one expects you to mourn for Billy, but you know that Father would never want you to mourn him by wearing black. He would want to see you attired in the most festive of colors to celebrate his reunion with Mother and meeting with his Savior."

"I would like to wear black for a while, for my own sake ... until after the hate inside of me has died."

Libby went to the kitchen to help herself to another piece of birthday cake. Becky dug a large scoop of peach ice cream from the churn and dropped it onto Libby's dish beside the thick slice of vanilla pecan cake.

"Miss Libby, I be so sorry 'bout Vie spillin' yo' personals," she apologized. "She musta heared Miss Clary and me talkin' 'bout you might be carryin' a baby. I know you probly don't want Miss Susanna ta know till you ready ta tell 'er."

Libby leaned over and planted a kiss on her cheek. "I'm not the least bit upset. Vie meant no harm, and Susanna would find out sooner or later," she assured her, placing her arm around her shoulders. "Becky, I would like to thank you for the lovely cake and especially delicious supper. You work *so* hard. You're worth your weight in gold, you know. You've been so kind and helpful to me while I've been here, and I want you to know how much I appreciate you. If you'll allow me, I would like to care for Vie on an evening of your choice and pay for your bill at the White Swan, so you and Abel may have some time alone. Will you allow me?"

"Why ... why, I don' know what ta say!"

"Say yes, of course. We'll talk more of this tomorrow. I should go bid our guests a good night." She picked up her plate and turned to see Justin standing in the doorway. By his tender eyes and smile, he let her know that he had been listening in on most of their conversation. When his eyes focused on her plate, she defensively explained, "I'm eating for two, Counselor."

He moved aside for her to pass and followed her down the hallway to the parlor. Charlotte and Susanna had just stood with the intention of departing.

"I know you have a big day tomorrow, Justin, so you need not see me home. I want you to go straight to bed now, to get a proper night's sleep," Susanna insisted.

Justin raised his eyebrows, surprised that she seemed concerned with the amount of rest he needed.

She looked across the room at Jeremy, who was sprawled out on the floor, sleeping soundly. "Charlotte will accompany me."

Charlotte appeared none too pleased by the suggestion, but since her darling had complained of a headache earlier in the evening, she knew it was in his best interest to continue sleeping. "Well, I suppose we had better leave now to be home before sunset." She turned to Libby. "I hope you had a lovely birthday, dear." She looked over at Clary, who was sitting on the couch close to Ben, the two of them absorbed in reading a chapter from a book on horticulture. "Are we still going to make spice candles tomorrow, Clary? *Clary*?" she asked.

Clary quickly looked up. "Oh ... oh yes. Ben will help us. He says that we didn't add enough stearine to the first batch. That's why they smoked so heavily."

Libby set her plate down on the tea table to hug Charlotte. "This party was a wonderful surprise, and I had a lovely time. Thank you so very much for the beautiful cameo brooch. I never owned one before." She looked at Susanna, who seemed to stiffen at the prospect of being hugged, so Libby held her hand out to her. "And thank you, Susanna, for the beautiful valise. It was so very thoughtful of you."

"Come," said Justin, taking Susanna's arm. "I'll see you and Charlotte out to your buggy."

After everyone said their good-byes, Clary closed her book, stood up, and offered Ben her hand. "Come with me to the kitchen. I give you permission to impress me with more of your exceptional knowledge while I attend to washing the dishes, and Miss Libby may play the piano to entertain us."

"Suppose Libby helps you with the dishes, and I'll entertain you with a Chopin etude," Ben suggested.

"Suppose Ben and I wash the dishes while Clary takes a warm, relaxing bath," suggested Libby.

"Suppose everyone goes to bed so that I may sleep in peace," a groaning voice complained from the floor on the other side of the room.

"Charlotte hasn't taken off yet, if you wish to kiss her good-night," Clary informed him, to which he was on his feet and out the front door in two seconds flat. "You play the piano also, Ben?"

"Why, yes, I do, and quite well, I might add. But please don't ask me to sing. Do you play an instrument?"

"My *stars*, what a talented family! Justin!" she called the second she spotted him coming back inside. "It seems that Ben is also an excellent pianist. Shall we ask him to play?"

"Well, *do* you play an instrument, Clarissa?" Ben asked again, curious as to why she was avoiding his inquiry.

Blushing, she looked down to the floor. "Well, um ... you see ... I had four brothers." Barely audible, she simply mumbled, "Trombone."

Ben tried to keep a straight face, but when a snicker escaped, she slapped his arm in embarrassment.

Justin shut the front door behind him and took out his pocket watch. "I have an hour to spare for entertainment and to speak to our birthday girl alone for a few moments. Court is in session at eight o'clock tomorrow morning, so I'd best retire by nine thirty in order to be chipper enough to catch the early morning train."

"Shall we wait for Jeremy?" asked Clary.

"No. He's following the ladies home on horseback. He'll be gone for hours since Mrs. Dupont is residing in Washington for the week."

CHAPTER 22

Justin turned to see Libby still standing beneath the arched entrance to the parlor. "Well, young lady, pick up your plate and follow me to the library, unless you're finished and ready for a third helping."

"I believe *we've* had enough," she said with a giggle while following him down the hallway.

He closed the door behind them, escorted her to the love seat, and then went to retrieve the journal from his desk. With a warm smile, he sat down beside her. "You seem to be well accepting the prospect of your child."

She nodded. "Ben has made me see that this is a miracle baby, that despite the fact that I've been beaten, tortured, and thrown from a train, it's God's plan that it still lives within me, and ... and I've taken the attitude that through my baby a part of my precious father will live on. While I despise Billy and hate that this child was conceived with cruelty, the little one is still innocent," she said, resting her hand on her lower abdomen.

With a light caress to her cheek and a certain admiration in his smile, he offered her the journal. "I'm giving this to you with instructions. When I come home in ten days, I'll check to see if you followed through with what I asked of you."

She cocked her head sideways and furrowed her brow in mock seriousness. "Will this project be within my ken, Counselor," she asked, "or will I be expected to research?"

"This project can only be from within your ken. You're to

make an entry into this journal when first you wake in the morning and immediately before retiring for the night. You're going to search your past with Billy and write down one good memory of him with each entry and dwell upon that memory for at least five minutes." When she gave an exhausted sigh and rolled her eyes, he firmly said, "I expect to see twenty entries when I return home. I believe you'll overcome your hate for Billy by doing this, and then the nightmares will vanish."

"And the guilt I harbor in creating the monster?"

"The war created the monster, but make a place in the journal where you'll record all of the reasons why you feel this guilt and what motivated the reasons. Writing is very effective. We ask our clients to record all of their memories and thoughts concerning the facts of their case. It helps to cleanse the mind, rather like housecleaning the brain."

"But what if I'm just sweeping the dirt out the door, only for it to become tracked inside again?"

He laughed. "You're being overly analytical. I guarantee that the nightmares will desist, but only you can release the guilt. Pray for that freedom, Elizabeth, as I will on your behalf."

She smiled and nodded. "Thank you. I'll do as you ask. I have one bit of information I didn't care to speak aloud with others in attendance. I asked the sheriff if Josiah Staples had been questioned concerning whether or not he ... he ... " She blushed.

"Violated you," he finished for her.

"Yes," she said softly, looking down at her lap. "The sheriff said that he had been questioned on all charges and claims he never touched me in that ... that sort of way. In his own words, he kept insisting to the sheriff, 'Had a woman of my own for that.'"

"Do you believe him?"

"The sheriff does, because he's been candid in his confessions. On my part, I cannot determine, for I've not spoken to him. Is it wrong for me to wish the death penalty for him? I'll never be able to expel Lottie's final moment from my mind, lying there, so beaten and battered, with no one by her side who dearly loved her." Tears pooled in her eyes.

"No," he reassured her, "it isn't wrong to want Lottie's death avenged. I wish I could speculate what his end will be, but I've come to learn, of late, that true justice lies low in the minds of those given the power and authority to uphold the righteousness of God's commandments. We've become a self-serving, depraved society, composing unrighteous rules and laws to suit the moment. Lately there seems a trend that deems right as wrong and wrong as right."

She rested a calming hand on his forearm. "You're thinking of Captain Wirz. You're troubled over him, aren't you?" she asked. When he nodded, she added, "Jeremy says the Northern press are fabricating their stories and making a mockery out of his defense. I know very little of the Andersonville trial but would like to know more if it will help to alleviate your anxiety."

"After reading the trial transcript, I believe that sitting in that courtroom day after day and not having any authority whatsoever to lend credence to the travesty that this trial has become may serve to persuade me to change my field of endeavor."

"You don't believe your appointment is God's leading?"

He shrugged. "I want to believe that it is. But for now I can only see myself viewing a murder in the making and rendered helpless in assisting the victim. As an alternate and mere spectator, I'll be given no voice whatsoever ... and I know I'll be riled to no end. The problem with military trials is that too much of the allowable evidence is hearsay, without presentation of proof to the credibility of the witness."

He looked into the beautiful eyes that were riveted to every word that came from his mouth, and smiled. "Young lady, this evening we celebrated your birthday, and I ask forgiveness for ending it on so sour a note. I shouldn't be so concerned with this trial because there may possibly be a turnabout as it progresses ... God willing." He squeezed her hand and stood up. "I'm sorry the only gift I have to give you is the journal. Perhaps when next I'm home, you'll allow me take you to the White Swan, where you may eat your heart's desire of their famous liver and onion pie."

She stood up to face him and placed her hand lovingly on his cheek. "You've given me gifts that money can't buy: shelter from the storm, a peaceful haven of love and friendship, and hope to face my tomorrows with strength and determination. For all of this, I deeply thank you." She folded her arms around his neck and pressed her cheek to where his heart lay.

His arms encompassed her, and they held each other for one long moment. "My dear little friend," he softly said. "In the short amount of time you've been with us, you given us a certain great joy in you just being you." He strengthened his hold on her and, in an emotionally charged whisper, avowed, "You're *so* very lovely, Elizabeth. You taught me a lesson this evening, you know."

"And what would that be, Counselor?" she asked with a surprised grin, pulling away just enough to look up at his face.

"You taught me that I've taken certain people in my life for granted. Your kind and thankful words to Becky shamed me, because they're words Clary, Jeremy, and I should be telling Becky and Abel on a daily basis. They've given us more than their all, and we've never heard even one small complaint from either of them. So, sweet lady, you've inspired me to purchase all of the building materials required for them to completely build their home as a bonus for going beyond the call of duty."

"That's marvelous!" she exclaimed. "Will it be a delivered surprise, or will you give them *carte blanche* to purchase the materials on their own?"

"*Carte blanche*, most likely. Hmm… French. Parlez-vous Francais, Madame? I'm curious because of your Martinique ancestry."

"Mais oui, Monsieur, mais seulement un peu. Et vous?"

"Probably much less than you. Your mother didn't help you to achieve fluency?"

"No, she was far more concerned with cultivating my singing voice and teaching Ben and me to play the piano. I believe she resented her ancestors because they disowned her father. The only link she kept to her culture was an old, framed French flag, which displayed the fleur-de-lis symbol. Mama told me the three petals of the iris represent the Trinity. Justin? Why is it that you don't call me Libby? I've only heard you use my given name."

"Do you know the meaning of your name?" When she shook her head, he said, "God's oath."

"You're quite knowledgeable," she said with an amused grin. "Did that just happen to pop out of your brain?"

He laughed and, releasing her to go to the bookcases, came back and handed her a book. "I looked up the meaning."

"*Names, Their Origins and Meanings*," she read from the cover.

"Suppose you look through this to help you find a noble name for the baby." When she said nothing but regarded him with questioning eyes, he said, "I call you Elizabeth because it has a lovely, womanly sound to it and because of its strong meaning and principle."

She hugged the book to her breast and regarded him with a shy smile. "I'm going to miss you these next ten days. You've become *so* dear a friend," she softly expressed. *Lord, forgive me for wishing to feel his lips on mine. I know he's not mine to kiss.*

He moved closer to her, cupped her chin to tilt her face upward, but upon hearing a knock on the library door, pecked a kiss to her forehead and turned to respond.

"The kitchen is spotless, and it's time for Ben to perform," Clary announced, barging into the room before Justin reached the door. She stopped to stare at Libby's red face for a few seconds then shifted her eyes over to Justin's face, and she felt like kicking herself.

"Where is my brother this morning?" Libby asked, sitting down beside Clary on the glider.

She laughed. "He's inspecting the soil in the gardens. The man is literally in love with the dirt in my backyard."

"That's because you've managed to grow things that shouldn't grow well in this area, especially at this time of year. When I was sixteen, we moved from Philadelphia to Wellesley because my thoughtful father bought a house with a large expanse of property for my brother's sake, so that Ben would have some acreage for his botany experiments. Papa also intended to grow poppies for their medicinal value. While his heart was in the right place, he should have taken Ben with him to make the purchase, rather than surprise him. The soil quality was so poor not even fertilizers could cultivate it. It only proved capable of producing wild weeds, sticker bushes, and allowing a few trees to barely remain alive. To Papa, dirt was dirt." Tears welled as she smiled to herself at the fond memory.

Clary rested a comforting arm around Libby's shoulders. "As soon as you're ready to pay homage to your papa, I'll accompany you to Wellesley."

"Perhaps in a couple of weeks. I didn't hear Justin leave this morning."

"He left at sunrise, attired in blue. He looked mighty handsome in his uniform."

"I imagine he would. He's a very handsome man," she said shyly. "I remain puzzled by the fact that your family was divided by the war, yet your bond remains unbroken."

"Jeffrey and Josh greatly respected Justin for his tribunal service. They were fighting for a particular ideal, but Justin was fighting for justice for the entire country. Decisions made through tribunals were for the benefit of the North and South. Living so close to Washington is unlike residing in the Deep South. The population surrounding the city is compiled of people with a variety of political views and ideals. We try to respect each other. We must if we're to live peaceably together."

"My father sheltered me from the complexities of the war. I was only taught that we were fighting to free the slaves and that slavery was against God's will. Clary, what was Mary Anne like? Was she as beautiful as Susanna?"

"I believe there could not be a woman so unlike Susanna. It's not that Mary Anne wasn't pretty. She had golden brown hair, light brown eyes that sparkled with vibrancy, and a certain air of contentment about her. She always appeared to be happy. Small, sentimental things meant much to her, and she was truly a product of her father's upbringing. When she died, you would have thought she and Justin had been married for years the way it touched him. The life seemed to drain from him. If I were to speculate, I would say that Justin set his sights on Susanna because he knows he could never love her the way he loved Mary Anne. Deep down he's afraid to really love again."

"But he's such a strong man ... "

"Not when it comes to matters of the heart. I believe that men find it every bit as difficult as women to rebound from a lost love, perhaps even more so."

Libby nodded. "You *are* correct. When Mama died, she took a vital part of Papa with her. He was never the same. He also felt such guilt that he couldn't have prevented her death with his medical skills. I don't believe he ever could have loved another woman the way he loved her ... and here I am ... not able to muster up even *one* regret that my husband has recently died."

"But your circumstance is like no one else's. Did you make an entry into your journal this morning? Justin told me I might have to prod you."

"Yes. I started from the point where I had just met Billy at a church picnic. No matter where I turned, I could see that his eyes were upon me. I thought him a fine-looking man with disconcertingly bold blue eyes. He came to my father that very evening to ask permission to court me, carrying with him a bouquet of daisies and a kitten in a basket. He had heard me tell a friend that my cat had just died, so he took it upon himself to replace it."

She smiled wanly at the bittersweet memory. "It's very difficult to think of myself as a recent widow, for our marriage died the day he went off to war. Nothing was the same from that day on."

Clary squeezed her shoulder. "You'll be just fine, my darling girl," she soothed.

Libby kissed Clary's cheek. "I know I will. With God and all of you as my guardians, how could I not be? You and Ben appear to have become nearly inseparable in the few days you've known each other."

"That's because I am he, and he is me," she said in a deeply mysterious voice, then burst out laughing. "Have you ever met two people who are so frighteningly alike? I do plan on asking him why he calls me by my given name, though."

Libby laughed. "I asked your brother the same question last night, and he said it was because Elizabeth sounds womanly and has an impacting meaning: 'God's oath.' I looked up Clarissa in a book of name meanings that Justin gave to me to help find a name for my baby. Did you know your name means 'brilliant'? Quite befitting, I would say. Ben must like your given name and most likely thinks it sounds more womanly than Clary."

"Aha! So you think Ben regards me as more than just a female version of himself?"

"Do you wish for it to be so?"

She looked thoughtful. "I believe I do. At least I have the confidence that I wouldn't frighten him, as I have done to so many others. Well, enough talk of men. Shall we go inside for a nice breakfast?"

"Yes. I really feel quite well this morning. I need to speak to Becky about something."

"Justin told me of your offer to care for Vie and a night on the town for Becky and Abel. He was correct in his assessment that you put us to shame. I've been thinking for some time now that because Vie is so bright, perhaps Becky will agree to allow me to teach her to read and learn her numbers and sums."

"Becky cannot read?"

"Barely, and Abel can't read at all. It would be a shame not to educate a child as intelligent as Vie. She can teach her mother and father all she learns."

They were quiet for a few moments, each deep in thought.

"Clary, do you ever feel pity for Susanna?"

"No. Why should I?"

"Because she'll be married to a man who isn't interested in developing a deeply spiritual love relationship with her. I thought much on the subject of spiritual love the entire time Billy was away, and even more so when he came home. I realized it *might* have come about had he stayed home with me and not gone off to war. If Susanna is denied an integral part of marriage, is it fair to her, and shouldn't she be pitied? From what you've told me of Justin and Mary Anne, I believe they had found a spiritual love, and that's why Justin was so wounded by her death. They had become so much a part of each other. I fervently craved that all important element in my marriage, the deep intimacy, what I saw in my parents."

Clary removed her arm from around Libby's shoulders and took her hand. "I suppose I haven't pitied her because I've never thought of marriage as being *spiritually* intimate. But I *do* believe in what you're saying. Perhaps Justin chose Susanna because he knows *she* doesn't care about true intimacy. As long as she's able to live her life the way she chooses, she may simply be content to acquire the matron title so that she's not deemed a spinster. In her social circle, there's a certain stigma at being an aged maiden lady."

"This is tragic for both Susanna *and* Justin, for he denies himself also."

"What are *your* feelings for Justin?" she softly asked. "I believe I know. I saw it from the beginning."

"He's my wonderful friend, and I love him as such, nothing more," she answered, avoiding eye contact with Clary.

"You deny yourself. You need to read it in his eyes, as I've observed."

"Our time together has been too short for anything more than friendship, and I find myself in a position that won't allow a relationship to develop."

"Why? Is it because you're carrying another man's child? What has that to do with anything?"

"Please ... may we speak no more of this?" She stood up. "I'm going inside now. Ben is coming toward us from the field. He probably wishes to be alone with you."

CHAPTER 23

This was a dreadfully painful moment for Libby. She clung tightly to Ben, her face wet with tears, wishing she could beg him to stay a while longer. But she knew he had responsibilities, and life had to move on. Pressing one last kiss to his cheek, she backed away so Clary could bid him farewell.

"I'm confident that you'll give my little sister the best of care, and I thank you profusely for your kind and generous hospitality," Ben warmly said to Clary, while reaching for her hand. "Truly, Clarissa, I've never met a lady quite as special as you. May I kiss you good-bye?"

"I expect you to," she said, giggling coquettishly.

When he went to kiss her cheek, she threw her arms around his neck and made certain the kiss landed on her lips. Then she stepped back and burst into laughter at his red face and somewhat dumbfounded expression. But he assured her with a broad grin that she hadn't stepped out of line. He had thoroughly enjoyed her aggressiveness.

"Wire me when you plan on accompanying Libby to Wellesley," he told her. "If I'm able, I'll meet you there."

"It will be for only one night," Libby informed him. "I merely wish to visit Papa's grave and gather a few of my belongings. You need not come all the way from Boston for a single night."

"Unless you want to," added Clary, staring anxiously into Ben's eyes.

"I believe I'll want to, Clarissa," he responded with a gleam in his eyes.

"Ben ... Ben!" He jerked his head around to look at his sister. "Your train is about to leave."

He grabbed his valise and ran up to the platform and through the only open train door precisely in the nick of time. They giggled as he tried to free the back portion of his coat that was wedged between the closed doors.

"He's so ... so," Clary sighed, "utterly charming."

Libby furrowed her brow and studied the face that was still fixed upon the train that was slowly moving away from them. "Charming" would never have crossed her mind if someone were to ask her to describe her brother.

When the train was beyond their sight, Clary turned to Libby and dreamily asked, "And what would *you* like to do on this incredibly beautiful Saturday morning?" She linked her arm through Libby's.

She shrugged. "Whatever you would like to do. I wonder how Justin is faring," she mused, while climbing up into the carriage and sitting down.

"Today he'll be too busy with his seminar to think about the trial, and I'm certain that Susanna has their evening well planned." As she took her place in the driver's seat, she glanced over at Libby's pale little face. "Aren't you feeling well?"

When her lower lip began to quiver, she pursed her lips and shook her head. Then the tears began to spill. "I ... I suppose it's just the inside of me ... changing ... the baby," she sobbingly said. "I'm having difficulty in controlling my behavior from one moment to the next."

"I've never had a baby, but I'm sure what you feel is as it should be. You're most likely low because Ben and Justin have left us. We'll have dinner, and then perhaps you should take a nap while I complete a few unfinished chores. We'll take a nice long walk after that. Have you ever fished?" Libby shook her head. "We'll go down to the pond to fish for trout and cook them for supper. Would you like to do that?"

Libby nodded. "I wonder where Charlotte and Jeremy are today."

"Aha!" Clary laughed. "I see! You don't care to be alone with me."

Libby laughed through her tears. "You know that isn't so. You're my dearest friend, and I love you. I'm just curious as to where Jeremy and Charlotte go. We've hardly seen them for the last few days. I heard Jeremy tell Charlotte that he was going to live at your parents' house even after Ben returned to Boston."

"I could not care less. Rest assured we'll see him at every meal though."

Once home, Clary suggested that Libby go sit at Justin's desk to read, knowing she would derive a certain sense of comfort and closeness to him.

"You don't want help in preparing dinner?" Libby asked.

"No. It should take me but a few moments to prepare a cold meal made from leftovers. We'll have our hot meal tonight, when we fry the fish. I've never fished in the pond without catching something, the same for my brothers. Go now," she said, gently shoving Libby through the library entry.

She sat down behind the desk and scanned its expanse, taking notice that Justin's "at home" Bible was placed at its usual spot. She drew it in front of her and turned to the book of Psalms, chapter fifty-eight. A large number of notes were written in the margins that hadn't been there one week earlier. *Evidently this passage holds great meaning to him*. She read the entire chapter then sat back to contemplate. Justin had written the word "imprecatory" after the words, *Psalm 58*. She went over to the bookcases to choose a dictionary. The meaning of "imprecation" was "spoken curse." Justin had written *David's cry to God for revenge* and *seven curses on men in authority who abused the judicial system* and *seven (God's special number) equals perfection.*

"Hello, Libby," Jeremy mumbled in a dejected tone. He sauntered into the library and threw himself on the love seat.

"Oh my! You startled me," she answered, closing the Bible and sliding it up to its appointed resting place. "Where is Charlotte?"

"She's preparing to return to Washington with her parents. They insist she attend the White House reception with them tomorrow afternoon."

"Why don't you go? I'll wager you'd be admitted if you mention the Dupont name."

"If circumstances were different, perhaps. I'm no fool. I'm well aware that the Duponts don't fancy the idea of Charlotte and me becoming close. Even though her mother doesn't like me very much, I still might have a chance. But now there's no chance of them accepting me, for Charles and I had quite a heated argument before he saw me to the door, and Charlotte ran upstairs to her room ... weeping. Where is my sister? I need one of her magic headache remedies. Sometimes it pays to have a witch for a sister."

"For that unkind remark, you have no hope that I'll help you," Clary said from the doorway. "Where is Charlotte?"

He repeated his story and added, "It all had to do with my coverage of the Henry Wirz trial. Charles thinks that I'm not seeing the situation clearly. He's such a scalawag! He believes the Northern press is reporting the details accurately. I told him that my reporters and I would print only truth and refuse to fabricate falsehoods just to write a sensational story for our readers. Then he accused me of calling him a liar! How is it that he and Justin have never argued over the fundamentals of this trial? Justin and I equally see the travesty."

"Justin knows better. He's a gentleman and not a hothead like you. But in your defense, you *are* reporting the facts accurately and without sensationalism. The press has far too much power in influencing the reader's thinking," Clary firmly stated. "This has truly become a witch hunt." She looked at Libby. "Please don't misunderstand me. I feel great pity for the Union soldiers that struggled to survive under the given conditions at Andersonville Prison, but—"

"You're not offending me," Libby insisted. "Justin told me the mortality percentage rates in several of the Union camps were as great as Andersonville, some even higher."

"But will the commission take those statistics into consideration? Suppose we eat and put this oppressive topic of conversation aside," suggested Clary. "We're going fishing after dinner, Jeremy, if you care to join us."

"Nothing better to do," he said with a shrug. "I'm going to the city on Wednesday and will stay overnight with Justin, in case either of you should want to send him a note." He stood up. "After we eat, I'll dig up some worms."

"Entry number eight," Libby mumbled aloud. Resting against the propped pillows on her bed, she began to write a few lines about the first Christmas she and Billy spent together as husband and wife. He had helped her prepare Christmas dinner then so thoughtfully waited on her and her father for the remainder of the day, making certain they were happy and comfortable. Papa had even commented at how pleased he was to have Billy for a son-in-law. *But that was so long ago... so long ago.* She leafed through the pages to the section of the journal she designated to be used as a diary, addressing all of her thoughts to "Dear Papa."

Dear Papa,
This morning Ben returned to his teaching position. I believe he's smitten with Clary, or should I say that they're equally smitten with each other. No two are as alike as they. You would love her, Papa, as I do.

I caught my first fish this afternoon. Unfortunately, taking him from the hook caused me to vomit, and not having the heart to eat him for supper, I settled for a bowl of grits (ugh!). But they're not too distasteful if covered with a good bit of butter and syrup.

Only six more days until Justin comes home for the weekend. I fear that I'll live for his visits home. He's always in my thoughts, as are you. His instruction to record happy thoughts of my time with Billy seems to be helping to quell my nightmares of the bad times with Billy. My dreams are still troublesome, but they're of different fears—fear of bearing a child that may be disabled due to Billy's addictions and my physical trauma, fear of raising my child by myself, fear of having to face Josiah Staples in a courtroom, fear of having to face the day when I must leave here for good, forever separated from Justin. I love him, Papa, so very much. I pray that the Lord gives me peace and that I'm able to discern and follow his direction.

Justin picked up the note Jeremy left on his night table. One glance at the flamboyant handwriting told him it had been written by Clary. He removed some of his cumbersome uniform and flopped down the bed to take a short rest before court was to commence, immediately following the dinner hour. Two more days … only two more days, and he could return home, away from the hustle and bustle, the noise, the unpleasant smells of the city, and most of all, the trial. The tension was so grating on his nerves that his head throbbed. He longed for his home haven, with its simple pleasantries and comforts—fresh air; the fragrance of birthday cake baking; sweet giggles; a beautiful, clear soprano voice; his little friend, Elizabeth, such natural loveliness. He no sooner fell asleep when he jolted upright thinking he heard a knock on his door. Once certain that he had, he rushed over to open it.

"Sorry. I didn't mean to disturb your rest. I left my keys on your dresser," said Jeremy. "I've decided not to stay the night and just wanted to inform you. Charlotte's going home this noon to pack for her trip to North Carolina, so I would like to accompany her on the train."

"Are you certain that's a wise idea? According to Susanna, Charles wants you nowhere near Charlotte. It appears that Nathan Wentworth has asked to court her."

"She didn't tell me this in the moment I spoke to her this morning. My stars! Charlotte is nearly twenty-one years of age and old enough to choose her own suitor. Nathan Wentworth is fifteen years her senior!" He slammed his fist on the dresser top then grabbed his key and said, "I've finished my business here, and we'll see if anyone can keep us apart!" He was out the door and down the stairwell before Justin could offer any brotherly words of advice.

"I sincerely hope he doesn't decide to do something foolish," Justin mumbled to himself as he shut the door and went to lie down again and read his note. He unfolded it to read:

> *Justin, we hope you're well enduring the tediousness of the trial and look forward to your return home in two days. We pray for you and Dr. Wirz daily.*
>
> *Libby and I saw Ben to his train this past Saturday morning. It was difficult for Libby (and me) to bid her brother good-bye. While our girl seems to be feeling much better upon waking, I find her to be wan and most melancholy. She anxiously accepts each chore I assign to her, but when not engaged in occupation, she sleeps away far too many daylight hours. I've been unable to coax her to sing and practice the piano, and the couple of times she attempted to, the quality was quite lackluster.*
>
> *After church service this past Sunday morning, I shook Reverend Crabtree's hand and after moving on turned to see Libby hug him and kiss his cheek. The remaining con-*

gregation who stood behind her appeared taken aback by the display, but not the Reverend. Libby simply said to him, "For Mary Anne," and the tears began to flow from his eyes. She sees him as a father who has lost, as she sees herself as a daughter who has lost; thus the common bond. It was quite a touching scene, and he thanked her for her caring disposition. Yesterday he visited to see how well she was faring and to pray with us.

Perhaps I should not say so, but I'm pleased that Susanna will be traveling to North Carolina this Thursday for her cousin's wedding and that she has accepted the fact that the trial presents this as being an inopportune time for you to accompany her. We wish to keep you for ourselves this weekend, and I feel no shame at my selfishness. Love from your sister.

"And I feel no shame that I wish to spend the weekend at home and am not traveling with Susanna, little sister," he said aloud, folding the note and slipping it into his pocket. Every night for the last week he had been dragged to a social gathering, and last night, dragged kicking and screaming. He and Susanna had made an agreement that she would not visit his suite without a chaperone, but this past week she had violated their agreement on several occasions. It surprised him that she no longer appeared concerned for her pristine reputation. Everywhere he turned she was there—at his door when he awoke each morning, waiting outside the courtroom for the trial to adjourn for the day, and *affectionate*. She had been more affectionate during these past eight days than she had been the entire time they'd been engaged. Strange, but while most men would joyously relish this positive change in temperament, he, for reasons unknown, found it overbearing. Oh well. He had the entire weekend to get over his miserable attitude. Blame it on fatigue.

Court would only be in session for half a day on Friday. He decided he would stop at a shop that sold sheet music before boarding the train back to Barrister's—home by three o'clock with a surprise in hand to cheer Elizabeth.

Dear Papa,

This evening I cared for Vie and sent her mother and father on their way to town to enjoy a wonderful supper and much needed time of quiet. This is not mentioned lightly, for Vie is a chatty explosion of energy! But she is so dear! Clary and I were able to teach her the alphabet and some of the letter sounds in a mere one hour. She amazed us with her knowledge of numbers. Clary gave her a small purse of pennies for use in learning her sums, but I believe the child thought the purse was intended as a gift, for it was nowhere to be found when she left us. I expect we'll see her eating a good deal of candy over the next few weeks.

Papa, Justin will be home late tomorrow evening. I feel my spirit begin to soar again at that very fact.

I know you're happy where you are, Papa, but I still cannot help wishing that you had been able to remain with me for many more years. Love to my father and the Father.

CHAPTER 24

Justin dropped his valise and surprise package for Elizabeth on his desk, headed to the kitchen to help himself to a molasses cake, and then went out the back door to stand on the stoop to survey the expanse of property. Becky was picking apples, but Clary and Elizabeth were nowhere in view. When Becky caught sight of him, she pointed to Clary's work shed.

He went to peek into the shed window, and seeing that Clary was working alone, he decided to sneak in from behind and grab her. But when she screamed and thrust her fist back hard against his throat, he realized he had made an unwise decision. She turned to face him with hands on her hips and a look so threatening, he backed out the door, choking all the way. When she saw that her assailant was Justin and not Jeremy, her face brightened, and she went to give him a hug of greeting.

"You do realize that thirty-year-old men should not be playing such childish pranks, do you not?" she asked, giggling with delight to see him.

He laughed. "And with four brothers, you should know that men never really grow up completely. Where is Elizabeth?"

"Sleeping. You're home much earlier than expected. We didn't think you would be home until late tonight."

"Court dismisses at noon on Fridays. How long has she been asleep?"

"Since dinner. She exhausts herself with work for the entire morning, eats dinner, and then literally drops off to sleep until supper. She didn't even care to assist me in making beauty creams and lotions with the enormous container of Italian olive oil Mother sent. Oh, and you now own enough garnished handkerchiefs to see you through to the turn of the century since she spends her evenings engrossed in needlework."

He chuckled. "So she's been asleep . . . *three hours*?"

"That's how it has been every day since Ben left." She sighed. "I asked Dr. Flanagan what he would suggest to give her for her melancholy, but because of her condition, he instructed me not to give her anything except the rusty nail broth. She doesn't realize I add it to her morning tea."

"It's understandable that, now she remembers all of the last few tragic months, she would like some relief from the horrific memories. Few have ever experienced what she just endured. From experience, I know that when the pain begins to subside, she'll eventually return to her stalwart self."

Wait until you see how she perks up now that you're home! "I know she'll be pleased to find you home earlier than expected," she said with a broad smile. "How is the trial progressing?"

He took a deep, disdainful breath. "I prefer not to discuss the trial this weekend. I'd like to devote my time home to lifting Elizabeth's spirit. However, I will tell you that this trial could not be headed more downward. The prosecution habitually tears each defense witness' testimony to shreds. I can barely look at poor, broken Wirz . . . but no. No more talk of him. This weekend is devoted to my family, Jeremy included, since Charlotte has gone to North Carolina."

"I expect that you weren't too put out that he imposed on you for an extra night?"

He raised his eyebrows. "What do you mean? He didn't spend *any* night with me, not even Wednesday, as planned."

"How odd! We've not seen him from Wednesday morning breakfast until dinner this noon. I assumed he decided to stay in Washington for yesterday also. Most of our conversation at dinner today was centered on the subject of planning a Christmas family gathering for Mother and Father, and he mentioned he wouldn't be courting Charlotte this weekend because she was going to her cousin's wedding."

"So he didn't tell you Charles gave Nathan Wentworth permission to court Charlotte."

Clary regarded him with disbelief. "You're not serious! Nathan is an old man!"

"Clary, he's not *that* old—"

"You understand what I mean, too old for Charlotte. Something is strange," she said, shaking her head. "That sort of news would provoke Jeremy to unbridled fury!"

Justin shrugged. "I agree that his reaction is not what I would expect. Well, he is a grown man ... rather ... Shall we wake up our little mama-to-be and take her to supper at the White Swan or another of her choice?" he asked, about to go back to the house.

"That would be lovely, but you go wake her. I'll need another half hour before I'm able to leave here. Also," she called after him, "please help Becky by carrying the bushel basket of apples she picked up to the kitchen."

He set the basket on the kitchen counter, then chose a perfect apple from the top of the pile and sunk his teeth into its crunchy sweetness. He could almost smell the spicy fragrance of the cinnamon apples stewing for canning and the pies baking in the oven. There was truly no place like home, most especially with autumn almost upon them, his favorite time of the year.

"Justin!"

Startled, he reeled around to see Libby standing in the doorway, her face aglow with a brilliant smile, rosy cheeks, and anxious sparkling eyes that appeared completely devoid of even a hint of melancholy.

She laughed. "I didn't mean to startle you. Finish swallowing your bite of apple. I was simply surprised to find you home." Her eyes devoured him from head to toe. He was the epitome of handsome, so regally attired in his blue uniform. She came fully into the kitchen to stand before him and took a bite from his apple, which he had pressed to her lips. "Incredibly sweet," she commented.

"None sweeter, Elizabeth," he affirmed, his eyes taking in every inch of her. "I'm home early because court adjourns at noon on Fridays. I was just about to go upstairs to awaken you and see if you would fancy dining at the White Swan. Clary is agreeable."

Her eyes lit up. "Yes, thank you, I *would*... but tomorrow evening. Tonight, *you,* Counselor, shall rest up from a long, tiresome couple of weeks. Becky had planned on making her famous juicy fried chicken, and with several of these fine apples, I'll make you an apple pandowdy topped with fresh cream. Will that be suitable temptation to persuade you to change your plans?"

Touched, he gently pressed his hand to her cheek and said, "You're so thoughtful."

"No, it is *you* who is thoughtful," she softly said, placing her hand over his as her eyes met his gaze. Intense as was the moment, the clear picture of a fair-haired woman with icy-blue, admonishing eyes stood between them, discouraging either from taking the initiative to embrace the other. Both dropped their arms to their sides. She went to the back door then turned to suggest, "Suppose you change into your comfortable clothes while I talk with Clary for a moment."

"I believe I *will* do that, young lady. What say we meet on the porch glider in ten minutes? I have a surprise for you."

She gave him a radiant smile. "How very sweet of you. I look forward to it," she said shyly. "I'll pare the apples and mix them with the spices while you dress and then meet you out on the porch."

He first followed her to the door, and a faint smile played on his lips as he watched the way her skirt swishy-swayed from side to side and her curls bounced up and down with every step she took toward Clary's shed. *Lord, she has to be the most adorable little creature you ever created. I'm so thoroughly torn between the commitment I've given to Susanna and the undeniably deep attraction I feel to Elizabeth. Give me wisdom and direction. I want to be just in all of my decisions. May I always make thy will my will.*

Libby stuck her head out the front door and, seeing Justin waiting for her on the glider, went to sit beside him.

"I finished making the pandowdy. Clary promised to keep an eye on it so it doesn't burn." She regarded the parcel sitting on his lap. "My surprise?" she asked bashfully.

He set it on her lap, and she untied the string and peeled back the brown paper.

"Music! All sorts! From all eras!" she exclaimed excitedly as she leafed through the pile. "Vivaldi… Schumann's preludes and fugues… Oh! And his eight duet Polonaises for you and me to play together, and… and Brahms' 'Piano concerto #1' and Hungarian dances… W.C. Peters, 'The Frankfurt Belle'… I've always wanted his book of quadrilles! However did you find the soprano only parts for Mozart's 'The Magic Flute'? Mama loved to sing the 'Queen of the Night' arias. This will most certainly be a challenge. Do you realize the range that these cover? I'm not sure I'll be able to reach the notes. I always wondered if a flute could be used to play the highest notes if the soprano's range couldn't reach that height… and… " She looked up at him and could see by his smile that he couldn't have been more pleased with her reaction to his gift. "All of this must have cost a small fortune!" Her cheeks burned red with excitement. She stopped to take a breath and then looked deeply into his eyes. "You're *so* very kind to me. I'll never be able to repay you, you know," she said with such heartfelt expression, it took all of his strength to keep from taking her in his arms to kiss her.

He held his index finger up to her. "I have one more surprise." He reached over the arm of the glider to retrieve a small gift box tied with a silky ribbon and handed it to her. When she just stared at it, he coaxed, "Go on and open it."

She untied the ribbon and slowly lifted the top off to find a small, highly polished mahogany box, its corners etched with gold filigree. When he reached over and lifted the lid, she caught her breath.

"A music box that plays 'Fur Elise'! Oh, how beautiful!" she exclaimed. And when she threw her arms around his neck to hug him in appreciation, his lips found hers before they were even aware of what was taking place. So velvety soft... so incredibly sweet... lingering, yet so thoroughly heart wrenching. She pulled back and looked down at her lap. "It was meant to thank you," she whispered.

"It was I who took the initiative," he said as softly. "Forgive me for taking advantage of your high spirit. I had no right." He took a labored breath and looked up. *Lord, what have I done?*

Tears blurred her vision as she shook her head and waved her hand in the air in an attempt to dismiss the intensity of the previous moment. "Shall we not talk of it again?"

He somberly nodded.

"Beethoven was never one of my best-loved composers, but I've always cherished 'Fur Elise' and played it on the piano quite often. After all, it's 'for Elizabeth,'" she said, with a short, faint giggle.

"Exactly. That's why I had to buy it for you," he said, thoroughly realizing their conversation had become strained due to his action.

"Please... *please*," she earnestly implored, resting her hand on his wrist. "May we please not allow one small indiscretion to become a barrier to our friendship? I would hate so to lose the ability to find comfort in conversing freely with each other."

"You're able to read my mind. We'll forget what took place from this moment on," he said with forced cheer. He took the music box from her and placed it back in its packaging, then stood up and offered her his arm. "Suppose we take a walk. The days are becoming noticeably shorter. We should take advantage of the daylight while we may."

As they walked along the path that led to the pond, he asked, "Elizabeth, what is it that you pray for most? I'm speaking of a need... something that you feel is necessary to be able to derive peace and contentment in your life."

She stopped walking for a moment to ponder. "I believe what I need the most at this juncture in my life is understanding... on my part, that is. I would like to *understand* the purpose for the progression of events in my life from the time Billy returned home to me and why my precious papa had to die. Oh, Justin! I wish you had known him. He was so tenderhearted. His patients loved him, for he was a genuinely compassionate man. I miss him so!" she tearfully exclaimed.

"There, there," he said soothingly, patting her hand. "It wasn't my intention to upset you."

"I... I would like to go home next weekend to visit his grave, since Lydia and Josh will be here the following weekend. You may find this nonsensical, but I've been using the back of my journal to write letters to him. It's a diary of sorts and helps me to feel close to him. I speak to him just as I did every day of my life."

"There's nothing at all strange in that. Clary told me you made all twenty entries."

"Yes, and I have to admit that following your instruction eliminated the nightmares completely. I've come to realize that what had been good in Billy outweighed the bad, and I need to cherish the better times for the sake of my child. My biggest fear now is facing Josiah Staples in a courtroom. I've received no communication from Mr. Campbell or the district attorney concerning my testimony. Do you find that to be odd?"

"Campbell must be ill again, although you'll only be speaking with the district attorney, and Campbell will have to come to him for a transcript of your pretrial testimony. So much for Staples' right to a speedy trial. If I were to wager, I would say that his indigent station and the fact that he's a mulatto that killed his lowborn, common-law wife places him at the bottom of the prosecution's priorities list. They would prefer that he rot in jail before the state has to appropriate the funds to cover his trial costs," he said bitterly. He ran his fingers lightly over her cheek. "But you're not to worry for one moment about his trial, for I'll make certain that I'm with you throughout its entirety."

"And what is it that you pray most for, Counselor?"

"Wisdom, Elizabeth. Wisdom."

Dear Papa,

I believe that your son has captured the heart of my best friend, for you should have seen her face glow with pleasure when the postman handed her a letter from Ben. He must have been scarcely home a moment when he wrote it. It contained a few fine words for me but was otherwise written in a language that was meant for only the two of them to comprehend. Would you believe that he promised to send her crushed minerals of different colors to replace the clay dust she adds to tint her beauty crèmes? Minerals? Clary informed me that mineralized beauty potions were used as far back as Cleopatra's time! Ben convinced her to give up her notion of merchandising scented candles, because they're far too costly to make. He suggests that she only make them for personal use and special gifts.

Justin so appreciated this quiet evening spent at home. I love the way he's completely devoted to his Lord. We had devotions and prayed as a family before bedtime. It was a pleasing time of closeness. I had never experienced this with Billy, prompting me to wonder, had we practiced sharing our faith, maybe our situation might be far different than what has come about. I also cannot help but wonder whether Susanna will allow Justin to communicate with her on a spiritual level. What sort of marriage will they have, Papa? Will either of them find fulfillment in merely existing together? I believe Justin to be wise in all things except for matters of the heart. He must have powerfully loved Mary Anne to be so fearful in fully opening his heart again, but Clary says he always honors his commitments. I have no right to expect him to support and raise a child that is not his own, so a union between us would be unlikely. I will always be his "little friend." Am I content in this? No. How could I? For I love him, and not merely as a friend.

CHAPTER 25

"Would you care for some company?" Justin asked Libby. He shut the front door behind him and went to stand next to the glider where she sat contemplating that the weekend was nearly at a close. The sun had just disappeared over the horizon, and a cool, gentle, dry breeze reminded them that summer was transforming into autumn.

Libby could feel the gloom of melancholy slowly wash over her again, knowing that Justin would be leaving for Washington in the morning. The past couple days of his companionship had been glorious, its moments spent in meaningful, fulfilling conversation, gay laughter, and joyous music. It was difficult to accept the fact that *Susanna* and Justin would be sharing the glider this time next week.

"Or would you prefer to be by yourself?" he asked, when she failed to respond.

"Of course I would like for you to sit beside me," she said demurely, smiling up at him and patting the vacant seat.

"May I bring you something, more dessert or milk?" he asked before taking his seat.

"I'm fine, thank you, and not hungry for a change."

He chuckled a bit but said nothing. They remained silent, each somberly pondering the fact that their time together was nearly over, and it might be weeks before they could find a few moments to spend together … alone.

"Will you be whiling away most of the upcoming week's

daylight hours in my bed, Elizabeth?" he asked. "Allow me to rephrase that question," he added with a laugh when she looked at him sharply. "Will you be wasting the daylight hours by sleeping away your problems?"

"I'm sorry if you find me slothful. I … I'll try to do better," she said with teary eyes.

"That was not my meaning at all," he said gently, taking her hand, "and you know it."

"Sleeping makes time move faster," she simply said.

"And when would you like for time to finally slow down?"

The well of tears overflowed onto her cheeks. "When all of the painful memories have gone," she sobbed. "It's time for me to go home to pay homage to my papa and put him to rest," she said in a way that tugged at his heart.

"But not to stay," he blurted with a certain anxiousness.

She shook her head. "No. No, I'm not ready to live alone. But perhaps if Ben were able to live with me … " She looked at her lap, relieved it was now too dark for him to read the frustration on her face at her inability to put the weight of her heart into words.

He casually rested his arm around her shoulders. "You can't seem to accept the fact that you're not imposing on us by living here. You're our little friend, and we enjoy having you with us," he said soothingly, kissing the top of her head in a brotherly manner. *Tell her what you really mean to say, you bumbling fool!*

To his surprise, she stood up, squared her shoulders, raised her chin, and swiped away her tears with her fingertip. "I'll send a telegram to Ben in the morning informing him that I plan to go back to Wellesley at the end of next week. I'll say goodnight to you now. I'll pray that your week goes well, and I imagine I'll see you again the weekend following when Lydia and Josh are here. Goodnight." Without waiting for him to respond, she walked swiftly and determinedly back into the house and up to her room.

It didn't take him any time to realize the gravity of her reaction to his latest comments. The way he had kissed her on Friday afternoon made it impossible to simply brush the moment aside and forget, by either of them. That heart-rending moment could not have left any doubt in her mind that he considered her more than *merely* his little friend. A hypocrite! That's what he considered himself, pretending to hold her with brotherly affection. And he knew by the way she had returned his kiss that she could not be content in *being* merely his little friend. He wasn't sure if he was ready to allow this sort of confusion to barge into his secure little world.

Before Elizabeth had come into his life, things were organized and simple. He knew where he was headed, and he didn't need to be concerned that there might be a chance of experiencing a broken heart again. It had taken far too long—seven years—to heal. Seven years to finally be certain that there could not be another woman on this planet who could so fully take the place of his precious Mary Anne ... until Elizabeth. In the short time he had known her, she had captured him—body, soul, and spirit. He realized that she had invaded every one of his thoughts and dreams over the last couple of weeks. But none of the emotions that he was experiencing seemed rational to him. He'd hardly known her for any decent length of time, yet he felt as if he had known her for his lifetime.

Only last month she had been another man's wife, and was even carrying that man's child. But he didn't care about all that. He only knew that he wanted and needed her, that he couldn't be whole without her. The pure irrationalness of the entire situation went harshly against his grain. He couldn't fathom how finding himself in love with Elizabeth could be God's will, even though he knew that God's will didn't always appear rational to an ignorant human being. And surely it couldn't be God's will to hurt Suzanna.

But the voice of wisdom inside of him told him that he had no right to become engaged to a woman whose values were so dissimilar to his in the first place, and it reminded him that there would always be a penalty to pay for willful disobedience. Perhaps it was good that he and Elizabeth wouldn't be seeing each other for two weeks. It would give each of them time to clear their heads and start afresh. But he knew he was fooling himself. Before this weekend, he had been separated from her for ten days, and she had only nestled herself more deeply into his heart. *Give it time*, he told himself. *See what plays out.* He decided to go to his office for a quiet time of prayer and meditation so that God could speak to him.

Dear Papa,
This evening I did something that I later realized to be reprehensible. I shunned Justin, and for no reason at all on his part. He is, after all, engaged to marry another, and I am but a guest in his home. I have no right to expect him to treat me as more than a friend. How could I display such audacity?

You always taught me that men react differently than women to "affection." I believe I may have misread a kiss between us. To me, it seemed deeply spiritual. I regard Justin so highly that I'd forgotten the fact that because he's a man, he simply may have considered the kiss a moment of physical pleasure. After all, I'm the one who threw myself at him to thank him for his gifts. Most certainly he would have "seized the moment." Yet my heart continues to tell me that the kiss meant so much more.

Much as I regret a two-week separation from him, perhaps it's for the best. I must protect myself for the well-being of my baby. The day will arrive when Justin and Susanna marry, and I must make certain that my wits are still intact and my heart has remained strong. Does it not appear strange to you that I should fully love him in so short a time? I believe it's his strength of character that I find to be so com-

pletely compelling. There's a certain power in the integrity of his character, and I'm certain that others will benefit from it as time goes on. He's been naturally gifted with qualities that most men can only hope to someday aspire to. I pray that God grants him the wisdom to make ultimate use of these gifts.

She closed her journal, set it aside, and then took out a sheet of stationery from the drawer of her bedside table. Justin deserved a note of apology.

Dearest Justin, I beg that you forgive me for the display of disrespectful behavior that you witnessed on my part earlier this evening, for no one could be more undeserving of such an exhibition. Who am I that I should take liberties in presenting myself in such a way? You have always been kind, thoughtful, and generous to me in every respect, and it pains me to think that I may have wounded you. I am truly blessed and grateful in that you are my dear friend, and I thank the Lord daily for your precious fellowship. Yours always, Elizabeth

She folded the note, went out into the hallway to slip it under the door of the guest room, and then knocked on Clary's bedroom door.

"Come in. I'm just reading."

Libby went in to sit on the edge of Clary's bed. "Are you comfortable with my decision to go to Wellesley next weekend? The trip will take more than half a day, so perhaps we should think about spending the entire weekend, Friday to Monday. I hope Ben will be able to meet us, but it *is* a very long train ride from Boston."

"I promised I would go with you. I finished writing a letter to Ben only fifteen minutes ago and invited him to spend Thanksgiving here. Do you realize your aunt and uncle live only twenty-five miles from my parents? Your family lives in Somerset, mine in the neighboring county of Gloucestershire. Have you ever visited your aunt?"

"Once, but I wouldn't recall as much as Ben, for I was only ten years old. What I remember most was that Mama and I were seasick for the entire time coming and going. Had we first-class accommodations, rather than a cabin below deck, it may have not been so hard on us. I do recall finding it amusing that the names of my aunt and uncle are Sarah and Clive Wellborn. If you saw their home, you would know 'Wellborn' is a descriptive adjective. I found it rather palatial, far too many rooms for two people. Is your parents' home large?"

She shrugged. "It's said to be so, but I've never seen it. Someday… Why are you not occupying your time with Justin? The evening is still young."

Libby giggled. "Why are *you* not occupying your time with Justin … or Jeremy?"

"I'm not in an argumentative frame of mind this evening, so I wouldn't be able to tolerate Jeremy. He's probably in his room at Father's house, pining over Charlotte. He certainly was quiet and pensive for most of this weekend, *and* I wish for *you* to be alone with Justin."

"Why?" she softly asked. "Why should I? What purpose would it serve?"

"Because you and he shall marry someday." She stared hard into Libby's eyes. "Do you think me blind? Be honest with me, Libby, and I'll be completely honest with you concerning my regard for Ben. What we privilege to each other will remain within our confidence only. I will tell you that despite the nominal amount of time I've known him, I'm certain that there could not be a couple more suited to one another than Ben and me. But because he's a man, I may have to make him realize so."

Libby had to smile. "I don't believe you'll have to try very hard. You so utterly charmed him with your interests and intellect, and I'll tell you that he confided in me that he finds you to be very pretty and thoroughly captivating."

Clary's face beamed. "He's everything I've dreamed of as a husband and a kindred-kind. We spoke on every subject under the sun during his stay here, probably discussed more than most couples do over an entire lifetime."

"Then you believe you love him already, after only two weeks?"

She nodded. "I have no doubt that God made us for each other, as I have no doubt God made you and Justin for each other. You talked of a spiritual intimacy as being an integral part of a fulfilling marriage. I feel this with Ben, as I see it with you and Justin. But you may have to make him realize so. He's spent the last seven years protecting his heart. I believe you're even more suited to him than Mary Anne, for you also communicate with each other through your like-musical abilities, as Ben and I do through our like abilities. Will you confide in me that you love him, Libby?"

She nodded. "Yes, I love him," she softly admitted, "but I could never be as bold as you. Justin is engaged to marry Susanna. He's an honorable man who has made a commitment. I could never ask him to become less than what he is."

"You mean in breaking his engagement to Susanna? It would be dishonorable to *marry* her. You see that he's not content when he's with her. Their ideals are worlds apart. To marry her would be a travesty to both of them."

"I would like to allow God and time to bring my life into order. I'm too recently widowed to be considering a love relationship, and I'm carrying another man's child."

"Don't allow the dictates of society to regulate your life. Your situation is far different than a woman who recently lost a decent, loving husband. Your husband abused you and murdered your father. I know my brother. Your child would be his in every respect."

"Even so, I would like for Justin to have full knowledge of his preferences and to take the initiative in accomplishing his goals with no goading whatsoever. I ask that you please respect my choice in not actively pursuing him."

"I respect your choice because I'm confident my brother will do what is right."

Libby stood up and leaned over to kiss Clary. "I'm going to retire early tonight. I would like to be at the telegraph office as soon as it opens tomorrow morning. I'll post your letter to Ben. Goodnight."

"Pleasant dreams, dear."

Libby stepped out into the hallway and shut the door behind her the very moment Justin came out into the hallway from his room. She smiled sweetly at him and bid him a goodnight. But when she went to pass him, he took her by the arm and led her away from Clary's door and leaned her against the door to her room.

"I read your note of apology," he said with a grave expression. He took her by her shoulders. "Don't you ever, *ever* think that I'm deserving of an apology after the demeaning way in which I tried to manipulate your thinking by pretending that our relationship is less than what it really is. The truth being I don't consider you a sister or mere friend. But you know this. I say it because you need to hear it, and my wish is to always be completely honest with you. That is the only way it can be between us. Do you understand me?"

She nodded. "I do ... but I suppose the only way we can come together freely is to ask God to direct us on to a clear path. You and I both have issues that need to be resolved, and it will take time. Because I'm newly widowed, I'll need time to put my past behind me before I'm able to face the future. I've not even laid my father to rest yet." She sighed. "And I should feel some sort of remorse for my dead husband, in memory of what was once good between us. I ... I don't wish to use you as a 'crutch,' Justin, and I know you realize the issues that you need to resolve."

He nodded. "I do ... and I will. I have to put my house in order before I'm able to ask you in, and I want you to know that I welcome you to lean on me any time you need a crutch. I'll always be here for you. I pray you have a safe trip. Goodnight, dear." He took her hand, kissed it, opened the bedroom door for her, and shut it behind her.

Thank you for Justin, Lord. She leaned against the closed door. *I long for the day when I'll finally hear those three glorious words from him: I love you. Please clear a path for us to come together. I pray for Susanna, because I know my heart would rip in two if I knew he wished to disassociate himself from me. Give her the strength to be able to move on with her life, and please grant Justin the wisdom needed in dealing with his issues. Because of the tremendous love he has for you, Lord, I'm confident that he possesses the great capacity to love me in the deeply spiritual way I need to be loved.*

CHAPTER 26

Clary popped the final bite of her sandwich into her mouth, folded the sack it came in, and rested her head against the back of the train seat.

"We're almost there. It's good we're heading north rather than south. At least the trains up here are running close to schedule. The Duponts must have found it grueling having to change modes of transportation so many times during their trip to North Carolina. It will take years to repair all the damaged tracks on the southern lines. You may want to place that sack between your head and the seat to protect your hair. The seat cover is gooey with hair tonic… and dear knows what else. Ugh!" Libby shivered. "I'm glad we're not overridden with those oily carpetbaggers up here. The trains in Washington were full of them. I never realized how big a problem they were becoming."

Clary unfolded the sack and wedged it between her head and the seat. "I should have worn a bonnet. I have a word of caution for you. *Never* mention the word 'carpetbagger' in Justin's presence. He believes they're one of the lowest forms of human life and will take up a good hour of your time explaining why. Oh, I can't *wait* to see Ben!"

"Don't be too disappointed if he can't be with us. He only promised to *try*. It's a long trip from Boston for so short a visit. Besides, you received a letter from him every single day last week. Won't they suffice in case he's unable to make the trip?" Libby giggled, knowing her friend was anxious to see Ben face to face.

"He'll be there," Clary affirmed with pure confidence.

"Prepare yourself. Only one more stop to go. You'll like Sally and Dr. Tim. They were friends to Mama and Papa from the time I was born. I believe Sally always hoped that Ben would marry her only daughter, Emma Jean." Sighting Clary's pouting mouth, she added, "Not to worry. Emma Jean married near the time I married Billy." She reached beneath the seat for her valise. "Next, a short ride by coach to where Sally will be waiting with her carriage."

"Do you suppose Billy's parents will come to visit with you?"

Libby shrugged. "My in-laws are queer people, the kind of folk that keep their distance. Mother Prescott's letter only stated how sorry they were at all that came to pass, and they wished to give me a more than fair price for my house. Billy's sister, Lavinia, would like to live in it. She has always admired the workmanship of her brothers. I'm thankful that Billy placed the deed in my name before the war started. I know that most husbands were not so thoughtful. I must record this thought in my journal for my baby to someday read."

Justin impatiently waited for the two o'clock train, although he was not so eager to return home for the weekend. While Elizabeth's precious presence would not be there to greet him, he was relieved to be away from the overwhelming tediousness of the week's courtroom drama. And what a drama it had been! It was inconceivable to him how any of the commission could have possibly found that last witness, de la Baume, to be credible. He had watched them nodding in agreement to the points made during testimony—a testimony that was so clearly contrived, only a fool could be taken in by it. Fools! That's what they were, and blind fools at that—the entire nine of the tribunal, every last one of them! Such *selective* use of evidence!

He reasoned that he should calm down, that he would never

be rid of his pulsing headache if he continued to allow himself to become so agitated. As his eyes perused his surroundings, he scowled. Carpetbaggers were everywhere, in every direction he looked, interspersed throughout the crowded station platform—leeches, lowlifes, thieves, preying vultures, every last one of them!

"Justin! Stop, please!"

Justin looked around to see Charles Dupont approaching. So they had finally returned from North Carolina. According to Susanna, they were to return to their Washington suite by Wednesday. He forced a welcoming smile and accepted Charles' outreached hand.

"Good afternoon. Susanna had said you would be back in town by Wednesday."

"We had transportation problems. Most of the rails heading south are in ruins. By the time we arrived at our destination, we nearly missed the wedding. We decided to take an extra day to recuperate before returning to Washington and didn't arrive in town until late last night. I promised Susanna that if I happened to catch up with you, I would tell you she'll be visiting with you this evening. If you would be so kind as to wait for the next train, I have a few topics I wish to discuss with you."

"Suppose we go out to the street and find a bench. It's far too crowded here." He gestured for Charles to lead the way.

"How is the trial coming along?" Charles asked when they were seated.

"Not well… for Wirz. But you and I stand at odds on the matter, and I would rather not offend you with my opposing opinions."

"That's what I like about you. You're a true gentleman and not a scrapper like your brother. Jeremy is one of the matters I would like to discuss. You're aware that I've given Nathan Wentworth my blessing to court Charlotte."

"I'm aware. However, if your desire is for me to persuade Jeremy not to pursue Charlotte, I'm afraid you're wasting your time. He has always been strong-willed, and he's twenty-two years of age, so I have no authority over him. The most I can do is to *suggest* that he honor your decision... and hers, if Nathan is who she wants."

"Sometimes young ladies don't really know what they want, so their fathers must decide for them. Nathan possesses the fortune to keep her in the manner to which she's accustomed. He may also be influential in changing her back to the lady that she once was," he added, with a sneering sort of smile.

Justin didn't respond to the remark. He liked Charlotte far more now than he had before... well, before Elizabeth had come into their lives. When Charles realized that he was getting nowhere concerning Jeremy, he moved on to the next topic of discussion.

"How much longer do you think the Andersonville trial will go on?"

Justin shrugged. "I can't honestly say. But by the way it's progressing, I don't see how it could last too much longer. Why? Has your workload become so great that you need my help? I have time in the evenings and Saturdays to assist you... if Susanna will allow me that time," he added anxiously, with a hopeful smile.

"No. The case that I'm about to explain to you will be all your own. I only found out about it this morning, but the district attorney assured me there's no rush for you to begin working on it. This will be your personal pro bono case, and as soon as it has completed, you'll be given a full senior partnership."

"Tell me of the defendant."

"His name is Josiah Staples, and I'm already aware that you're well acquainted with his case and crimes."

The color drained from Justin's face. He could feel his heartbeat accelerate to a tempo that pounded like a gavel against his throbbing temples. "But... but," he sputtered, "I can't take his case. Elizabeth Prescott is living in my home!"

Charles chuckled. "I was fairly certain you wouldn't be too pleased with your assignment when it was handed to me."

"How can I defend the man who assaulted and robbed my houseguest?" Justin asked. A wave of nausea swept over him, and he could literally feel the beads of sweat break out on his forehead. "Will there be two trials?"

"One. Staples beat and murdered his . . . whatever she was . . . because she wanted to return what he had stolen from Mrs. Prescott's person after he assaulted her. The charges are assault leading to second-degree murder of Lottie Harmon, assault and robbery of Mrs. Prescott, and robbery of Miriam Bingham."

"But . . . but he's guilty!" Justin exclaimed incredulously.

Charles laughed. "I believe you could use some rest, my man. Ninety-eight percent of your clients will be guilty. You know that."

But this case is personal. How will I ever explain this to Elizabeth? "Who . . . who is Miriam Bingham?" he asked, arduously trying to hold on to his composure.

"Staples climbed into her first-story bedroom window and stole a diamond ring and necklace from her dressing table. Both pieces of jewelry have been confiscated and returned to her."

"I thought Arthur Campbell had been assigned this case."

"So you didn't hear that he died this past weekend."

"No, no I didn't. Poor man," he mumbled. *Lord, how did this happen? Why me?* He silently prayed instead of standing up and shouting to the sky, as he felt compelled to do.

"You might want to consider sending your houseguest back to her home in Pennsylvania if you feel that you can't perform adequately in her presence. She can always be wired to return to Washington when comes time for her to testify." He studied Justin's anguished face. "You and I both know that Staples is guilty and will most certainly spend the better portion of his life in prison. All you need do is see that he receives his rights and that the trial goes without a hitch. I can't understand why you're distressed so."

"Distressed" doesn't begin to describe what I'm feeling at this moment, he thought. *I made a promise to Elizabeth to be her guard-*

ian throughout this trial, not to harm her by defending her perpetrator. And send her home? Unthinkable!

Charles gave him a light slap on the back then stood up. "You appear exhausted. I'll request that Susanna allow you to rest this evening. Suppose tomorrow evening you come to our house for supper. We'll talk more about the case then. The district attorney asked Campbell's associates to gather his paperwork and send it to you by messenger. Also, he'll be speaking to Mrs. Prescott next week, upon her return from Wellesley. I told him he'd best see her soon, just in case she decides to go home for good... or unless you weary of her and send her packing," he added with a laugh.

Justin stood up with eyes flared. He clenched his fists to the sides of his body. It was all he could do to keep from using one of those fists to give Charles a swift hook to the eye. Send her packing! Who did he think he was that he could regard her in so disrespectful a manner?

"Elizabeth Prescott is going to stay *exactly* where she is until she feels it's time for her to move on. And she is anything *but* an imposition," Justin sternly informed him.

"So you *are* fond of her," he simply replied, but in a way that incited Justin to know that Charles and Susanna had had a discussion concerning the possibility that he and Elizabeth might be coming too familiar with each other and the fact that Charles had been informed that Elizabeth was in Wellesley for a few days.

But Justin didn't care. "I'm *quite* fond of her, as is my family. She's a lovely young woman of character. Everyone who comes to know her is fond of her."

"I see," Charles said somberly, with a slight nod of his head. The men stared hard into each other's eyes, each one knowing that not another word need be spoken. They understood each other precisely.

Justin abruptly nodded his farewell then turned on his heels to make his way back to the train platform.

"I cannot imagine where Sally could be. She's always punctual," Libby said, searching the landscape with worried concern in her eyes. She perused the length of street before them, hoping to glimpse Sally Morrow's carriage coming toward them. They had been waiting for nearly an hour.

A young girl stood by the side of the road with a pail of bunched flowers. Libby handed her valise to Clary. "I'm going to buy flowers for my father's grave. Please wait here for me. I told Sally I would be waiting for her on this spot beneath the bridge."

When she had distanced herself some twenty yards from Clary, she heard a delighted squeal, and turned around to see Clary held in the arms of Ben. She smiled at the sight. How endearing a moment! Clary had been correct in her assumption that Ben would be there. She decided to take her time in choosing the flowers to enable them a few moments of intimacy.

"Are you surprised, little sister?" Ben asked when Libby returned to them. He handed her a brown paper bag, and she handed him the flowers.

"I am, but my friend was confident that you would be here." She opened the bag and peeked inside. Immediately her eyes lit up. "Pretzels!" she exclaimed, taking one out to hand to Clary. "A Philadelphia tradition for over forty years now," she explained. "One cannot come into the city and not buy at least one to nibble on. There are a half dozen in here. Thank you."

"Two bunches of flowers?" he observed aloud, returning the flowers to her so he could carry their valises.

"For Papa and Billy." When Ben's brow furrowed disapprovingly, she added, "I must lay Billy to rest also, if I'm to become whole again. Take us to the carriage now."

"This tastes very good... similar to a chewy bread," Clary commented as they followed Ben to a small lot where several buggies and carriages were hitched. "I'll wager they're best hot from the oven."

"Suppose we bake a batch when Lydia is with us next weekend? The men will be spending the entirety of Saturday installing the plumbing into your parents' home. Vie would probably enjoy helping also. I know Sally will have a pretzel recipe in her Amish cookbook... Where *is* Sally?" she asked Ben. "And how did you manage to persuade the school to give you the time to come to Wellesley?"

"I had no trouble being granted permission to take several days away from my teaching position. After hearing our tragic story, my superiors were more than happy to allot me the time. Besides, I knew you would need me here for moral support. I had wired Sally that I would like to meet you so that we might stop at the cemetery before we go home. Sally said she would be waiting there for us with a hot supper. She's mighty anxious to see you. How have you been faring, sweets? Are you still ill upon waking?" He stashed the valises beneath the seats.

"I feel in perfect health and have for several days. Mrs. Flanagan told me that I should be feeling my very best during my second trimester, which began a few days ago ... hm! And she would be correct!"

"You look wonderful," he commented, helping her climb into the backseat of the carriage. Turning to help Clary, he whispered into her ear, "And you, Miss Clarissa, you're looking even prettier than when I last saw you ... if that be possible."

She waved her hand and gave him a peck on the cheek before he helped her settle herself beside his driver seat.

Libby enjoyed listening to Ben and Clary chatter nonstop on topics to which she had no inkling. It was the amiableness in their way with each other that pleased her so. She sighed. Her heart ached to be near Justin, and she wistfully longed for the day when he and she would be free to truly enjoy each other with no holds barred.

When they arrived at the entry gate of the Wellesley Memorial Cemetery, Ben and Libby insisted that Clary accompany them to their father's gravesite because she had been somewhat apprehensive at first, feeling they should be permitted private time as a family. They walked fifty yards down a path that led to their mother's grave, and the very second Libby cast her eyes onto the large mound of bare soil beside her mama's resting place, she broke into a sob and hurriedly walked ahead of them. She dropped to her knees beside her papa's headstone and laid a bouquet of roses at its base. Ben came to kneel beside her and took her hand, while Clary stood back to observe the pair through misty eyes. Upon viewing tangible evidence of the tragedy's end result, the realization of what had taken place touched her fully for the very first time, and her heart went out to them.

After spending a lengthy amount of time in meditation and prayer, they stood up, but only Ben went to rejoin Clary.

"Billy's buried on the other side of the cemetery. Libby wishes to pay her final respects, so we'll head back to the carriage," he explained. Glancing upward to a gloomy gray sky, he hoped Libby wouldn't get caught in a downpour. "You're cold," he commented to Clary when she emitted a shiver. He encircled his arm tightly around her shoulders to walk her to the carriage.

When Libby came to the Prescott family section of the cemetery, she made her way over to the only mound of fresh dirt that had been packed between the gravestones of Chester and Harley, Billy's two older brothers. No marker for Billy had been placed at the end of the dirt mound, and she wondered if his parents expected her to take care of the matter. But no, they had only learned that she was alive a couple of weeks prior. She was curious as to what sort of reaction she could expect when she informed them that they were to become grandparents. How could they not be pleased? This grandchild would be their first. But still ... they were strange people.

She set the bouquet of daisies where his headstone should have been placed and stared ahead, wondering what she could say to put him behind her. *Forgive. Simply forgive.* Shivering in the frigid breeze, she pulled her shawl tightly about her shoulders and allowed her eyes to survey her surroundings. Dozens of dirt mounds in various degrees of aging scattered the expanse of the cemetery. Time hadn't even replaced all of the grass that once grew above where Billy's brothers lay. So many wasted lives—all victims to the most recent folly of man. So much love lost ... and so many lost loves. She looked back down to the mound that covered the one whose love she had lost, the one who had lost her love. But his face suddenly flashed before her; a radiantly smiling face, with tender, love-filled eyes; a face that she had seen so often ... so long ago. The tears and the rain began to fall.

"Oh, Billy!" she cried through her tears. "I want to always remember the very best in you, not so much for my own sake, but for our child's. You were every bit as much a victim as I, for the war robbed you of your wonderfully kind and loving nature. I must ask that you forgive me for not being the proper helpmeet that I had pledged to be before God, and I *must* choose to forgive you, because the Bible, Matthew 6:15, tells me that God will not forgive those who cannot forgive. It's far easier for me to forgive you for your treatment of me than it is to forgive you for taking the life of my dear father. But I *do* forgive you so that I may release you, and for the freedom and dignity that only true forgiveness can bring."

CHAPTER 27

Justin sat peacefully rocking on the porch glider, hoping that a dose of cool, crisp air might help rid him of a throbbing headache brought about by a solid week of frustration and tension. He figured Jeremy would know exactly which of Clary's many vials of medicinal powders would be a designated headache reliever. Seeing that Jeremy's horse was hitched outside his parents' house, he decided to mosey over to bring him back to prepare dinner together since Clary had given Becky and Abel time off from their chores while she accompanied Elizabeth to Wellesley.

Surprised to find his parents' front door unlocked, he entered without announcing himself. As he passed by the parlor, his nose and peripheral vision picked up a foul odor and a sort of chaos. Aged food-caked dishes, utensils, and glasses were piled up in every direction he turned. And when he happened to glance out the window, he saw that an unfamiliar horse stood grazing in the grass on the side of the house that couldn't be viewed from the other house.

Knowing that his mother wouldn't take kindly to Jeremy's thoughtless lack of responsible care for her home, he headed upstairs to deal a harsh reprimand. But upon opening the door to the guest room, he stood grounded, trying to comprehend exactly what it was he had happened upon. By the girth of what lay hidden beneath the bed covers, he knew that more than one individual had to be in occupancy. Taking a couple steps closer, he could see several long strands of golden hair caught between two pillows. Charlotte! And the only other possible occupant had to be Jeremy.

Well provoked to verbally make his presence known, he stopped short when he noticed that a large array of women's clothing hung in perfect view by the fact that the wardrobe door had been left fully ajar. But something inside of him told him to let them be and to question Jeremy later, in private. He stealthily backed out into the hallway but left the door open so Jeremy would know someone had discovered his secret rendezvous.

He hastily retreated back to his front porch, dropped down onto the glider, and exhaled a deep sigh. If his head wasn't aching so, he might be a tad more concerned as to when all of hell was going to break loose—when Elizabeth learned that he was to defend Josiah Staples, when Charles learned that his daughter and Jeremy had become intimately involved, or when he informed Susanna that he had come to dearly love Elizabeth far more than he loved her. Elizabeth's presence—now there was a sure anecdote for any manner of ill state. Just a mere mental picture of her seemed to bring a certain dose of relief from the pain. He wished he had been able to accompany her on her trip so he could lend her his shoulder to weep upon, his arms to hold her securely, his ear to vent her frustrations, and to see her lovely smile, warm expressive eyes, and soft, kissable lips.

"Justin!"

He glanced over to see Jeremy walking through the field between the houses. Holding up his hand in acknowledgement, he wondered how he should admonish his brother concerning his extreme indiscretion. Strangely, he felt little anger over the situation. He somehow knew that his brother's spiritual upbringing would never allow him to fornicate. When Jeremy came to the base of the porch steps, Justin merely looked down at him and asked, "When did you and Charlotte marry?"

Jeremy came up to sit down on the top step. "In Washington, the day before Charlotte went to North Carolina," he nonchalantly stated. "You're not going to beat me senseless or have me drawn and quartered?"

"I might give you a stern piece of my mind if my head wasn't about to explode. However, I do have one question that I'm compelled to ask: do you love her?"

Jeremy nodded. "Yes, I love her . . . just as you love Libby." When Justin raised his eyebrows, he added, "None of us are blind to your adoration, including Charlotte *and* Susanna. It can be read on your face every time Libby steps into your presence."

"So I'm that apparent," he softly said, his heart warming as he envisioned her loveliness in his presence.

"All too clear. I wasn't about to allow Charlotte to be courted by Nathan Wentworth, and because you'll most likely be disengaging yourself from Susanna within time, Charlotte and I knew we best marry now, before we were forcibly separated by Charles." He stood up. "Charlotte is dressing. I told her that you and I would begin to prepare supper. I believe some feverfew powder mixed into white willow bark tea should give you some relief. Clary keeps those two items in the pantry, since this family appears to suffer from an exorbitant amount of headaches." He opened the door for Justin. "Have you decided where you'll go for employment after Charles discharges you, disowns Charlotte, and orders a public flogging for me?"

"Perhaps now is the time to accept Richard's partnership offer."

"He would greatly appreciate partnering with you, more so now that Charles finally persuaded Nathan Wentworth to back out of his offer from Richard to accept his offer of partnership as Richard's replacement in your firm. Charles didn't tell you?" he asked, seeing a look of surprise on Justin's face. "Charlotte believes that her father may have an ulterior motive, to persuade Wentworth to use some of his wealth to endorse him as a Congressional candidate. She even feels that her father would be delightedly agreeable to her union with Wentworth in order to get to his money."

"No, he never said a word. I spoke to him for a few moments today, but he only expressed his displeasure with you and informed me that I've been assigned as Josiah Staples' defense attorney by the district attorney." He sat down on a kitchen chair and folded his arms on the table as a place to rest his head. "I'll make a deal with you," he mumbled. "You make my tea and supper, and I'll clean Mother's parlor."

"Deal," agreed Jeremy upon entering the pantry. "Did I hear you correctly?" he shouted. He came back to the table and sat down. "Did you say that you've been assigned to Josiah Staples?" he asked with astonishment.

"You heard correctly... and *please* lower your voice. Arthur Campbell died this past weekend."

"Hmm." He went back to the pantry to select his supper supplies.

Justin had heard that "hmm" enough times to know that his brother was in a suspicious frame of mind.

"Hello," Charlotte said timidly from the doorway.

"Charlotte," Justin said, standing up to greet her with an embrace. "Welcome to our family, sister. I hope and pray that all goes well with you and Jeremy, and we'll all find some peace when the dust settles."

"I'm fairly certain that I'll be disowned for disobeying my father, but my love for Jeremy deems it all worthwhile. And you shall see, Justin, while I have no desire to see my sister hurt, through Jeremy and me, you shall benefit... you and Libby."

"And when are you planning on informing your parents?"

"We'll tell them when we feel the time is right. My parents will be home from Washington late this evening to spend the weekend. I'll return home before they get there so they'll not become suspicious as to where I spend my time. Sadly, I'll only be able to see Jeremy in church this Sunday, but they'll be returning to Washington on Monday. I'll remain at home... and with Jeremy."

"I can't say that I approve of the deception involved here.

Who performed your nuptials, and how do you plan on avoiding Nathan when he calls on you?"

"Please bear with us for the time being. A Washington district magistrate married us, but we'll renew our vows before God and Reverend Crabtree when your parents arrive home from England, perhaps on Christmas Eve. As far as Nathan is concerned, I've only agreed to visit with him in my home on Saturday evenings. I feel badly that he's wasting his time, but there's nothing I can do about it. I promise we'll tell my parents as soon as possible. If I shun Nathan before he's a full firm partner, he may withdraw from my father's offer. I don't wish to hurt my parents either, but neither will I give up Jeremy. His love means more to me than my family."

"You were absolutely correct. Sally and Dr. Tim are a very likeable, thoughtful couple. I enjoyed our time with them immensely. But your in-laws! Do they ever display any sort of emotion? Your mother-in-law didn't smile once in the two hours we spent with them, and when you told her of the baby, she didn't even flinch," Clary commented while gathering their belongings from beneath the train seat. "Be ready. Our stop is next."

"My mother-in-law has always been aloof and unaffectionate, and my father-in-law is rather uncouth, as was Chester. They aren't people of faith, as you most likely surmised by the number of times my father-in-law used the Lord's name in vain. Billy, Harley, and Lavinia all attended church on their own. I hope you're not too put out by all that I'm bringing back with me. I really wanted to give some of my books to Vie and knew Becky would appreciate the fabric," Libby said, struggling to stand with her arms loaded up with parcels and luggage.

"Not at all. We'll rent a carriage rather than a buggy. Do watch your step. I'm concerned that you might fall. You're still not very steady on your feet."

"Clary, look out the window … to your right. It's Charlotte and Jeremy! They must be going into Washington. Evidently they care nothing of honoring Mr. Dupont's wishes. Let's try to hail them before they board."

Once out on the platform, Clary called to the couple just in time to keep them from passing through their train door. Jeremy rushed over to help them with their parcels, but Charlotte ran in the opposite direction.

"She went to stop Abel. He delivered us here, so he may as well take you home."

"I cannot believe that you and Charlotte are together! Charles will have both of you tarred and feathered if he catches you!" scolded Clary.

When Charlotte returned to his side, he put his arm around her waist and, with a great charming smile, announced, "Ladies, my wife, Mrs. Charlotte Chambers."

Clary just stood mute, her eyes bulging and mouth hanging open. After a long, strained moment, Libby began to giggle. She laid her parcels down on the platform floor and reached her arms out to hug and congratulate Charlotte. Clary laid her parcels on the platform floor and reached over to punch Jeremy in the shoulder.

"Have you gone *mad*?" she screeched. "What were you thinking, you … you *imbecile*!" she yelled with eyes ablaze.

"Don't get your 'red' up. I was thinking that because I love this lady, I would marry her before we were forcibly kept apart," he calmly informed her. "Justin is aware and agreeable."

"Do you honestly expect me to believe Justin gave you his blessing?" she asked with suspicion.

"He really has," said Charlotte, resting her head against Jeremy's shoulder. "He understood that I would be forced to be courted by Nathan, and … " she looked at Libby, "and for several other reasons that you will learn of in time."

"I cannot believe Justin didn't demand that you have your marriage annulled."

"Too late," Jeremy said with an impish grin. "He happened upon us while we—"

Clary put her hand up in the air to halt him from finishing. "No details! When were you going to tell Charlotte's parents? Does Susanna know?"

"We're going into the city to pick up a copy of the marriage certificate from City Hall. No, Susanna doesn't know, and the only time Justin saw her this past weekend was when he was invited to her house for Saturday night supper. She never showed at our house or church because her social schedule was full and most likely because she knew Libby was away." He glanced over at Libby's questioning eyes. "No one to compete with for his attention and affection the entire weekend," he explained.

Libby lowered her eyes and didn't respond, not wishing to be drawn into personal conversation.

"Here comes Abel," said Charlotte. "We best be going. I need to be home by early this evening. While I know the servants would never relay my manner of comings and goings to my parents, I choose to be as discreet as possible to avoid any suspicion."

Justin sat fidgeting in his chair, determined to restrain himself from a powerful urge to dig his fingernails into his itchy arms, neck, and chest. After being locked down tightly for the weekend, the courtroom seemed especially stifling and stuffy, and the wool blend of his uniform was driving him mad. *This is only the beginning of the week. Another week of being required to listen to packs of lies, flub-dub, and bloated testimony*. He already well knew how this trial was going to end, and when it was over, he planned to kick up an awful fuss by voicing his opinion in writing an elaborate article to be published in Jeremy's newspaper.

Sitting here day after day after day, witnessing the pained expression on Wirz's face at every slanderous falsehood... Psalm 58... *Lord, is there a righteous and just man to be found anywhere?*

He wondered how righteous Elizabeth would find *him* to be, once she learned he was to defend her enemy. If he were not so responsible an individual, he would beg that she allow him to whisk her off to his parents' home in England and stay there with her for good ... as her husband. *May this week pass swiftly, Lord. I long so to be with her. Grant me wisdom ... please!*

Dear Papa,

Our train trip back to Barrister's moved quite smoothly, but upon our arrival, we learned that Jeremy and Charlotte had been married for twelve days! Clary's aura of euphoria (brought about by your son) instantly vanished upon hearing this information. While the situation might be deemed as foolhardy, they are adults who love one another. Charlotte is not concerned that she may be disinherited from her family—therefore the one I pity is Justin. As soon as the Wirz trial is finished, he must face Charles Dupont on a daily basis, whereas Jeremy and Charlotte never need face her father again. Oh, that I could face my father again! And then there is Susanna. I pity her also, Papa, for one day Justin will separate himself from her and he'll be mine, Lord willing.

Before returning to Washington this morning, Justin left a note of encouragement on my pillow, along with the verses of Proverbs 3:5–6, "Trust in the Lord with all thine heart; and lean not to thine own understanding. In all thy ways acknowledge him, and he shall direct thy paths." Justin explained that this passage liberates me from the need to understand, so therefore, I must pray for the ability to trust more fully.

Only four more days until he's home again!

CHAPTER 28

"So, Miss Libby, I've calculated that you should experience your baby moving sometime during the first half of November," declared Lydia as she lay the sleeping Laurel in Clary's eager arms.

"Clary is ever so miffed with President Johnson for mandating December 7 to be the official Day of Thanksgiving, because she'll have to wait an extra two weeks to see Ben," said Libby. "I hope you'll be here also. I would like for you to meet him."

"I'm afraid that every other Thanksgiving is spent with my parents," explained Lydia, "and this year we belong to them. We'll look forward to meeting Ben at Christmas."

"Ben is the epitome of intelligence and charm and is quite handsome," Clary informed her sister-in-law. "And I freely declare that I love him."

The ladies giggled at her candor. "So much has changed since I was here last," said Lydia. "Everyone is in love ... or married," she said, smiling at Charlotte.

"Hawoe, evwy peoples." Vie ran into the kitchen to greet the woman and to deliver a letter to Libby. "Dis be fo' you, Miz Lizzybits." She eyed their cakes and teacups.

"You may sit with us," invited Clary, "but you'll have milk with your cakes." She placed the baby in Charlotte's arms then set a place for Vie. "I wonder where Justin could be. He should have been home by three o'clock, and it's nearly four. I know he wanted to spend part of the afternoon helping to lay the pipes for the wash closet. Who is the letter from, Libby?" she asked, glancing over at Libby's flushed face.

"It's from my Aunt Sarah. She writes that Ben had wired her with complete details upon learning of my whereabouts. She ... she would like for me to *accompany* Ben to England for the upcoming summer and would be pleased if my baby and I would live with them, as I have no known kin, save Ben. She offers her full support in place of the care my father would have bestowed upon us. I ... Ben never told me he was going to spend the summer in England. Did he mention his intentions to you, Clary?" she asked, looking bewildered.

"No ... no, he did not," she somberly stated, and then turned to look out the window to hide surfaced tears from the women.

"Don' cwy, Miz Cwary. You go wif Misser Ben too. Mama an' me take good care of da house," offered Vie, with a cake-stuffed mouth. When she saw that four pairs of eyes were suddenly fixed upon her, she stopped chewing and stared back wide-eyed.

"Could there be a more perceptive or sensitive three-year-old child in existence?" Charlotte commented in awe.

"If only life were that simple," Clary said, turning to look back out the window.

After a moment, she turned back to the women and shrugged. "But why *should* he tell me? We're not engaged, and I've not known him for very long. Although, I *am* surprised that he didn't inform you of his plans, Libby, and ... and I hope you won't consider your aunt's offer." She sniffed. "I'm sorry! Forgive me for that selfish wish," she apologized before hurriedly exiting the room.

Libby went to follow her to the stairs but stopped short of her ascent when Justin came in through the door to the foyer.

"Justin!" squealed Libby excitedly, now torn between following Clary upstairs and staying below to properly greet Justin.

He removed the hat to his uniform, placed it on a coat rack hook, and then turned to face her. All the stress and strain of the week instantly disappeared from his eyes at the very sight of her lovely, welcoming face. With an adoring smile, he reached over to caress her cheek. It took all of their strength to restrain from intimately embracing one another.

"I know," he softly said, reading the eagerness in her sparkling eyes. "You would like for me to take you in my arms and greet you as your lover. I ask you to trust me ... that it *will* happen."

"I *do* trust you," she as softly and simply returned. "Will you spare a few moments to speak with me later this evening? I know you're anxious to help your brothers and Abel for now, and I need to console Clary. I'm afraid Ben unknowingly hurt her by not sharing certain pertinent information with her."

I hope you're not hurt when you finally learn that I visited with Josiah Staples this afternoon, dear one. "Go to Clary. We'll meet after the household retires for the night. I'm anxious to learn the details of your trip." He watched her ascend the stairs, pleased to see her attired in deep blue rather than mourning black. He dreaded having to relay to her certain information concerning Susanna, but it must be told for the sake of honesty.

Libby lightly thumped on Clary's door. "May I come in?"

"Please, do," responded Clary with faux cheerfulness.

Libby opened the door to find her sitting at her dressing table searching through the contents of a small box that Ben had left with her while in Wellesley.

"This box is filled with small tins of finely crushed minerals that Ben promised to me ... mica, titanium oxide, ultramarine, zinc, iron oxide. See how lovely the colors are, pinks, peaches, cream, and sand tones. He suggested applying them with a brush rather than a puff, similar to a man's shaving brush but with much softer bristles for the more delicate skin of women. I'll blend them with fine corn silk powder. Perhaps after we bake our pretzels tomorrow, we'll experiment with beautifying our complexions."

"Whatever you wish. Clary, Ben would never consciously hurt you. You do know that," Libby said soothingly.

Clary smiled. "Pay me no mind. I've finished with my little tantrum. I honestly don't mind that Ben is going to England, as long as he doesn't decide he loves the country and would rather reside there. I have plans of my own that include him. I may simply have to postpone them until a later date. Suppose we go help Becky prepare supper. Fried chicken, sweet potatoes, greens, and cornbread is the fare. The men will be ravenous."

"I'll be down to help in a moment. I have an envelope from Ben that I promised to give to Justin."

Libby went to search through her valise until she found the envelope Ben handed her upon his departure, and opened it to sort through its contents. She knew there would be a sum of money for her personal use, and she figured there would also be a check to give to Justin for her keep. When she found a folded note with her name written on it, she unfolded it to see several scribbled lines—

> *Libby, I nearly forgot to inform you that you may be receiving a letter from Aunt Sarah and wanted to head off any information that I plan to spend the summer in England, should Sarah refer to the fact. A portion of the trip will be for pleasure, the remaining to work on behalf of the Academy, as they will be funding the expedition. I don't wish for Clarissa to know of this, for I intend to propose marriage to her this Thanksgiving holiday. I could never leave the country for three months without her and know she would relish the journey… and, I hope and pray, as my bride. I place this information in your confidence so as she's properly surprised. Ben*

Libby bounced up and down on her toes, so delighted with the information. But keeping it a secret for the next few weeks would be a great feat, especially if Clary happened to pine over the fact that he would not be visiting with her in Barrister's for the entirety of the summer. It was going to be difficult to witness her melancholy day after day and not be permitted to soothe her by serving up the remedial knowledge. She tucked her spending money and the note in a dresser drawer then bounded down the steps to place her room and board check on Justin's desk.

"Have you something to say to me?" Justin asked, coming into the library behind her. When she caught her breath, he said, "Forgive me for startling you. I was just about to go help the crew but saw you enter this room."

She turned and handed him the envelope. "Here's a check for my keep ... from Ben."

He opened the top desk drawer and held up the first check Ben had given him. "I refuse to accept payment for your room and board but, knowing that Ben wouldn't accept my refusal, decided that all funds given to me on your behalf be banked under your name until the baby is born. Use it toward a future need or education." He took the check from her and placed both in the desk drawer. Seeing that she was about to protest, he said, "Elizabeth, surely you must realize that if I accept payment for your care it would place a mercenary element into our relationship. My desire is that you're secure in the fact that I'm well able to provide for you and enjoy doing so because I care deeply for you."

She smiled and blushed. It was enjoyable to her merely to hear the words "I care deeply for you."

He came around his desk to give her hair a playful tug. "Well, I'm off. I don't want the rest of the troops to accuse me of shirking my duties."

"Are you able to spare a few moments now, Counselor?" asked Libby, peeking around the doorway to the library.

He looked up from where he was seated behind his desk, motioned for her to enter, and then looked back down to pen a few more words.

She approached his desk and asked, "What are you doing? Perhaps I should come back tomorrow..."

"No, no," he said, rising to escort her to the love seat. "There's no rush to finish this. It's an article to be published in *The Beacon*, but it must wait until the Wirz trial is finished. Is everyone down for the night?"

"Josh, Lydia, and Laurel are nicely settled into Jeremy's room, Clary is upstairs writing a letter to Ben, and I believe Jeremy is still attempting to smuggle Charlotte back into her parents' house, since they won't be home from Washington until tomorrow. Charlotte doesn't wish to place the Duponts' servants in a compromising position by having to lie about her whereabouts should her parents ask them where she spends her evenings. They certainly would have heart failure at the knowledge of how she spends part of her days," Libby added wryly with a giggle.

Justin raised his eyebrows and chuckled at her dodging a more frank description of Charlotte and Jeremy's daily "activity."

"I honestly don't care for all of the deception, but they're adults not living under my roof, so I have no right to interfere into their lives. Now, young lady, did your week go smoothly? It surely must have been a painful visit. I only wish I had been able to accompany you," he said soothingly, lifting a lock of her hair to play with as they spoke.

"The only truly painful portion of my visit was facing the reality that my father, who was so well and chipper only a short while ago, lay buried beneath the ground," she said sadly. She looked up into his eyes. "But not really, right?" He nodded to her that he understood that she meant that the "real" part of her father, his spirit, was alive and well.

She went on. "But part of my stay was amazingly satisfying! Because I had recalled so much good that had once been in Billy, I was able to fully forgive him. I learned that there's *such* great freedom in forgiving, enough that I also was able to feel pity for him at the realization that he had been every bit as much a victim as I. The war had robbed and ruined him. His treatment of me was the only way he was able to vent his frustration at knowing he would never again be the man he had once been," she explained tearfully.

What a lovely soul she has, that she's able to rationalize his cruel behavior toward her. She's so lovely in every way. Help me to explain to her, Lord. He took her hand and comfortingly patted it.

"Well, enough said about my visit to Wellesley. It's finished, and now I'm free to attempt to move on. Do I dare ask about *your* week, Counselor? For I could see it in your eyes the moment you stepped though the front doorway."

He laughed. "I seem to be a very transparent individual." He suddenly became sober. "Elizabeth, I don't wish to discuss Henry Wirz's trial during my time with you. I will only say that I believe it will be over soon, but none of the end result will be to my satisfaction. I would like to shift my frustration into the article that I'm preparing to be published before the man is hanged."

Her eyes widened in horror. "*Hanged!* How can you be certain?"

"I know … I just know. I have two other topics to discuss with you, unless you've not told me all you care to," he said, abruptly changing the subject.

"No. I have nothing more to say," she said tensely, reading from his facial expression that she was not going to be pleased with the matters he was about to relay.

"I spoke to the state's prosecutor this past week concerning your pretrial testimony. He gave me a form of questions that he requires you to answer. He also asks that you write a complete account of what took place on the night of August 22. I'll deliver it to him when you finish."

She looked at him as if waiting for him to continue.

"That's all for that matter."

"Oh," she simply said. "I'll attend to his request tomorrow." When he remained silent, a feeling of gloom and doom set in. "And the final matter?" she cautiously asked.

"It has to do with Susanna." He took a deep, cleansing breath before continuing. "I was asked to supper at the Dupont home last Saturday evening, while you were in Wellesley. Nathan Wentworth was there also, and I must admit that I found it rather disconcerting to find myself in the presence of my new sister-in-law and her 'suitor,'" he first said offhandedly.

"But for the matter, Saturday evening was the only time I spoke with Susanna over the entirety of the weekend, and even then, only in the presence of her parents. She appeared to be apprehensive at being left alone with me, and I had a hunch as to why. It all had to do with a discussion that took place between her father and me the day prior, concerning my fondness for you. Charles led me to believe that he and Susanna had previously discussed my growing closer to you, which explained why she was determined that we not be left alone together so that I wouldn't have the opportunity to voice my intent to break our engagement.

"Before I departed from her, she informed me that she planned on returning to Washington the next morning and would visit with me after court on Monday evening. I was surprised and disappointed that she wasn't waiting for me outside the courtroom, because I had planned to openly and honestly discuss my regard for you and the fact that I had no right to propose marriage to her when I didn't feel for her the way a man should feel for his wife. Please don't think me callous, Elizabeth, for I *do* take blame for bringing my relationship to Susanna as far as engagement, and I planned to tell her so, that I had been working directly against God's will. I was very wrong and feel great guilt and remorse that I had led her to that point.

"When I returned to my suite, I was *astounded* to find her lying naked between the sheets of my bed. She told me the time had come for her to *demonstrate* her love for me, and perhaps she might be able to please me by giving me a child of my own, knowing of my desire for children."

"And… and were you at all tempted?" Libby timidly asked, clearly visualizing the beautiful Susanna offering herself to him.

"I can honestly say to you no. I was too overwrought by an overwhelming combination of disgust at her tactic to manipulate me and feeling great pity toward her. After gathering up her clothing, I laid them on the bed then headed for the door, informing her that she was to dress while I waited out in the hallway and she was not to leave before we discussed the matter, but downstairs in the glassed visitor's room, in public view. I was well aware that I had humiliated her by not accepting her proposition, but I wasn't prepared for the onslaught of attacks against you and my person."

She fidgeted a bit at the thought of what was to come next, then braced herself and focused her attention back to him.

"I have no intention of repeating her comments regarding you, because I'm fearful that you would dwell on them and possibly allow yourself to take them to heart and consider them as truths. With every bitter word that came from her mouth, I became more and more confounded as to how I allowed myself to become attached to a woman whose nature had no comprehension whatsoever of what it meant to be indwelled by the spirit of God."

"I won't coax you to repeat her statements. Her anger toward me is understandable, though, for I've also humiliated her. She set an ultimatum, I would imagine?"

"Yes, she did," he said somberly. "She has refused to accept a break in our engagement, and if I make any attempts to do so or attempt to form a bond with you, she'll make public that I ill-used her by taking *you* to my bed, that the child you're carrying may be mine, that I 'knew' you before you came to my door begging that I take you in, and that she would see to it that her father discharge me in disgrace. And then she had the gall to inform me that I didn't realize what was best for me yet, that I wasn't clearly seeing that she and her family had the influence to station me into a high position of power, that someday, I quite possibly might be vice president to her father, the president of the United States! Such *pomposity*!" he exclaimed, shaking his head in disgust.

Libby sat wide-eyed, wondering what her reaction should be. Should she laugh at the preposterousness? She felt like laughing hysterically. Should she be afraid of the influence that the Dupont family had on Washington society? No, she felt no fear whatsoever. Should she cry at how tragic this situation had become? She felt like sobbing uncontrollably. So she decided to laugh and cry simultaneously. He watched her for a moment and then, deciding that her reaction was the only sensible one, took her in his arms and did the same.

"Do you suppose she composed the threatening oration in the short time it took her to dress?" Libby asked him once she had calmed.

"I believe she had already fabricated it should I decline her advances."

"I cannot comprehend why a woman would hold on so tightly to a man who didn't love her enough to want to marry her, and, not wishing to offend you, she obviously doesn't love you. But perhaps it's not mine to opine."

"I'm not offended, and you have every right to voice your opinion, for you're the crux of the matter. It surely must have to do with pride."

"Most likely you're correct. Clary told me of Edward Wentworth breaking their engagement."

"He's part of it, I'm certain. To be driven to the point of desperation at the prospect of a *second* rejection—"

"That's why I pity her, and also because she's to lose you. I'm able to feel great empathy for her in that," she tenderly added. "How could I not? It's difficult to find a truly good and righteous man these days." She sighed.

"I doubt she would be impressed with 'righteous.'" The name Josiah Staples crossed his mind, prodding him to ask, "Do you trust me, that I would never do or say anything that would harm you in any way?"

She looked into his eyes and smiled. "I most certainly trust you," she assured him. "This is the second time today that you've spoken of trust. Is there more I should know?"

He kissed her cheek and stood up. "No. Not at present. It's time for us to retire for the night. Tomorrow is going to be a long day of heavy labor. Sleep peacefully, sweetness, and pray for God to set things right for us."

Dear Papa,

He still hasn't told me he loves me, but he tenderly regards me in every way, and while my heart is certain of his adoration, I still long to hear those three glorious words. Are they so difficult to say? Perhaps he's still holding on to his love for Mary Anne. Perhaps… no! He will, in time, I'm certain… when he finally "puts his house in order," as he is fond of saying. My heart goes out to Susanna, for despite the wretched person that she is, she will have lost greatly. I believe Justin to be the man of any woman's dreams, and I hope and pray to God that he may someday be mine.

I face a dilemma besides my own, Papa. It's painful to see the look of hurt on Clary's face at the fact that Ben did not inform her of his plan to spend the summer in England. I'm certain that she has come to think that he doesn't care for her in the way she had believed. I could so easily ease her pain, but if I did so now, I would be robbing her of her joy in the morning. I best write to Ben so that he might remedy the situation, for he wouldn't want for her to fret so until his Thanksgiving marriage proposal.

CHAPTER 29

"I would say that our hard labor resulted in perfection," Josh affirmed to his brothers as they surveyed the completed wash closet. "I'm anxious to see the look of relief on Mother's face at not having to wait several weeks to have a commode installed or having to bathe in the kitchen. Attempting to lay pipes when the ground hardens would have greatly impeded our efforts had we waited until December to undertake this task."

"I know that Charlotte will be pleased. No more trips to the privy, and you need not worry," Jeremy said at the sight of a stern expression on Justin's face. "We promise to keep it spotless. Suppose we go to the parlor to talk. I'm anxious to hear your news, now that the ladies have gone back to the other house. I have news for you also, Justin."

"We best not stay here too long," said Josh, dropping down onto a comfy chair. "Justin and I have to be up at dawn to catch the early trains, and it's nearly ten o'clock now. What have you to say, Justin?"

Justin told his brothers of Susanna's ultimatum, her attacks on Elizabeth and him, and the extent of her action at offering herself to him.

"Whoa! That must have been tempting! And here we thought she was a cold fish. It's good you managed to keep your wits about you," commented Jeremy when Justin finished his tale.

Justin grimaced his disgust at Jeremy's attempt at humor. "I realize that your brain will be focused below your belt for some time, since you're a newlywed. I don't care what Susanna does to me or what gossip she spreads about me, so long as she causes no anguish to Elizabeth. She's innocent and vulnerable and undeserving of any sort of ill treatment. Now what information have you for me, Jeremy?"

"Charlotte discovered that Charles has been buying political endorsements with money and favors, and she's livid that he sees no harm or wrong in it. It appears that you were unknowingly aiding him by delivering contracts and at times, money. It seems that he owed the Perry and Glass firm a favor, and upon Campbell's death, *you* came to be assigned to the Josiah Staples case. State prosecutors didn't assign it to you; it was *bought* for you by Charles. And because Staples is a 'nothing,' no one seems to care who is assigned his case. The Perry and Glass firm were certainly relieved to be rid of it. Charles also felt that he would be doing Susanna a favor, because he thought that Libby wouldn't stay in your home if she knew you were defending Staples. Charlotte said that Susanna was overjoyed at the news. So, brother, I suppose you'll refuse the case, resign from the Dupont firm, and go into partnership with Richard."

"And you would be wrong, little brother. I've already suspected some of what you've told me, but I'm not resigning from Charles until after the Wirz trial, and I do intend to represent Mr. Staples."

Jeremy's and Josh's eyes widened. "Are you daft?" asked Jeremy. "Libby will head back to Wellesley the moment she hears. She wants him to be sentenced to the death penalty for what he did to Lottie."

"He would never receive the death penalty because the most serious charge is *second*-degree murder. I spoke to Staples on Friday afternoon and determined by my interview that I have no reason *not* to represent him, and that is all I'll be doing, representing him. There really *is* no defense strategy involved. You'll see, in time. Meanwhile, I prefer that Elizabeth know nothing of this until I'm able to explain to her why I accepted the case and that it will ease her if I accomplish what I set out to do. I want her to trust that I'll take care of her... completely."

Libby lay in the dark wishing she had not agreed to go to her room when Clary and Lydia decided to retire for the night. Justin would be leaving for Washington at dawn, and she hadn't had the opportunity to bid him farewell for the week. After tossing and turning for a good half hour, she lit her bedside lamp in order to read a passage or two from her Bible and maybe a few poems from a book she had brought from home. After some time, she heard a light knock on the door.

"Elizabeth?" whispered Justin.

"Come in," she softly called, reaching into the side table drawer for a handkerchief.

He partially closed the door behind him but stood still for a moment, watching as she dabbed her eyes.

"Why are there tears?" he tenderly asked as he approached the bed.

She giggled. "Pay me no mind. I've been reading poetry, and one of the poems was particularly touching," she explained with a short succession of sobs and sniffs.

He sat on the edge of the bed and took the book from her. "Hmm... *Joy Comes in the Morning*," he read, then set the book on the night table. "I saw from outside that your light was still lit. I thought I should tell you I won't be home until near supper on Friday. I have business to attend to."

"How will you avoid Susanna for the week?" she asked. "I would wish, for our sakes, that she would stay at her estate for the week rather than in Washington, but I'm afraid that would upset Charlotte and Jeremy greatly, for they couldn't come together."

"Would it distress you if I played into Susanna's hands for a while? I have my reasons for doing so and don't wish to rile her any further at present."

She laughed. "Counselor, because you managed not to allow the beautiful naked temptress to lure you into your bed, I have no reason *not* to be rest-assured of your fidelity."

He reached over to rest his hand on her cheek. "You're the beautiful temptress in my bed, you know. But you lure me with so very much more than just your body."

She blushed and looked away from him. "It would have to be more than my body, for in another few months, I'll look like the fatted calf. Have you given thought to that?" she asked, focusing her eyes back on his.

He lightly chuckled. "I certainly expect that you would eventually become all round and rosy. I've not given it any actual thought, however, but I want to assure you that you'll always be lovely to me." He stood up and leaned over to kiss her cheek. "I see that you placed your pretrial testimony on my desk. I'll make certain that it's in the state prosecutor's hand while on dinner break tomorrow."

She nodded and, looking up to lovingly focus on his face, said nothing. He stared down into her longing eyes for a moment and, finding that he was becoming consumed with the desire to take her in his arms to passionately kiss her, decided he had best vacate the room as quickly as possible before temptation took them even further.

"Goodnight to you, dear. I pray you have a pleasant week," he wished her on his way out the door.

Once he had closed it behind him, she snuffed the lamp and nestled beneath the blankets, thinking, *He still hasn't told me he loves me.*

"What is so humorous?" Jeremy asked from the entryway to the parlor. He went in to wedge himself between Clary and Libby on the divan. "I could hear you ladies laughing from out in the kitchen."

"This issue of *The Beacon*," said Clary, looking up from her morning newspaper reading. "Are you trying to compete with *Harper's* or *Godey's*? Beauty and fashion tips... letters from the lovelorn... the most asked questions concerning proper social etiquette?" She and Libby burst into laughter again.

"I see no hilarity in any of that," he indignantly remarked. "Circulation will soar once women know what is offered. Do you see who is editor in charge of the new columns?"

"Yes," Clary said. "C.C. I take it that C.C. is Charlotte Chambers?"

"Correct. These columns are her idea, and who better to give advice, considering all of her highbrow education. Only there will be a surprise that comes with the etiquette column, for all of the answers to the questions sent to us with be answered in a satirical manner. Then I'll find you laughing yourselves to tears. I've learned that Charlotte has quite the sense of humor."

"If her humor matches yours, the two of you will end up being tied to a rail and run out of town," Clary sarcastically commented. "And if you're allowing her that much coverage, then why did you balk when I asked for a small block to sell my beauty items?"

He pinched her cheek and stood up to leave them. "I will bestow my favor upon you and grant you your wish, dear sister, if you'll patent what you plan to sell. I'll not set myself up to be accused of soliciting quackery."

"You're not toying with me?"

"I am not, my lady," he responded with a bow.

"You seem to be in high spirits," Libby acknowledged.

"Because I'll be with my wife for the next two days. Oh, I nearly forgot to tell you, Libby. Susanna has been home with Charlotte for the last three days, away from Justin, which should please you greatly, and which explains why Charlotte hasn't been with me. Nathan Wentworth asked Charlotte to accompany him to a formal soiree last evening, in honor of the governor's birthday. She agreed to go with him if he asked Susanna to chaperone her, and he was agreeable. I'm anxious to hear if it went well."

"I suppose Susanna will be returning to Washington today if you say Charlotte is to be with you?" Libby asked, picturing Susanna possessively hanging on to Justin's arm.

Jeremy nodded.

"I think it a crime that you and Charlotte are deceiving Nathan. He's a gentlemanly person who is truly undeserving of such antics of deception," declared Clary. "Society will deem him a fool when it's finally learned that Charlotte has been married to you while he thought he was courting her."

"That's why she hasn't agreed to be alone with him in public. If Susanna is with them, it merely looks as if he's accompanying them as a friend. We've seriously considered informing Nathan of our marriage, hoping he would understand that because the Duponts consider me unfit to even wipe their boots on, we had no choice but to marry on the sly." He looked at Libby and winked. "However, a few more outings with Susanna as chaperone, and who knows what new relationships might develop, especially since my sweetheart is doing her best at playing an ice queen," he said, heading for the front door.

"If none of us can tolerate Susanna, what makes you so certain Nathan can?" Clary called to him.

"It's worth a try," he called back, slamming the door shut behind him.

"Jeremy forgets that Susanna was engaged to Nathan's brother," Clary said to Libby. "And Nathan most likely knows the secret why Edward detached himself from her."

Libby fidgeted uncomfortably. "I would rather not discuss Susanna."

"You're very pale. Aren't you well?"

"I... I'm feeling somewhat melancholy. I'm sure it must be due to bodily changes."

"Just keep thinking that Justin will be home again in two days, and not too many more weeks until Thanksgiving, Ben will be here," she said dreamily. "Have you felt any movement yet?"

"No, but my lower abdomen is no longer flat. There's a distinct hard bump," she said, standing up and taking Clary's hand to place over the small mound. "Can you feel it?"

Clary's eyes brightened. "Why, yes, I do. How exciting! It must seem mysterious and awesome to you to have another human being growing inside of you."

"Would you like to have children someday?"

"I would like two girls ... preferably. No boys! It's strange, but the subject of wanting children was never a topic of discussion between Ben and me, and we certainly have discussed and written to each other about *almost* everything. He's your brother. Do you know if he wants children?"

Libby giggled. "I never thought he would want a *wife,* let alone children. Oh, forgive me!" Libby exclaimed when she realized the tactlessness of her comment. "What I meant to say was that Ben never showed much interest in forming relationships with women, until he met you. I'm certain it took him no time to realize that you are his ideal in every way. I know you've received several letters from him since we parted ways in Philadelphia. You're *certain* that he failed to mention or even *allude* to a trip to England in any of them?" she asked, wondering why Ben hadn't honored her request to at least *hint* to Clary of his plans.

"No mention at all," she said sadly. "If he's separated from me for the length of a summer, his affection for me may cool."

"I know my brother well enough to see by his manner that he considers you and he were meant to be together," she soothingly offered. "We shouldn't worry, just pray and have faith that God will bestow us with a trusting nature as far as our men are concerned." She lightly giggled. "I do believe you're correct in the fact that men seem to need a bit of prodding. I would feel so much more secure if I could only hear those three binding words ... I love you. You also, I would assume."

Clary nodded. "If I had to choose a curriculum to be taught in school during the middle teenage years, it would include money management, what to expect in child rearing, and understanding the needs and proper treatment of the opposite sex."

"All of that can be found in the Bible; therefore, everyone should be taught to read," Libby said upon standing. "I'll help you take the clothes from the line as soon as they're dry. Right now I would like to practice my part of the duets that Justin promised to play with me this weekend. Have faith. I'm *certain* that all will go well for you."

A pair of large, warm hands clamped over Libby's eyes just as she was about to turn from the counter to set a platter of sliced roast beef on the kitchen table. "Guess who?" a husky male voice whispered into her ear.

Her heart began to race, and she set the platter back down on the counter. "Mm … a hint, please."

"I'm the blessed man who you've so thoroughly captivated," he continued to whisper, then pressed a firm kiss on her cheek.

She began to bounce up and down on her toes, so anxious to turn around to throw herself into his arms. "I can't imagine who that might be … although the scent of your hair is vaguely familiar," she said with a giggle.

"You can't think who it is that holds you in adoration and finds you to be lovelier than any woman on God's earth?"

"But will you still adore me and find me lovely if I choose to wantonly embrace you in the very unladylike manner that defies the rules of etiquette, since you're still engaged to another and are not my husband?"

He took his hands from her eyes, took her by her shoulders, and turned her around to face him. "I'm no longer engaged to another, and she's living in a world of delusion. Besides, those foolish rules were made by foolish people, so they're meant to be broken." He drew her tightly to him and held her quietly and snuggly for a good length of time. They both sighed contentedly in unison. "So meant to be," he whispered into her ear. "I find such peace and fulfillment just being in your presence."

"I missed you so," she honestly confessed. "I miss you more and more with each passing day that you're away from home." She placed her hands on his shoulders and pulled back a bit so that she could look at his face. "I know Susanna went back to Washington yesterday morning. Did you—"

Reading the anxiousness in her eyes, he touched his finger to her lips. "You are not to concern yourself with Susanna. Last evening she asked me to take her to supper at a new restaurant in Washington. Over the entire evening she behaved as though nothing had changed in our relationship, despite the fact that I barely spoke a word for the entire evening. I let her talk herself into oblivion about a wedding that will never take place. All I could think about was how brutal a day it had been in court and the fact that tomorrow I would be standing in my kitchen, or any other room in the house, holding you close."

She put her arms around his neck and rested her head on his shoulder. *Why! Why can't he tell me that he loves me? Perhaps if I told him first... but no, I don't want him coerced into saying it.* She pulled away from him. "I must put supper on the table. Please tell Clary that supper is ready. She's lying down. Another headache, I would imagine." *Or an aching heart... Oh, Ben! Oh, men!*

He didn't move from the spot where he stood, just sharply observed her, wondering what he had said to cool her affection.

She dumped the string beans from a pot into a bowl, gave him a swift glance, and then set the bowl on the table.

He grabbed her wrist. "What is wrong, Elizabeth? Is it that I took Susanna to supper?"

"Certainly not. It's obvious to me; it's obvious to *everyone*, except Susanna, that you don't love her."

"She knows I don't love her the way a man should love a woman he intends to marry, and I don't believe she cares... although I can't imagine why. No. Something is tormenting you. I wish you would tell me. Please be honest with me," he implored, taking her into his arms again.

"It's for me to know but not say, and for you to realize. Honesty has nothing to do with it, yet it has everything to do with it," she simply said.

"Are you presenting me with a riddle?"

She stared into space for a few seconds. "No riddle, only realization."

"Well, I certainly hope I quickly realize, for I don't relish separating myself from your good graces."

She stood on her toes to give him a peck on the cheek. "You haven't, and I trust that you *will* realize."

He burst out laughing. "Well, now I'm becoming perplexed by all the mystery. I best go change into comfortable clothing before I become too embroiled by frustration and perchance say something to further irk you."

"You've said nothing to irk me. It's what you've *not* said that irks me, but you must realize on your own. Go change, and please inform Clary that dinner is on the table." She pecked his cheek again and pulled away from him. "Hurry. Dinner will be cold in another few minutes." She turned away from him to resume her chore.

CHAPTER 30

Dear Papa,

Less than six weeks until Thanksgiving, and Ben will be arriving in Barrister's the evening before the holiday to propose marriage to my dear friend! Clary has resigned herself to the fact that she and Ben may be merely "friends" for a good long while—a year, perhaps, until he returns from England, at least. She no longer appears wounded. Clary is a woman of tremendous fortitude, and I admire her greatly for that one attribute alone. I believe Ben has already realized that quality in her.

This past weekend was absolutely delightful! Justin and I spent hours absorbed in playing piano and singing duets. On Sunday morning Reverend Crabtree asked the two of us only to sing a cappella a stanza of a lovely old hymn. I wish you had been there to hear, for God made our voices to perfectly and gloriously blend together. Susanna was absent from the service. I believe I would have found it difficult to sing with him while in her presence. I hear you telling me that this is wrong, that my songs of praise should be directed to my Lord, and her presence should bear no influence whatsoever, and you would be correct.

Susanna elected to stay clear of Justin this past weekend, most likely due to not wishing to be anywhere near to me. I suppose she'll make it a point to spend this evening with him while they're both in Washington. I must trust him. It is her that I cannot trust.

Poor Justin! This trial has weighed so heavily upon him. I've learned that he literally takes injustice to heart, almost as if it were a personal confrontation. He's writing a piece to be published in all the Washington area newspapers, which he has entitled, "Descent from God's Grace." He should have it ready to publish as soon as the trial is through and hopes to do so before Henry Wirz is hanged. He's not optimistic that it will in any way help Wirz to escape the gallows, but he's determined that the public should be informed as to the truth of the whole matter, so they might learn for next time—next time a commission wishes to take to trial an individual to be used as a pawn to the anger and vengefulness of the victors of war. How tragic and shameful!

Then there are those who are so obviously guilty. Woe be to Josiah Staples if my "knight in shining armor" was to have any authority in imposing the punishment so well deserving of his crimes… I so dread that trial, Papa. Lottie's battered face is still in my mind's sight.

Clary's mother and father sent me a wonderful letter expressing their wish…

She looked up when she heard the clomping of hooves, closed her journal, and slid it beneath the glider beside her book of poetry. *Oh dear, not Susanna!* She nervously glanced over at the elder Chambers' home and could see that Charlotte's horse was hitched to the post. Clary and Becky had gone to town for supplies. She could see that Abel was pushing Vie on the oak tree swing between the two houses, so she knew that Charlotte and Jeremy were alone in the other house. Abel lifted Vie off the swing when his eye caught sight of Susanna, and he sent the child to warn the couple of her unannounced arrival.

But Susanna didn't appear to notice her sister's horse. By the determined expression on her face, Libby was nearly certain that the sole intent of her visit would deal in a personal confrontation with her alone.

"Clary isn't home," Libby immediately called to her.

"Good morning, Miss Libby," she pleasantly greeted while climbing down from her buggy. "Please stay where you are, for it's you I've come to visit, not Clary. The weather is fine, is it not?" she asked as she royally ascended the porch steps in her frock of Scotch plaid wool.

Libby shifted as close to the glider arm as she was able. "Good morning, Miss Susanna. Yes, it's a lovely autumn day. Do sit down. Would you like a cup of tea?"

"No. No thank you." She plunked herself down beside Libby, took a deep breath, and then shifted in a way to better view her victim. Her lips broke into a broad, exaggerated grin, and she reached over to very lightly pat Libby's hand. "We ladies have a dilemma, have we not?" she asked with a breathy giggle.

Don't give her the upper hand! She forced herself to stare into Susanna's limpid pools of blue. "Have we?" she asked with large, inquiring eyes.

"I would like to be completely frank with you. I'm certain that Justin has expressed to you my thoughts concerning you residing in his home and your desired 'relationship' with him."

"Somewhat. I'm confident that he was too concerned for my feelings to relay all of your … your innuendos. But I give you leave to express, in complete detail, all that you've entrusted to him."

"No innuendos, merely facts. How long have you known Justin, two months, perhaps? Well, I've known him for over two years now and am well aware of his strengths and weaknesses. I've tried to place myself in your position, Miss Libby, so that I might be able to imagine and understand how it is that you've come to cling so to one who does not belong to you.

"You may find this difficult to believe, but I'm well able to sympathize for your cause. You were an abused wife who had been able to take shelter in the arms of her father. Now that he's no longer available to you and you find yourself carrying your abuser's child, you're alone and lonely, desperately trying to fathom how you'll be able to support and care for your child. So certainly it's effortless to delude yourself into thinking that you're in love with Justin or that he might be feeling love for you by any expression of tenderness or concern for your well-being. It's perfectly natural that you would cling to Justin, for he's a truly caring, tender man, who wouldn't have the heart to turn you out. But you would do well not to confuse his manner with love.

"I've learned that the only one he could ever truly love lies buried in a church cemetery. I will admit openly to you that Justin has never been able to actually say the words 'I love you' to me. But this doesn't concern me to the degree to which you might think. A certain sense of caring and love comes naturally to a couple after they've been married for a length of time, and I'm content in the knowledge of that fact.

"What is important is that I have the ability to offer much to Justin that will be of benefit to both of us in the future. And what is it that you have to offer him? You've not even shown enough concern for him to vacate his home while he's preparing his defense for the Staples trial. Do you not realize that it may hinder his future prospects if it's learned that you influenced a certain bias in the handling, or perhaps I should say *mishandling*, of the case when Justin finds he's unable to fight for the man because you've manipulated his thinking?"

She stopped when she saw that Libby's face had blanched, and the look of anguished wonder in her eyes told her that Libby knew nothing of Justin being assigned as Staples' defender. "He hasn't told you, has he? Nor the state prosecutor?" She emitted a short, wicked laugh and threw her hands up in the air. "So much for honesty! You have every right to be *outraged* at such blatant disregard and negligence!"

"I'm certain that he has his reasons, and I trust . . . " Her eyes followed Susanna's eyes to where Jeremy stood passionately kissing his wife on the porch of the other house.

Susanna bolted to a standing position, clenching her fists in rage when Charlotte and Jeremy stopped for a second to wave to her. Immediately she stomped down the porch steps and headed over to where they appeared to be luring her.

Libby wasted no time in packing her valise and decided not to take time fathoming what was playing out between all to whom she was acquainted. She would think about them and the meaning of "trust" during the train ride to Philadelphia to stay with Sally until summoned to testify at Staples' trial.

After counting her money to make certain she had enough to cover the fare, she scribbled a few lines to Clary then went to ask Abel to deliver her to the train station. He reluctantly agreed to do so, but only after she informed him that she would walk to the station if need be. As the carriage headed up to the road, Charlotte, Jeremy, and Susanna were nowhere in sight, but she could certainly hear them, as could the entire county, she reasoned.

"I pway fo' Jesus to bwing you home, Miz Lizzybits," Vie said to Libby when they arrived at the train station.

"I promise I'll see you again, Vie. I can't explain why I must leave for now. It's for a reason that only an adult would understand," she explained, giving her a hug.

"But Misser Jussin be sad an' cwy dat you don' want him to take care o' you an' stay wif him ... 'cause he wuvs you."

Tears freely flowed from Libby's eyes at the earnest reasoning in the child's voice. "All will be fine, dear. Please don't fret over this. I'll see you soon." She planted a kiss on the child's cheek, nodded a good-bye and thank you to Abel, and then boarded the train.

"The president will see you now, Mr. Chambers."

Justin followed President Johnson's secretary from the waiting hall into the Oval Office.

"Justin!" Andrew Johnson stood up from his desk and came

around to shake Justin's hand. "It's so good to see you, my man. I tried to speak with you at the governor's reception in September, but your lady seemed to be continually pulling you from one corner of the ballroom to the next, and always opposite to where I was."

Justin smiled wanly. "Not my lady anymore. Our engagement was a mistake and is now broken, but that's a story in itself."

"Pity. The wife and I were looking forward to an invitation to the wedding."

"You'll still get your invitation, Andrew, but my bride will not be Susanna Dupont."

"Hmm ... I see." He studied Justin's face for several seconds, then clapped his hands together and took a deep breath. "I received a letter from your father last week. Jason is to be commended for the excellent job he's doing. The Chambers men can always be counted on for their honesty and integrity. I only read *The Beacon* if I want to read truth."

"I'm pleased to hear it, sir."

"I'm not the only one who believes so, for General Grant suggested your name as serving on the tribunal for the Henry Wirz trial. Your reputation preceded you, young man. Grant claims that your character is flawless, that he had seen you at work in the war tribunals, always striving for justice."

Justin furrowed his brow. "Are you speaking of the *actual* tribunal or tribunal alternate?"

"The actual, but when it was learned that you had returned to civilian life and had chosen to associate yourself with the Dupont firm, your name was replaced with another. Would you like a glass of water?" he asked, regarding Justin's pasty face.

Justin dropped down onto a chair, accepted the glass of water, took a sip, and handed the glass back to him. "The reason I've come to you today concerns the Wirz trial. I was asked to serve as an alternate, and—"

"You accepted, and now it's eating you up. Am I correct?" he asked gently.

"It is . . . more and more each day, to the point where I'm about to explode from the indignation that has built up inside of me. Have you *any* idea of what has been taking place in that courtroom?" he asked, feeling a bit ill and guilty at the thought that he might have been on the actual commission had he not strayed from God's will by becoming engaged to Susanna and accepting a position in Charles' firm. But the odds still would have been eight to one, he reasoned—eight on the commission that had their minds set against Wirz before the trial even began.

"I know through my sources. I also know that I'll be expected to sign the man's death warrant. It's a responsibility that will haunt me until my dying day," he said bitterly.

"That's why I'm here. I have no say whatsoever in determining the man's sentence, and you and I well know that he'll be sentenced to hang. But you *do* have the authority to grant Wirz amnesty. I *plead* that you send him back to Switzerland, if you must. That may serve to cool the volcano."

"The only way the volcano is going to be cooled is to sacrifice the virgin, I'm afraid. Justin, do you realize what damage will be done if I refuse to sign his death warrant? I've already granted pardons for all other prisoners of war crimes, and my actions have caused a cataclysmic eruption of anger among Northern politicians. Haven't you been listening to the political gossip imposed by the House and Senate? They try to determine among themselves whether I should be impeached for cozying up to the seceded States at my desire to take them back into the fold given only a mere slap on the wrist. The Union's teeth are bared for a blood punishment! That is the only way their anger will be quelled, and then I'll be given more leeway to bring peace to this country, once and for all. They may finally stop wrestling with my every decision, and we might finally become a whole nation once more."

He rested his hand on Justin's shoulder. "Do you understand? Please believe that I do see the great tragedy in this. But what am

I to do? If my office is taken from me, this country may have to reckon with a radical tyrant as my replacement."

He went back to sit behind his desk, an indicator to Justin that their discussion had reached a climax.

"I do understand your position, Andrew. Wirz's death is for the good of this country in the long run. But somehow that doesn't ease my mind... no, not one bit." He stood up and went to reach across the desk to shake the president's hand. Their eyes locked.

"I'm *dreadfully* sorry. Please believe me when I say so," he somberly begged.

"I do believe you, and I bid you a good day." He turned to follow the secretary out of the Oval Office.

Justin slowly trudged up the stairs to his third floor suite and reached into his pocket for his key.

"Justin!"

Startled, he quickly looked up the remainder of the flight and, upon seeing Clary standing at his door, experienced a certain sense of panic beginning to set in. The last time she had come to his suite was months ago, to help see him comfortably settled into his new residence.

"What has happened?" he anxiously asked.

"It's Libby. She went to stay with the Morrows until she's called to testify at the Staples trial."

He unlocked the door, gently pushed her inside, and then closed the door behind him. She punched him in the shoulder the second he turned to face her.

"Have you lost your mind?" she shrieked. "Why did Libby have to hear it from Susanna and not from you? I didn't even know about it until Jeremy informed me, after Susanna ran home to tell her mother that Charlotte and Jeremy had married in secret—"

"Slow down and *sit* down. Now tell me all... slowly."

"Susanna paid a visit to Libby early this morning, while Becky and I were in Barrister's, and Jeremy and Charlotte were alone in Father's house. When Vie warned them of Susanna's arrival, they came outside to lure her away from Libby, but the damage had already been done. Libby hightailed it back to Pennsylvania, leaving me a note with the Morrows' address so she can be wired when comes time for her to testify. How is it that Jeremy knew of you becoming Staples' defender, and not me ... or Libby?" She handed him Libby's note.

He read it, slid it into his pocket, and then threw himself on his bed and commenced to massaging his pulsing temples.

When he didn't answer her questions immediately, she asked, "Justin, do you love Libby?"

"Love her? I love that little woman hundreds of times more than I thought I could *ever* love again."

"*Men!*" She rose from her chair and approached his bed. "Roll over," she instructed him. "I'll rub your back and shoulders. It's obvious your muscles are tied into knots. Did it ever occur to you to *tell* Libby that you love her? She doesn't know where she stands with you." She reached into her pocket, took out a folded sheet of paper, and handed it to him. "I probably shouldn't have, but I tore this poem from Libby's book. She read it to me once, and I'm aware that she reads it over and over again. I understand why there are tears in her eyes every time she reads it."

He read the poem, refolded it, and slipped it into his pocket.

"I'm going after her," he informed her while rising from the bed to go get two sheets of blank paper from his desk. Several minutes later, he slid one folded sheet into each envelope, addressed them, and then handed one to her. "Please drop this by the firm. It's my resignation. I promise to explain everything to you when I return home *with* Elizabeth. I will tell you now, however, that there will be no trial for Josiah Staples. Court is back in session in twenty minutes, so I must return to the courthouse. As soon as the session is through, I'll request a day of personal leave and head directly to Philadelphia."

"What about *that* envelope?"

He handed her the second letter. "Will you post it, please? It's addressed to Susanna, a written, formal break in our engagement. Let her do her worst, for I simply don't care anymore. I leave it in God's hands." He opened the door for her and slammed it shut behind them. "I'll bring Elizabeth home with me," he called back while racing down the stairs. "Thank you, sister."

CHAPTER 31

By the time Libby reached Philadelphia, her common sense had convinced her that she had no reason not to completely trust Justin and that he really hadn't the heart to send her away after finding himself burdened with the Staples case. She knew it couldn't have been his choice to represent the man and determined that she would be providing him some relief by staying at Dr. Morrow's home until Staples' judgment days.

But she couldn't be certain that he truly loved her. The man's motives, so tenderheartedly driven by his righteous nature, could very easily be misconstrued. Perhaps the greater portion of his heart still lay buried with Mary Anne, and his conscience restrained him from professing an honest proclamation of love. But what was she to do? She knew for certain that she loved him, but she was in no way similar to Susanna. She could only accept the man if he relinquished his whole heart to her. Yet, she was certain that their spirits touched and had become even closer with each added moment spent together.

She pulled her valise from beneath her seat, stood up, and focused out the window to the only horse car parked by the busy station platform, hoping it would not be fully occupied by the time she reached it. The train door opened for the crowd to begin their ritual of push and shove, and before Libby realized what had happened, she found herself face down on the platform floor with her foot caught at a sharp angle between the bottom train step and the platform. Thankfully, the thick brim of her bonnet had acted as a barrier between the cement and her face. People stopped to stare as a porter rushed to assist her.

"Here, here, miss. Allow me to help you," he offered. He set her valise to the side then attended to releasing her foot. When she screamed out in pain, he placed his hands beneath her arms, turned her over, and sat her up. In this position, she managed to free her foot on her own.

"Oh no! I believe my ankle is sprained," she told him.

"I'll help you to stand." He clenched her waist and pulled her upright.

When she attempted to put her weight on her foot, she found it futile. "Yes... yes, I'm certain it's sprained!" she exclaimed, wincing with pain.

The porter looked helplessly about them, hoping to catch the eye of a kindly lady who might help him in tending to the distressed young woman. But when he turned back to Libby, he found her bent over, her hands clutching her abdomen, and a panic-stricken expression etched into her face.

"Please, sir!" With labored breathing, she cried, "My baby!"

"What seems to be the trouble?" a man asked. "Perhaps I can be of help. I'm a physician's assistant."

"This lady fell and sprained her ankle, but I think she's worried about her unborn baby," the porter explained.

"Bring her valise and follow me," he instructed, then put his arm around Libby's waist and carried her over to a bench. "I'll hail a carriage and take you to the hospital. It's only a couple of blocks away. Hold still, now. I'll be back in a moment. Stay with her," he said to the porter.

Finally seated in a carriage beside her rescuer, she covered her face with her hands and wept until devoid of tears. About the same time, she arrived at the hospital door. The man went into the reception area and came back with an orderly and a wheeled chair. He apprised the head nurse of Libby's condition as the orderly wheeled her to a room where another nurse removed her shoes, frock, and petticoat, then helped her into a bed.

"I'm bleeding!" Libby exclaimed, seeing spots of blood on the back of her petticoat.

"Hush, miss," the nurse said calmly. "Try to remain as still and relaxed as possible."

"But I'm concerned that I'll lose my baby!" *Please, Lord. Permit me keep my baby, for I've already come to love him. After bringing us through so much, I cannot believe that you would allow me to lose my baby due to a mere fall.*

The nurse left the room for a moment then came back with a chart to record Libby's statistics and symptoms. "Are you still in pain?"

"My ankle aches and is swelling, but I no longer have abdominal pain. Does that mean that my baby is still safely situated?" she anxiously asked.

The nurse smiled caringly and patted her hand. "The calmer you stay, and the more bed rest you receive, the more likely you'll keep your child. It is all up to you. I'll ask the doctor to give you something to help you sleep."

"Please... will you please telegraph Dr. Tim Morrow of Addison Street in King of Prussia and inform him of my whereabouts? I came by train from Washington to stay with him and his wife, but without their knowledge."

"I know Dr. Morrow. I've tended to several of his hospitalized patients, and he delivered my sister's baby last month. I'll do that for you, Mrs. Prescott."

"And please thank the physician's assistant for me, for he so kindly brought me here... How did you know my name? I've told no one."

The nurse looked perplexed. "I know of no 'physician's assistant' who brought you here. We nurses are the only ones who assist the doctors. Our head nurse told me the man who brought you here said your name is Elizabeth Prescott." Her face suddenly lit up, and she expelled a light laugh. "I believe you may have met your guardian angel today, young lady."

“Wait here,” Justin directed the carriage driver. “I’ll pay you extra if you’ll wait a few moments.” *I must be mad to wake these people at this hour. The house is pitch-black.* He looked into the Morrows’ parlor window. *Still… he is a doctor and most likely used to being wakened at all hours of the night.* He knocked on the front door then looked up when he heard a second-story window being unlatched and opened.

“Who is it?” a male voice groggily inquired.

“I’m terribly sorry to disturb your sleep, Dr. Morrow. My name is Justin Chambers, and I’ve come to take Elizabeth back to Barrister’s Junction with me. I’m on a very precise schedule and must be in a courtroom in Washington by early Wednesday morning. Otherwise I would have waited until morning to come for her.”

“*Elizabeth?* I have no Elizabeth in my home.”

“Libby Prescott.”

“Justin … Justin! I’ll be right down to let you in.” Upon opening the door and seeing the carriage, he told Justin to send the driver on his way. “Come into the parlor and sit. I don’t quite understand why you’re here. I understood that she was residing in *your* home.” He regarded Justin with a look of fatigue and confusion. But as he witnessed an expression of fear and trepidation grow on Justin’s face, he instantly came to attention. “She … she’s not in your home, and you believe she’s here.”

He took Libby’s note to Clary from his pocket and handed it to the doctor.

“Sally and I haven’t seen or heard from Libby since she and your sister came up to visit Caleb’s resting place several weeks back.”

“Do you suppose she decided to stay in her father’s house?”

“Now there’s a possibility. She may have stopped here first and, finding that we weren’t home, moved on. We were visiting with our daughter.”

"May I have directions to Dr. Shaw's home, and might I borrow a horse and buggy?"

"Certainly. The Shaw house will be easy to find. You need only stay on Route 30 for a full five miles then … but let me write it out." He left the room and came back with written directions and a key to Caleb's house. "Come. Follow me back to the shed, and I'll hitch my mare to the buggy. Why did Libby come back to this area?"

"I'll explain to you when I find Elizabeth and bring your buggy back. It's a long story, but I believe she's harboring falsehoods that are causing her to feel insecure concerning my regard for her."

"I thought you were engaged to some socialite."

"No longer. Elizabeth's presence in my home has made me realize that I had made a grave mistake. I've come to love her dearly and want to make her my wife."

"She's an enchanting little person, that Libby. I'm pleased she's found a decent man to love her the way she deserves to be loved. Hold the lantern up while I hitch Nelly."

Justin sat outside the Shaw home strategizing how he would awaken her without frightening her to death. He could faintly see the house across the field that she had shared with that brutish animal of a husband. *It's depressingly desolate and dark out here … despite a three-quarter moon*, he thought as he jumped down from the buggy, grabbed the lantern, and reached into his pocket for the key. The plan would be to enter as quietly as possible, search the house for her, and then take her in his arms to hold her snuggly until her fear subsided at the unannounced intrusion. What else could he do? Banging on the door seemed out of the question, for that might only startle her into doing bodily harm as she clamored in the darkness.

But after searching the entire house and not finding her, he began to panic. He knew she couldn't be in her former home, because it had been bought and paid for by Billy's sister to move into when she married in a few weeks. He loudly yelled her name several times, then went outside and climbed back into the buggy to survey the vast nothingness all about him. He gulped hard and could literally hear the uncontrolled pounding of his heart, the *only* sound to be heard in the macabre stillness of this night. He prayed. He begged and pleaded with God to help him find her, that she was safe ... somewhere ... *somewhere.* He finally headed back to the Morrows' home, only to find Dr. Tim sitting in his reading chair waiting for his return.

"I knew you wouldn't find her and would be back here in no time," he told him. He handed him a note. "This telegram was wedged in my kitchen door. I wouldn't have found it until tomorrow if the dog hadn't barked to go outdoors to relieve himself ... first time ever during the night ... strange."

"Elizabeth Prescott informs you that she had a small accident and was taken to Jefferson Hospital. Please be in touch. She would like to stay in your home for a while," Justin read. He looked up. *Thank you! Thank you, Lord! I promise to tend to her with the very best of care. I realize tonight, more than ever, that she is to be my cherished gift from you, and I take an oath to treat her as such.*

"Well, time for a few hours of shuteye. The hospital doesn't allow visitors until eight o'clock in the morning. You'll sleep in our spare room. Sally will wake you at six for breakfast then take you to a coach."

"I'm forever grateful to you. Thank you!" he exclaimed excitedly, so relieved to know where she was and that she was safe. After he was shown to his room, he spent a good half hour in praising prayer.

"Mmmm," Libby hummed, her eyes still closed and a broad smile plastered across her face. She stretched her arms above her head and sighed contentedly. The most vivid and sweetest dreams were the dreams that always ended with Justin's lips on hers. She ran her fingers lightly over her mouth, still able to feel his warm, moist kiss.

"There are more from where that one came," he whispered into her ear, and then kissed her long and tenderly once again.

This time she was awake enough to realize his presence and threw her arms around his neck to properly welcome his offering.

When he finished, he took her face in his hands and looked deeply into her eyes. "I love you so very much, Elizabeth. I offer my heart to you, asking that you'll honor me by agreeing to become my wife."

Tears rolled down her cheeks. "I wasn't sure … I couldn't quite tell … " she said, sobbing.

"Hush, sweetness. I know you were confused. If I hadn't had so much on my mind, I might have realized. I simply assumed that you knew my adoration for you. But that's no excuse! When a man loves a woman as I love you, she should be told so, and often. I promise to never again take you for granted. You're so precious to me … my perfect mate in every way. God sent you to my home as a gift, a gift that I'll cherish unto death." He took her in his arms and held her close.

"I love you also, Justin … so dearly. And there's nothing more that I want than to be your wife, but … but … "

"But what, dearest?"

"You'll be a father to a child that isn't yours, a child that you may not be able to love and raise as your own. I've thought of that so very often."

"Then put your mind to rest. The child will have you in him or her, so how could I not love it and want to raise it as my own?"

"And I thought that perhaps you found it too difficult to tell me that you loved me because you still couldn't release Mary Anne—"

"I've put her to rest. My heart belongs to you alone, if you'll accept it."

"Susanna—"

"No more Susanna. I sent her a letter that formally broke our engagement and gave my blessing that she may tell the entire world that she officiated the termination."

"Charles—"

"I'm resigned from him."

"Josiah Staples ..."

He rested her head back down on her pillow. "I need to know why you left my home. Did you leave because Susanna said something to you that broke your trust in me?"

"No ... although that may have been her intention in order to prod me to depart. When she told me that you were to defend Staples, I immediately knew you hadn't taken him of your own volition but wondered if perhaps you were too kind to send me home until the trial. I thought I would be doing you a service by leaving on my own."

"I'm relieved to know this. I want you to always trust me, and I'm pleased to know that Susanna hadn't influenced your thinking. However, when I asked you to trust me, it was because I had a plan to follow through with before I could tell you that I had become Staples' representative. I accomplished what I set out to do yesterday morning. The district attorney sent word to me that there would be no trial. Staples had pleaded guilty to all charges, relinquished his right to a trial, and thrown himself on the mercy of the court, as I had advised him. His assigned judge sentenced him to twenty-five years in a maximum security prison, with no chance of parole until twenty years served." He studied her face. "You don't look relieved. You won't be forced to testify, and I won't have to attempt to represent him as 'not guilty.'"

"I was willing to testify if it would have helped to ensure the death penalty for him, for Lottie's sake."

"I couldn't see going through the whole trial process because he was only charged with second-degree murder, so he never *would* have been sentenced to death. He was drunk when he beat her, and he hadn't any intention of killing her. It was not premeditated."

He caressed her cheek while she contemplated what he had just told her. "Do you believe that Billy made plans to murder you during the times that he was drunk and abusive?" he gently asked. When she gravely shook her head, he said, "I've spoken with Staples for hours at a time, and I'm convinced that he's genuinely remorseful for his crimes because Lottie was the only friend he had in the world. He was well able to accept his punishment. He'll be spending twelve hours a day at hard labor and most likely wishing that he *had* been sentenced to death. Death would have been the easy way out. And had he gone to trial, his sentence might have been lighter because twelve men with different opinions regarding the testimony may have arrived at a compromise."

"Did you question him as to whether he—"

"He didn't. As soon as he knocked you unconscious, he yanked your rings off, and he and Lottie moved to another boxcar for fear of being discovered once you had regained consciousness."

She nodded, knowing it was best to put the past behind her and trust that his judgment had been well used to resolve the matter. She smiled. "However did you find me?"

"I never worried as greatly or prayed so fervently at the helplessness I felt in not knowing where you were." After he told her all of the last night's happenings, he smiled down at her. "Would you like to know when I first began to love you?"

"I already know, for it was the same time I began to fall in love with you ... before we ever laid eyes on one another. It was in the darkness of your bedroom, the first time I heard your voice."

He nodded and laughed. "When I heard that sweet voice and giddy little giggles coming from my bed, promising me she wouldn't reveal to Clary that I had awakened her, my heart began to open again after seven long years."

"Well, I couldn't see the sense in her beheading a perfectly good attorney, Counselor," she lovingly told him.

"Oh, but I did lose my head over you, my love," he tenderly informed her.

Looking longingly into his eyes, she softly said, "Take me home, please."

"I will the moment your doctor gives his permission. The baby seems to be doing well, but the long train ride home might prove too tiresome for you. Sally and Tim ask that you invite them to our wedding, and I've already promised an invitation to the Johnsons."

"I don't believe I know them."

He whispered into her ear then sat back to view her reaction.

"No!" she exclaimed with eyes as round as saucers.

He nodded and smiled warmly at her pleasure. "The sun has broken through the clouds, my darling, and it's time for us to share in the joy of the day."

"It seems odd that Justin is required to be in court so early on a Monday morning," Libby commented to Clary as they sat discussing their day's plans. She stood up and began to hobble-pace on her still aching ankle. "I suppose I'm rather on edge because today is Dr. Wirz's sentencing. While Justin knows he'll be sentenced to hang, actually *hearing* those damning words pronounced by a judge … My poor dear will be so distraught. I'll have to think of a way to soothe his frazzled nerves when he arrives home this evening."

Jeremy joined them in the parlor and handed Libby a newspaper, folded to emphasize a specific article. "This will interest you, Libby. Charlotte and I decided to sponsor a 'most admired individual' contest, offering a two-dollar prize for the best story.

Charlotte chose to write this one as an example, and it's remarkably good. I hope you won't be too put out that she had to relay personal details so that our readers are touched by your travel through adversity."

Libby's face blanched. She stared at him for a few seconds, and when he nodded for her to begin, she read through the article. When she finished, she looked up misty-eyed.

"Charlotte has made me out to be a saint! If only I had had the faith, hope, and trust in the Lord that she claims to have seen in me. Why did she choose to write about me?"

"Doesn't the article speak for itself?" he tenderly asked. "Your shining example, your altruistic nature, and all that you've brought to our household places you as the most admired person to Charlotte ... to all of us." He looked to see Clary nodding her affirmation.

"But all of you are my good Samaritans. If it were not for your charity and emotional support, I might possibly have died or lost my baby or ..."

"We didn't find you; you were sent to us, by God. Your sweet, spirit-filled character helped bring me to the knowledge of the loving nature in my Charlotte. You brought to Clary the only possible man who could wish to be romantically involved with her ..." He shot his sister an impish grin. "And you brought Justin to the realization that there exists a woman even more suited to him than Mary Anne, besides saving him from a charade of a marriage. I could name many more reasons why you're so admired, but the article tells all. I suspect that when Susanna reads it, she'll realize that she's been robbed of her bravado in any attempt to discredit your person."

"It's true, Libby," Clary said with conviction. "You've helped to make life so much more fulfilling for all of us, even Becky and Vie. I cannot tell you how much they love and admire you."

Libby smiled. "Suppose we leave this discussion with the thought that we mutually admire each other, but God is to be praised for orchestrating it." She suddenly caught her breath and clapped her hand onto her abdomen. "I felt my baby move for the first time!"

Arriving home later than anticipated, Justin entered the dining room to find everyone had already begun to eat supper. By his staid demeanor, they were able to discern that Henry Wirz's fate of doom had been mandated. He took his seat at the table, and Libby glanced about her with warning eyes and a slight shake of her head. Mealtime was not the proper time to discuss such issues.

"I've kept your food in a warm oven," Libby said, going to the kitchen. She came back and set his plate in front of him then hugged her cheek to his in order to communicate that she realized his state of anxiety. She sat back down and, with a broad smile, said, "This morning I felt our baby move for the very first time."

He wanly smiled back at her attempt to cheer him. "That's *wonderful* news. It's reassuring to know that he or she is strong and developing on schedule. And it pleases me greatly to hear you say *our* baby, sweetness." He flashed another smile at her then looked down to say grace.

After tidying the kitchen, Charlotte, Jeremy, and Clary elected to go to the elder Chambers' home to play parlor games, knowing of Libby's desire for private time to bring cheer and offer sensitivity to her lover.

Libby peeked around the library doorjamb to see Justin sitting stoically in a wing chair with one hand cupped across his forehead, staring down at a two-cent coin held in his other hand. She quietly approached him and dropped to the floor to wrap her arms around his leg and hug her head to his knee. Resting his hand on the side of her head, he lightly massaged her temple with his thumb. After several moments of silence, he reached down and lifted her up to draw her onto his lap, then pressed her head to his shoulder and wrapped his arms snuggly about her.

"I so need to hold you close for a while, precious," he informed her in a decisively needy tone. After several more moments of silence, he said, "I will never forget this day: the heart-wrenchingly mixed expressions of horror, disbelief, anguish, and loss written on his face, the fact that he knew he would be forever separated from his beloved family. Such a sham of a trial, such shame to his sentence." He took a deep, quivering breath.

"I believe we may be living in end times, for there is little justice, and our consciences have become numb to God's laws of righteousness. It wouldn't surprise me at all if, someday soon, the name of God and his commandments were banned from our coins, our schools, books, and every judicial institution in this country, for there are few seekers of *truth* to be found anywhere. They don't wish to see the name 'God,' perchance it might awaken their sleeping consciences and possibly interfere with their ignoble practices and causes. We've become a society of self-serving vultures. How *can* God continue to bless us as a nation if we continue on as we are? Henry is to be hung this upcoming Friday morning, and I've even been given one of the 250 tickets to witness the ghoulish spectacle. I forwarded my pass to Charles," he said with a bitterly sarcastic grunt of a laugh. He then nestled her to himself and became silent once more.

After several moments of meditation, she soothingly said, "You're exhausted right now and need to rest. You strain yourself so, by taking on everyone else's burdens and neglecting your own needs. I ask that you give this to the Lord and move on trusting in the Father's wise bestowment. You've been asking yourself for the last couple of months what purpose it served to be rendered speechless and helpless in a situation where you knew your input might have made a difference. But God has his reason for placing you there, for certain. Over this time you've learned that you cannot, in good conscience, defend the guilty, and you cannot prosecute one who you know to be not guilty. Both go against your sense of obedience as a child of God."

"I suppose I'm to accept Richard's offer. Is that what you're communicating?"

"No. I'm saying that you may never find peace and fulfillment as an attorney, for prosecution *or* defense."

"You're saying that I'm best suited as a research attorney only."

She took his face in her hands and gently kissed his lips. "*Oh* no, Counselor! I believe God has far *greater* things in store for you. You must simply wait patiently upon the Lord to make plain his will for you. This sad and sorrowful time will pass by," she said soothingly, "and your days of gladness will come again."

CHAPTER 32

"Miss Clary, git yo'self in this kitchen and help me d'cide what the menu be fo' tomorrow," shouted Becky, trying to draw Clary away from the hall window. "He'll git here when he gits here!"

Clary commenced to jump up and down, ignoring Becky's pleas. "I see him!" she called up the stairs. "Libby, Ben is rounding the path!"

Libby had just limped out of her room when a pair of strong arms suddenly appeared from behind to sweep her up to carry her down the steps to meet her brother. He set her on her feet, and they watched as Clary could contain herself no longer. She went outside, paused for a second, and then ran to throw herself into Ben's *beckoning* open arms. He swung her around then pressed his lips tightly to hers.

Justin put his arm around Libby's shoulders and hugged her to his side. She looked up at him and said, "He's going to propose to her during his stay."

"For certain?" When she nodded, he added, "So she's been moping for weeks that he'll be going to England for three months *without* her, and all the while you knew and could have so easily relieved her anxiety by—"

"Ruining the surprise? I would have deprived her of the great joy she'll experience shortly, along with a little lesson in learning to trust the one she loves and wishes to commit herself to. Instant gratification doesn't always guarantee happiness. Sometimes *anticipating* the desire of your heart brings a greater sense of fulfillment when it's finally granted and received. I speak from experience."

"Among your many admirable qualities, you're also wise. When I prayed for wisdom, I wasn't expecting it to be delivered to me in so fine a little package."

She giggled. "I believe, sir, that you were *already* blessed with the gift of wisdom *before* God sent me to you."

He escorted her out onto the porch. "Do you suppose he'll ever release her? It's nearly suppertime. I know this because Jeremy and Charlotte are coming this way, and they never miss a meal."

"Charlotte hasn't shown for breakfast for the last few days. Jeremy says she would rather sleep than eat and that breakfast is repugnant to her…" She caught her breath and looked up at him. "Do you suppose?"

"Ask her. Ben! Welcome!" Justin exclaimed, extending his hand to his future brother-in-law.

Ben shook his hand and kissed his sister. "How are you, sweets? Your ankle is still troubling you? You do realize that it was very foolish to just pick up and travel by yourself… No?" he asked when she stubbornly shook her head.

"It was the wisest move I ever made, although it appears it takes far more time to recover from a sprain than a break. You may not believe this, but immediately after my fall, I had the pleasure of meeting my guardian angel. He's *the* Physician's assistant."

"The fork goes on this side and the spoon beside the knife. The serrated part of the knife always is turned in toward the plate," Libby instructed Vie. "Thank you for providing our Thanksgiving centerpiece. It's lovely!" she added, observing the clever use of a carved-out pumpkin as a vase for a bouquet of bright red chrysanthemums.

"I gots somethin' mo.'" She ran out to the kitchen and returned with a small pile of colorful leaves, each one bearing the name of an attendee to the feast. "I put Misser Jussin here, wif you nex' ta him." She placed a leaf above each plate.

Libby stood astounded. "Every name is spelled correctly! Who helped you?"

"Mama an' me do it. Miz Cwary give us a book ta teach us."

"You amaze me, young lady!" Libby praised, bending down to kiss her cheek.

"Dinner is ready," Clary called from the kitchen.

After everyone was seated at the table and Justin had given thanks for the food, Clary gave him the honor of carving the bird.

"I hope you don't mind a pile of hacked pieces. They forgot to teach us meat-carving at law school." He placed a portion on each of the nine plates then held up his water goblet. "Here's to those who prepared," he looked up, "and he who provided. So you'll be enjoying two feasts today," he commented to Jeremy and Charlotte. "I'm amazed that Charles didn't disown you, Charlotte, considering you foiled his plans by running off to marry this young upstart," he said, throwing a playful glance over to Jeremy.

"Thanks to you. You turned from Susanna just in time to send her running directly into Nathan's welcoming arms. She'll be a far better agent than I in assisting my father to gain access to his wealth, for Nathan much prefers her companionship to mine, him being an avid art collector and appreciator. She's telling her circle that she chose to break with you for a more worthy and sophisticated suitor. I hope that doesn't wound you."

"Not at all. I deserve her disdain. I don't care what she tells her circle, as long as she does no harm to my Elizabeth."

"Also," she continued bashfully, "I told my parents I may be with child ..."

Everyone's eyes turned to Jeremy's red face. He smiled sheepishly. "I didn't do anything wrong," he defended himself to his older siblings. "We're married."

"Evry peoples have babies in der bewwies!" Vie exclaimed. "Miz Lizzybits, Miz Charwit, Mama ..."

All eyes turned to Becky. "She be tellin' the truth. Due two months after Miss Libby."

"Congratulations!" Justin looked at Abel. "We'll have to get that house erected before the big day. I would be happy to help you until I find gainful employment."

"There's always Richard," Jeremy reminded him.

"We'll see what God has planned. I'm not so sure Richard still wants me since my editorial has stirred up so much dissension among the judicial community. At this moment I'm simply thankful to be reveling in the peace and contentment that comes from knowing that this precious woman is to be my wife," he said, reaching over to squeeze Libby's hand.

Ben took hold of Clary's hand. "How would you feel about a double wedding when your parents arrive back in the States?" He chuckled at her dumbstruck expression.

"You're speaking of Libby and Justin, and Jeremy and Charlotte renewing their vows before God and Reverend Crabtree, correct?" she asked cautiously. "Well, they've *already* decided on Saturday, December 23, a mere sixteen days from now. I have no say—"

"You disappoint me," he interrupted, on the verge of a laughing fit. "And here I thought you were the most intelligent woman I had ever come across—"

With scarlet cheeks and clenched fists, she shrieked, "Are you proposing to me?"

"Well, I realize sixteen days is short notice, but yes, I am proposing to you. I'm aware that Libby told you of my summer retreat to Great Britain. I certainly couldn't take you with me for three months unless we were married. I have to think of my reputation, you know, so it will have to be a triple wedding, unless you prefer to wait until closer to summer, but then your parents will have gone back to England—"

"Will you hush up? Yes, I'll marry you!" She grabbed his face and kissed him so hard his lips turned purple.

"And I declare before God and these fine people that I love you, Clarissa, with all of my heart. I couldn't bear the thought at not seeing you for three long months."

"And I love you, so completely!" she exclaimed, her face radiating joy. She looked at Libby. "You knew and were able to keep it secret?" Libby nodded. "Thank you for not ruining the surprise. I had resigned to the fact that I might *possibly* be asked by Ben to marry in a year or so, but this is much more than I could have hoped for. It will just be a small, quiet wedding—"

"With President and Mrs. Johnson in attendance," Libby added with a giggle.

"I told you the truth, my darling. Andrew is expecting an invitation, so I sent him one," Justin affirmed.

"Mother and Father won't believe three of their children will be marrying at the same time!" Clary exclaimed, clapping her hands excitedly.

"I'm *already* married," Jeremy grumbled, ducking to avoid her swat.

"It's so pleasant to be permitted to speak during mealtime," Charlotte softly commented. "Many problems that plagued my household might have been resolved had we been encouraged to speak when we all came together."

"Will we visit with your aunt Sarah while we're in England?" Clary asked Ben.

"Early summer will be spent quite leisurely. We'll start out in Cornwall, explore the Gardens of Heligan, and then visit the Wellborns and your parents. Then we'll head north, up the Cotswold Way to tour Thornbury Castle. The second half of the summer will be spent in Scotland, Ireland, and Wales, mostly discovery camping, visiting with museum curators, and lecturing to museum boards on behalf of the science academy. If you'll make a list of the sites you wish to visit, I'll incorporate them into our itinerary."

He smiled tenderly at the excitement he read in her eyes, patted her cheek, and then directed his attention to Justin. "I've decided not to take a semester's leave of absence from teaching and hope Clarissa will agree to live with me in Boston during that time. The added income will make our trip more enjoyable, so my wife may indulge herself in buying any trinkets that she might fancy. We'll visit with you to meet our new niece or nephew before we sail to England from New York harbor."

"Your plans are well laid out," Justin acknowledged.

"Charlotte and I will continue to live next door," offered Jeremy. "You and Libby will have this house to yourselves."

"Much appreciated."

Libby sat in silence staring pensively at the face of her lover. Almost four weeks had passed since Henry Wirz was hanged, and she was relieved that he had finally calmed enough to relax and enjoy this day of thanksgiving. He even appeared to revel in the stir he caused at publishing his article citing a good number of Bible passages to defend his views that society was fast falling from God's grace by failing to adhere to his righteous laws for perfect justice. He didn't even scoff when a few of the Northern press labeled him a "religious fanatic." She couldn't help but be concerned that the passions of his nature might cause him to wear before his time and knew it would be her responsibility to find ways to alleviate the stress he placed upon himself. As David asked of God, "*Can a righteous man be found anywhere?*" *Yes. He sits beside me, and he's ours, little one,* she thought, feeling the faint fluttering in her womb.

Dear Papa,

I'm determined to invest the money made from my house sale into the iron works and railroad industries. It seems a wise choice, considering we've become such an industrialized nation. With the westward expansion of the railroad and the rail repairs that must be made in the South, I believe I've made the most profit-rendering choice. By the time our children are grown, I'll have made enough money to educate them without hardship to our budget. I would also like to educate Vie, if Becky and Abel will allow. She is extremely bright, and black children have so few opportunities offered to them.

After writing to you for nearly three months, I've come to the last page of my journal, so this must be my final entry addressed to you on this Thanksgiving evening. But not too sadly, for it really is time for me to leave you so that you may bask in the companionship of friends and ancestors gone by, my beloved mother, and our Lord. I'm confident that I'm able to move on now, for it's a wife's duty to share her heart, soul, and spirit with her husband, and I realize I'm blessed with a most avid listener. He eagerly hears my every thought put into words and has a keen insight into what I fail or cannot put into words then anxiously assists in helping to place my world in perfect order. "Perfect order." Those are the key words, Papa. Those words alone have led me to believe that there can be only one calling to which Justin is best suited—judgeship. As a mediator, his wisdom and power will be well implemented to ensure that both defense and prosecution are kept in perfect order so that pure justice might prevail.

"This is lovely," commented Libby the following morning. "This is the first time we've ridden two upon a horse."

He tightened his arm around her waist and nestled his face to her neck. "Fifteen days, and you'll be mine. Time can't move fast enough for my liking. I'll be glad to be back in my own bed."

She laughed. "You've never complained before. Is it so much more comfortable than the bed in the guest room?"

"Comfort has nothing to do with it, my dear."

She giggled. "Ah, so you're anxious to share your bed with your soon-to-be enormously plump wife."

"Stop!" he gently chided. "You mustn't be concerned that your expanding middle is going to repel my desire for you. We have our whole life together to intimately enjoy each other. I just want to be with you. You so fulfill me," he said tenderly, pressing his lips to her cheek. "And Dr. Flanagan informed me that we may have several weeks of intimacy with no harm to you or the baby—"

"Aha ... so you asked!"

"Certainly I asked. What man, who dearly loves his woman, *wouldn't* be anxious to consummate his marriage? Are you tired of riding, dear? Would you like to return to the house?"

"No. I'm enjoying the brisk air."

"It *is* true, you know. There's something especially beautiful about a woman with child, your glowing pink cheeks, the sparkle in your eyes—"

"Has nothing to do with the baby. You put the sparkle in my eyes and glow of excitement in my cheeks."

He raised her hand to his lips. "You're hand is icy cold," he commented. "You'll have to warm it in my pocket. No, not that pocket," he said, taking her hand out of his outer coat pocket and transferring it into the coat-lining pocket.

"What is this?" she asked, bringing her hand back out clutching a folded piece of paper and miniature box. She unfolded the paper. "So *you're* the one who tore the page from my poetry book! And why, Counselor?" she demanded with mock sternness and a charming smile.

"I didn't tear it out. Another of your guardian angels did the deed and gave it to me. I'll always carry it with me to reprimand me if there ever comes a day that I neglect to tell you of my love for you and to remind me to thank God every day of my life that he brought us together through adversity then blessed us with abounding joy. Elizabeth," he huskily whispered into her ear, "when I think of the mistake I may have made if you hadn't come into my life ..." He wrapped his arms tightly around her.

Her arms encircled his neck, and she pressed her cheek to his. "God rescued both of us," she softly said, "and all of the pain was well worth the reward."

"Now open the box," he coaxed. When she lifted the lid, he took out the ring of engagement and placed it on her finger.

"I wasn't expecting an engagement ring!" she exclaimed. "I would have been content with just a wedding band. I've never seen so beautiful a setting, a diamond-crowned heart! Thank you, my darling! It's exquisite!" Her eyes focused over his shoulder to another equestrian. "There's a messenger on horseback. He's dismounting to go to the front door, but there's no one home to receive him."

They rode back to the house where he dismounted and lifted her down to stand by his side. "Who are you looking for?" he asked when the man turned to greet them.

"I have a special delivery document from President Johnson to be placed in the hand of Justin Samuel Chambers."

"I'm Justin Chambers," he said, accepting the letter. He turned to Libby. "Must be our wedding invitation acceptance," he said, prying the wax presidential seal from the paper. He unfolded it and held it to where they both could read:

> *I, Andrew Johnson, President of the United States, do hereby request the presence of Justin Samuel Chambers to dinner and then a conference to be held in the Oval Room of the White House, Monday, December 11, 1865, at 1:00 p.m. The purpose of said meeting will be to discuss a presidential appointment to occupy a recently vacated District Court Judge position. A response is expected via this courier…*

Libby smiled lovingly at her betrothed. "Verily, there *is* a reward for the righteous, Psalm 58:11."

And then Justice Chambers took "God's Oath" to be his…

FEBRUARY 14, 1912

(Late afternoon)

"For nearly thirty years your grandfather moved up through the judicial courts to higher and higher judgeships, stopping just short of accepting a Federal Supreme Court nomination offered by President Grover Cleveland. The name 'Justice Chambers' became renowned as one that bestowed true righteousness upon all.

"But as I had contemplated, there would be a price to pay for such passion. He suffered a mild heart attack at the age of sixty, and even *he* realized he was spent. His mother died about that time, having survived his father by two years. She willed this house to us, so we decided to retire to the peace and quiet of the English countryside to enjoy intimate time together... until he died of heart failure, two years ago," Elizabeth said sadly.

"Clary and Ben were already living in the enormous, old Wellborn house, the perfect place to have raised their five boys. And when they introduced our son to the lovely English girl who would someday become your mother, he married her and stayed in this country. It seemed only natural that we live here among our loved ones. I do greatly miss my other children, though, and look forward to their visit this summer." She kissed Justin's picture then held it to her breast. "How I loved this man and still do! I feel his presence at all times, as if the Lord is allowing him to watch over me still."

"Oh, Grams!" Julia began, on the verge of tears. "I ... I had no *idea* of your life before Grampa. I realize you're telling me that Billy is my biological grandfather, but it makes no difference *whatsoever*. Now I know why Father's name is Jeffrey *Prescott* Chambers ... to commemorate Grampa's brother and to pass on Billy's name. Father once told me that 'Prescott' is a family name but would offer no details. My loving grampa will always be my perfect grandfather, just as Father refers to him as his perfect father."

"That he was. I told you of Billy for two reasons, so that my only granddaughter would know of the marvelous way God worked in my life and to see the great joy and light that followed my dark time. Always be steadfast in the Lord, Julia. He has vowed to stay beside you through your dark times to bring you to a greater understanding of his power and then promises to bring you joy in the morning.

"I also felt you should be given the Prescott medical records I've documented. They're very different than the Chambers' medical histories. I was compelled to do this, being my doctor-father's daughter. Also, your aunt Clary left you a small parcel of her newest beauty products. One item is a particular favorite of Queen Mary, an herbal fizzy stone for your bath."

Julia laughed. "A *Fizzy* stone? What *will* she come up with next? So, did Andrew Johnson come to your wedding?"

"We three couples were married late in the afternoon of December 23, 1865, with a mere forty guests in attendance. The President, Mrs. Johnson, and their daughter, Martha, came, along with two security guards. After the ceremony Mother Chambers held a lovely banquet supper in her dining room. The Johnsons came for hors d'oeuvres but had to leave because Mrs. Johnson didn't feel well. Charles and Mrs. Dupont came to the service for the sake of Charlotte, but not to the house ... for obvious reasons. They *did* bring us a gift from Susanna, however ... a lovely, green crystal pitcher and goblet set, etched with a silver renaissance scene, imported from Prague. But... green is *my* favorite color," she added with a giggle.

"Did Susanna marry Nathan Wentworth?"

"Yes, on the day that she and Justin were to wed. Her wedding plans had not been interfered with. Only the groom changed. Edward Wentworth was Nathan's best man, and he brought with him his wife and six children all the way from Maine. Edward's obvious great love for children explained why he had broken his engagement to Susanna, having realized her inability to be a nurturing mother.

"Her marriage to Nathan didn't last long, however. I had delivered your father, your aunt Jeanette, and your uncle Christian before Susanna ever became pregnant. Sadly, her son was stillborn, and Nathan was killed in a hunting accident before she was able to conceive again. She never remarried, and I heard, through Charlotte, that she died five years ago, all alone in her great mansion. She never became a politician's wife, nor did her father ever reach any height of greatness. Due to his unethical ways, his political career was over before it ever began.

"I'm so pleased you decided to honeymoon in the States. Niagara Falls is lovely in springtime, and Charlotte and Jeremy are so looking forward to spending time with you and Will. You chose a fine husband, a strong, God-fearing man who truly loves the Lord, just like your father and grandfather. Your days will be blessed, as mine were with your grandfather, for he will love you dearly in the deeply spiritual way you need to be loved."

"Will *is* one of those rare men, isn't he? Oh, Grams! Your story has worn me out. I don't believe I could have endured all the adversity you have fought your way through."

"Yes, you could. I had been a sheltered young woman with all of my needs met. Except for losing my precious mother at an early age, my life was quite comfortable and secure. You don't realize the 'stuff' you're made of or the amount of strength you can draw from God until you're blessed with adversity... yes, *blessed*. For conquering adversity is what *makes* the man, or woman. It builds faith and character. You will go through times of adversity, but if you keep your eyes on your Savior, he will guide you through it. He's your only hope."

Misty-eyed, Julia went to hug her grandmother. "You're my hero. I want to be just like you."

"You're still up here, ladies? You must be having a jolly good time," Will called from the attic doorway. He entered carrying Elizabeth's wrapped wedding gift and set it on a storage box.

"Will!" Julia exclaimed, rushing over to throw her arms around his neck. "Grams just told me a love story, and quite a gripping one at that, of her and Grampa. I'll tell you the remarkable tale later this evening. What's in the box?"

Will looked over at Elizabeth for her approval. "Is it all right?"

"Certainly it is. Will already knows what the gift is, Julia. Did Viola give any indication as to when supper will be ready, Will?"

"She says all six dishes will be ready in twenty minutes, and we may make three choices for our reception rather than the two she usually gives to her clients. Plus, she made a steak and potato pasty for you to take home to your mother, dear."

Julia giggled. "If I don't eat it first. Viola promised dishes that are the latest culinary rage of the Cordon Bleu." She took the wedding gift over to sit beside her grandmother. "This is heavy!"

"You may have the mantilla comb as 'something old,' and there's 'something new' in with your wedding gift. What about the 'borrowed' and the 'blue'?" asked Elizabeth.

"I would like a small flounce cut from your old blue gown to be sown onto my petticoat... to remind me of the look of love Grampa gave to you when you were dressed so regally, and because blue has always symbolized love and purity throughout the centuries. And may I borrow your lovely, inspiring poem to carry in my wedding purse?"

Elizabeth patted her hand. "Of course. Now open your gift."

Julia untied the ribbon, lifted the lid, and took out a white handkerchief with an intricately crocheted lace border, embroidered pink initials "JSC" on two corners, and a blue fleur-de-lis embroidered below each set of initials. A silver six pence piece for her bridal shoe was tucked in its fold.

"Oh, it's lovely! My 'something new,' with my initials... the same initials as Grampa's. Thank you." She lifted out a journal with roses on the cover.

"That's the journal in which I recorded my thoughts of Billy in happier days, and the diary to my papa. I thought you might enjoy reading my ancient writings."

Julia kissed her grandmother. "I certainly will." She reached into the box again and lifted out an enormous family Bible.

"There's a Prescott and Chambers family tree in there. Everyone is listed: Josh and Lydia's two daughters, Charlotte and Jeremy's son, Clary and Ben's five sons, your aunt Jeanette and uncle Christian and each of their two sons, even Lavinia and her daughter and son, all of their children's children, and so on. You may continue on with your own children. Now turn to the back page."

Julia flipped the heavy Bible over, removed an envelope, and then looked up to see the smiles of anxious anticipation on her grandmother and fiancé's faces.

"Remember I said I invested in the railroad and iron works?" Elizabeth asked. "Well, I also invested in gold. But after educating three children, five, including Viola and her sister, Gracie, there were little funds left. But in 1901, your grampa suggested we invest the little into Pittsburgh Steel, and our returns have been phenomenal, enough that I'm able to give you a wedding gift that will give you a lifetime of memories."

Julia unsealed the envelope and took out a small packet with two tickets attached to it. After reading *what* the tickets were, she looked up at her grandmother and Will through enormous, glistening, dark eyes. "I don't believe it! This is astounding! Oh, thank you! *Thank you*!" she exclaimed, bouncing up and down on the wing chair. "They're two *first class* cabin fares to sail to America, Will, aboard the *RMS Titanic*!"

EPILOGUE

Barrister's Junction—April 22, 1912

Dear Grams,

At this moment I'm sitting on the newly painted and restored glider that you were so fond of sharing with Grampa, trying to imagine what it was like to live here in the "olden days."

Aunt Charlotte and Uncle Jeremy are wonderful hosts and have cared for my darling Will as if he was their own son. Aunt Jeanette paid us a visit this morning, and Uncle Christian and his family will be joining us for supper this evening. All are anxiously looking forward to visiting with you this summer.

I'm compelled to write this letter because even though you were informed that both Will and I arrived here safely, I wanted to relay the outstanding details of what took place on the night of April 14, 1912. Please keep this letter so that I may someday show it to my grandchildren.

On that evening, Will and I entered the foyer to the dining room and were about to descend the grand stairway, when an elderly gentleman, Mr. Isidor Straus, and his wife stopped to speak with us. Mr. Straus believed he had previously met Will through a business associate and began to read off a mental list of dozens of men to which Will might possibly be acquainted. As we four slowly descended the stairs, I was all too aware that Mr. Straus had difficulty in keeping his saliva in his mouth as he spoke, and Will's face was becoming damper by the second. I routed through my purse for something to casually wipe away the spittle the very moment the old gentleman departed from us and took out the lovely handkerchief embroidered with your famous fleur-de-lis design. When it slipped through my fingers and fell to my feet, Will hastily stooped down to retrieve it at the very same time Mr. Straus surmised we were moving on. He knocked into my poor dear, sending him sprawling down the entire stairway! I rushed down to his aid, only to see that his arm was bent at an unnatural angle, his hand still clutching my handkerchief. He was immediately taken to the infirmary, his arm having been broken and knee badly sprained.

Six hours later, when the ship hit the wall of ice, Will and I were transferred directly from the infirmary into a lifeboat. If I had not dropped your gift, Grams, with its embroidered symbol of the Trinity, I might not have my husband today. My heart goes out to all of those who lost their loved ones! There is no way that anyone can imagine the horror (except maybe for you). I will never forget that night and will remember it as clearly fifty years from now as I can picture it now. Hours of piercing screams! Such anguished cries for help! Then silence—dead silence. As we sat from afar, watching the great "indestructible" ship being swallowed up by the ocean, I could hear the very haunting melody and words of a hymn you and Grampa used to sing so beautifully together.

O the deep, deep love of Jesus,
vast, unmeasured, boundless, free,
rolling as a mighty ocean
in its fullness over me!
Underneath me, all around me
is the current of Thy love.
Leading onward, leading homeward
to Thy glorious rest above!

Will had been made helpless to help himself during the catastrophe, so he was instructed to join me in the lifeboat with the women and children. God certainly works in mysterious ways, as you so well know. I had been so angry and bitter that our wonderful honeymoon voyage was ruined by Will's fall but now am jubilant and ever so grateful that we have been blessed with the joy of seeing the sunrise together after a tragic night of weeping. Praise the Lord!
Your loving Julia

BIBLIOGRAPHY

Futch, Ovid. *History of Andersonville Prison.* Gainsville: University of Florida Press, 1968. Wikipedia

Harper, Frank. "*Andersonville: The Trial of Captain Henry Wirz.*" MA Thesis, University of Northern Colorado, 1986. Wikipedia.

Hoemann, George. *The American Civil War Homepage.* compiled: University of Tennessee, Knoxville, 2008.

William Marvel. *Andersonville: The Last Depot.* 1994.